THE
BOOK
OF
URIEL

THE
BOOK
OF
URIEL

ELYSE HOFFMAN

ISBN 978-1-952742-06-4

Project 613 Publishing

Project613Publishing.com

PROJECT613

E.M. TIPPETTS BOOK DESIGNS

emtippettsbookdesigns.com

1.

Uriel wished he could scream.

Normally, he could. A scream was one of the few noises that ever emerged from the boy's lips. No words ever escaped, but he could summon a scream.

Yet his lungs couldn't gather enough air to produce a cry. They struggled to supply enough oxygen to keep the child awake. Smoke invaded his throat and clawed at his lungs. Although screams pierced the air from every angle, he couldn't add his own to the din.

He still felt the pressure of mother's fingers locked around his hand, even though she was gone. Uriel's golden eyes darted to and fro, searching for her face. His fingers twitched as her warmth faded. He strained his ears, trying to hear her call to him, but her voice did not rise above the ruckus.

Mama! Uriel thought, his tears allying with the smoke and assaulting his eyes. He wanted to cry out for her. Perhaps if she heard him, she would find him, and they could get to safety. But his voice had never worked before, and though he opened his mouth to call out, all he could do was pant and cough.

Gunshots rang out. The fleeing villagers clung to their families and their few precious possessions, shoving one another out of the way as they tried to escape the flames enveloping the little town and the murderous mob cutting down the Jews. Young and old, women and men, little children and babies were thrown to the ground, beaten with clubs, shot, stabbed, and slaughtered. Their blood mingled with the warm ash coating the cobblestones.

Uriel stood in the midst of the mayhem, still as a statue, alone. His right hand yearned for his mother, while his left clutched the one possession he had snatched before fleeing his house. His little golden notebook. Small enough to fit in his pocket and filled with stories he couldn't leave to burn.

Although the villagers would normally never leave a small child alone in the street, concern for their own lives and the lives of their families caused them to stampede. Uriel was pushed against a brick wall, and his golden notebook flew from his hand. He gasped, inhaling an army of ash. The boy desperately tried to crawl to his notebook. Boots and shoes stomped on the cherished book, but Uriel reached it. He grabbed the notebook and held it to his chest, shielding it with his body.

The child was trampled and kicked. His lungs began losing to the smoke and ash entering through his nostrils and silent lips. He felt as though his insides were on fire, as though every bone in his body was about to shatter. When darkness finally took him, all he felt was gratitude.

2.

Uwe Litten had never seen so many trees. He had never stepped foot outside his tiny hometown, and the area surrounding his village consisted of flat, boring farmland. The sights of the Polish woodland were refreshingly alien to Uwe's rural senses.

He leaned against the window, smiling like a small child and drinking in the forest's beauty as the trees zoomed by. He wished he could open the window and breathe in the fresh air, but the major had said to keep the window closed. He didn't want wind in the car to distract their driver.

Still, it wouldn't hurt to ask once more. They had been driving for hours, after all. Surely the major and the driver were thirsting for a breeze.

"Major Brandt," Uwe said. Major Günter Brandt, who was sitting in the passenger seat, idly drumming his fingers on his knees, looked in the rearview mirror and smiled at Uwe.

"Everything all right, Herr Litten?" he asked, his eyes twinkling amiably.

"I'm fine," Uwe said. "I wish we could lower the windows, though. It's getting stuffy in here."

Brandt's smile became slightly skewed, and he looked at his driver. The driver shrugged.

"We're not driving that fast, I suppose," he said. "It won't be that distracting."

Brandt nodded and waved for Uwe to do as he wished.

"We wouldn't want our little linguist to choke," he said with a wink.

Uwe thanked him and happily lowered the window. He considered taking off his thin-rimmed glasses, lest they fall out of the car, rendering him blind and useless, but he decided he wanted to enjoy the scenery and kept them on. The wind gently whipped at his blond hair, and he inhaled deeply.

A chuckle rumbled in his throat when he thought of the pet name Brandt had bestowed upon him: our little linguist. He wasn't sure if he was fond of or annoyed with that epithet. On one hand, he thought bitterly, his linguistic skills were the reason the *Ordnungspolizei* had taken him away from his home and family. He sighed heavily and tried to imagine what his wife and children were doing. He hoped his daughters wouldn't use his absence to start dating. The very thought made him shudder. His son would be lonely without somebody to wrestle with him and help him with his reading.

Still, so far, it wasn't nearly as bad as he'd expected. There hadn't been a whiff of danger since they crossed into Poland. No sign of partisans or enemy soldiers. Brandt had assured Uwe that he and his men would take care of the "nasty business."

"We only need you to tell us what they say once we capture them," Brandt had explained. "You won't be in harm's way. You have my word."

Although Uwe wasn't fond of the National Socialists, Brandt had been affable since picking him up, nothing like the hard-hearted soldier he had expected. Uwe would much rather work for a man like Brandt than for the frightening fanatics of the SS.

His wife, though, had been quite distressed at Brandt's arrival. She had gazed at the major with fear flooding her soft brown eyes.

Just keep your head down and do as they say, she had whispered to her husband just before he left with Brandt. *You'll be safe that way.*

"Herr Major…" Uwe started to say.

"You really ought to call me Günter, Herr Litten," Brandt interrupted.

The linguist smirked.

"But you refer to me as Herr Litten. That's quite formal."

Brandt laughed. "Fair point! But I refer to you formally out of respect."

"But as a major, you certainly command more respect than me!"

"Not necessarily," said Brandt with a shrug. "After all, if I don't understand what the criminals we capture are saying, I won't hold my position very long. I have to admire you for learning so many languages. Russian, Polish…Yiddish, even! You can read Yiddish, can't you?"

"Yes."

"And it has a different alphabet! I can hardly ask for a cup of water around here! You must be very intelligent, Herr Litten."

"Not really, Herr Major," said Uwe. "My town's at a crossroad. We had merchants from everywhere passing through to do business. If you wanted to succeed, you had to be able to speak to your patrons. Not intelligence so much as…economic necessity."

"What about your children?" asked Brandt. "Have you passed on your knowledge?"

Uwe swallowed and hesitated, knowing that as far as the National Socialists were concerned, the languages he spoke were those of inferior people, *untermenschen*. Few proud Germans would dare sully their tongues by speaking the language of a lesser race. Uwe was only treasured for his knowledge because his lips could serve the *Reich*. Teaching such things to his children, however, that would be frowned upon.

"Not really, sir," said Uwe, subduing a stutter. "My daughters know a few words of Polish and Russian, but naturally, I haven't taught them an ounce of Yiddish."

Much to Uwe's surprise, Brandt shook his head.

"That's a shame."

Uwe blinked at the Major's back.

"But sir," he said, "Yiddish is a Jewish language."

"Yes." Brandt craned his neck and smiled warmly at Uwe. "But there's no sin in learning the language of the enemy. Even Adolf Eichmann knows Yiddish."

Uwe felt his tight stomach uncoil when Brandt flashed him an easygoing grin.

"I didn't know that," he confessed quietly, looking down at his lap.

"At any rate," said Brandt, turning back to the road. "If you insist on respecting me, call me Herr Brandt, but not Herr Major. Herr Major is so formal it's suffocating."

Uwe opened his mouth to agree, but at that moment, a foul odor replaced the sweet scent of pine. The driver and Brandt noticed too.

"Ugh!" The driver gagged, waving his hand in front of his nose while the major inquisitively sniffed the air.

"Smells like…brimstone," whispered Uwe, peering out the window. The trees continued to fly by, but the sickening scent wafting into the car overpowered their pleasant smell.

"Shut the window!" the driver commanded. "It smells like hell!"

Uwe obeyed and rolled up the window, his eyes scanning their surroundings, trying to spot the source of the stench.

The trees vanished, and a small village appeared on a hill by the road. Smoke billowed from the town, a gray cloud of death hanging above the area.

"Stop the car!" Uwe shouted. The driver was so startled he slammed on the brakes without even consulting the major. Brandt was nearly smacked against the windshield, but he gripped his seat and avoided a collision. His hat fell off, and he huffed in annoyance as he put it back on and adjusted it. Before he could scold Uwe, the little linguist was out the door and dashing towards the smoldering village.

Uwe saw a sign, an old wooden board with faded paint and chipped sides that read 'Zingdorf.' Uwe stared at the Hebraic letters and realized this was a Jewish *shtetl*.

He stepped into the street, and the sight that greeted him almost made him vomit. The buildings smoked, and some still crackled with dying flames. Broken furniture, glass, and wood littered the streets, clear signs of plunder. But even more horrifying were the bodies. There weren't many, at least not that Uwe could see, but the few he saw made his legs shudder and his heart shatter. There were old men, young women, and youthful boys who looked just old enough to wed. Their skulls had been bashed in, their clothes ripped apart, and their bodies broken and left in the streets like rubbish. Blood coated the cobblestones like rain. The scene was a nightmare brought to life.

Brandt strolled out of the car and observed the smoking *shtetl* with a curious tilt of the head.

Odd, he thought. *I didn't order any action against this town yet. Hm…must have been the Poles.*

He marched up the hill to sate his curiosity. It wasn't unusual for the local anti-Semites to vent their hatred. The Nazis wouldn't stop them from doing so.

It also wasn't unusual for the Germans to rile up the Poles and turn them loose on the Jews. It saved them bullets and time.

Perhaps my boys encouraged this? Brandt thought, wandering the streets and stepping over the battered bodies like they were logs obstructing his path. He finally reached an area of blackness. Singed scrolls and pews were strewn about, along with hundreds of charred corpses. Women, men, little children. Brandt looked down and saw a plaque with a Star of David. He gave it a light push with his boot and realized this had been the village's synagogue. Anybody who hadn't been butchered in the streets had been herded to the synagogue and burned.

The smell was nauseating. Brandt covered his nose and shook his head. *Definitely the Poles,* he thought. *My boys wouldn't do it like that.*

He kicked the plaque and turned around, waving the smoke away as he looked for Uwe.

Meanwhile, Uwe stared at the gory scene, unable to move. He had only seen a dead body once in his life, after his father passed. His father had gone peacefully in his sleep. Uwe had seen him at the funeral in his casket, dressed in a fine suit. He had kissed his father's forehead and said goodbye right before the casket had closed. But these people had died in a miasma of fear and panic. There was nobody left to kiss their bruised foreheads.

His eyes traveled to a brick wall, and one body caught his eye. He pushed his glasses up and forced his legs to carry him to the wall. He knelt before the body, his heart trembling as he examined the still form.

It was a boy, not a day older than ten, with soft ebony hair and gentle features. He looked as though he was sleeping, curled on his side with something under his arm.

As Uwe looked at the serene child, he could think only of Jürgen, his little boy. This child looked so much like him. As he stared at the child, Uwe couldn't help but picture Jürgen curled up in his bed with his favorite toy lion under his arm, breathing softly as he slept. Except this boy was dressed in tattered brown and gray clothes instead of soft pajamas, and when Uwe looked at the boy's chest, he couldn't see him breathing.

Uwe's stomach churned. This little boy was nowhere near the age of death. He could only imagine what thoughts had gone through the child's mind as his short life was snuffed out. He wasn't nearly as battered as the other bodies, but a small stream of blood dribbled down the side of his face, and bruises covered his arms, which held something gold to his chest.

Uwe, curious, carefully pulled the golden item from under the boy's arm and was surprised to see it was a notebook. The cover and the edges of the pages were gold. Unlike everything else in the destroyed village, the notebook was perfectly intact. Beautiful, in fact. He flipped through the book and saw that, except for a few blank pages at the very end, the notebook was filled with Yiddish writing in a childish yet neat script. On the cover was a name written in large, black letters:

URIEL

"Uriel," he whispered, looking at the boy. He swallowed and slowly reached out, hoping beyond hope that perhaps the child was alive and he would feel a pulse.

"Herr Litten!"

Startled, Uwe shoved the golden notebook into his pocket and stood up just as Major Brandt found him.

"There you are!" Brandt sighed, a carefree smile on his face. He noticed Uwe shaking, and his smile disappeared, replaced by a look of sympathy.

"Yes, it is brutal," he said. "But this is war."

"D-d…" Uwe stuttered, struggling to find his voice and the courage to ask his question. "Did your men do this?"

Much to Uwe's relief, Brandt smirked and shook his head. "No, I highly doubt it. This isn't how we handle our enemies. We're the *Ordnungspolizei*. We keep the order. This wasn't done with order."

"Who…?"

"The locals, likely," said Brandt. "The Germans aren't the only enemies of the Jews."

Uwe choked and looked back down at the boy, Uriel. Who would ever consider him to be an enemy?

"Come along, Herr Litten," said Brandt. "I'm sorry you saw this, but don't worry. This will be the last grisly sight you witness."

Brandt started to lead him back to the car. Uwe slowly followed, the golden notebook weighing down his pocket. He looked back at the boy, praying he would move, but the boy's body was still. He prayed for a whimper or a plea for help, but the child was silent.

Dedicated to my mother and father, who have always supported and loved me.

To my grandfather, whose stories I never heard.

To my teacher Mr. Feinstein, who nurtured my interest in history

To my friend Eliana, who always listens to my stories

And to God, Who makes all stories.

"Herr Litten!"

Inhaling deeply, causing the smoke to clog his throat, Uwe turned away from Uriel and Zingdorf. He got back in the car and kept the windows firmly shut as the driver eagerly stepped on the gas. The linguist looked behind him, keeping his eyes on the dead *shtetl* as it disappeared into the distance. Once it was gone, he settled down with a sigh and shoved his hand into his pocket.

He pulled out the book, Uriel's notebook, and opened it to the first page.

Stories Told to and by Uriel

Interested, he turned to the next page.

The Story of Michael the Archangel

With a heavy heart and an intrigued mind, Uwe tore his eyes away from the radiant forest and began to read Uriel's stories.

3.

Hardly had the car pulled away when Uriel stirred. His mouth opened, allowing his singed lungs to fill themselves with cool air. The smoke clouds slowly drifted away, allowing Uriel to breathe without choking. His every sinew throbbed as he regained consciousness.

The first thing he noted was that his book was gone. He brought his hands to his heart, but his precious book was no longer nestled against his chest. His eyes, which had been struggling to revive themselves, snapped open. He looked down at his dirt-caked coat and the ash-covered stones beneath him, but to no avail.

Uriel slowly pushed himself up, his body screaming for him to be still so it could recover. He disobeyed its wishes long enough to sit up and lean against the brick wall, panting as though he had run across the country.

He wrapped his empty arms around himself and looked up at his village, his home. Zingdorf was decimated. Bodies were strewn across the village like feathers from the geese his mother used to pluck. He would always delight in chasing the feathers about, trying to catch as many as he could while the wind

11

scattered them across the streets. Now dust and corpses were scattered across the streets, the corpses of his neighbors lying about like slaughtered geese.

Mama…Papa…Everyone…

His eyes, already burning from the lingering smoke, filled with scalding tears. He buried his face in his knees and sobbed, his chest aching with every wail that wracked his little body.

Uriel cried until he had no more tears, and when that happened, he just sat, his face hidden, unwilling and unable to look up at the world around him. He was alone, hopeless, lost.

He didn't know how long he sat there, his sobs and the tauntingly cheerful songs of the birds being the only noises that echoed through the dead village.

Eventually, however, the birds stopped singing, the smoke dissipated completely, and the drab village seemed to brighten. Even Uriel, without looking, could feel it. He raised his head, opened his eyes, and saw the crimson cobblestones bathed in light. Not the sun. This light was no mere celestial beam. It replenished his spirit, killed his sobs, and strengthened his heart.

He looked to the side and saw the source of the holy light. Four people. They looked like humans, but it was clear they weren't. No human could be so perfect. The light obscured their faces as they approached, yet it didn't hurt his eyes the way the sun did. The light slowly dimmed, and he could see that they were men, clad in armor that shimmered so brilliantly that it seemed to be made of stars.

They stood on the street in front of him, staring at the *shtetl's* remains. One of them spoke:

"*Hashem…Hashem…*" he muttered sorrowfully.

"Awful," said another. "It's a miracle we can walk through here. So much evil, even with the sinners gone."

"Gabriel, it hurts…"

"I know, Raphael. We will not tarry, but we must search for Michael."

"*Hashem* help him if he's here. He must be in agony."

One of the men knelt before the corpse of a young woman and reached out, gently brushing his fingers against her bloodstained bangs.

"These poor people…" he whispered, his voice hoarse. "Gabriel, please, is there nothing I can do?"

"I am afraid not, Raphael. It is too late. Their souls are with Him now."

"Gabriel," said one man, pointing to Uriel. "That one still draws breath."

"Ah, yes. But he is wounded. See the blood? The bruises? Poor child…"

"Gabriel, may I heal him?"

"If God wills it, you…"

The man's voice trailed off as he realized that the boy was staring directly at him. Uriel's golden eyes glistened with wonder. He refused to blink even once. The light that hid the man's features vanished so that Uriel could finally see his face.

The Archangel Gabriel locked eyes with the child.

"Can you see me?" he whispered.

Uriel barely felt himself nod.

Gabriel and Raphael looked at one another, just as amazed as Uriel.

Raphael slowly walked over to the boy and knelt down in front of him. He carefully reached out and touched the child's forehead. A wave of soothing energy washed through Uriel's body. He felt his aches vanish, his broken bones repair themselves, his bruises disappear. The little stream of blood that cascaded down his face stopped as his cut healed and the blood itself evaporated. Uriel sat in front of the angel, dirty and healthy. The boy gawked at the angel for a few seconds before a smile broke out across his face. Raphael's eyes twinkled.

"God wills it…" he quietly proclaimed.

Gabriel ordered the other two angels to go search the village. He knelt beside Raphael and looked at the boy, wonder in his eyes. Uriel gazed at the two angels, unable to decide which one was more breathtaking. He had always believed in angels, and now he was seeing them, basking in the warmth of their holiness.

"This is very impossible, you know," Gabriel said to the boy, stern and gentle, like a father teaching his child a worldly wisdom. "Normally humans cannot see or hear us unless we reveal ourselves."

Uriel's smile twitched.

"Can you talk?" Gabriel asked.

Uriel shook his head.

"Have you ever been able to talk?"

Again, Uriel shook his head.

"A mute boy…" muttered Gabriel. "What could this mean?"

"Is there a way you can tell us your name?" asked Raphael. Uriel looked down at the dusty ground and used his finger to carefully write.

'U-R-I-E-L," Raphael read once the boy was done, barely able to get a glimpse of the letters before the wind scattered the dust once more.

"Uriel," said Gabriel. "You are a Jew?"

Uriel nodded.

"And this village…this is your home? This was a Jewish town?"

Uriel nodded, his smile wilting.

"Gabriel," said Raphael. "*Hashem* let me heal him. He has given this child the ability to see us…that must mean something."

"Indeed," Gabriel concurred, looking back at the boy. "The angels of the Heavenly Host can neither save nor kill if it is against God's will. If God did not want Raphael to heal you, then his hand would have never reached your forehead. We have no power of our own; it comes from *Hashem*."

"And," Raphael added, "even we aren't all-powerful. Gabriel, this boy is good and innocent. His presence takes away some of the pain…but still…"

"Be patient, Raphael," ordered Gabriel. Uriel raised an eyebrow. Angels could feel pain? What was hurting them?

Noticing the confused look on the child's face, Gabriel elaborated. "Uriel, you must understand that some things are too holy for human eyes or human hands. When the Ark of the Covenant was carried, humans had to be cautious not to touch it lest its sanctity overwhelm them. If a human looked at the face of God, he would perish. We angels are holy beings. We can stand to see and be near such incredible holiness."

"But evil, now, that is different. Evil is as painful to most of us as fire on mortal flesh. It burns us, corrodes our hearts. And some places, particularly now, have become so thick with sin and evil that we cannot even enter without being blinded by pain. A great evil deed took place here, and so it is painful to stay. The only reason we could enter at all was because the murderers who caused this horror are gone…"

"But," Raphael interrupted, "there's so much evil here, so many horrible things happening everywhere in this land. So much sin…we can't even go near the Germans without doubling over. Perhaps that's why we haven't been able to find Michael…"

Uriel's eyes sparkled. Michael, the greatest of all the angels, the one that his father had always told stories about.

He leaned forward and his fingers twitched, begging for more information on the Archangel. His heart sunk, however, when he saw the misery that crossed the angels' faces at the mere mention of the great angel's name. They saw the question in the boy's eyes and Gabriel spoke up.

"Michael has gone missing," he explained. "We have no clue where he could be, though we think we may know who is responsible."

Uriel trembled with anxiety and eagerness. He grabbed the hem of his shirt, twisting it so much that he nearly ripped it, and leaned in so far that he nearly fell against the angel's shoulder. Gabriel, seeing his desperate desire to know, explained.

"Michael is the Guardian Angel of God's Chosen People, your people. Many centuries ago, he was the Guardian Angel of Jacob, the Patriarch, the father of the Jewish People. Jacob was a righteous man, loved by God, but he had a wicked twin brother named Esau. And Esau too had a Guardian Angel, one named Samael."

"Naturally, Esau and Jacob were opposing forces, one good and the other evil. And so their angels, too, were adversaries. One day, Samael attacked Michael, and the two came to blows right before the Throne of God. God, in His wisdom, stopped the fight and punished Samael for his murderous behavior. He decreed that Samael would no longer be the Guardian of Esau. Instead, he would become the Angel of Death, a grueling and thankless position."

"Without his Guardian Angel to protect him, Esau and his family were wiped from the face of the Earth. Samael was distraught and furious, and he blamed Michael for his woes. He swore that he would do to Michael what he did to him. Samael wants to get rid of Michael so that his people, the Jewish People, will be wiped out like Esau. It is impossible to kill Michael, but he can weaken and imprison him so he cannot protect the Children of Israel. For centuries, Samael has plotted and fought against the Jewish People, but he has never succeeded. Michael has been weakened, but never to the point where he could be captured by the Angel of Death."

"But now…now it is different. The Children of Israel are being butchered, and the persecution has weakened Michael so much that it would have been easy for Samael to capture him. If Michael is not found and freed, then the Jewish People…without their guardian…"

The angel's voice trailed off into oblivion and Uriel's blood congealed at his unspoken words.

"Samael is the Angel of Death," sighed Raphael. "He can go to areas we can't without feeling even a twinge of pain. If he's hidden Michael near the sinners…"

He looked down at the child and his eyes gave a glint of realization. He put a hand on Gabriel's arm.

"Gabriel," he said, "perhaps that's why Hashem has sent us this child. He is not an angel, so he can walk among the sinners without burning."

"Raphael…"

"Hashem wouldn't let him see us if there wasn't a reason!"

Gabriel looked down at the child, gazing straight into his eyes. Uriel felt as though his soul had been laid bare before the angel's star-like irises.

"Child," Gabriel said at last, "what Raphael says is true, but it is your decision. Would you be willing to serve Hashem and your people? Will you find Michael?"

Without a moment's hesitation, Uriel nodded.

"Be warned," said Gabriel, "you will have to enter an area overflowing with sin and slaughter. There will be horrors there that no innocent eyes should behold."

Uriel nodded.

"And," Gabriel added, "the Angel of Death will confront you if you search for Michael. Are you prepared for that? Are you still willing to go through with this?"

Uriel paused and looked towards his beloved Zingdorf, now nothing but a graveyard of bodies and buildings. He had nothing else to do, no other purpose, and if he met his end, he could at least join his family and friends.

He nodded.

"Hold out your hand," Gabriel ordered. Uriel obeyed, and the angel dropped a pendant into his palm. Uriel examined the necklace closely. It was a *hamsa*, the Jewish symbol for good luck. The pendant was shaped like a hand and in the middle of the small, ornate silver palm there was a golden jewel.

"Put it on," said Gabriel, and Uriel slipped it around his neck. The hamsa rested at his breast and he gently touched the gem.

"This hamsa," Gabriel explained, "was forged on the First Day of Creation by Hashem Himself. Its true owner is not with us anymore, but perhaps you will be a worthy wearer. Keep it on and only the righteous will see you, but to the wicked you will be invisible. Do not take the hamsa off for any reason, particularly while you are among the Germans, or else they will see you and they will kill you."

Uriel wrapped his fingers around the warm necklace and nodded. Invisible. He had always wondered what it would be like to walk among men unseen. He touched the golden stone and sighed happily as his fingers brushed against the holy jewel. It fit perfectly, as if it had been made for him.

"Be brave, Angel-Finder," Raphael whispered to the boy.

"God be with you, Angel-Finder," said Gabriel. He and Raphael rose, and the world was filled with light once more. There was a powerful *crack* and the light rose like an upturned flash of lightning, disappearing into the skies above and taking the angels of God back to the Heavens.

Uriel slowly stood, his eyes glistening as he stared up at the cumulus clouds above, wondering if the angels were still watching him.

He reminded himself how to move his stiff legs and reached the edge of Zingdorf. He slid down the hill, further dirtying his already sullied clothes. He looked around at the forest. The birds chirped, the crickets sang, and Uriel stood silent, wondering which way he should go.

The thin road up ahead caught his eye. He darted to the dirt trail and noticed fresh wheel tracks. Somebody had passed by Zingdorf since last night and they had been driving a car. The Jews in Zingdorf and the other nearby villages were either too poor or too traditional to own cars of their own. On the rare occasions that he had seen a car in the past, a wealthy gentile had owned the vehicle.

Although he couldn't tell which way the car had driven, he knew enough about the area to know that other villages—many Polish, many Jewish, and some mixed—lay south of Zingdorf. If the Germans had been driving the car, then they would have been going to those other villages to commit their crimes.

Uriel looked back at Zingdorf. The smoke was gone, and at a distance, with the birds singing in the background, it was hard to tell that the village was no more. He almost wanted to run back. Perhaps if he did, he would find that his imagination had taken him far from home. His mother and father would be waiting to scold him for staying out so late, reminding him that they had synagogue tomorrow…

He crushed the wish before it could carry him back to his old home and instead forced his legs to follow the car tracks, leaving Zingdorf standing alone, with only the twittering birds for company.

ZINGDORF

It seemed to be an ugly place. Gray and brown, musty, the smell of goats and cats marinating the air, filled with old wooden buildings that looked ready to fall over at any moment. It didn't seem like the sort of town that any prudent person would want to visit, much less live in.

Yet all one had to do was stand by the synagogue during choir practice, and the true beauty of the little shtetl would fill their ears.

The choir of Zingdorf was famous even outside of the teeny village. People from other neighboring towns would often pass by just so they could pause and listen to the practice sessions. The people of Zingdorf were well known for being wonderful singers, and their choir sounded more like a chorus of angels than a chorus of mortals.

Joining the choir was a rite of passage for every child born in Zingdorf. It was part of being a member of the community. Every boy, no matter how naughty on normal occasions, treasured the part they played in the choir and always showed up to sing.

Every boy, that is, except for Uriel. The village mute.

Uriel couldn't count the number of times he had felt an ache in his heart as he heard the lovely sound of children's voices coming together in perfect harmony. He couldn't count the number of times he had peeked into the synagogue during the practices he couldn't attend and shed tears, knowing that he could never sing with them.

He would never sing God's praises with the others. He would never stand at the front of the synagogue, shoulder to shoulder with the other boys, and feel his voice meld with the others before ascending to the Heavens. His parents would never sit in the audience and applaud after his performance was done.

And even though he had been born in Zingdorf, even though the town's every nook and cranny were engraved onto his mind, he would never completely belong. Not while he couldn't add his voice to the melodious din. Not while he didn't have a voice to add.

Uriel, though, was not one to drown in self-pity. Although he would always feel alienated, and although he wanted nothing more than to join the choir and sing God's praises in front of everyone, he wouldn't spend all of his time moping outside of the synagogue.

Uriel couldn't sing. He couldn't speak.

But he could write. And writing became his outlet. While his mouth would never utter a single word, his hands could create entire worlds with only a pen and paper. He could craft people, stories, places, countries even. He could make animals talk and angels appear. He could do whatever he wanted.

With a pen and paper, he had a voice.

But even so, he wished he could sing.

4.

"**H**err Litten!"

Brandt's outburst and the slam of a car door yanked Uwe out of Uriel's world. He shoved the book into his pocket before Brandt could see, knowing full well that the National Socialists were fond of Jewish literature only when they could use it for a bonfire.

Disappointment welled up in his stomach. The small child was a surprisingly good writer. He had been completely wrapped up in the boy's tale and immediately wondered when he could get to a secluded place so he could finish and figure out what punishment that foolish Simon would receive for deceiving the Archangel Michael.

Brandt opened the door for Uwe.

"*Après vous, monsieur,*" said the Major. A crooked smile came to Uwe's lips.

"French?" he said, narrowly avoiding the roof of the car as he climbed out. "I thought *I* was the linguist."

"Those three words are the extent of my foreign language knowledge," replied Brandt. "Well, I know a few dirty words in English, but let's not count that."

Uwe had to bite his tongue in order not to laugh. He looked up at the house they had parked in front of. Two stories high, pleasant, and to Uwe quite large. He realized that it was no manor, but Uwe could tell that it was big as the biggest building in his little hometown.

"Nice?" asked Brandt, standing beside Uwe.

"Very," Uwe confirmed. "Is this where you and your men live?"

"This is where *I* live. The rest of them sleep in a house a little down the road from here."

"Why?"

"They insisted," said Brandt with a glitter in his eyes. "They said I deserved a space to myself, to do my work in peace. Personally, I think they just said that because they wanted to get rid of me. Now they can party and drink all they want without me wagging my finger at them…"

"Not so, Uncle Günter!"

Two guards that had been standing by the house's door scurried up to the Major, boyish grins on their faces. They, like Brandt and Uwe, weren't very young. They were middle-aged, maybe slightly younger than Brandt but older than the average soldier. In fact, they looked somewhat out of place in their uniforms. Uwe thought they would have been more comfortable in a clockmaker's clothes or a milkman's outfit.

"'Uncle Günter'?" Uwe repeated, watching with surprise as---rather than clicking their heels, throwing up their arms, and barking 'Heil Hitler!'---the two policemen cheerfully shook their superior's hand and slapped him on the shoulder like an old friend.

"Their nickname," said Brandt with an amused grin. "If you call me 'Major Brandt' around here, Herr Litten, you'll be the black sheep."

"Herr Litten?" said one policeman. "So you'll be our linguist then?"

"To the best of my abilities."

"Very good to meet you!" he said. Uwe shook hands with the two officers. Both told him their names, but he forgot them almost immediately. He had always been bad with names.

"Uncle Günter," said one soldier. "I think we should get you up to speed on everything that happened while you were away."

"I was hardly gone for a week! Unless the Führer decreed we're not allowed to drink anymore—which would concern *you* more than me…"

The soldiers both laughed. "No, no, sir. Just a few things. It won't take long."

"Very well. Herr Litten, I'm sorry, but could you perhaps just get your bags together, put them by the front door, maybe look around the backyard if you wish? I'll be right with you and I'll show you around the house…"

"Of course," replied Uwe, nodding to the two policemen before scurrying to grab his bags. He left his luggage right by the front door and then decided to have a look around.

"Don't stray too far now," Brandt called after him. "We're right by the forest and there may be partisans nearby."

"I'll just be behind the house! Just getting some air and stretching my legs."

"All right! I'll be a moment!"

The backyard of the house was nonexistent. Instead, there was a small forest that led into the larger forest. Trees stood so close to the house that their branches scraped against the bricks and windows. Uwe hoped that wouldn't be a nuisance on windy nights.

He looked up at one tree, which was only slightly smaller than the house. Several of the branches were low. The tree was almost perfect for climbing. Uwe made an attempt, but his upper-arm strength left much to be desired and he couldn't hoist himself up. He chuckled at his futile attempt and wondered if Jürgen would enjoy having such a tree in his yard. Were Uwe not concerned that his sprightly child might leap out of the tree and break all his bones, he might have planted one near his house.

"We passed a village on our way here," said Brandt once Uwe was gone. "A little Jewish town. Do either of you know anything about it?"

"Little Jewish town? Where exactly?"

"It was on a hill. Burned to the ground. All the Jews were killed in the synagogue."

"Ah, that! Right, I think the place was called…Zi…Z something…"

"Zo…Christ, I can't remember either."

"Was it us or the Poles that did it?" asked Brandt.

"A little of both."

Uriel was surprised by how fast he ran without tiring out. He rushed down the road, slowing down only when he felt the need to catch his breath for one moment before sprinting once more. He spotted a house and his golden eyes glinted as he followed the tracks right up to the shiny black vehicle he had been pursuing. He stared at the car for a moment, having never seen such a beautiful, sleek machine in his life. It shimmered in the sunlight like a black diamond. He ran his fingers over the ebony surface and wished that he could ride in such a vehicle.

"What do you mean by that?"

The query snapped Uriel out of his daydream. He ducked behind the lovely car and peeked out at the speakers. He could tell right away that they were Germans, and he was surprised that he could understand them despite the fact that he didn't know a word of German. His finger brushed against the golden gem on the hamsa, and he wondered if it did more than just hide him from the wicked.

"Ackerman knew we were gonna have to clear out that town eventually, but the Pollacks in another village apparently did a lot of business there. He talked to the mayor, and the mayor said that he and his folk would clear out the Jews. They practically begged to burn the place, so he let them have at it. Said it would save us time and ammunition."

Uriel slowly stood up and stepped to the side. He should have been visible as day, and yet none of the policemen noticed him.

"Hm. Well, I'll have to talk to him about that. Enlisting the Poles is fine and all, but he shouldn't make decisions like that without an order from me or the higher echelons. At least that's one village off our list. It'll be smelling over there for weeks, though."

Praying that the hamsa would work, Uriel warily walked up to the three Germans. Their eyes didn't divert from one another for even a second. They didn't hear the quiet patter of the child's footsteps, his intakes for air, his rapid heartbeat. They didn't see his eyes shining with a dozen questions as he stood right beside Major Brandt. Uriel looked up at the German, examining his dusty medals and slightly wrinkled uniform, looking into the sharp green eyes that never once shifted to the Jewish boy.

Uriel's face broke into a grin. The wicked men couldn't see or hear him, just as Gabriel had said. The boy placed his fingers on either side of his mouth, stretched his lips apart, and wiggled his tongue at the Nazis. None of them saw him. The boy did every funny face he could dream up, waving his hand in front of their faces and jumping up and down, and yet their pupils never shifted to him.

Uriel decided to do one last test and carefully tapped one Nazi on the arm. Brandt's brow furrowed and he looked down, his eyes right on the child.

"What is it, Uncle Günter?" asked one policeman. The Major looked at the seemingly empty space behind him and shook his head, turning back to the soldiers.

"Nothing," he said. The Germans continued to converse. Uriel looked behind them. The door to the huge house beckoned to him. Michael could very well be imprisoned in the manor. It would be the best place: right where the wicked men slept. Gabriel and Raphael wouldn't be able to step foot there.

He scurried to the door and was relieved to find it unlocked. He opened it a crack and slipped in.

The inside was warm, the air clear and free of any forest smell. Uriel gazed about, overwhelmed by the splendor of it all. The only buildings he had ever been in had been made of wood and old bricks, little buildings with short roofs and musty air, usually saturated in smoke from candles and the fireplace.

This palace seemed six stories tall. Uriel gazed up at the giant staircase and wondered how anybody could run up and down those stairs without becoming exhausted and falling. The walls were painted white and lined with colorful pictures and portraits. The floors were covered with a soft blue carpet that Uriel couldn't help but brush his fingers against. Instead of candles, the house was lit with bulbs and lamps that glowed like man-made stars. Uriel had only seen an electric light thrice in his young life and seeing so many bathing the entrance hall in light almost made him dizzy. He looked up and saw a cluster of diamonds as big as a man dangling from the high ceiling and had to wonder where they had gotten so many shimmering jewels and why they would hang them all the way up there.

Slightly afraid that the diamonds would fall and crush him, Uriel moved to the next room, which turned out to be the sitting room. The chairs and sofas were bigger than his bed and he wondered if anybody slept there. He pressed his finger against a petunia on the floral-print couch and smiled when he saw how cushy it was. He sat down and nearly yelped in surprise as he sunk into the cushion. He adjusted his position and, much to his delight, found that it was as bouncy as it was comfortable. Keeping his dusty shoes on, he hopped onto the couch and jumped six times, a giggle occasionally escaping from between his teeth.

Before he could bounce a seventh time, however, his eyes fell upon the rich red curtains that hid the window. He jumped down and approached, pulling the curtains away. He looked out the clear window and saw the trees in the backyard and the forest that lay barely five yards from the house. Uriel pressed his nose against the glass, wondering if perhaps he would find something in the forest that would point to Michael.

The sound of a door slamming and German voices caused the boy's stomach to lurch. Although he knew that they couldn't see him, he instinctually ducked behind the curtain. If he hadn't had the hamsa, the curtains wouldn't have done a very good job of hiding him.

He stayed behind the velvet fabric, clutching it tightly as he listened to the two men that had entered.

"Are you thirsty, Herr Litten?" asked Brandt as Uwe dropped his bags by the stairs.

"Parched, actually," the linguist replied. "I don't suppose you have any beer…"

Brandt laughed. "I'm afraid the boys have probably bled me dry by now, but I'll see what's left."

Uwe prepared to thank him, but as he stood up his eyes landed on a large picture of a woman and a little boy embracing and waving at the camera.

"Is that your family?" Uwe asked, pointing to the picture. Brandt's pupils followed the linguist's finger and his eyes shimmered fondly when they fell upon the mother and child.

"Yes," he confirmed. "They're in Hamburg. I miss them, but they write enough to keep me from stealing a car and driving there without leave. Hans is just learning to write by himself. Very smart boy. You have a son as well, Herr Litten."

"Jürgen," said Uwe with a nod. "He's ten. My daughters are sixteen and fourteen."

"Oh, dear," chortled Brandt. "Two teens, two *daughters*! I don't look forward to that stage."

"I'm sure yours will be fine," Uwe assured him. "How old is he?"

"Five."

"Then he has a long time to go."

"True! By the time he's a rebellious teen, London will be a vacation site for the Reich. I have another on the way, so he may get a sister to argue with."

"Congratulations!"

"I hope I can get leave when that happens, but for now, come, you can have a seat and a drink. Your room is right upstairs, first door to the left. We have people come over every other Wednesday to clean…"

"Poles?" asked Uwe, following the Major into the sitting room.

"Mainly ethnic Germans," said Brandt.

"Would it be all right if they didn't clean my room?" asked Uwe. "I'm used to keeping my own area in order, and if anything's moved from its proper place it grates on my nerves."

"I understand completely," said Brandt. "I feel the same way, actually, but it's not possible for me to keep this whole place clean by myself. Just lock your door before you leave every day and nobody will disturb your space."

"I app…" Uwe started to say, but at that moment a shadow caught his eye. He looked over his shoulder and met the eyes of a little boy. The boy from Zingdorf.

The child was partially hidden behind the scarlet curtain, and when the German saw him his lips parted with surprise.

He can see me? Uriel thought, bewildered. *A German can see me? But only the righteous can see me…*

Uwe had no clue that being able to see the boy was significant. To him it seemed that the child had, somehow or another, followed him here and was hiding behind the curtain.

Fear, confusion, and even a spark of relief clashed in Uwe's mind. The Jewish boy was alive, but if Brandt saw him, knew that he was in his house, knew that an 'enemy of the state' was there…what would he do? Deport him, of course. Uwe had heard enough rumors about the camps and ghettos to know that they were brutal. A little orphaned boy wouldn't make it there.

Although Uriel knew that he was in no danger so long as he wore the hamsa, he pressed his index finger to his lips. *Shhh…*

Uwe obeyed the silent command, unsure of what to do.

"Herr Litten," said Brandt, causing Uwe's heart to somersault. The Major looked at Uwe with concern as he asked, "Is something wrong?"

Six words threatened to vault from Uwe's vocal cords: *There's a Jew behind the curtain.*

Instead, six different words emerged: "No, nothing's wrong, Major. Just thirsty."

He was astonished that he had the ability to stay so calm. Even as his heart threatened to implode with fear and sweat beads formed on his forehead, his voice stayed neutral. The Major's smile returned and he clapped his hands together.

"Ah, stupid me! Right, I'll see what I can salvage. You wait here, I'll be right back."

Uwe sat down in one chair and nodded. As soon as Brandt left, however, his calm façade melted, and he flew to the curtain.

"What are you doing here?" he hissed to the boy, ripping the curtain from his grasp. Uriel just stared up at him, stunned and silent.

"You…" whispered Uwe, examining the child closely and realizing without an inkling of a doubt that this was the boy who wrote in the golden notebook. "You're the boy from the village, from Zingdorf…"

Uriel blinked and scrutinized the German's features. He couldn't recall ever meeting this man before.

Uwe grabbed the child's arm and yanked him away from the window.

"Run, now," he ordered. "Up the stairs, first room on the left, lock the door behind you and don't open it until I knock seven times!"

Something about the urgency in the German's tone caused Uriel to obey. He skittered out of the sitting room and up the stairs, quietly shutting and locking the door.

Uwe collapsed onto the chair and started gnawing on his fingernails. *What the hell am I doing?* he thought. *If Brandt finds out…*

There were laws that dealt with this sort of thing. If he was caught harboring a Jew, he would either be killed on the spot or deported to a concentration camp. Jews were enemies of the Reich. By hiding one he was betraying Germany, and the only sentence for a traitor was death.

Still, he wasn't quite at the point of no return. If he told Brandt that he had seen a Jew running up the stairs, he wouldn't get in trouble. In fact, he might even be rewarded for helping to catch an enemy of the state.

I have a family at home. I have children of my own to take care of, he thought. *I can't leave them. I can't die. I can't get caught hiding a Jew.*

And yet the more he thought of his family, the less possible it seemed to turn Uriel in. He heard footsteps and quickly brushed his hair back, sitting up and forcing a friendly smile onto his face as Brandt returned, his arms laden with a pitcher, two glasses, and a large old book.

"Water!" the Major declared, tipping the pitcher. Uwe compelled himself to chuckle. Brandt set the pitcher and glasses down on the coffee table and sat across from Uwe, holding the book in his lap like a precious treasure.

"You'll have to forgive me," said Brandt, pouring some water for Uwe, a few ice cubes clinking against the glass as they fell into the cup. "I should have known that the boys would raid my icebox while I was gone."

"I-it's fine," said Uwe.

"I can swipe a real drink off one of the boys tomorrow while we're at the base. Until then, let's have a toast."

He raised his glass and Uwe copied him, trying his best to keep his hands from visibly trembling.

"To your health," said Brandt. "To the health of your family and mine, to Germany, and to a greater, safer Reich."

"Cheers," said Uwe, tapping his glass against Brandt's and taking a sip. The cool water struggled to make it down his tight throat as his thoughts lingered on the Jewish boy in his bedroom and what would happen to him and his family if he didn't tell Brandt about the child.

Uwe's eyes darted to the book that Brandt had brought. He gestured to it and asked, "What book is that?"

Brandt's eyes sparkled like those of a child eager to show off his drawing. He set his glass down and handed the book to Uwe. The linguist had to stifle a shudder when he saw that it was the Führer's book, *Mein Kampf.* He carefully flipped through the black hardback, scanning the gothic script with intrigue and fright.

"I show this to everyone," said Brandt. "Have you ever read the whole thing?"

"I…ahhh…"

Brandt laughed and waved his hand dismissively. "That's all right, neither have I. But this one is special. Look on the front page."

Uwe did so and his eyes fell upon two hastily scrawled words that separated this book from the millions of other *Mein Kampfs*.

Adolf Hitler

Uwe almost dropped the book. He carefully shut it so the damning name wouldn't make his already pounding heart beat any faster.

"He signed it…" Uwe muttered. "Did…you get him to sign it in person?"

"Me? Ha! No, a small man like me has never met him face to face."

"Then how did you get this?"

"I killed one of my men for it," replied Brandt so quickly and seriously that Uwe's head snapped up and his eyes bulged. Brandt burst into laughter.

"The look on your face!" he cried, nearly doubling over. Uwe wasn't sure if he should laugh or apologize, so instead he just sat silently until Brandt got a hold of himself.

"I'm kidding, of course," said the Major. "A good friend got it for me on a trip to Berlin. It's very precious to me, but you're free to flip through it anytime you like. My office has plenty of other books as well if you feel like reading something a little less political."

"Thank you, Herr Brandt," said Uwe. "Though won't I be too busy to read?"

"Oh, we won't overwork you," Brandt assured the linguist.

"Pardon me, Major, but I know what *I'm* doing here. May I ask what you and your men are doing here?"

"Of course," said Brandt, taking another sip of water. "As you know, Herr Litten, I am the Major of this battalion. We are the *Ordnungspolizei*, the Order Police, and that's exactly what we're here to do: keep order."

"How so?"

"Most of the regular army and the SS men are further east, fighting the Russians or guarding the camps or handling the major population centers like Warsaw," explained Brandt. "But they left behind some scraps in the countryside. In the little villages there are many Jews and partisans, enemies of the state who would rise up against us and kill our men. But these villages are far from railways and cities and civilization as it were, and so we've been tasked to crush the partisans and resettle the population."

"'Resettle'?"

"This is very good land, Herr Litten," said Brandt, leaning forward and clasping his hands together, speaking calmly and slowly, like a teacher trying to get a dimwitted student to understand a basic concept. "We have millions of poor, homeless Germans back in the Old Reich. We won this land, we drove the Poles back, and so we can do what we like with it. We can build this land up and settle hundreds of German families here and send the Poles and Jews to settle in another place."

"You'll take them from their homes?" muttered Uwe.

"It seems harsh," replied Brandt. "I realize that, but our people are our first priority."

"But this is their home, their land…"

"And need I remind you, Herr Litten," said Brandt, still calm, though a touch of irritation could be seen in his eyes, "that this was *our* land first? Don't you remember Versailles? How they took this land from Germany? They *stole* our homeland and now we're taking it back, with some interest. That's only fair."

"Yes," mumbled Uwe. "Right, I didn't consider that. Forgive me."

For a moment, the Major's expression remained severe, but then the impatience melted from his irises and a smile pulled at his lips once more.

"Quite all right," he said. "I know you meant no offense. You have a good heart, Herr Litten."

Uwe bowed his head and was barely able to choke out, "Thank you."

"And with that said," said Brandt, scooping up his book and standing up, "I shall leave you and your good heart to your own devices. Go wherever you like, but stay on the grounds for your own safety. Take some time to get acquainted with the house. It's your home too, at least for the time being."

Uwe thanked Major Brandt once more and watched as he exited the sitting room. Once he was gone, Uwe leapt from his seat, ran up the stairs, found his door locked, and knocked seven times.

Uriel fumbled with the doorknob for a few minutes before he spotted a key sitting on a nearby desk and locked the door. His mind reeled with baffled bewilderment.

That German had seen him.

God thought that man was righteous. Uriel didn't question the Lord's wisdom, yet the fact that a *German* could see him still confused him. What made *him* righteous?

Uriel thought of the fear that had glistened in the man's eyes as he ordered him to go upstairs. The German didn't know that his wicked comrade couldn't see the Jew.

Then he was trying to rescue me, thought Uriel with a small smile. A noble, if unnecessary, gesture. Uriel was in no danger, and even if the German decided to 'take a risk' by hiding the Jew, he would be fine so long as Uriel had his hamsa.

Uriel hoped that the German's kindness wouldn't get in the way of finding Michael. The Jewish boy glanced around the large, cozy room. Although it was unlikely that Michael would be hidden here, he needed to look everywhere.

The bed had no less than six pillows. He wondered why anybody would need so many and giggled as he thought of a man with six heads snoozing on the large bed. The covers were thick and dull gray, nothing like the thin, scratchy blue blanket that Uriel's mother had tucked him in with every night. He touched the silky gray bedspread and decided that he preferred his blue blanket.

He got down on his knees and looked under the bed, but there wasn't even a dust bunny down there to greet him. He checked the closet, which was almost as big as his room back in Zingdorf, but it was empty.

Uriel's amber eyes shifted about, eventually falling upon the window. He walked over and after a brief struggle, he managed to undo the lock and throw it open. The smell of trees swept into the room, and Uriel took a deep breath. He saw a tree right in front of the window, which somewhat impeded his view of the forest. The tree was tall, but as he looked down, he could tell that it would be climbable. He and the boys from Zingdorf had climbed higher. True, many of those higher climbs had ended with bruises and broken bones, but Uriel was confident that he could make it down unscathed if the need arose.

A bang on the door caused his heart to jolt. The boy turned away from the window as six more knocks followed.

He darted to the door and swiftly unlocked it. The spectacled German pushed him away from the threshold and slammed the door shut, locking it once he was inside. The German sighed, breathing heavily and leaning against the door. Uriel watched him with fascination, standing in the middle of the room and rocking back and forth on his heels.

Finally, the German turned to face him, his blue eyes locking onto the Jew's and shimmering with wonder and aggravation.

"You're alive," he muttered, staring at the boy suspiciously. Uriel looked down at himself as though to confirm this before looking back up at the German, lifting his brow as if to ask why his continued existence was worthy of indication.

"But I saw you," said the German, pointing to the boy like a lawyer would a criminal. "I saw you in Zingdorf; we passed through there and I saw that you weren't breathing!"

Uriel's head tipped to the side.

"What are you doing here? Why are you here? How did you even get this far without getting caught?" the German demanded, each question bursting from his lips like a bullet. Uriel took a step back, slightly scared of the spark that flared in the frustrated German's eyes.

"Well?" Uwe demanded when the boy didn't respond.

Uriel touched his throat and shook his head. Uwe's visage discarded its impatience.

"Oh," he muttered. "You can't talk."

Uriel shook his head. Guilt jabbed at Uwe's heart.

Yelling at a little mute kid. Real nice, Uwe, he thought to himself. *The poor boy's lost everything and all you do is interrogate him.*

"I'm sorry," said Uwe. "It's just…I…agh!"

He clenched his fists and began pacing back and forth. "You're here now, that's that. Brandt said that I could have my privacy here as long as I keep the door shut and locked. So…I can hide you here and smuggle you some food… Christ, this is insanity! If I get caught…damn, damn, damn! But I can't send you off or you won't make it. I can keep you here until…until…I don't know! Until something changes and I can put you somewhere safe! But as long as you're here neither…"

His rant was interrupted as a small finger tapped his shoulder. He stopped and glanced down. Uriel smiled widely, looking almost amused as he offered Uwe his hand.

Uwe gazed at the child's hand and his ire departed. A smile forced its way onto his face as he carefully grasped the child's hand and gave it a small shake.

"Where are my manners?" he chuckled. "My name is Uwe, Uwe Litten."

Uriel's eyes sparkled as if to indicate his understanding.

"And you," said Uwe, "must be Uriel."

Uriel's smile shifted into a surprised frown. Seeing the boy's bewilderment, Uwe released the child's hand and reached into his pocket.

"This belongs to you, doesn't it?"

As soon as he laid eyes on the golden notebook, Uriel snatched it from the German's hand, holding it to his chest like a mother would her child. Uwe couldn't help but inwardly chortle as he watched the boy flip through the book to make sure that no pages had been ripped out. Uriel kissed the cover when he confirmed that every precious word that he had lovingly etched into the notebook was still there.

Overwhelmed with gratitude, Uriel suddenly embraced Uwe. The German, startled, leapt back. Although his hug had been rejected, Uriel grinned up at Uwe, who noted that the boy had a small gap between his front teeth and was missing one tooth on the bottom row.

"You're welcome," said Uwe, adjusting his glasses, his fond smile slowly returning as he looked down at the gap-toothed boy. "I was reading some of your stories…"

On hearing that, a look of utter horror came to the child's countenance. His lip wobbled and the blood left his face as he squeezed the notebook to his chest and tried to hide it from Uwe's sight. He had never let a soul glance at his writing. Not even his mother and father, although they had always wanted to read his stories. He was too embarrassed, afraid that his tales would be less than perfect. Besides, they were *his* words, his and his alone, and he didn't want to give them to anybody else.

Seeing the terror and shame that crossed the child's face, Uwe almost gave a rather dark laugh. He looked so frightened at the very concept of having somebody else read his words, and yet he had seemed so *calm* when Major Brandt was only feet away from his hiding place.

What a strange child…he thought, carefully touching the boy's shoulder and turning him to face him.

"Uriel, calm down," the linguist said. "It's not a big deal…"

Uriel shook his head and Uwe could see small specks of water forming at the corners of his golden eyes.

"I thought they were good," said Uwe. "Very good. You have a gift. I've never seen a child write so well."

The threat of tears left, and the boy's eyes shimmered with suspicious surprise as he blinked up at the German.

"I mean it, really," Uwe assured him, reading the child's apprehension. The boy's lips parted in awe. He, Uriel, had written something that another person enjoyed. The very thought made his smile return with twice its normal strength as his heart fluttered up to his throat and a sigh of joy exited his otherwise silent lips.

"And you know, Uriel," said Uwe, putting a hand on the golden notebook and giving it a slight tug. Uriel at first tightened his grip, not willing to let go of his words, but Uwe gave him a gentle smile, one that begged for his trust. Slowly, the child released his precious notebook, allowing Uwe to once again hold his tales.

"Stories are meant to be shared," said Uwe. "Have you ever read your stories aloud, Uriel?"

Of course not. He couldn't read them aloud himself. The child's lips tightened bitterly as he shook his head.

"Well, right, erm," muttered Uwe, realizing his poor phrasing. "What I meant to say was: has anybody ever read them aloud *to* you?"

Again, Uriel shook his head. Uwe sat down on the bed and leaned against the headboard.

"I usually read to my son before bedtime," he said. "You remind me of him, you know. You look the same, and you're around the same age."

He patted the space beside him. "Come. If you want, I'll read your stories to you. We'll have to keep it quiet, though."

Uriel's eyes glistened at that. He had never *heard* his stories before, and he wondered if listening to them would make the experience any different. He crawled onto the bed and sat beside Uwe, making sure to give the German an inch of space.

"Very good," said Uwe with a curt nod. "One story and then you need to sleep. We'll figure this out more in the morning. Let's see…well, might as well start back at the beginning."

"There was once a small village. This village had all the members that every village has. It had its rabbi, its teacher, its baker, and, like every town, it had its fool. The town fool was a man named Simon, whom everybody called 'Simon the Fool.' No one remembered his last name, so they just called him 'The Fool.'

He was certainly foolish, though kind at heart, and yet nobody trusted him because he was known to be such a halfwit. His landlord, a man named Aaron, trusted him the least…"

PAPA

His withered eyes had seen many things, and his aged ears that often couldn't hear his own name being called had heard many stories.

He would sit Uriel down on his lap and Uriel would lean back, giggling as the hairs of his papa's long beard (which, when he stood, went down to his bellybutton) tickled his ears and the back of his neck.

Once the boy was still, Papa would start speaking. He would tell Uriel stories of his childhood, tales from the Torah and Talmud, folktales passed down for generations, or a story he would make up as he went along. No matter what he told Uriel, if it was a story, Uriel remembered it. Rules he wouldn't always remember, but stories would always stay in his mind. Papa noticed that and had plenty of fables and moral stories on standby.

When Uriel began to write he, at first, merely transcribed the stories Papa had told him. Then, gradually, towns and people and creatures of his own creation began to form in his head and would bother him endlessly until he succumbed to their wishes and wrote their stories as well.

Still, even after he started writing his own tales, he would eagerly hop onto his papa's lap at the end of each day and wait for wondrous stories to spill from his lips. Uriel could only dream of being such a storyteller. The tales he told were, like him, silent. Seen, but never heard.

Yet one day, Papa came home to find Uriel in tears. Mama told him that another boy had mocked their son.

"He said, 'God mustn't care about you, Uriel. If He cared about you, then he wouldn't have forgotten to give you a voice!'"

Tears were still streaming down Uriel's cheeks as his father lifted him onto his lap. He expected a story to make him feel better, but instead Papa looked right into his eyes.

"God forgets nothing," he declared. "Uriel, you were made perfectly."

5.

When Uwe awoke the next morning, he rushed to his closet and peeked inside. The boy was there. It hadn't been a dream.

The child was lying on a pile of Uwe's socks in the corner of the closet, the hanging coats and shirts partially obscuring him from the German's view.

Uwe crept downstairs and made it to the kitchen without running into Brandt.

"Up, Uriel, wake up!"

The child yawned and his heart sank a centimeter when he remembered where he was and when he realized that his mother hadn't woken him.

"Eat this, Uriel, you must be hungry," said Uwe, handing the child a small loaf of bread. The linguist's assumption was certainly accurate. As soon as he saw the food, Uriel's stomach seemed to remember itself and started snarling like an angry wolf. He gobbled up the bread in three bites, nearly choking until Uwe gave him a cup of water to clear his throat.

"All better?" he asked. The boy nodded, smiling gratefully.

"Good," said Uwe, allowing his worried eyes to wander to the door behind him, half afraid that he would open it and find Major Brandt pressing his ear against the flimsy barrier.

"Listen," he said to Uriel, his eyes hard as stones. "Major Brandt and I are going to meet his men today. We'll be gone all day. You stay in this room and don't leave for any reason!"

Uriel stood up and did a little dance from one foot to the other. Uwe looked down at the boy as though he was mad for a moment before he realized what the child was trying to get across.

"Bathroom?"

Uriel nodded. Uwe sighed.

"There's one right across from here…but don't go until we leave! Hold it! Your life is at risk and so is mine, so we both need to tread carefully. If either of us makes a wrong move then we'll both die, understand?"

Uriel nodded, though he didn't look as concerned as Uwe would have liked. He seemed rather nonchalant about the prospect of getting captured.

*Strange child…*Uwe thought. He reached into his pocket and handed the boy the golden notebook.

"Here," he said. "You can write while I'm gone. We can read more tonight. Okay? Would you like that?"

Uriel, although he knew that he had no time to write, smiled and nodded. He had enjoyed hearing his own words, and Uwe's voice seemed to have been fashioned for the task of reading them aloud.

"Very good…"

"Herr Litten!" came a shout from downstairs, causing Uwe to flinch.

"I have to go!" he hissed, rushing out of the room and locking the door behind him, not bothering to say goodbye.

"Come along then," said Brandt with a chipper smile as Uwe joined him downstairs. "Can't leave our little linguist behind, not when my boys are so eager to meet you. You'll love them, Herr Litten. They're rambunctious and talkative as little children, but they can be very intelligent conversationalists once they warm up to you."

"I'm sure we'll get along," said Uwe, forcing his pupils to focus on the Major instead of wandering restlessly back up the stairs. He followed Brandt outside and climbed into the car, his mind firmly pinned on Uriel as he prayed that the boy wouldn't get into any trouble while he was gone.

Uriel waited until he heard the sputter of a car's engine before he moved. Once he heard the vehicle drive off, he tried to open the door. He huffed when he realized that Uwe had locked the door from the outside and taken the key with him, which meant that Uriel was stuck.

He glanced about for an escape route and his eyes fell on the window. He pried it open and looked down as a long, sturdy branch from the tree in front of him tickled the bricks right under the windowsill.

He hesitated only for a second in order to discern if the branch would support his weight before climbing onto the windowsill and slowly stepping onto it. It wobbled and strained. Although Uriel was by no means a large child (in fact, he was fairly skinny), the branch wasn't so sturdy and was only barely able to hold him without snapping. He slowly inched his way towards the trunk and from there it was easy to climb down. He made a small jump, landing effortlessly on his feet. His hands were slightly sore from the jagged bark, but he had gotten worse injuries while at play.

Uriel ran back to the front of the house and was pleased to discover that the front door was open. The Major must have been overconfident. He had two guards stationed near the gates, and they would surely see any intruder. As it were, the boy was easily able to slip back into the manor without either of them even hearing his footsteps on the wooden porch.

Once inside, he had the whole house to himself. He began his hunt, checking every nook and cranny, every room, being careful not to get lost in the huge house and being extra careful not to linger beneath the hanging diamonds. The kitchen was filled with more food than he could dream of, but he didn't touch a crumb. He had to search, not snack.

He looked in the Major's room, the sitting room, every bedroom, being careful to put everything he moved back so that the Major wouldn't get suspicious and Uwe wouldn't get in trouble.

Search as he might for a sign of the Archangel, however, he found nothing. He finally came to the last unexplored room, the basement. It was dark, and Uriel's stomach roiled rebelliously, but he forced his legs to move him down the stairs. He managed to find and turn on the light, but the basement wasn't worth the fear and effort. It was almost completely empty except for a few boxes in the corners. One wall was blank, not a box leaning against it. He could assume that nobody ever spent time in the basement since the blank wall didn't even have a picture hanging upon it to make it seem less drab. Uriel examined the crates, but although he shook them, they never rattled or felt heavy. There was no sign that an angel was trapped inside any of them.

The basement started to give him an eerie feeling. The shadows seeped into his skin. He shuddered, shoving the last crate back into the corner before scurrying back up the stairs.

He released a heavy sigh as he slammed the door shut behind him. Michael wasn't in the house then.

So where could he be? wondered the boy, wandering back into the sitting room and pacing back and forth, trying to think of another place that the Angel of Death might have hidden the Archangel.

Uriel's eyes shifted to the rose-colored curtains. He swiftly moved to them and pushed them aside, allowing the bright sunshine to spill in through the glass. He rubbed his eyes as the light assailed his pupils before his vision adjusted to the brightness and he was able to look at the forest that lay right in the backyard.

That might be the place, he thought. He pushed the curtain back over the window, plunging the room into darkness before he scuttled to the front door and exited.

He dashed right into the forest, being careful to remember where he walked. He didn't want to get stranded in the woods. Uwe, benevolent as he was, certainly wouldn't go looking for him.

The trees shielded the sky with their long branches and emerald leaves. Only some sunlight was able to slip through the holes and land on the ground, creating patterns of light and darkness at Uriel's feet. Eventually, even the light that clung to the forest floor faded as the sun sank under the horizon.

I'd better head back, thought Uriel with a sigh. Perhaps he could continue the search tomorrow.

He took only ten more steps forward and found himself in a little circular clearing. The orange light from the setting sun splashed itself across the grass and dirt, causing the blades of grass to sparkle like sharp gems as they swayed in the approaching cool night breeze.

For a moment, Uriel stood in the circle, admiring the sky above and the dancing foliage that surrounded him.

But soon the last sliver of sunlight vanished, only traces of its glorious light remaining as night began to take over and the stars peeked out of the not-quite-black sky. He stood in the middle of the circle, watching as the trees' shadows stretched over the glittering grass, causing it to stop shining.

Uriel was about to turn and leave when he noticed that the shadows kept stretching even though the light wasn't changing position. He pursed his lips and took a cautious step back as the shadows congregated in the center of the circle, stretching, writhing, and then, much to his surprise and horror, transforming.

The shadows seemed to rise from the ground and swirl, twisting themselves into a humanoid shape. The figure of darkness opened its eyes, violet and filled with a ferocious hate. Color came to the figure, and Uriel's eyes bulged as he beheld the being that stood before him.

The angel was clad in dark armor, with a long sword strapped to his side. A smile formed at the corners of his lips as his dark purple eyes locked onto the boy. Slowly, the Angel of Death drew his blade.

"Little snoop," he purred. His sword looked like a sliver of the moon. It glowed with grim malice as its master raised it and pointed its sharp end at the boy. Uriel tried to back away, but a tree obstructed his path. He backed up against the trunk, his eyes dancing in desperate terror.

"Interesting," mused Samael. "You can see me, can't you, child?"

The sword got closer to his neck. Uriel whimpered, too afraid to nod.

"And yet I didn't reveal myself," whispered the demonic angel. "Fascinating. Gabriel sent you, didn't he? He sent a little Jew-boy to find Michael! Amusing... and rather clever."

Uriel clutched the bark of the tree. As the Angel of Death drew near, he couldn't help but recall one of his papa's admonitions.

Remember, Uriel, don't stop praying even when a knife is at your neck.

The child shut his eyes and prayed. *Sh'ma Yisrael Adonai Eloheinu Adonai Echad, Sh'ma Yisrael Adonai Eloheinu…*

He heard the Angel of Death grunt in aggravation and opened his eyes a millimeter. Samael held the sword right at Uriel's throat, and yet, though he obviously tried to, he couldn't stab the child.

Finally, the Angel of Death gave up, lowering his blade.

"He won't let me," Samael snarled. "He doesn't will it."

The angel sheathed his sword. Uriel mentally thanked the Lord. Samael, meanwhile, looked at the smiling child with wrath.

"*Israelite,*" he hissed as though it were a curse. "Jew-boy. One of the *Chosen.* You're here for Michael. That's why you've been snooping around."

Uriel nodded, his courage returning, knowing that Hashem would not let the Angel of Death touch him.

"As it were," scoffed Samael, "it's not your time yet. I can't lay a hand on you."

Uriel smiled widely, and Samael noted his lack of pompous bragging.

"You can't speak, can you?" he asked. Uriel's smile faltered slightly. He shook his head.

"A mute Jew-boy," sneered the Angel of Death. "Gabriel could have sent better. Why not a strong man? A rabbi, at least. A mute little Jew-boy, that's all you are. Why you?"

Samael stepped back and a resolute glow blazed in Uriel's amber irises. He couldn't let Michael's kidnapper go so easily. The boy rushed forward and tried to grab Samael's wrist. The Angel of Death saw him coming, however, and pulled away before the child could lay a hand on him.

"Filthy human!" barked Samael. "Filthy Israelite! Do you wish for death?"

Uriel glared at the Angel of Death, his eyes steely, unyielding. Samuel's fury melted into scornful amusement.

"Persistent," he chortled. "You want your precious angel back, is that it, child?"

Uriel nodded.

"And why," asked the Angel of Death, "should I give him back to you? He's getting what he deserves. You all are."

Uriel stomped his foot and attempted to growl, but all that came out was a furious huff. Samael gazed down at the child, his eyes smoldering with hatred. As he looked into the dark angel's violet orbs, however, Uriel could see a trace of something else: sadness.

"An eye for an eye, that's what this is!" Samael declared. "You Hebrews, God's Chosen People! He looked after you! He favored Jacob! Not Esau, never Esau! When the Jews whined about a little work in Egypt, He rushed to their aid and rained fire and brimstone down on their oppressors! Did He do that for Esau and his family? No! *I* had to protect him! *I* cared for them! But because of Michael I became the Angel of Death…and they had no one."

Hate and anguish mixed in his eyes, forming a deadly concoction that he turned towards Uriel.

"You'll never know what it's like," Samael said. "Being forced to take the souls of the people you cared for one by one until there are no more left to take!"

For the briefest moment, Uriel felt pity for the Angel of Death. That pity expired quickly, however, as Samael's cruel smile returned and sadistic satisfaction drowned the sadness in his eyes.

"Taking the souls of your people gives me pleasure, Jew-boy," he declared. "I hate them. Michael loves them, so I hate them. I've been waiting centuries for this time, and now it is happening. Rest assured, I'll let Michael out eventually, but only after your people are wiped out. Once he's free, he'll have nothing. Just like me."

Tears stung Uriel's corneas, but he held them in. Samael scrutinized the little boy and his amethyst eyes rested on the hamsa around the child's neck, which was emanating a holy aura that he could see clear as any star.

"Ah," he said. "The hamsa. From Gabriel, no doubt. That would explain how you made it this far without the Germans giving you over to me."

Uriel grabbed the hamsa, pressing it against his palm. Samael's eyes shifted from the shielded hamsa to the boy's determined expression and his smirk stretched.

"Hm," he muttered, a devious gleam coming to his eyes. "You're a funny little Israelite. You've got spirit. Perhaps I can have some fun with you."

Uriel quirked his head to the side.

"You want your angel back, little Israelite?" asked Samael. "Then let's make a deal. God gave Abraham ten tasks, but since you're a child, I'll only give you five. You will bring me five items, but *you* have to get them. No help from Gabriel or Raphael or any of your angel friends. *You* will venture to their hiding places and *you* will brave whatever obstacles are in the way. If you complete every task I give you, then I will tell you where Michael is."

Uriel's eyes gleamed.

"But," Samael said, his voice dripping with malicious mirth, "if you fail or cheat, you must give me that pretty hamsa around your neck."

Uriel's heart plunged at the mere thought. If that happened, he would die for sure. The Germans would see him, and Samael would have both his hamsa and his life.

Samael offered the boy his hand. Uriel inspected the Angel of Death's appendage. Samael had long, thin fingers that reminded Uriel of spider legs. The child shoved his hand into his pocket.

"Come now," Samael said. "You'll never find Michael otherwise. I've hidden him too well."

Uriel gritted his teeth and warily narrowed his eyes.

"Ah, you don't trust me," said Samael with a small chortle. "Wise, but not to worry. I swear to God that I will fulfill my end of the deal, and an angel can't go back on an oath made to God."

Uriel examined the angel's shadow-flecked eyes and slowly pulled his hand out of his pocket. He inhaled deeply, trying to calm his heart as it beat on his chest, begging him not to make such a deal.

No choice, he thought. *Hashem protect me.*

He grasped the Angel of Death's hand and a dark sort of energy shot through his body. He gave Samael's hand a single shake before he quickly yanked his hand out of the angel's grasp.

Uriel's hand stung, and he quickly wrapped his fingers around the hamsa. The holy pendant soothed his sore flesh like ice on a burn and he sighed. He looked at Samael and was surprised to see the Angel of Death hiss and grab his hand, as if Uriel's touch had hurt him just as much as his touch had hurt the child.

Samael recovered swiftly, however, and his spiteful smile returned.

"Excellent," said the Angel of Death. "Now, your first task: Bring me the Book of Blood."

Uriel felt fear and confusion grip his mind at once. *The Book of Blood? What's that?*

He looked at the Angel of Death and realized that he could expect no leniency or hints from him. The clueless child would have to figure out what and where it was by himself.

Uriel gave an obedient nod.

"Good boy," said Samael. "Once you find it—*if* you find it, that is—bring it right back here. If I can, I'll arrive once the starlight hits the shadows. But don't expect me to come at your beck and call. After all…"

He grinned and his eyes glistened wickedly. "I'm *very* busy these days."

With that, the color vanished from his body and the Angel of Death slipped back into the shadows. Uriel shivered and ran his fingers across the hamsa, praying that this Book of Blood wasn't very far. He looked up at the moon and realized that Uwe would surely be back at the house by now.

The boy turned and ran towards the house, trying his best to avoid the shadows.

MAMA

Every night she sang to him.

"Sleep, my little bird

Shut your little eyes

Eye-lu-lu-lu

Eye-lu-lu

Sleep soundly, my child

Sleep and be well

Eye-lu-lu-lu

Eye-lu-lu..."

It always struck him as ironic that she called him her little bird when he couldn't sing. Nevertheless, she always sang him that song to lull him to sleep, holding him close and kissing his raven hair when he started to drift.

She loved him more than anything. She always said that he had been a gift from God. Before Uriel was born, she had given birth only once, to Adina, his older sister. But after that, for eleven long years, no matter how much she tried, she didn't get pregnant again.

In Zingdorf, it was unheard of for a woman to have only a single child. Most houses had at least five, many had over ten. Children were considered to be the greatest of blessings, and having only one was a gloomy, embarrassing prospect.

Mama had cried to Hashem every night for years, pleading and bargaining with Him for another child, just one more. She swore that she would teach her child to follow all the Commandments. She swore to sell her nice clothes and give the money to the poor. Anything for a child.

Then, finally, one night she sobbed that she would love any child that God gave her no matter what. Even if he was blind, deaf, lame, and mute, she would love him more than her soul.

Barely nine months after making that vow, Uriel was born. Blind, deaf, and lame he was not, but he couldn't speak.

His mother was true to her word. Uriel was her precious treasure, her loan from the Lord, and she loved him. She was always there when he fell and scraped his knee, prepared with a bandage and a tissue to wipe his tears away.

There was always love in her eyes, but there was also worry. Her dearest boy was a mute, and that would make life hard for him. What would he do when he grew up? What could he work as? Who could he marry? Who would ever give their daughter to the village mute?

Still, as long as Uriel was smiling, she would smile. And if anybody caused her baby's smile to dampen, they would pay dearly. The children who bullied him had to tread lightly, for if Uriel's mother caught them, she would drag them by the ear to their parents and wouldn't leave until they had received a satisfactory spanking.

Hashem had stayed Samael's hand, but Uriel couldn't help but think his mother had also been there. Uriel was her precious baby, and she would never let anybody lay a hand on him. Not even the Angel of Death.

Brandt and his men had taken control of an old schoolhouse which served as their base. As Uwe followed Brandt through the halls and struggled to remember the names of the policemen he was introduced to, he couldn't help but inwardly chuckle. The school didn't seem like the intimidating structure that he would normally associate with the National Socialists. They hadn't even bothered to take down the children's artwork, and so sloppily painted puppies and goldfish smiled at the Germans as they sauntered down the hallways.

All the policemen were friendly, if not memorable enough for Uwe to recall their names. The youngest of the bunch was a twenty-three-year-old with a fiancée back in Hamburg (a good half of the men were from Hamburg). The rest, however, were middle-aged, and almost all of them had wives and children at home.

Wives and children that they were more than eager to talk about for hours. By the time he met all forty-six of them and chatted with them all, it was nightfall.

"All right," sighed Brandt with a scolding smile, "I'm officially counting this as a day off for *all of you* since *all of you* have been jabbering away instead of working."

"Uncle Günter! You didn't give us an assignment for today!"

"You could have taken Herr Litten to the prisoners to interrogate them instead of blabbing about your son's spider collection for an hour."

"Now, that's an exaggeration…" the policeman said, but Uwe looked curiously up at Brandt and interrupted.

"Prisoners?"

"Of course," said Brandt. "You think we're in this schoolhouse because we enjoy being reminded of math class?"

"I didn't see any prisoners. How many are there? Who are they?"

"Poles," Brandt explained. "We're still searching for the Jews that are hiding out, but the Poles have been a thorn in our side for the last couple of weeks. At least some of them. Many are docile, but there's a whole gaggle of them hiding somewhere in the woods. They only ever come out to murder our men, but after that they go running back to their hiding place. We've caught some of them, but naturally we haven't been able to interrogate them to figure out where the rest are squatting."

He clapped Uwe on the shoulder. "But that will change…tomorrow. For now, it's late, and since *a certain group of men* raided my ice box while I was gone…"

The other men smiled innocently.

"I have a promise to keep. Do you still want to get a drink, Herr Litten?"

Tired and thirsty Uwe was about to agree when the golden-eyed child that hid in his room came to his mind. Little Uriel was still at the house, stuck in the room, probably famished at this point. The very thought of the child being so miserable made Uwe's already arid throat become even drier.

"Actually, Herr Brandt," he said, yawning for emphasis, "I'm quite tired. I think I'd like to go back to the house and sleep, especially if I officially get to work tomorrow."

"Need your rest? I understand," said Brandt, "Then let's head back."

"Goodbye, Herr Litten!" said one policeman.

"Look forward to working with you!" said another.

"Me too," said Uwe, following Brandt past the children's pictures. The linguist's eyes landed on one particular drawing. It depicted a lion with a fat ovular body, orange mane, and a giant toothy smile. Uwe's eyes glistened fondly. Jürgen loved lions. One of his favorite games was 'Eat the Zebra', where he was the lion and Uwe the zebra. He couldn't count the number of hours he had spent running about the house, trying to avoid his growling, giggling son.

Brandt noticed Uwe's eyes lingering on the picture and he inquired why. When Uwe explained his son's love of lions Brandt's eyes twinkled.

"Hans is the same way, except he's obsessed with tigers. He's a much better artist than that, though."

He pointed to the picture and Uwe nodded. The linguist looked down at the child artist's nearly illegible signature. His smile faded.

I wonder, he thought, *where he is right now.*

His eyes traveled to the other drawings. *Where did they all go?*

As soon as he unlocked the door to his room and entered, Uwe's stomach twisted itself into a knot.

The window was open. A bitter breeze was creeping in. The boy was gone.

He slammed the door behind him. The room trembled.

Uriel, you stupid boy, he thought, rushing to the window, the cold air further freezing his already icy blood.

He looked down, his weak eyes desperately searching the shadows for a sign of the child. He heard a mighty rustling of leaves and craned his neck to look behind the tree. Relief flooded his heart when he saw the boy emerge, whole and unhurt, from the thicket.

"Uriel!" he hissed. Uriel's head snapped upwards and even in the dark Uwe could see the boy's eyes glowing happily, like two little suns in the dead of night.

"Come back here! Now! Quickly!" Uwe ordered, as quietly and firmly as he could. Uriel nodded and scuttled to the tree trunk. He froze, however, when a sound hit his ears: boots marching across the grass. Uwe leaned out of the window and his heart cartwheeled when he saw a shadow approaching. One of the guards must have heard the crackle of branches and was going to investigate.

Not daring to urge him on with words, Uwe gestured desperately for Uriel to hurry before he was spotted. Although he knew that the policeman wouldn't be able to see him, Uriel obliged and scurried up the tree like a squirrel escaping a predator.

As soon as the boy was within arm's reach, Uwe grabbed him, threw him onto the ground, and slammed the window shut. The policeman arrived just in time to hear the slam of the old windowpane and looked up at Uwe's room just as the curtains were drawn. He stood there for a moment, but when he didn't hear any sounds of a struggle coming from the little linguist's room, he shrugged the sounds off and went back to his post.

Uwe knelt beside Uriel, pulling him away from the window and holding a hand over his mouth. Faintly, he knew that such a gesture was pointless since the child couldn't say anything that would alert the policemen to his presence, but the act was instinctual. He didn't remove his hand until five minutes had passed and he was certain that they were safe.

Once the sensation of relative safety returned, the hand that had been used to shield the boy's mouth smacked the child on the head. Uriel winced, his own hand flying to his throbbing skull. Uwe had not hit him very hard, but Uriel, the well-behaved darling of his parents, wasn't accustomed to corporal punishment. The sheer shock that the slap gave him was enough for him to look up at Uwe with pained confusion, his eyes watering.

"Don't you look at me like that, boy," growled Uwe. The fear and anger that swirled in his azure irises caused Uriel to lower his head like a submissive puppy.

"How dare you run off like that?" Uwe said, outrage overpowering his anger as he stood up, towering over the boy. "How dare you, right after I told you not to? You realize what I'm risking, keeping you here like this? I have a family of my own at home, and I will not put their safety and mine on the line if you're insistent on suicidally running off!"

He was no longer yelling, instead he spoke in a deadly hush that frightened Uriel more than any bark or snarl. Tears escaped the boy's eyes and ran down his cheeks, landing on the carpet fibers like drops of dew. He grabbed at Uwe's leg, bowing his head, pleading for his anger to abate, begging for forgiveness.

It was truly incredible, Uwe thought, how the mere sight of salty water in the child's doubloon-colored eyes could cause his fury and indignation to abandon him almost instantly. He pulled the boy's fingers off his leg and carefully stood the weeping child up.

"Stop crying," he ordered, gently as he could, dusting the dirt from Uriel's coat. Uriel struggled to obey, taking deep breaths to get his agitated lungs to go back to their usual rhythm.

"Why were you even out there?" Uwe asked once the boy had gotten his breathing in order. Uriel clamped his lips together in a thin, contemplative line. He couldn't tell Uwe the true reason. Even if he could speak of all that had happened and who he was searching for, Uwe would never believe him.

Instead, he hopped from foot to foot, lying as he did a little dance. Uwe's stern countenance almost shattered as he watched the boy.

"Bathroom?"

Uriel nodded. Uwe sighed.

"Yes," he muttered, reaching into his pocket and running his index finger along the jagged edge of the key. "I locked you in here. Hm…what to do about this…?"

He thought for a moment before pulling the key out of his pocket.

"Here," he said, grabbing the child's hand and pressing it into his palm. "From now on, you keep the key. When I come home, I'll knock seven times and you let me in. When the Major and I are gone, you can use the bathroom across the hall, but don't go downstairs or the guards at the door might hear you!"

Uriel examined the silver key, stealing a glance at the German as he rolled it in his calloused palm.

He trusts me enough to give me this, Uriel thought, guilt scratching at his chest. *I'll have to be here when he comes back. I don't want to worry him again.*

He tried to calculate how long it would take to run to the spot where Samael would appear when the starlight hit the shadows. Would he have enough time to go there and get back before Uwe arrived? The Jewish boy heaved a sigh and offered the German a crooked smile.

Poor man, he thought. *Poor, good man.*

"Here," said Uwe, reaching into his pocket and offering the boy a slightly squashed piece of bread. "I'm sorry. Major Brandt was downstairs, that's all I could grab. I promise to give you more before I leave tomorrow."

Seeing the Angel of Death had done a number on Uriel's appetite, and the little loaf was more than enough to satisfy him. He smiled and tried to give Uwe an assuring pat on the shoulder, but he was only tall enough to reach his forearm.

"Well," sighed Uwe, rubbing his weary eyes. "That near heart attack sapped my remaining energy. Let's get some…"

Before the suggestion of sleep could even make it out of his mouth, the boy shoved a small rectangle into his hands. He looked down at the golden notebook. Uriel's matching golden eyes glittered eagerly.

"Ah…yes…" Uwe muttered with an amused and fatigued sigh. "I made a promise, didn't I?"

Uriel nodded.

If Uwe was nothing else, he was a man of his word. He sat down on the bed, trying to ignore the almost overwhelming desire to lie down and slip into sleep, and patted the place beside him. Uriel obediently sat down, looking at his notebook and imagining what all his stories would sound like.

Noticing the child's indulgent eyes, Uwe smirked. "Only one tonight, and a short one. I'm exhausted."

Uriel nodded.

"Any particular story you want me to read?"

Uriel tapped his chin in contemplation before eureka came to his irises. He grabbed the book from Uwe, expertly flipped to the desired page, and once he had located the tale, he tapped the heading.

"*'From Papa: Elijah the Prophet Angel,'*" Uwe read aloud, glancing at the boy to confirm that this was the right story. Uriel nodded, adjusting himself so he was comfortable and looking down at the page, gazing at the Hebraic letters and waiting for them to come to life.

"All right…" Uwe said, clearing his throat and beginning.

"'Long ago, when Hashem still spoke with men, in the land of Israel, King Ahab took an idolatress for a bride. The Queen, named Jezebel, hated God with all of her black heart. She wanted the people to only worship her and her false gods. She banned the worship of the True God. Any person who dared to preach in His name was swiftly put to death. Hundreds of God's prophets were murdered.

But one prophet, a man of God named Elijah, evaded Jezebel. He hid and fled from her, until one day Hashem said, "Until this time, I have shielded you. Now go, confront Jezebel and her priests, for she has the blood of My people on her hands and the men of Israel are too frightened to stop her."

Elijah, who had complete faith in God, obeyed. He challenged Jezebel's priests to a contest in front of Israel. He said, "Take an ox, slaughter it, and if your gods are real, then surely they will send fire from Heaven to consume the sacrifice."

The priests of Jezebel tried in vain, for their gods were false. When Elijah laid an ox onto the altar and invoked the Lord, however, fire came from Heaven. All the people of Israel saw it, and faith and courage came to their hearts again.

"The Lord, He is God!" they all proclaimed. When Jezebel heard of this, she became furious.

"I will kill Elijah," she declared, "just as I killed every other prophet of God. Then no mouth will ever utter 'The Lord is God' again!"

Elijah was forced to flee, and Hashem kept him hidden. Yet Elijah never remained in hiding for long. Until the end of his days, he would come out to help the Children of Israel, and then slip back into hiding before Jezebel could catch him. Because of him, faith was spread through Israel again, and Jezebel's plot was devastated.

And when the day came for Elijah to die, the Angel of Death was all too eager to take his soul away. But Michael, the Guardian of Israel, pleaded on Elijah's behalf.

"Hashem, Sovereign of the Universe," Michael begged. "This prophet has given life and hope to Your people, to Israel. Do not let the Angel of Death lay a finger on him! Let him join us, the Heavenly Host, and let him continue to help Israel."

Hashem agreed, and when the time came for Elijah to die, Hashem sent a chariot of fire to take him straight to Heaven. He is the only person who went to Heaven without dying, and he is the only human who ever became an angel."'

Just as he finished, Uwe felt a breach of his personal space. He looked down and saw that Uriel, fast asleep, was leaning against his shoulder.

Uwe only ever allowed his own children to lean on him like that, yet as he looked down at the sleeping child, he realized that he wasn't as uncomfortable with Uriel leaning on him as he thought he would be.

Carefully, he set the book down on the nightstand beside him, examining the child's face all the while. Uriel's nose was scrunched up. Occasionally, the child fidgeted, as though he was running from something. Without a doubt, his dreams were unpleasant.

That's to be expected, I suppose, Uwe thought. He looked closely and chewed on his lip when he saw that there were bags under the child's eyes. Normally, Uriel's golden eyes were the focal point of his face, and thus the linguist hadn't noticed the bags previously. But now that the golden eyes were hidden behind his pale eyelids, Uwe could see how haggard the boy was.

Children should be carefree, Uwe thought gloomily as he moved the boy onto his side and picked him up, carrying him to the closet and laying him down on his crude bed of socks.

They shouldn't have bags under their eyes.

ELIJAH

Every Passover, Uriel would be careful not to blink too often. It would only take one unnecessary bat of his eyelids for him to miss seeing the Prophet-Angel.

He came every Passover, Mama said, but Uriel was always so busy running around like an agitated kitten that he never spotted the elusive Prophet-Angel. Elijah could be in and out of a house in the time it took a fly to blink, she said, and flies were swift blinkers.

Uriel could see his violet reflection in the undisturbed cup that they always left out for the Prophet-Angel. He often wondered why they left the wine out for Elijah. Was he tired and thirsty from running around the entire world, looking for Jewish homes to visit? And if he needed it so badly, why did he never seem to drink any?

"He only drinks a drop at every house," Papa said. "He would get drunk if he drank the whole cup at every house he went to! Besides, our wine isn't very good. Not fit for a Prophet-Angel to drink more than a drop of."

Yet as Uriel stared at it, he didn't see the surface of the liquid move even slightly. Not a drop had been taken.

Slowly, a knot formed in his throat. Perhaps they had done something wrong this year. Perhaps they had committed some sort of sin, and Elijah had thus decided to ignore their offering.

Or maybe he just didn't like to be watched while he was drinking. That's what Mama said, at least.

"Instead of gawking at the cup, little bird," she suggested. "Go open the door and welcome him in."

Her suggestion caused Uriel's throat-knot to uncoil ever so slightly and his heart filled with hope once more. Every year his parents told him to open the door and welcome Elijah in. Yet every year the Prophet-Angel wasn't there.

Perhaps this year, however, he would come. He would sense how much the little boy wanted to lay eyes on him and would allow the child to see him.

Just for a second. One little second was all Uriel wished for. He opened the squeaky door and offered his brightest smile. Nobody was there.

By the time Uriel awoke the next morning, Uwe was already gone for the day. The German had left a plate of bread and a tall cup of water on the nightstand for the boy, along with a note.

Little writer,

Left with Brandt. Will interrogate prisoners today. Will probably be gone all day.

Remember: open only when you hear seven knocks. Stay away from downstairs.

Be good,

Uwe

Uriel's mouth quirked into a curious smile.

Little writer, hm? he thought. He supposed it was more accurate than 'little bird.' Less affectionate, perhaps, but still there was a touch of fondness in the title that Uwe had bestowed upon him. The boy's chest swelled as he looked at the two words.

Writer...I'm a writer. Hm...I guess I am.

He carefully folded up the paper and stashed it away in his pocket, the two little words bringing him such pride that he couldn't find it in himself to toss it in the wastebasket. He ate the food Uwe had left, not wanting to get hungry during his search, and once he was sated, he dashed downstairs to begin his hunt.

The Book of Blood then...well, I suppose the first place to look would be a library.

He recalled that the other day, when he had been searching for Michael, he had entered an office with a large bookshelf. Deciding that would be the best place to start, Uriel scurried about, retracing his steps until he finally found the Major's office.

The shelf was so tall that even if he sat on Papa's shoulders, he wouldn't have been able to reach the top row. He scooted the Major's chair to the bookshelf and stood on it, but still couldn't reach the top shelves. Uriel pursed his lips and glanced at the books that he could reach. There were several hardbacks. Large ones, too.

He grabbed a group of hardback books and stacked them on top of the chair until he had made himself a small tower. *Climbing books is much harder than climbing trees,* he decided as he cautiously crawled on top and slowly stood, the tower trembling at his feet.

He stabilized himself and sloppily perused, sighing in disappointment and tossing the book aside when it showed no sign of being anything but bound paper.

The Book of Blood would look different, he thought, slowly climbing down from his stack. *It would have to be...darker, somehow.*

He looked at the books that he could reach without the unstable aid of his book building and paid particular attention to the ones with red spines, pulling them out and lazily dropping them to the ground when they turned out to be normal books.

Finally, his arms started to hurt, and his fingers stung from the paper cuts that served as his only reward for all his trouble. He collapsed beneath the bookshelf, sitting in the midst of the red-bound books and wondering where the Book of Blood could be.

His eyes fell upon the Major's tidy desk and focused on a black rectangle that rested ominously on one corner. He rose, approached the desk, and a spark of hope struck his heart when he saw that it was a book. He glanced at the two gray words on the cover.

Mein Kampf

Hm. Perhaps…

He touched the book and shuddered as dark energy seemed to crawl onto his skin and scrape at his flesh. *It feels like it did when I shook Samael's hand.*

Careful not to touch it more than necessary, Uriel picked up the book and opened it. Somebody had scrawled in the book, but he couldn't read what he or she had written. The scribbler must have been a rude person, he decided. Papa had never tolerated defacing books in such a manner.

As he stared at the signature, though, the black ink slowly turned scarlet. It began to run, dripping down the page and landing in small pools on the Major's formerly spotless desk. Uriel's eyes widened. He flipped through the book. The gothic script became crimson and dribbled down the pages, forming a small stream that soon created a lake of blood on the smooth oak.

He slammed the book shut and ran out of the Major's office, so excited that he didn't even bother to clean up the blood on the table or the books he had thrown about.

Uriel knew, though, that he couldn't take the book to the forest right now. Samael had specifically stated that he wouldn't show up until the starlight hit the shadows. Until then, Uriel would have to wait. He stashed the book beneath his bed of socks and shut the closet door, sighing and wondering what he should do until the stars came out.

He glanced at the sunlight, which was dying much too slowly for his liking, and a realization came to him.

It's Friday.

The eve of the Sabbath, the holiest day of the week. He needed to welcome the Sabbath Queen, and to do that he would need to have a feast prepared. Or at least something close to a feast. He couldn't afford to be indolent when it came to the holy day. Hashem wouldn't be pleased if His Angel-Finder ignored one of His primary Commandments. *Observe the Sabbath day and keep it holy.*

I'll make preparations, and Uwe can join me. Maybe…if I do everything right…she'll come.

The drive to the school was long, bumpy, and insufferably boring. The tall trees that framed the road had lost much of their allure, and before long Uwe's eyes were roaming about the car for something even mildly intriguing to focus on. He looked at Brandt just as the Major took a long draw from a flask and put it back at his hip.

"A flask, Major Brandt?" said Uwe. "I didn't notice you had a flask."

"As of today, I do," replied the Major. "Since *certain policemen* won't let me have a drop of liquor to myself."

"Was that emphasis directed at me?" queried the driver. "If you're looking for a guilty party, Uncle Günter, look elsewhere. I don't drink."

"If it were up to the rest of the boys, I wouldn't either," said Major Brandt. "More for them. Still, I dug this out of my old suitcase. Took an hour to clean, but now at least I'll have something to myself."

"Unless they swipe it off of you," Uwe pointed out with a slight smile.

"Ha! True," laughed the Major. "I wouldn't put it past them, but still, even I'm not that much of a doormat!"

They finally arrived. Brandt quickly ushered Uwe inside and started leading him down a long, cobweb-clad staircase.

"Now then, little linguist," said Brandt as Uwe ducked to avoid the unfortunate flies that had gotten caught in the spider webs. "This is fairly simple. I'll ask the question, you translate it for the Pole. When he talks, you tell me exactly what he says. Nothing that should cause any headaches for any of us…except perhaps the prisoner, though believe me he already has quite the headache!"

Several *Ordnungspolizei* men clambered up and down the stairs, some with vaguely familiar features. Uwe recognized the one whose son had a spider collection and the one with a fiancée in Hamburg, though he couldn't remember their names. He cursed his poor moniker memory and politely greeted them. All the men, without exception, were smiling cheerfully.

The schoolhouse's basement had at one point been a hallway of storage closets. Now, however, policemen paced the hallways where teachers had once rushed to grab paper and pencils, the keys of the closets-turned-cells jingling from their belts.

Brandt led him straight to a door that had been labeled 'Interrogation' in clumsy calligraphy. Uwe had to shake his head when he imagined the middle-aged, working class policeman who had probably written that and compared his legibility to that of the ten-year-old Uriel.

He wasn't given much time to dwell on the letters, though, as Brandt threw open the door. The interrogation room was fairly large and almost empty save for one teeny chair in the center of the room.

A man sat in the chair, his arms bound to the armrests, his head high and his shoulders sagging. His face was stern and determined even as his overall posture was faltering. He had several visible bruises and a few barely-healing cuts. His clothes, which were covered in dark stains that might have been a mixture of blood and mud, were worn and ripped.

He was in worse shape than Uwe had anticipated, but he hadn't exactly been expecting any prisoner of the Nazis to be in great shape, especially if that prisoner was a member of an inferior race. Besides, he was a partisan. Living in the woods and fighting in battles would inevitably lead to some injuries.

The bruises, though, were deliberate and fresh. He could see that they had been produced by fists and boots. Bile rose to his throat. He had heard many horror stories of what it was like to be questioned by the Nazis, but actually seeing the result of such an interrogation made his stomach churn.

Just keep your head down and do as they say.

His wife's words caused him to take a deep breath and regain control of his gut. He looked at the smiling Major while another policeman handed his chief a cigarette and a lighter.

Uwe tilted his head to the side. "Major? I didn't know you smoked."

The Major turned to him, still smiling, though something had changed about his smile. The friendliness was still there, but something else had crawled onto his face. A flicker of malice, a smidgeon of sadism.

"I don't," he replied.

Uwe swallowed and, without even realizing it, slowly stepped behind the tied-down Pole, holding the headrest of the chair, practically using the Polish man as a shield.

"Th…" he began, but before even a single word could leave his lips, Brandt tucked the cigarettes and the lighter into his pocket and clapped his hands together.

"Let's begin! Herr Litten, please ask our guest where his comrades are hiding."

Though he was still curious about the cigarettes, Uwe didn't dare disobey the Major. He looked down at the Pole.

"Please, sir," he said in his politest Polish. "Where have your comrades gone? Where are they?"

The Pole answered curtly, and Uwe translated for the Major.

"He says he doesn't know."

"Of course. That's what I suspected he had been saying," replied the Major, still seemingly in good spirits, shifting his weight from leg to leg as if he was getting antsy. "Little linguist, tell the Pole that if he tells us what we want to know, we will consider it in his merit. He'll be allowed to go home unmolested."

Uwe reiterated the Major's message in Polish. The partisan answered sharply.

"He replies that he has no home to go back to because of us—and by *us* I presume he means us Germans."

The Major shook his head and clicked his tongue disparagingly. "Now... that's just rude, lumping us all together like that. Tell him, Herr Litten, that he has my deepest sympathies, but we of the Order Police are only doing our duties, and we had no part in the destruction of his home. In fact, I've been very kind to the Poles I've encountered so far. Why, I spared him, after all! Even though he tried to murder me and my men."

Uwe gave the Pole Brandt's response. The Pole's eyes flared like a fire as he retorted with a snarl and a string of curses.

Brandt, amused by the Pole's obviously furious rebuttal, chortled.

"Am I to assume, little linguist, that our guest's comment was impolite?"

"I…would hesitate to translate most of it, sir. Simply put: he won't tell you a thing."

Brandt brought his flask to his lips and took a long draw. Uwe felt the chair shake slightly as the Polish man shivered. Though his eyes remained determined, the prisoner was visibly dreading the punishment that his refusal to cooperate would entail once the Major finished his drink. The Major seemed to know this and, as if to draw out the suspense, took a very long time to finish his sip.

Finally, he put the flask back at his side and his hand swiftly disappeared into his pocket. He pulled out the lighter and a cigarette and clumsily lit it.

"Herr Litten, do you smoke?" he asked, not bringing the cigarette even close to his lips. In fact, as the smoke gently snaked up to his nostrils, the Major wrinkled his nose, as if the scent disgusted him.

"No, Herr Brandt," Uwe mumbled in response, his eyes locked onto the glowing end of the cigarette. "I detest the smell, actually."

"Small world. You and I have much in common, Herr Litten," said Brandt, slowly walking towards him. Uwe felt his heart rate speed up exponentially, but Brandt wasn't looking at him. Rather, the Major's maliciously glittering eyes were on the Pole.

Major Brandt bent down so that he was at eye level with the prisoner.

"And what about you, sir?" he asked in the same affable tone that he always used with Uwe, except now his friendliness was laced with derision.

"Do you smoke?"

The Pole said nothing. For a few moments, there was an unholy silence.

Brandt jammed the cigarette right between the Pole's eyes, shoving the burning end into his flesh.

Uwe could only watch in horrified silence as the man screamed and writhed, the tight ropes digging into his wrists, the horrible smell of burning flesh reminding Uwe of Zingdorf and little Uriel lying on the bloody cobblestones.

Brandt continued to smile as though he was engaging in pleasant conversation with the man even as he threw the used cigarette to the floor and lit another. He stuck that onto the prisoner's skin.

Then another.

Another.

Another.

Until the poor man's face was covered in horrible black burns and Uwe felt as though he was going to pass out from terror and disgust.

"Herr Litten," Brandt finally said after ten cigarettes, ten burns, and ten fits of agony. "Tell the man that he's trying my patience. Tell him that if he doesn't tell me where his comrades are, this next one is going in his eye."

Uwe felt his throat seize up. He looked from the weeping prisoner to the Major, who casually prepared to light the next cigarette. The prisoner had tears leaking from his blue eyes, and if he continued to scream instead of confess, those eyes would be burned like his skin.

Like Zingdorf.

Uwe's throat opened enough for him to speak, and yet the words that Brandt ordered him to say did not come out. Instead, one German word emerged.

"Stop."

Brandt, who had been fumbling with the lighter, finally managed to light the cigarette. "Tell him I will if he just…."

"*I'm* telling you to stop!"

Brandt looked up from the cigarette, his eyes forming question marks as he gazed at the straight-backed, trembling translator. Uwe tried his best to seem firm, but he couldn't help but quiver as his eyes wandered to the prisoner and he was reminded that he could very well share a worse fate if he displeased the *Ordnungspolizei.*

Head down. Do as they say.

"What was that, Herr Litten?" asked Brandt, a smile on his face and ire in his voice. "I'm afraid I didn't quite hear you properly."

"Stop torturing this man," ordered Uwe, ignoring the echo of his wife's command that continued to ring in his ears.

Head down…head down…

He kept his posture straight. "It's not right. Please, enough."

He expected Brandt's chipper smile to fade into a sour frown. He waited for the Major to order him to shut his mouth and do as commanded or face the consequences.

Instead, Brandt laughed. "Ah! Herr Litten! There you go with that good heart again! You really ought to learn to keep it in check. Mercy for mercenaries only leads to trouble, you know. We have a job to do, little linguist, but since you're such a good friend, I'll humor you. Just give this man my message. If he still refuses, I'll only punish him one more time. Then we can send him back to his cell. I'll even poke his nose instead of his eye. Deal?"

Head down. Do as they say.

Uwe almost said yes, but the smell of scalded skin slipped into his nostrils and killed his agreement before it could even fully form in his throat.

"No," he said. "That's enough for one day."

Brandt's smile faltered for a full second and a flash of annoyance shot out of his eyes like a bullet, but his lips quickly quirked up once more as a snide smirk spread across his face.

"As you wish," he said. "Rather cruel of you, though. Forcing him to get punished without an advanced warning."

Brandt raised the cigarette, prepared to jab it into the prisoner's eye, but before he could Uwe started to jump in between them. In the process, however, the linguist's hand scraped against the chair and the splintered wood sliced his palm. He yelped in pain and dropped to his knees.

Brandt stopped, sighed, dropped the cigarette, and stamped it out with the steel toe of his boot.

"Herr Litten," he said, watching the blood drip from Uwe's wound with a patronizing headshake. "You shouldn't have done that. I might have hurt you. Your wife wouldn't be pleased if I returned you with only one eye."

Uwe growled, partially at the Major's taunting tone as he spoke of his wife, but also to repress another pitiful cry. His hand felt as though it had been ripped in half.

He heard a sigh of relief behind him and looked back at the Pole, whose scorched face now relaxed as he looked at the unused cigarette on the ground. His still-whole eyes met Uwe's for the briefest moment, shining with gratitude, and instantly the pain in the linguist's hand seemed to dissipate.

Two policemen ran in and darted to Uwe's side.

"Herr Litten!"

"Damn! Your hand! Are you all right?"

"I'm fine…" Uwe insisted, gnashing his teeth and pressing his palms together in an attempt to stop the bleeding. One soldier helped him to his feet while the other turned to Brandt, mutely requesting orders.

Brandt's lips were clamped together in a thin, irritated line. He almost reminded Uwe of his own father. When Uwe had been a small child and had broken the rules, that look of pure disapproval would always be the prelude to swift and harsh punishment.

Brandt scoffed and turned away. "Fredrick, you get Herr Litten some medical attention and then send him back to the house. Helmut, you take this prisoner back to his cell."

Uwe was quickly ushered out of the room. He looked behind him and saw the Pole being dragged back to his closet.

I won, he thought with satisfaction, though he quickly realized how minor a victory it was. The Pole was fine for now, but he would be back in the little wooden chair soon.

Uwe narrowly avoided a fly that was caught in a spider's web. The poor creature thrashed about, helplessly trying to free itself from the trap it had flown into. Uwe couldn't help but empathize with the insect. In a way, he felt that they were both stuck in a spider's web. Perhaps making a fuss about it would only speed up the inevitable.

Careful not to use his freshly bandaged hand, Uwe knocked on the bedroom door and was relieved when he heard a patter of footsteps inside that signified Uriel's presence.

Good boy, he thought. *Didn't go out into the woods again. Good boy.*

Uriel answered Uwe's seven knocks and welcomed the German home with a smile that made the sun seem dim by comparison.

"Hello, little writer," sighed Uwe, giving the boy a small pat on the head. Somehow or another, his comment was enough to make Uriel's already sky-sized smile stretch even further. Uwe stepped into the room and made sure to shut and lock the door behind him.

He turned and was about to ask Uriel what he had done all day, but before he could say a word, he saw something that nearly made him want to burst into laughter.

A 'feast' fit for a hiding Jew and his rescuer was laid out on the nightstand. Uriel had been busy, it seemed. He had swiped the necessary dinnerware and fare, set it up on the 'table', scooted the nightstand to the center of the room and put a chair on either side of it.

"Dinner?" asked Uwe. "What for? Oh! Wait! Today's Friday, isn't it?"

Uriel nodded, skipping to the 'table' and pulling out Uwe's chair for him. He waved in a welcoming manner.

"Well, thank you very much. I'm sorry I took so long," chuckled Uwe, taking a seat and observing the meal. The little banquet consisted of cut fruits, vegetables, and bread ornately arrayed on the plates, but he could surmise that Uriel hadn't been taught to cook and so he was rather impressed that the boy had been able to prepare the meal as well as he had.

"You made sure to cover your tracks in the kitchen, right?" asked Uwe. Uriel nodded.

"Well, if Brandt notices all the food that's missing, I'll just say I got really hungry. I *am* really hungry…"

He made a move for an apple, but Uriel swatted his hand away and wagged his finger at the German. Uwe's brow furrowed, but Uriel clasped his hands together and bowed his head, his ever-silent lips moving rapidly as he wordlessly recited the Sabbath prayer he knew so well.

"Oh, yes. Prayers first," whispered Uwe, bowing his head even as he kept his eyes pinned on the youth. He recalled all the times he had jammed little Jürgen into his fine clothes and dragged him to church. Oh, the misery! His son would huff and sigh so much it was a wonder his lungs didn't burn out. Never had he bowed his head and prayed as fervently as Uriel. Even the adults at the church hadn't been as reverent as this little boy.

As soon as the child lifted his head, Uwe asked, "Uriel…you still believe in God?"

Uriel looked at Uwe as though he was insane for even asking such a question. The answer was so obviously yes.

*After everything he's seen…*Uwe thought. *I would be questioning it a little, at least. Why would God let somebody as innocent as you get hurt so much, Uriel?*

Sensing Uwe's melancholy, Uriel examined the German to be sure he was in good health. He looked at Uwe's hand and gasped when he saw it wrapped in a bandage. He reached over the 'table', carefully grabbed Uwe's hand, and pointed to it, worry causing his golden irises to flash frantically.

"I got a cut today while I was working with the Major," explained Uwe, a stone of trepidation clogging his throat at the mere thought of all that had transpired earlier. He somehow forced a nonchalant smile onto his face.

"I'm fine, really," he insisted. Uriel gave the German a look that was far too stern for such a young face. Uwe almost fell to the floor with laughter when he saw Uriel's no-nonsense expression. The boy wasn't buying it.

Still, Uriel smiled once more, seemingly willing to let Uwe off the hook for his fib. At least for now.

Uriel planted a small kiss on Uwe's palm and gave it a gentle pat, as if to proclaim, "All better!"

"Kiss for a cut?" chortled Uwe. "Did your mother do that for you when you were hurt?"

Uriel nodded.

"I do that for my children, too. Thank you, Uriel, it does feel much better now."

Uriel released Uwe's hand and ran over to grab his golden notebook off the bed. He flipped to the very back and handed it to Uwe.

Uwe was impressed. Uriel had taken the time to write down the necessary psalms and prayers for the Sabbath dinner on some blank sheets in his precious notebook. Since Uriel, naturally, couldn't sing the songs, he begged Uwe to do it. Uwe, unable to deny the boy such a request, conceded and sang. Though his cheeks burned with embarrassment the whole time since he knew he was a terrible singer (his fifth-grade music teacher had made sure to let him know *that*), Uriel was more than pleased and gave Uwe as many smiles and claps as he needed to get through each song.

"Lecha dodi,

Guard and remember in a single utterance

Let us hear the special kind

God is One and His name is One..."

Uriel fidgeted and tapped his foot, glancing impatiently at the door.

"Get up from the ash

Shake it off of you

Wear your glorious garments, my people..."

*Tap, tap, tap...*Uriel's eager foot tapping quickened. He fiddled with the hem of his jacket and his eyes remained fixed on the door.

"Lecha dodi...

Enter in peace...

Enter, O Bride, the Sabbath Queen..."

The instant the final verse was sung, Uriel dashed to the door, his eyes overflowing with zeal. Uwe's heart back-flipped.

"No, Uriel! Don't op…!"

The boy threw open the door, smiling graciously, as if to greet the guest that would surely be standing at the threshold.

But his smile was only received by the other side of the hallway.

Uwe sighed in relief. "There's nobody there, Uriel."

As he too realized this, the excitement that had taken hold of Uriel turned into disappointment. He lowered his eyes, his racing heart slowly returning to its normal pace as he accepted that she had not come.

With his head bowed, Uriel closed the door.

THE SABBATH QUEEN

While Uriel and his fellow children suffered through school, the adults of Zingdorf would spend all day preparing for her.

He would run home, out of breath from his day of play and learning, and would be greeted by the sweet smell of baking bread and cooking meat.

His mother would be flitting from pot to pot, from the fire to the table. She would be preparing the meat, kneading the dough, cutting the onions until her eyes filled with salty tears. Still, she smiled all the way, humming softly as she prepared their Sabbath dinner.

He would sit and watch, mesmerized. To him, it was like watching an artist at work, seeing how expertly she prepared and presented the meal. She always timed it just right. The instant she was done and everything was ready, Papa would arrive and the ceremony could begin.

All because of Mama. She was the one who made the Sabbath holy. She would be the one who blessed their house, who waved her hand over the flickering candles and prayed for the family.

Papa, meanwhile, always sang 'Lecha Dodi.' Once he called out, "Come, O Bride, the Sabbath Queen!", Uriel was supposed to open the door and welcome her into their sanctified abode.

Uriel wasn't entirely sure who the Sabbath Queen was. The Rabbi and Papa and his teachers had tried to explain it many times, but everybody seemed to have a different vision of what she was.

Papa said she was the Bride of God. Rabbi said she was the Shekinah, the divine presence that visited all Jewish homes on Shabbat.

But whenever Uriel heard 'Sabbath Queen' his eyes would shift to his mother. She and God were the ones who made the Sabbath, and so it was only fitting that she should be the Queen. Whenever his Papa told him to open the door for the Sabbath Queen, Uriel would wonder why that was necessary when she was already sitting at the table.

He had hoped that if he did everything right, the Sabbath Queen would come back to him. She would hold his hand and kiss his brow. She would never let him slip from her grasp again.

But she hadn't come. And as soon as he gazed upon the empty hall, he knew that he would never again lay eyes on the Sabbath Queen.

By the time Major Brandt returned, the stars had awoken from their slumber and were glittering proudly in the sky. He hardly paid the celestial gems any mind as he entered the house and stretched his sore limbs.

What a day, he thought with a sigh. *I had planned on doing more interrogations, but since Herr Litten had to be a humanitarian and get himself injured, I suppose that will have to wait until tomorrow. I misjudged his endurance. It appears I'll have to be slightly more lenient with the prisoners when he's around. That or I'll just have to have a cordial talk with Herr Litten and explain how we operate here.*

He strutted towards his office. *Yes, that's likely preferable. He's just a civilian, after all. No worse than some of my boys when they first started out. Still, I don't like the way he just went against my orders, and then physically tried to stop me! Very impolite. Very dangerous. We'll talk. We'll have a long talk…*

The Major entered his office and his emerald eyes became wide.

His chair was beside the bookshelf, a small stack of hardbacks standing on the seat. Books lay strewn about the floor, undamaged and unorganized. He looked at his desk, and pursed his lips when he noted the absence of his precious signed *Mein Kampf*.

"Dear, dear…" he muttered, putting his cap aside and moving towards his desk. "Looks like a tornado passed through here."

Brandt's eyes fell upon his oaken desk and a small pool of brownish-red caught his eye. He dabbed at it with the tip of his index finger and examined the stain. It was not-quite-dried blood. Recently spilled enough that it was still liquid, but old enough that it was starting to take on a rusty color.

He wiped the blood off on his pant leg and scowled at the stain.

Yes, he thought. *We'll certainly need to have a long talk…*

Uriel slipped out of the closet, quieter than a cat on the prowl. He crept up to the sleeping Uwe and examined him closely. The German fidgeted and moaned in his sleep, a clear sign that his dreams weren't pleasant.

To be expected, I suppose, thought the boy. He didn't like hearing his helper whimper, and he wished that there was something he could do, but he was no master of dreams. He was an Angel-Finder, and he needed Uwe to stay asleep if he was going to make any progress in his search.

Once he was certain Uwe was asleep, the child slunk back to the closet and shifted through the socks until he unearthed the Book of Blood. Carefully tucking it under his arm, he tiptoed to the window and looked out. The stars were shimmering proudly, casting their light onto the shadows of the forest. Samael would be there by now.

The boy opened the window and winced when a gust of cold air burst into the room. Uwe groaned, but fortunately for Uriel, the slumbering linguist only pulled the blanket closer around himself without waking up. Uriel sighed with relief and hopped onto the branch. It was difficult to climb down while holding the Book of Blood, but he managed to do so without falling. Once his feet touched the earth, he scurried to the forest.

As soon as he arrived at the clearing, Samael appeared from the shadows. The Angel of Death's haughty smirk was still plastered onto his face even as he accepted the Book of Blood from Uriel.

"That was fast," he said. Uriel smiled proudly and Samael, seeing this, unleashed a condescending chortle.

"Don't get too confident, Angel-Finder. That was merely the first task, and it was a rather easy one. This next one won't be so simple."

Uriel impatiently waved for Samael to hurry up and give him his orders. The less time he had to spend in the presence of the Angel of Death, the better. Besides, he didn't want to be out for too long while Uwe was back at the house.

"Impetuous child," grumbled Samael. "Very well then, since you're so eager. Your next task is to bring me the Shamir. Can you handle that, Jew-boy?"

Shamir. Uriel knew about that. Papa had told him a story once. The Shamir was supposed to be a creature of some sort, one that could cut through rocks better than any tool. Papa had told him that King Solomon had used it to make the Temple in Jerusalem.

Then where did King Solomon leave it? Where can I find it?

Although he didn't even know where he was supposed to start, Uriel kept his countenance confident as he nodded.

"Good spirit. Hurry home, little Jew-boy. Wouldn't want your German guardian to worry."

Uriel's lips parted in horrified surprise. Samael's spiteful smirk widened.

"Oh, you thought I didn't know? I follow him and his countrymen everywhere, little Israelite. This place is drenched with death. I've been lingering in the shadows, listening in. Don't think you can hide anything from me. I'm keeping my eye on you, little Jew-boy."

Uriel looked back towards the house, his mind flashing to Uwe. The linguist was sleeping, his heart still beating, his breath still in his body. But if Uriel angered the Angel of Death…

Samael laughed. "Oh! But don't worry about him too much, Angel-Finder. He's not a part of our contest, at least not for now. Besides, it's not his time yet."

Although he didn't trust the Angel of Death, Samael's words calmed Uriel down slightly. He already had the weight of the world on his young shoulders. Having to worry about one more thing would break his back.

Without so much as a farewell to the Angel of Death, Uriel bolted back towards the house. Samael glared after him and muttered a curse under his breath before he and the Book of Blood disappeared into the shadows.

Before he could see the glowing windows of the house, a bright light caught Uriel's eye. He paused and looked up at it. It drew closer and closer, and for a minute Uriel wondered if he should approach the light or run away.

Deciding that a little exploration wouldn't hurt, he crept close and blinked with surprise when he saw that it was a bird. A dove, to be more precise. In its claw it clutched a small golden vial filled with some sort of shimmering liquid. In its beak, it held a letter.

Uriel took the letter first. The seal disappeared as soon as he laid eyes on it. He unfolded the paper.

Angel-Finder Uriel,

Word of your deal with the Angel of Death has reached the Heavenly Host.

Although I cannot help you personally, I can give you this.

King Solomon the Wise used to speak over seventy languages, including the language of the birds. Drink this and you too will understand them.

The birds are privy to many secrets.

May Hashem bless you.

Gabriel

The instant Uriel finished reading the letter, it vanished into wisps of golden smoke that drifted heavenward to join the stars. Uriel watched it ascend and then turned his amber eyes down to the vial.

The bird held out its claw and twittered, practically begging Uriel to take it. Uriel opened his hand, and the bird dropped the glass container into his palm.

The Angel-Finder hesitated, staring down at the vial as if it could be either medicine or poison.

Samael's words echoed through his mind. *You will bring me five items, but you* have to get them. No help from Gabriel or Raphael or any of your angel friends.

Is this cheating, then? Uriel wondered. If it was, Samael would win by default. Uriel would have to hand over his hamsa, which would be a death sentence for both him and Uwe, and the Jewish People would still be without their Guardian Angel.

But Gabriel wouldn't have sent him the bottle if there was such a risk. *I guess,* the boy thought, *Samael meant that they aren't supposed to tell me exactly where the items are or get them for me. This is different.*

He grasped the vial and reached for the cork. If he drank it, he risked losing everything. If he didn't, he might never find the Shamir or anything else. Then he would lose everything.

Gabriel sent this. Gabriel is the Messenger of God. I trust him, and I certainly trust God.

He uncorked it. It smelled foul, but he pinched his nose and drank it all. It took a fair amount of effort to keep it down since it tasted far worse than it smelled, but he managed. The empty vial turned to dust, which was swiftly blown away by the cold night air.

Uriel's stomach writhed, and he gagged, falling to his knees and grabbing his tummy, feeling as though he was about to vomit. He was reminded of the time he had devoured a rotten apple and had been bedridden for a week, unable to eat because of his brittle stomach.

Soon, though, the churning stopped and his urge to heave departed. Panting, the boy shakily rose to his feet, stumbling as his dizzy head adjusted to the world once more.

"Angel-Finder! Angel-Finder! Do you understand me?"

The small, high-pitched voice caused the mist of vertigo that clouded his mind to evaporate. Uriel turned to the bird, his eyes wide as the sun.

The little dove jumped from one foot to the other, waiting anxiously for Uriel to respond. Slowly, the child nodded.

"Baruch Hashem!" the bird twittered, and Uriel couldn't help himself. He burst into such a fit of laughter that he once again fell to his knees and grabbed his chest as his hiccups and laughs caused his stomach to ache. The bird's voice and the way it praised God in Hebrew…were all birds Jewish then? Or maybe just all doves? It was so bizarrely hilarious that the child was doubled over for well over three minutes.

The poor dove stared at the boy with its head cocked to the side, curious and worried as it watched the child wince and laugh and hiccup and wipe tears from his eyes.

Slowly, after the boy had gained some semblance of control over himself, the bird asked, "Angel-Finder…are you well?"

The sound of the bird's voice almost sent him into another bout of laughter, but the boy bit down on his tongue and remembered his mission. He rose to his feet, a silly smile lingering on his face, the ghost of his laughing fit. He nodded and waved for the bird to say what it needed to.

"Angel-Finder Uriel," said the dove, "I and my kindred know of your mission, and we wish to help you as much as we are allowed. The Shamir that Samael has charged you to bring him is not far, but acquiring it will not be simple."

Uriel, straight-faced now, nodded eagerly and gave the dove his complete attention.

"King Solomon the Wise used the Shamir to cut the stones he used to make the Holy Temple," said the dove. "After that, he kept the Shamir in the Hailstone Cup, a cup made from the hailstones that Hashem rained down on Egypt during the Seventh Plague, for the Shamir cannot cut through a stone that was sent down from Heaven."

"However, after Jerusalem was conquered and decimated, the Shamir and the Hailstone Cup were found and picked up by a creature called the White Eagle."

Uriel gave the dove a questioning look. Seeing this, the dove elaborated.

"The White Eagle is a great bird, as tall as a tree is high. It uses the Shamir to carve out nests on the tops of mountains for its young. Right now, it roosts at the peak of the Moving Mountain, which is not far from here. It has the Shamir with it. My kindred and I can lead you there in the morning, but you will have to climb it. You must be careful! The Moving Mountain is constantly changing, and if you are not watchful, you will either fall or be crushed. As for the White Eagle, it will not normally harm humans, but it may do so to protect its fledglings."

Uriel gave a slow nod, fiddling with the hamsa and looking thoughtfully down at his scruffy shoes. A small light of inspiration came to his eyes. He bowed to the dove to thank it for its assistance before running back to the house and climbing into Uwe's room. He was relieved to find that the linguist was still sleeping, unaware that the little boy had been up and about.

Smiling to himself and resisting the urge to chuckle as he thought of the little dove's voice, Uriel settled into his bed of socks and got the sleep he would need for his mission tomorrow.

CHEATING

He hated it.

He hated being the one and only honest student in class, keeping his eyes firmly locked on his own paper and plugging his ears when somebody tried to whisper an answer. Even if they were trying to help, it was cheating.

He didn't want a cheater's help.

When the teacher would laud and praise the other children for getting every answer correct, when the teacher would carelessly toss his imperfect test back at him like it was garbage, his stomach would twist with anger.

He had been the one to get those questions right. No help. No wandering eyes. Every question he got right represented the agonizing amount of time he had spent studying.

He had seen those other boys, though. They snuck into the teacher's classroom and copied the test. They passed each other notes with the answers on them. They looked over at his paper and copied what he had put down.

Whenever they did that, he felt furious. He felt cheated.

But he didn't have the voice to complain.

He hated it when he and the other children played a game with set rules, rules that the other boys would break just so they could have a hollow victory. Whenever they cheated, and then boasted about their worthless accomplishment, Uriel would become frustrated and storm away.

He didn't want to play with cheaters.

Cheating was abhorrent to him, and if he considered something to be cheating, he wouldn't do it.

And although he went to sleep with a smile after listening to the dove, his sleep became fitful as guilt nagged his heart.

Even if drinking the potion hadn't been cheating, it felt like it. Even if it was the Angel of Death he had cheated, he didn't like it one bit.

He didn't want to be a cheater.

7.

Although Uriel would normally refrain from doing anything arduous on the holy day of rest, since his work was for the sake of the Children of Israel and since millions of lives were hanging in the balance, he decided that Hashem would surely forgive him and prepared to set off

Once Uwe and Major Brandt left for the schoolhouse, Uriel scurried downstairs and into the kitchen. He tested several metal pans and spoons, and once he found a pair that made a satisfyingly loud *clang* when they were hit together, he tucked the spoon into his pocket and hung the pan from his belt.

With his kitchenware at the ready, the boy ran out of the house, the pan smacking against his leg as he did so. The two policemen that Uriel scurried past on his way to the backyard looked curiously around, as they could swear that they heard something, but when they saw nothing, they shrugged it off and went back to chatting.

Uriel ran to the tree that he normally climbed and smiled when he saw five doves flitting about in the branches. When their black eyes fell upon the boy, the birds tweeted with excitement.

"Angel-Finder! Angel-Finder!" they chirped. "Blessings upon you! Come quickly! The Moving Mountain is this way!"

The birds alighted from the branches and fluttered into the forest, being sure to fly low so that Uriel could see them and keep up. The child pursued, jumping over the claw-like bushes and ducking to avoid low-hanging branches. The pan at his side smacked his thigh so many times that it soon became sore, but he ignored the throbbing and kept his eyes trained on the birds.

This is fun, he thought with a smile as he listened to the satisfying sound of the branches cracking under his feet. He inhaled deeply, the cool morning breeze causing his lungs to wake up. Beams of sunlight filtered through the forest canopy and left a mosaic of color at his feet. He looked down for a mere second to admire it before looking back up and huffing in frustration when he saw that the birds were flying far ahead of him.

Sprinting to catch up, he didn't see a thick pool of mud and nearly fell over as his feet sunk down into the goop. The child managed to catch himself, but as he yanked his feet from the mire, his left shoe slipped off and got stuck in the muck.

Uriel hopped on one foot and looked back at his half-sunk shoe. He grunted in aggravation and prepared to dive in and retrieve it.

"Angel-Finder! Angel-Finder! Please, hurry!"

He heard the birds, but they were so far away by now that they were barely little dots in the distance. Huffing, he abandoned his shoe and ran as fast as he could to catch up.

"Here, here, Angel-Finder! Here is the Moving Mountain!"

Uriel gazed up in wonder at the magnificently tall mountain. The foot of the mountain was covered in grass, but the rest was made up of a reddish-brown rock that he could swear was quivering, as if it were anticipating an earthquake.

While the doves settled in a nearby tree, peeking out from behind the leaves, the boy started up the mountain. Clawing his way up the side of the grassy portion proved to be moderately difficult. The grass was weak, and he couldn't get a good grip on it without yanking it out of the dirt and nearly falling backwards.

When he finally made it to the russet rock, climbing became much simpler. The stones stuck out, forming smooth-ended spikes that were easy for him to grab on to. Uriel hoisted himself up and was even more delighted when he found a thin path. Rubbing the rusty dust that clung to his palms off on his pant leg, he started walking up the mountainside.

Just as he was getting close to the peak, however, the ground shook. Uriel stumbled and fell to one knee as the ground gave another mighty tremble.

Before the boy could rise to his feet, the ground seemed to pull itself away from the rest of the mountain with a mighty yank that caused him to fall to his side. Uriel shook his head and quickly sat up. The sight that greeted him made him gasp in both amazement and alarm.

The middle of the Moving Mountain had torn itself apart and all the rocks were floating in the air. Giant boulders and little pebbles soared here and there, rearranging themselves as if the mountain had been dissatisfied with the current order of its midriff and decided to switch the position of its own stones.

Uriel looked up and noted that the very top of the mountain hadn't moved. It hung suspended in the air, waiting patiently for the lower stones to arrange themselves to their liking. The boy looked down and saw that the grassy foot of the Moving Mountain also remained stationary.

He craned his neck upwards and his normally quiet lips permitted a squeak of fear to escape as he saw a huge stone hurtling right towards him and the stone he sat on. The boy looked wildly about for an escape and at that moment another rock passed by his perch. He leapt from his boulder just as the other rock crashed into it.

Uriel sighed, but he wasn't given much time to feel relief as another gigantic rock came barreling towards him. Quickly realizing that there wasn't another perch available, he took a deep breath and jumped as high as he possibly could, gripping the side of the rock just as it collided with his former stone seat. His fingernails dug into the copper boulder and he was only barely able to pull himself onto the flying stone. He panted, but there was no time to rest. He flattened himself against the rock as another soared by and missed him by mere centimeters.

Uriel was forced to leap from boulder to boulder, narrowly avoiding being crushed like a bug as he attempted to make sure that when the mountain became whole again, he was on the outside rather than the inside.

At last, the rocks came together and the Moving Mountain became still once more. Uriel gripped the face of the mountain, his heart pounding so hard that he felt as though it was going to lurch into his throat. For a minute he stood there, completely still, like an ant that had just barely escaped a human's boot.

Breathing deeply to steady his heart, Uriel started to climb. He needed to get the Shamir and get down quickly, lest the Moving Mountain shuffle its stones once more.

At last, after a grueling and anxious climb where even the slightest tremor made him wince and duck down, he made it to the peak. Panting, the boy yanked himself up onto the flat mountaintop and instantly his eyes fell upon the mighty bird.

The White Eagle sat beside its nest, its head lowered towards its squeaking young. Uriel hid behind a rock and peeked out, observing the White Eagle and her young as the great bird crooned and touched each of its three chicks with its beak. The nestlings were almost completely bald, only a few teeny white feathers dotting their wrinkled skin. Their eyes were closed, and they squealed helplessly as they moved towards their mother's beak. The blind bird babes were about as tall as Uriel.

Conversely, the mother was easily as tall as the Zingdorf synagogue. Her charcoal-colored eyes were the size of dinner plates and glittered affectionately as she gazed down at her young. Her brilliant plumage seemed to glow as the sun's bright beams struck the white feathers.

Uriel sat still, both enthralled and terrified, before he ripped his eyes off of the White Eagle and looked about for the Hailstone Cup. He smiled when his squinting eyes finally fell upon a large, smooth half-sphere that rested behind the White Eagle's nest. Listening closely and drowning out the squeaks of the eaglets, Uriel could hear a quiet hissing emanating from the cup.

With the knowledge that the Shamir was close, Uriel stood up. He hurriedly slipped the pan off of his belt and took the metal spoon out of his pocket. Gripping them in his hands, he stepped out from behind the rock.

The White Eagle noticed him almost instantly, stopped nuzzling her young, and turned her now-fierce black eyes on him. The White Eagle didn't speak (perhaps what it had in size it lacked in mental capacity), but instead crouched down and gave a mighty caw. Uriel didn't need to understand the language of the birds to know that the beast wasn't pleased with his presence.

The child inhaled and tried his best to keep his head up and his chest swelled so he would look bigger than he was. He raised his pan and spoon and suddenly ran towards the White Eagle, banging on the pan with the spoon, causing a horrible clanging noise to echo about the Moving Mountain.

In Zingdorf, whenever a murder of crows descended upon the town, the boys would always run at them, waving their arms and screaming curses as though possessed by some evil spirit. Their insanity always frightened the birds away. Since Uriel had no voice to curse with (and *wouldn't* have cursed even if he could), he hoped that his banging would have the same effect on the White Eagle.

It seemed to. The mighty bird was startled. It stepped back, eyeing the ostensibly deranged human with fearful curiosity, as though it didn't quite know whether to flee from the child or try to feed him to her young.

Confidence building at seeing the great creature's confusion and fright, Uriel charged again, waving his arms, shaking his head, jumping up and down, making as much noise as he could with a pan, a spoon, and no voice.

The White Eagle let out a surprised caw as the bold and possibly crazed creature once more came running right at it. Frightened by the small beast's noise, his wild movements, and his apparent fearlessness, the White Eagle leapt into the air. Loving mother though it seemed to be, it was still an animal. Its own safety was its highest priority. Leaving its younglings at the mercy of the maniac, it disappeared behind the clouds.

Uriel watched the White Eagle fly up and exhaled, dropping the pan and spoon and feeling proud of his craziness. The poor, blind little eaglets squealed pitifully, writhing about as they desperately called for their mother. Uriel felt a stab of pity and wished that he could give them something to eat, to make up for driving their mother away. But he had nothing to give them, and besides he could surmise that if he got close, he might end up *becoming* their dinner.

He cautiously crept around the baby birds and ran to the Hailstone Cup. It was easily as big as his chest, and inside there was a creature about as big as a large cat.

It was probably the ugliest thing Uriel had ever laid eyes on. It looked like some monstrous combination of a worm, a weasel, and a spider. Its body was long and covered in prickly black fur, with a wet black nose that twitched as it sniffed the air and six lifeless black eyes that dotted its forehead. It had short, stubby little legs that were as thin as Uriel's pinkies. Its mouth, which looked more like a rounded snout than a mouth, was circular, with six rows of spike-like teeth. Its perpetually open maw emitted unearthly hisses as it squirmed about.

Uriel was afraid to touch the hideous thing, but as he listened closely to its hisses, his heart was once again punctured with pity. The creature was in pain. Perhaps it was hungry, or perhaps it was losing its sanity. He certainly would if he was kept in a teeny cup for hundreds of years.

I hope that Samael treats it well, thought Uriel, gripping the sides of the Hailstone Cup and trying to lift it.

He only succeeded in nearly dislocating his arms. Trying to lift the cup was like trying to pull the mountain itself from the earth. It was heavier than a ton of bricks. Strain and struggle as he may, Uriel simply couldn't pick it up.

All right then, he thought, sucking in as much oxygen as his lungs could accept in one breath and trying not to focus on the feel of the creature's hair on his hands as he picked it up and lifted it out of the cup.

The creature wriggled only a bit before going limp in Uriel's arms. The boy released the air he had gathered, relief rushing through his body as the Shamir seemed to accept his assistance.

The second Uriel turned and started towards the path, however, the Shamir sunk two of its razor-sharp teeth into the child's arm. The boy yelped in pain and dropped the Shamir by reflex.

As soon as it landed on the smooth rock of the Moving Mountain, the Shamir turned its teeth downwards and gnawed right through the stone, digging a burrow and slipping into the mountain. Uriel dropped to his knees and pressed his ear against the rock. Listening closely, he could hear a scratchy pattern of crunches as the Shamir chewed.

Ignoring the small cuts on his arm (perhaps, he thought, the Shamir was slightly grateful to Uriel for giving it freedom; it could have chewed through his arm, after all, but it hadn't), Uriel bolted past the peeping younglings and ran down the side of the Moving Mountain, desperately searching for a cave.

STORK

She rested at the tip-top of the synagogue's roof, having carefully and precariously built her nest on the pointed pinnacle of the Holy House.

Why, of all the roofs in Zingdorf, she chose one so unsteady to settle on was a mystery. Nevertheless, she never fell. Her nest remained there, silhouetted against the sun as it rose and set and the moon as it appeared and faded.

The residents of Zingdorf would awaken to her soft singing and fall asleep when she tucked her head under her wing and drifted off, still keeping her balance. She would gaze down on the people as they went about their daily tasks, listening as the choir practiced in the synagogue.

She would turn her eyes down on Uriel as he crouched outside of the synagogue while every other boy was inside singing. She would watch him peek into the windows, his golden eyes tarnished with sorrow as he listened to songs he would never sing.

And, perhaps out of solidarity, she too remained silent during those practices, never singing a single note.

The boys of Zingdorf often said that if one climbed to the top of the synagogue and grabbed hold of the Stork's leg, she would fly him to Heaven and he would become an angel, like Elijah.

But the synagogue roof was horribly steep. Not at all suited for climbing. The boys would often try, much to the chagrin of their fathers and the horror of their mothers, to climb up and grab the Stork by the leg. All of them fell. Every single time.
And she would remain there, balanced as ever, calmly and almost condescendingly gazing down on them as they whimpered and nursed their shattered bones, as if to berate them for their stupidity.

The one time that Uriel tried to touch the Stork was at night. His mother would sooner jump from the synagogue roof herself than let her precious little bird climb up there, and so he had to sneak out. He felt guilty about it, but the desire to become an angel overpowered his hesitation as he slipped out of his room and made his way to the synagogue.

He hoisted himself to the roof and remained on his hands and knees, digging his fingers into the cracked clay tiles. Slowly, without daring to look up for even a second, he crawled in the direction of the nest. He tried to be like a cat as he cautiously crept across the roof: graceful, agile, able to balance on anything.

A small coo caused him to look up. His golden eyes widened when they landed on the Stork.

He made it. He was kneeling right beside her nest.

His eyes traveled from her night-black eyes to her long, sun-colored legs. All he had to do was reach out and grab one. Then she and he would fly up to Heaven together.

A teeny chirp made him stop. His eyes flitted to something pink, bald, and helpless that sat right behind the beautiful bird's leg.

A stork hatchling. Barely a week old. It blindly waved its not-quite-wings, cheeping softly for its mother. It chirped so quietly. Uriel wasn't surprised that nobody had known that the Stork had a youngling.

It found its mother's leg and rested its featherless head against her smooth flesh. She didn't pay her child any mind, instead keeping her eyes on Uriel. It seemed like she was asking him what he was going to do.

Uriel looked from the hatchling to the mother. He thought of Papa and Mama. How would they feel if they woke up to find that their boy had vanished? Would he be able to come back down after he became an angel? Would he be able to hug them once more?

And the little baby stork, well, it still needed its mother. Heaven would have to wait.

He slid down the roof and ran home.

The other residents of Zingdorf were quite surprised and delighted when they eventually found out that the Stork had a youngling. Soon, though, the baby grew up, and one day it was gone.

And after that, the Stork herself abandoned her nest. Perhaps she went back up to Heaven once the one who needed her left, or perhaps she realized how dreary and empty her nest was without her beloved nestling.

Either way, the Stork vanished, leaving her lonely nest on top of the Zingdorf synagogue.

"Major?"

"Hm? Yes, Herr Litten?"

"Ahm…it's still very early. May I ask why we're going home so soon?"

They were already halfway to the house, yet Major Brandt had been so distant and cold that Uwe had been hesitant to say anything but "Yes, Major" all day. Only once they were in the car and Brandt began to smile and crack jokes like usual did Uwe build up the courage to ask why their workday was so short.

Brandt looked over his shoulder at the linguist, a warm smile on his face, his eyes gleaming affably once more. "*We* are not going home, in fact, Herr Litten. Only *you* are."

"Why only me? Don't you still need me for today?"

"Ah, your eagerness to help out is appreciated, little linguist," said Brandt. "But no, we won't be needing you for the rest of the day."

Uwe had to work hard to conceal his relief. The less time he had to spend helping the *Ordnungspolizei* interrogate prisoners the better. Although Major Brandt had been considerably less brutal today, only giving the prisoner the occasional slap when he refused to cooperate, he had made it clear to Uwe that he was only being 'gentle' today for his sake.

"You'll have to get used to our interrogation techniques, I'm afraid, Herr Litten," he had said. "I can't always afford to be so gentle. We have important work to do for the Führer. Besides, if I don't get rid of these partisans posthaste, my men will be in danger. You understand, don't you?"

Uwe had, of course, replied with an obedient, "Yes, Major." He was already in the spider's web. Best not to gain the spider's attention by struggling.

Head down. Do as they say.

Still, he was already struggling in a way. Keeping Uriel in his room could hardly be considered anything but quiet sedition on his part.

He smiled slightly when he thought of the boy. At least with the Major gone he would have some time to read to him. Uriel would be delighted to see him back so early.

"Where will you be going, Major?" Uwe asked.

"After we drop you off? The woods. We're going to use some of the information you and I extracted from the prisoners to try and find the Polish partisans. If we're lucky, we might even stumble across some hidden Jews."

They finally pulled up to the house. The two guards at the door waved to their 'Uncle Günter.' He smiled and gave them a tiny salute. Uwe eagerly jumped out of the car.

"In that case, I wish you luck," he said, "Goodbye, Herr Brandt!"

"One moment, little linguist," said Brandt, causing Uwe to grit his teeth in disappointment and stop before he could bolt to the front door.

"Yes, Major?"

"In case I come back late, I think I should give you advanced notice," said Brandt. "The higher echelons have given us orders to clear out a small Jewish village just west of here. Tomorrow's going to be a busy day."

He smiled brightly. "So be sure to get plenty of rest! Don't stay up too late!"

Uwe's heart sunk at the prospect of being part of such an operation. Nonetheless, he swallowed his reluctance and smiled as he said, "Yes, Major."

"Very good. Ah! Also!" Brandt cried just as Uwe turned towards the house. Uwe suppressed an aggravated hiss and looked back at the Major with a smile forcefully planted on his face.

"Yes, Major?"

"I was wondering…did you borrow my copy of *Mein Kampf*? It's fine if you did, I had just been meaning to ask you."

With a genuinely confused glint in his eyes, Uwe shook his head. "No, Herr Brandt, I haven't touched your book."

For the briefest second, Uwe could swear that he saw a toxic look pass across the Major's face, but it was quickly replaced with a cheerful grin.

"Ah! Never mind then!" he said with a friendly, dismissive wave. "Must be my fault! This is what I get for being so disorganized! My father nagged me about it no less than a million times, but it never quite sunk in! Well, it'll turn up. Goodbye then, Herr Litten."

Gratefully bidding the Major farewell, Uwe ran into the house. He entered and waited a moment to hear the car drive off before he ran up the stairs and knocked seven times.

"Uriel!" he cried, "I'm back early! Open the door!"

No response.

"Uriel! Are you asleep? Wake up and open for me!"

Still nothing. Uwe raised a concerned eyebrow. He got down on his knees and peeked under the door but didn't see the boy's shadow or the bottoms of his feet.

His chest tightened like a boa constrictor. He ran down the stairs. Not wanting the guards to see him go into the backyard, he hurried into the living room and opened the window. Carefully climbing out of the house into the tree-speckled backyard, he ran below his bedroom and released a sailor-dictionary's worth of curses when he saw that the window was wide open.

Damn that boy, damn that boy, damn that boy!

He practically seethed as he gazed up at the gaping window. He looked over his shoulder at the woods and clenched his teeth when he thought of the boy running around, putting his life in danger, doing exactly what Uwe had told him not to.

Then the Major's words came to his mind and his anger turned to dread.

Oh, Christ, he's going into the woods!

The Major and his men could find the boy. They could catch him. Send him to a camp.

But that wasn't Uwe's fault. He had done all he could, and if the boy was captured, then his blood was on his own hands. He had disobeyed Uwe, and Uwe was not obligated to run into the woods and put his own life in jeopardy just to find the boy. Uriel was not his child.

Not my responsibility. I'm not his father.

He was ready to go back inside and hope for the best, but he looked closely at the threshold of the forest and saw a broken twig. Stepping closer and peering into the seemingly peaceful woods, he noticed a trail of broken branches and crushed leaves. A human had been through there. A little one.

Uriel…

He looked down at his injured hand and the boy's bright smile and treasure-like eyes flashed through his mind.

And even though his instincts objected to such foolhardiness, his heart would not let him abandon the child.

Damn it.

He ran into the woods, trying his best to move fast, keep track of Uriel's trail, and watch out for partisans and the *Ordnungspolizei*.

He didn't dare call out for the boy, worried that if he shouted, he would attract unwanted attention. Instead, Uwe rushed through the thicket, trying to remain as quiet as Uriel, biting down on his tongue to keep himself from cursing when a tree limb smacked his face.

Finally, he stumbled out of the bushes, a few leaves clinging to his clothes and hair even as he tried to sweep them off with his hands. He looked up, and his eyes fell upon a short, grassy hill.

He narrowed his azure eyes at the hill and tried to assess if it was even big enough to have a cave in it that the curious boy might have been tempted to explore. He circled the base and was surprised to find one hidden behind a jungle of weeds. He had to duck to avoid hitting his head on the rock roof and to keep the dangling weeds out of his eyes, but once he was inside, he could stand up straight.

Unfortunately, the inside was practically pitch black. The only light the cavern offered was the sunlight that managed to slip past the weeds that guarded the entrance.

"U-Uriel!" Uwe whispered, cringing as his voice echoed horribly throughout the cave.

"Uriel! Are you there?" he hissed. He slowly walked forward, the cave growing darker and darker until he could hardly see where he was going.

By the time Uwe reached a fork in the cavern, he was nearly blind. He could see well enough, though, to realize that he was standing in front of two divergent paths. He hesitated, not wanting to go deeper into the cave and get lost.

Just as he was about to turn back and leave, a strong pair of hands grabbed his shoulders and slammed him onto the stone ground so hard that his teeth rattled. The pain made him moan and caused his mind to become hazy, but he was lucid enough to hear voices above him and recognize the language that his attackers were speaking.

"A spy!"

"Is he German?"

"Kill him!"

"Hang on! Hang on! We should let Matthias talk to him!"

Yiddish! Uwe thought, realizing with dread that he had found the fugitive Jews.

Hardly had Uwe entered the cave when Uriel finally made it down the Moving Mountain. He slid down the mountain's grassy base and looked up when he felt a great shaking and heard a great grinding. He sighed with relief when he saw the Mountain once again rearranging the stones at its center and thanked Hashem that he had made it down in time.

Uriel landed in a small patch of weeds. He cringed and looked down at the plants with horror as their scratchy leaves rubbed against his soft skin. He stood bolt upright and hastily tried to dust the weeds off of him, rubbing their residue off his hands. He got horrible rashes whenever he touched weeds, and the very last thing he needed was to be itchy while trying to fulfill Samael's quests.

The child heaved a sigh of pure ire as he looked down at his already-tingling hands. *Terrific. I lost my shoe, got a rash, and I still don't have the Shamir!*

The boy looked over his shoulder and his face lit up when he saw a cave directly behind him.

Well, maybe I'm not cursed after all!

Hoping that the Shamir was hiding inside, Uriel crept into the cave. The air was so moist that it caused him to sneeze several times, but he tried his best to ignore his stuffy nose and prickling hands as he ventured deeper into the cavern.

The further he went, however, the more light he lost. He almost didn't see the diverging paths that eventually appeared in front of him, and when he did manage to make them out in the dark, he pursed his lips together, wondering which one he should take.

He glanced at the left path and pricked up his ears. Uriel had always had very good hearing (perhaps to make up for his missing voice), and so when he listened closely, he could hear distant voices speaking in what he could swear was his own native tongue, Yiddish.

Jews? Uriel thought, gasping with happiness and almost darting down the left path to greet his kindred.

He stopped himself, however, when another sound echoed down the opposing hallway. A long, frightening hiss. He glanced at the right path.

*The Shamir...*thought Uriel. He looked longingly down the left hallway, listening to the Yiddish words as if they were lyrics to the most beautiful song in the world. He bit his bottom lip so hard that he almost hurt himself and turned away.

I can't, he thought with sorrow. *If I meet them, they might try to keep me with them. They might stop me from doing Samael's quests. I can't let that happen. I have to find Michael. For their sake. For everyone's sake.*

With a heart that felt heavy as the Hailstone Cup, Uriel followed the Shamir's hissing.

Darkness consumed the cave and Uriel had to hold out his arms so he didn't run into the stone walls. Walking quickly and blindly, he followed the hiss until, much to his relief and delight, he spotted a beam of light. He ran towards it, arriving in a small section of the cavern. There was a hole in the cave's roof, one that seemed to go all the way to the top of the mountain. Sunlight flew into the perfectly circular tunnel and traveled all the way down into the gloomy cavern below.

The light allowed Uriel to see the small area clearly, and his ears directed him to the corner. He instantly saw the creature, its slender body curled up in the corner. He took a step forward, thinking that the creature was asleep, but the instant he did so the Shamir raised its hideous head and bared its many rows of teeth, giving off a threatening hiss that echoed throughout the cave.

Uriel jumped back, fearfully throwing his hands behind him. He stepped out of the light and remained still as stone. The Shamir continued to hiss, but then slowly lowered its head. Its hisses became soft, like snoring.

Uriel sighed in frustration. He couldn't just pick the creature up. If it woke and bit him again, he could lose his arm, and besides trying to grab it could cause it to burrow even deeper into the earth, where the child wouldn't be able to catch it.

Maybe, the boy thought, *there's some way to knock it out or trap it. There must be some way. Maybe the birds will know.*

A small smile returned to his face at the thought. Moving slowly so as not to wake the Shamir, he turned and stumbled through the dark cavern once more, trying to find the exit and praying that the Shamir would stay where it was until he figured out a way to capture it.

Uwe's glasses nearly cracked when the Jews slammed him onto the cold ground. His skull throbbed in pain as it met the cave's floor and his nose started to bleed. Though his brain was thoroughly rattled, he could still hear and understand what the Jews were saying.

"Watch his head!"

"Oh, he's alive! German son-of-a-bitch deserves to feel a little pain."

"Enough."

A voice like frozen steel caused all others to fall silent. Uwe pushed himself off the ground and one of the Jews, seeing this, grabbed the back of his collar and forced him to his knees.

Uwe grunted and looked up at the man who had given the frigid, curt order.

The apparent leader of the renegade Jews was less ragged than his fellows. The candlelit cave revealed that, while the others were a disheveled lot with only tatters for clothes, he only had a bit of stubble and wore a slightly ripped gray army outfit. He crossed his arms behind his back rather imperiously and gazed down at Uwe with his chillingly lifeless gray eyes.

Previously, Uwe had been too terrified to speak, but now he straightened his back and looked the man in the eye, trying his best to look and sound calm as he spoke in Yiddish.

"Please release me," he said in the language of the Jews, earning several blinks of surprise from all but the Jewish commander.

Uwe's forehead became moist with sweat, and yet he kept his expression composed as he looked up at the severe Jewish man, searching his rigid face for a hint of what he was thinking.

The Jewish man's brow lifted so subtly that had Uwe not been examining him closely he wouldn't have noticed.

"You speak Yiddish well, but you have an accent," the commander observed. "What are you? German? Jewish? Polish?"

"I…am German," Uwe confessed. Although he hesitated to admit his nationality, the Jewish leader's forbidding eyes almost seemed like a pair of x-rays that could see right through him. He was afraid that the man would easily recognize a lie, and when he did so Uwe would be in even worse trouble.

The Jewish man inclined his head ever so slightly, almost as if he wanted to give Uwe's honesty a nod of approval but didn't remember how to show that much emotion.

"What are you doing here and how can you speak Yiddish so well?" he asked.

"I-I'm a linguist," Uwe replied, "I know languages. The Major that runs this area, Major Brandt, he forced me to come here so I could be a translator for him…"

"You see?" blurted the Jew who seemed particularly frustrated by the fact that the German was still alive. "He's a filthy spy! He's going to tell the Germans about us if we don't bash his skull in!"

"*Enough.*"

Two syllables from the Jewish leader cut through the suspicious one's rant like a blade. The other Jews huddled together, trembling with fear. Uwe couldn't be certain if their terror was caused by the suspicious one's prophecy of doom or their leader's single word.

The linguist's attention was drawn away from them as he became aware of something sharp dangerously close to his jugular. Not daring to move his body, he directed his pupils downward and realized that the Jewish leader was pointing a knife at his throat.

Meeting the Jewish man's icy irises, Uwe quietly pleaded, "Please…don't kill me."

"Is what he said true, German?" asked the Jewish leader, his head giving a barely noticeable nudge to indicate the suspicious one. "Are you going to tell the Nazis where we are? Are you going to get us killed if we free you?"

Not daring to swallow while the knife was at his throat, Uwe stuttered, "I…I don't want to hurt anybody. I don't want anybody to get killed. I have a family and I just want to go home…"

A flash of emotion passed over the Jewish leader's face, but it happened far too fast for Uwe to identify whatever sentiment it might have been. After it vanished, though, an ominous aura wrapped itself around the man, causing Uwe to shudder and shut his eyes.

He sensed the knife being moved away and heard a small sound as it was sheathed. The Jewish man knelt down so that he was at eye level with the German.

"Then why are you here?" he asked.

Uwe, quite surprised and grateful to still have an intact neck, inhaled deeply and replied, "I was looking for someone."

"Nobody else has come in recently," said the Jewish leader. "Who…?"

But before the Jewish commander could even complete his question, the suspicious one cried out, "Wait, you're not going to kill him?"

Standing up, his dull eyes seeming oddly irate, the Jewish leader replied, "No. I believe him. Besides, killing him would only cause the Germans to come looking for him, and if they find us with his dead body that will just give them another excuse…"

"They don't need an excuse, Matthias!" barked the suspicious one. "They'll kill us either way, and he's going to lead them…!"

"Matthias, is that your name?" Uwe interrupted, looking up at the Jewish leader, widening his eyes and twitching his head towards the bellowing man, nonverbally begging the Jewish commander to get him away from his accuser.

The Jewish leader, Matthias, nodded. "It is," he replied. He offered Uwe a rather stiff hand and said, "Come, we'll talk more in private."

Uwe grasped Matthias' hand and the Jewish man pulled the German to his feet. With the suspicious one growling and cursing under his breath as he watched, Matthias led Uwe to a small section of the cave. There was a lice-ridden mat spread out on the ground, along with several maps and notes that were lying dangerously close to the flickering candle. Were he not still recovering from his near-fatal encounter with Matthias' men, Uwe would have scolded the Jewish man for leaving flammable papers so close to a flame. Instead, he kept his mouth shut and sat down on the floor when Matthias gestured for him to do so.

"So…" muttered Uwe after Matthias didn't speak for some time. "You're the Jews that Major Brandt's trying to find."

"I assume, though I don't know who Major Brandt is," said Matthias. "You know him well, I presume."

"A bit. He's nice to his men, but to his enemies…"

The memory of the interrogation caused a shiver to slither up his spine. He could practically smell the burning flesh.

"He's ruthless."

"And he's the one running the German unit in this area."

"The *Ordnungspolizei*."

Matthias' head tilted ever so slightly to the left, expressing his desire for Uwe to elaborate.

"The Order Police. Brandt is their leader, and right now he's looking for you and the Polish partisans."

"Polish partisans?" Matthias repeated, genuine surprise forcing its way into his metallic voice. Uwe nodded.

"Yes. They've apparently been causing him a lot of trouble."

The Jewish leader's deadpan expression faltered as a bitter smirk tugged at the far corner of his lip.

"I see," he said, his mirthless voice sounding darkly amused. "So they finally discovered that we're not Hitler's only target, hm? Fools. Evil fools."

"Evil?" Uwe repeated, his mind promptly summoning up the face of the poor man that Brandt had been tormenting.

"The Poles helped the Germans when they first came," Matthias said. He gestured to the despondent Jews and explained. "Most of the people here, Poles and Germans attacked their villages. The Poles destroyed my home."

With eyes like a snowstorm, he looked at Uwe and declared, "If this Brandt person is too busy hunting down the Poles to focus on us, I'm fine with that. Let them kill each other."

Uwe opened his mouth, prepared to defend the Polish people by rationally arguing that surely not all of them hated the Jews.

He stopped, however, when he noticed Matthias' gaze lingering on the Jews he protected. Uwe followed his eyes and examined the Jews closely. He noted that they were all men, and young men at that, ranging from sixteen to thirty years old. They were also emaciated. Only the men who had dragged Uwe to Matthias looked strong enough to carry their own weight. The others laid about the cave, their wide, tragedy-filled eyes bulging from their sockets as they grasped their snarling stomachs and stared at nothing.

"How…long have you and the others been here?" the German asked slowly. Matthias didn't answer immediately and didn't look at Uwe when he finally responded.

"I don't know," he said, his voice exhibiting a morsel of distress. "Long enough that our food supply is gone."

"You have no food?" Uwe whispered, his eyes flickering to the rail-thin runaways. Matthias nodded.

"I can send my men out to hunt sometimes," he muttered, anger slowly coming to his iron voice, building up like a volcano ready to erupt. "But every time I do, I risk the Germans finding them and killing them, or following them back here and killing us all! And even when that doesn't happen, they can't bring enough food for twenty people! When somebody eats, somebody else goes hungry! This is what the Germans are doing to us! They're turning us into mice, forcing us to hide in a hole and either go hungry or risk getting caught in a hawk's claws just for a crumb! We're sick, we're starving, and I can't do anything about it!"

Pain and fury melded in the Jewish man's eyes like two liquid metals. For a moment, looking from the distraught man to his famished charges, Uwe almost offered to bring them something. Even if it was measly, a few bits of bread smuggled from Brandt's overstocked kitchen might do wonders for the Jews, if only for their morale.

But Uwe quickly shook his head to rid himself of that idea. He had one Jew to worry about. He was already putting his life on the line. He simply couldn't make his precarious situation even more dangerous.

He was already twitching. Thrashing about would only cause the spider to notice him faster.

He stood up.

"Please, Matthias," he begged, "Major Brandt is out in the woods looking for the Poles. If I'm not back before he returns, he'll come looking for me…"

Matthias' rage boiled down and his eyes became icy once more. He glanced over at the guards.

"Let him leave," he ordered, not shouting, but speaking loudly enough that the other Jews would hear.

Immediately, the suspicious one started to argue against such an edict. While he and Matthias quarreled, Uwe slipped past them, thanking the Heavenly Host for the mercy that Matthias had given him. He still wasn't quite out of trouble yet, though. He needed to find Uriel.

Uriel.

He paused, looking back at the now-exasperated Matthias and his men. A group of Jews. They had avoided the Germans for so long. Perhaps he could leave Uriel with them. Then he wouldn't have to worry about him anymore.

One cursory glance at the other Jews in the cave banished such a proposition from his mind. They were sick and starving. The very last thing they needed was another mouth to feed and another soul to worry about. A child wouldn't make it amongst them. Though it seemed surreal, Uriel was much safer in Major Brandt's house.

Sighing and glancing over at Matthias one more time, he bit his bottom lip and suppressed the humanitarian offer that threatened to burst from his lips.

Instead, he turned his back on the unfortunate Jews and exited.

"Yes, Angel-Finder," said the doves once Uriel successfully mimed out his situation. "The Hailstone Cup cannot be cut by the Shamir, but it would take the strength of three men to lift it. The White Eagle is mighty enough to carry the cup, but you…"

Uriel sighed, absentmindedly scratching his now maddeningly itchy hands as he looked up at the birds with pleading eyes, begging them to give him some sort of solution to his dilemma.

One bird, a gangly dove, piped up. "Ah! Wait! What about Elijah's Mantle?"

Upon hearing the name of the adored Prophet-Angel, Uriel's smile stretched to a breaking point. The other birds didn't seem as excited by the prospect. Well, two of them twittered in cheerful concurrence, but the other two shook their little heads.

"But we have no inkling…" one dove started to say, but he noticed the eager and curious expression on the child's face and looked down at him.

"Angel-Finder," he said. "When the Prophet Elijah was taken up to Heaven to become an angel, he left his cloak behind on earth. His cloak is imbued with great spiritual power. It cannot be cut or torn by anything, man or beast. If you could get the Mantle, you could use it to catch the Shamir."

Uriel nodded eagerly, but his optimism deflated a tad when the bird lowered its head sadly.

"However," the dove said, "we do not know where it is."

Uriel pursed his lips. He was perfectly willing to search for the Mantle, but it would help if he had a hint of some sort. Even though he could go running around the countryside looking for it, it would be much more convenient if he didn't have to.

Fortunately, the gangly, confident dove seemed to recognize this and declared, "Then we'll search for it all day and all night! We have to, for Michael and Gabriel! We'll figure out where it is and lead Angel-Finder Uriel to it once we find it. If we spread out and search thoroughly, we should be able to locate it!"

His suggestion seemed to give the other doves the encouragement they required. Uriel nodded keenly.

"Very well," said one dove. "Then we must hurry. Farewell, Angel-Finder. Hopefully, we will return soon."

Uriel gave them a cheerful wave as they alighted from the branches and fluttered up into the steadily darkening sky, disappearing behind the clouds.

"*Uriel!*"

A voice too familiar for the child to mistake caused him to spin around and gasp in shock when he saw the shouter. Standing at the mouth of the cave, haggard and yet clearly relieved, was Uwe.

Uriel wouldn't have been too surprised had it been Gabriel, braving the sin-filled lands to give the Angel-Finder a message from Heaven, or even Samael there to scold him for talking to the birds. Seeing Uwe in the middle of the woods, his azure eyes filled with slowly receding worry, caused the child's jaw to drop.

Uwe saw the boy and could hardly believe his luck. Uriel was standing in front of a tree, staring at the sky. When he called out to Uriel the child turned, his eyes bulging as he gawked at the German in disbelief. Uwe wasn't entirely sure what surprised the boy so much, but at the moment he didn't care. He was just relieved that he had found Uriel safe and sound.

He ran to the boy and grabbed his shoulders, giving him a small shake, as if he wanted to make sure that the child was real and not a hallucination that his still-aching head had summoned up. The child barely reacted to being jostled in such a way. He merely gazed up at Uwe, awe consuming his amber eyes.

Then tears. Uriel smiled a wobbly smile and startled to sniffle, joyful tears running down his cheeks.

He came looking for me, Uriel thought. *I thought he would never…*

Uwe saw the child's tears and misinterpreted them. Giving the boy another shake, this one gentler than the last, he cried, "Uriel, what's wrong? Are you hurt? Agh! I know you can't talk, but gesture or something! What in the name of the living God were you thinking, Uriel? Why are you out here? And don't you dare do the bathroom dance again, that is *not* a sensible excuse!"

Uriel looked up at him, smiling and crying merrily. Uwe noticed that Uriel wasn't trying to wipe the tears from his face. In fact, the child had his hands behind his back.

Arching a suspicious eyebrow, Uwe asked, "Uriel, what's behind your back?"

The child's smile twitched. His cheeks became red with embarrassment.

"Uriel," Uwe ordered. "Let me see your hands!"

Uriel took a step back and stubbornly shook his head.

"Uriel!" ordered Uwe, his tone rising to a reprimand as he grabbed Uriel's arms and pulled his hands in front of him. "Let me see…!"

His voice trailed off when he saw Uriel's hands: red as a pair of tomatoes, with some skin beginning to peel off from the child's scratching.

Uwe's anger immediately transformed into exasperation.

"Uriel…"

The child could only smile bashfully.

"Unbelievable! You run off when I tell you not to, you cause me to stumble across the hiding Jews, you worry me half to death, you get a terrible rash on your hands, and to top it all off, you lose your left shoe!"

Uwe scolded the boy while simultaneously standing at the sink and trying his best to clean the child's clothes the old-fashioned way. Since Uriel didn't have any other clothes and since he was, frankly, starting to stink as a result, Uwe had ordered him into the bath while he tried to scrub the dirt from the child's apparel. The very last thing he needed was for Brandt to *smell* the hiding Jew.

Uriel sat in the tub, giggling with delight as he tried to pop all the soapy bubbles that covered the surface of the water, enjoying his overdue bath.

What a bath it was! A gigantic marble tub, nothing like the old pewter one he had bathed in back in Zingdorf. Uwe hadn't even needed to run down to the well and haul a bucket of water back five or six times to fill it. All he did was twist a little silver knob that was attached to the tub and water came right out of a faucet! Uriel had quite a bit of fun playing with the knob and faucet until Uwe ordered him to stop, saying he would flood the bathroom if he kept goofing around with the water.

Uriel took a deep breath and dove under the water, squeezing his eyes shut so the sudsy water wouldn't sting them. He wondered how long he could hold his breath.

Uwe glanced at the boy as he dunked his head under the bubbly water and couldn't help but smile. Back home, he practically had to wrestle his little Jürgen into the bath. Apparently, lions weren't too fond of baths, and so neither was Jürgen. Uriel, on the other hand, seemed to be enjoying himself. He had only put up a fuss when Uwe urged him to take off the odd necklace that hung around his neck. The boy had steadfastly refused to do so and Uwe, wanting to avoid any unnecessary trouble, let the boy keep it on while he bathed. He had warned Uriel that it would rust if it got wet, but the child hadn't seemed very concerned.

Uwe's smile slowly turned into a frown when the child didn't emerge for a full minute. Concerned, Uwe hung the clothes on the towel rack and knelt beside the tub.

"Uriel?" he said. The boy promptly surfaced, taking in a huge gulp of air before grinning widely, proud of his breath-holding accomplishment. As he sat up, he splashed Uwe in the face. The German smirked and got his revenge by attacking the boy with soapy water.

"Yes, yes, very good," said Uwe as the boy giggled and shielded his eyes. "But try not to make me think you're drowning in a foot of water. I've done enough worrying today."

Uwe grabbed the shampoo and said, "Lean your head back. Your hair is probably a lice neighborhood."

Uriel obeyed, cheerfully wiggling his toes as Uwe rubbed the scented material into his hair. This almost reminded Uriel of how his mother used to help him bathe. It wasn't exactly the same, especially since Uwe kept muttering in German about lice and Major Brandt and all the trouble he had to go through for Uriel's sake, but it was still nice to have somebody to take care of him.

"All right, dunk," Uwe ordered once he finished his part. Uriel obeyed and submerged his head once more to get the shampoo out. Once his hair was free of suds, he emerged. Uwe was already handling another tube.

"Hands," the German ordered briskly. Uriel pulled his scarlet hands out of the bathwater and held them out to Uwe, who rubbed some sort of cool cream on the irritated flesh.

"I managed to snatch this medicine," he explained. "It should help. Just try not to scratch the rash, even if it itches. Understand?"

Uriel nodded. Uwe retrieved the boy's clothes, which were thoroughly soaked but much cleaner now, and set them beside the bathtub.

"All right, bath time's over. Get dressed."

Uriel hugged himself with one arm and shook his head, gesturing for Uwe to turn around first. Nodding obediently, Uwe turned to the wall. He heard a slight sloshing and a bit of fumbling before he felt a small tap on his shoulder.

"Done then?" he asked as he turned around to look at the fully clothed and dripping wet child. The boy nodded happily, but Uwe sighed and shook his head.

"You're still drenched," he said, grabbing a towel, "Here, let's try to dry your hair at least."

He rubbed the towel through the boy's ebony hair, causing the boy to grin and giggle when he looked in the mirror and saw how crazy he appeared with his locks sticking out every which way. Uriel tried to straighten out his hair while Uwe tried to dry the boy's clothes.

Uwe did the best he could, though the child's clothes were still wet by the time he gave up. He threw the towel aside and emptied the bathtub before he returned to Uriel's side and pulled a comb out of a drawer.

"Here, let me," he said, moving the boy's hands away from his hair and quickly brushing it so it was semi-tidy. The child's eyes gleamed. He thanked Uwe with a spine-shattering hug. Uwe gagged and nearly dropped the comb, but decided not to verbally object. He was through with scolding for the day.

"Okay, come now," said Uwe once he cleaned up the bathroom, yanking Uriel back to his room and locking the door behind him.

"There, all clean and safe," he said, looking down at the boy with a small nod of approval. Water dripped from the child's clothes, forming a small puddle at his feet.

"And wet," Uwe added. "But you'll be dry by tomorrow."

Uriel certainly hoped so. He wasn't looking forward to sleeping in wet clothes. He hoped that they wouldn't shrink because of this mandatory washing. It was bad enough that he had lost his shoe today. He didn't need *more* garb-related trouble.

"The important thing is," said Uwe, exhaling as if to banish the strain from his body, "we're both safe, we're here, and we're happy. Now, let's do some reading."

Uriel nodded eagerly and ran to grab the golden notebook, speedily flipping to the desired page while Uwe sat down and waited for the boy.

"Have a specific one in mind tonight?" he asked with a smile. The boy nodded. Since they had read about Elijah last night, he thought it was only appropriate for them to read about his friend Obadiah.

The child jumped onto the bed and handed the book to Uwe. Uwe watched with an amused half-smile as the boy got settled and drenched Uwe's blanket in the process.

Oh, well, he thought, allowing the boy to lean his head against his shoulder without objection. *I guess we both get to sleep soaked tonight.*

He glanced down at the title.

From Papa: The Story of Obadiah the Righteous
Once Uriel was still, Uwe cleared his throat and began to read:

"Long ago, when Hashem still spoke with men, in the land of Israel, the King made a godless woman his wife. The Queen, named Jezebel, was a ruthless and wicked woman. She wanted to purge Israel of its faith and replace the True Lord with her false gods.

To do this, she banned the worship of Hashem, and anybody who was caught preaching in His name or praying to Him instead of her abominations was slaughtered.

During this time, hundreds of faithful men and women were put to death. God's precious prophets were slaughtered by the thousands.

But two faithful men were spared from Jezebel's sword. One was Elijah, the great prophet who would one day become an angel. The other was his friend, Obadiah.

Obadiah was a kindhearted man, a convert from the House of Esau. Because of his family's idolatrous origins, Jezebel and her husband made him their advisor, never suspecting that his loyalty was with the Lord.

Obadiah was a wealthy man, with a large family and a job that gave him much power. Yet when he saw the oppression of God's people, he decided that he could not stand by. He took a hundred of God's prophets that Jezebel had designated to die and hid them, fifty men to a cave.

Obadiah was forced to feed those hundred prophets for many years, and the stress that such a task caused nearly killed him. He had to keep them hidden from Jezebel even as he stood in her presence every day. Gathering food for a hundred men was no simple or cheap task. He was forced to drain his wealth just to buy bread for the prophets.

Yet Obadiah did not regret it. Even though he toiled to keep the prophets hidden and alive, he felt proud.

Then, one day, Jezebel was at last slain and her evil reign came to an end. By that time Obadiah's health had withered, and he died just as the prophets could finally leave the cave that he had used to keep them safe for so long.

And although he died without a coin to his name, his wife and children could speak of him with pride. His name and deeds were written in the Holy Books, never to be forgotten."

Slowly, Uwe shut the golden notebook. For a moment, he sat in silence, mulling over the story.

"Obadiah, hm?" he finally whispered. Realizing that the young author of the story that was troubling him wasn't moving, Uwe glanced down and saw that the boy was fast asleep. It seemed as though hearing his own stories was practically a lullaby for the little writer.

Carefully, Uwe set the book aside and patted Uriel on the head, wondering distinctly if the child somehow knew everything that happened to him earlier, right down to his almost-offer to bring bread to Matthias' men. He doubted it, but then again Uriel was a strange child.

FISH IN A BARREL

It was a rather entertaining and smelly affair. His mother was always adamant about only cooking the freshest meat. She liked to personally pluck her geese and hesitated to buy any meat that she had not seen alive. She insisted that the fresher the meat, the better it was for a growing boy like Uriel. Besides, meat was a gamble. It could either be healthy or, if poorly prepared, deadly.

Because of this (and perhaps because the Zingdorf butcher had a bit of a reputation for not keeping his workplace comfortably clean, as poor Old Man Yitzhak could testify since the day he had discovered a beetle wiggling about in his beef), Mama preferred to buy her meat freshly killed and her fish alive.

Of course, while there were many benefits to buying the fish alive, there was the problem of where to keep the wriggling creatures until the time for their demise came. Mama's solution to this problem was rather unorthodox.

Getting water in Zingdorf was quite a hassle. Mama would keep a barrel in front of their house and run back and forth to the very-crowded well, pumping the water into buckets and running back home to dump the liquid into the barrel. She would repeat this process until the barrel was full and then she and her family would have their water for drinking, cooking, and washing clothes for the week.

They would also have a place to keep their fish. Since it would take too much time to fill a separate barrel for the fish, she stored the creatures in their drinking water. Since people often bathed and drank from the fish-filled lake without getting sick, she didn't see any reason why they couldn't put up with the aquatic animals sharing their water supply.

It actually wasn't too much of a problem. Aside from the fact that their water always tasted like fish (which Uriel became so used to that he often wrinkled his nose when he drank water without that distinctively fishy taste), and the fact that their clothes ended up smelling like fish (which even the other children became accustomed to eventually), Uriel's family didn't mind keeping their fish in their water barrel.

Uriel often enjoyed watching the fish swim around in the barrel. He almost felt a strange kinship with them. Perhaps it was because their scent and taste clung to his clothes and tongue, but whatever the reason, he cared for them. He still ate fish, but he didn't like to watch when Mama ended their lives, and he hesitated when she offered him the creature's cooked corpse on a plate.

The relationship that developed between him and the fish was odd. He would give them little bits of bread and even gave them names, yet he never considered them to be his pets. He wouldn't let Mama kill them if he thought of them as pets.

No, it was more pity than anything else. Pity and empathy caused him to act compassionately towards the fish even though he knew that they would die. He would try to be kind to them, to make their last few days on earth a bit more pleasant, all while knowing full well that they were going to perish.

Perhaps that was what he was to Uwe. A fish in a barrel.

8.

Uriel sat on the bed, his hand flying across the paper, elegantly drawing out his letters, pausing only to make sure he had selected the perfect word to describe what was going on in his world.

He was waiting for the birds to arrive with news on Elijah's Mantle, and in the meantime another story had been beating on his brain for the past day or so, begging to be put on paper. Since he had time, he decided to oblige. If he didn't, he would eventually go insane. That was what happened whenever a fresh idea or place or person was born from his imagination. It would practically become patricidal, assaulting its creator's brain, pleading and whining until he simply needed to write it down.

He didn't entirely mind, though. He loved to write. The only issue that arose was when more than one story was born at once. When that occurred, the tales would become fratricidal, fighting over who would get written first, and it would be nearly torturous for him to decide which one he liked more. After all, like any good parent, he loved all of his creations.

At last, Uriel finished. He read over his story once and corrected one or two spelling errors that he had made in his haste to fulfill his creation's wish.

Once it was finished, he beamed like a small star, his heart feeling warm and full. He always got that feeling when he completed a story. That feeling of relief, contentment, and pride always washed over him when he could look at something he had written and proudly proclaim he had finished another one.

I hope Uwe likes this one, he thought, setting the golden notebook aside and sighing. Uwe had been gone by the time he woke up, but yesterday the linguist had told Uriel that he would be going with the Major on some sort of important mission. What the 'important mission' was he hadn't said. Uriel could safely assume, however, that if the Major was in charge, it would be bad for his people.

I hope they're all right, he thought. *I hope Uwe is all right too. I hope the Major doesn't make him do anything bad. I hope he doesn't get hurt if he tries to do something good...*

There was a teeny tapping at the window, and Uriel smiled widely. He had been waiting for that sound all morning.

He darted to the window and threw it open. Five doves stood on the branch before him, hopping from foot to foot and twittering ecstatically.

"Angel-Finder! Angel-Finder!" they chirped. "We have found it! Elijah's Mantle is near! Please, come quickly!"

Eager to get the Mantle and finally fulfill his second quest, Uriel nodded and climbed onto the branch. It was harder to climb down while he only had one shoe on, but he did so without falling or getting injured. Once he had safely reached the bottom, he waved for the birds to lead the way.

By the time Uwe arrived on the scene, the operation was in full swing.

The driver pulled up to the tiny village and looked at the rearview mirror. He noted that his passenger was clasping his hands in his lap, his posture stiff as he nervously looked out the window.

"Herr Litten," the driver said with a half-smile. "We truly appreciate your help here. It will make things much easier for all of us. Not to worry, this is a small place. This operation is going to be very quick and very clean."

Uwe hardly paid him any mind as he gathered his courage and opened the car door. He stepped out without bothering to bid the driver farewell.

The village was indeed petite, half the size of little Zingdorf, and surrounded by no less than sixteen small trucks. Uwe hadn't even known that the *Ordnungspolizei* had trucks, but he wasn't surprised. After all, if their chief purpose was to deport and resettle people then it only made sense that they would be given some way to transport them.

Major Brandt was already at the village, having left early with his men to get the operation started before Uwe could arrive. One policeman cheerfully greeted Uwe and led him into the village so he could meet up with the Major.

The sight that greeted the linguist caused him to freeze. The *Ordnungspolizei* men were shoving, smacking, and shouting at the village's residents. They yanked them out of houses and buildings, hustling them to the middle of the village. Many windows were broken. Glass shards lay scattered across the cobblestone streets.

Although it wasn't nearly as hellish as Zingdorf, there was a heavy cloud of fear that hung in the air, one that was almost worse than the smoke and ash that had strangled Uriel's home.

The policemen led the Jews out of their homes at gunpoint. Little children clung to their mothers with one hand while keeping the other raised. Religious Jews who bore long beards and clutched scrolls and books were taunted and shoved, the holy texts knocked out of their hands.

"Step on it!" one policeman barked at a Jewish man, giving the Torah a vicious kick for emphasis. The poor Jew trembled, tears flooding his uncomprehending eyes.

"Moron," said another policeman to his comrade, pressing his boot down on the holy book even as he scolded his fellow soldier. "He doesn't speak German! He can't understand you. That's why we have Herr Litten."

For one horrible moment, Uwe thought they would see him and ask him to give the Jew their cruel command. Before they could, however, a shot echoed through the air, followed quickly by several screams.

Uwe gasped and spun around. One policeman had fired, and now the body of a young man lay in the street, blood pouring from his ear, his eyes still open. They were blue, just like Uwe's.

Uwe's eyes shifted to the killer, who heaved a deep sigh and looked up. Seeing his comrades shaking their heads with disapproval and Uwe gawking at him in revolted shock, the policeman offered them a rather embarrassed smile.

"Sorry," he muttered, sounding more like a schoolboy who had put down a stupid answer on a test than a man who had just killed a fellow human. "He resisted."

Uwe couldn't speak. All he could do was stare, aghast, as the crimson liquid crept between the cracks in the cobblestone road, forming a small river of blood.

Major Brandt, who had been standing near the village doctor's house and speaking to another soldier, heard the gunshot and an annoyed expression came to his face. He gave the soldier he was speaking with a subtle wave and the soldier gave an obedient nod before scurrying into the doctor's house, pursued by several policemen.

"Hermann…" Brandt said. His voice, which was more reminiscent of a mentor admonishing his charge than a commander scolding his subordinate for murdering a man, brought Uwe back from his state of appalled paralysis. The linguist turned his face to Brandt, willing himself to look away from the corpse and instead keep his eyes on the irate Major.

The killer's smile dissipated. His eyes briefly flickered down to his boots before he forced them to rise and meet Brandt's emerald irises. His chief shook his head disparagingly, looking down at the Jew's bleeding body like it was a stubborn stain on an expensive carpet.

"Sorry, sir, he resisted…" the policeman said.

"I realize that, and I understand," said Brandt, speaking in a firmly considerate tone that Uwe could easily picture him using while rebuking his five-year-old son for being naughty. "But I've told you a million times that if you're going to shoot a Jew, refrain from doing so while we're rounding them up, and *especially* refrain from doing so in the middle of the street where the Jews can all see and hear! You'll scare them into sedition. We already have enough chaos to wrangle in here."

"Right," said the killer. "Sorry, sir."

"All right. Somebody move that eyesore out of here," ordered Brandt.

"I've got it!" the murderer volunteered, grabbing the Jew's leg. Another policeman helped him to drag the Jew's body behind a building where the already-panicking Jews couldn't see it. They left a trail of blood in their wake. Uwe stared at the scarlet streak, his hands beginning to quiver as the gruesome image burned itself onto his corneas.

"And you two, knock that off!" Brandt barked impatiently at the two soldiers who were stomping on the Torah and ordering the religious Jew to do the same. "We already have enough disorder, don't add to it by acting like small children! Get him to the well with the others!"

"Right! Sorry, sir! Just having some fun!" said one policeman, kicking the Torah to the side and harshly grabbing the Jewish man. "Come on, swine! Get with the others!"

The Jewish man's mournful eyes met Uwe's for the briefest second before he was shoved towards the conglomerate of terrified Jews that the *Ordnungspolizei* had forced to gather around a small well in the center of town.

A powerful slap on his shoulder and a joyful cry of, "*There's* our little linguist!" caused his attention to revert to Brandt, who, it seemed, had just realized Uwe was present. Uwe looked up at the Major and tried his best to force a friendly smile, but his lips stubbornly refused to fake happiness in such an environment.

He started to open his mouth to greet the Major, but his words were prematurely killed when the muffled sound of several guns being fired caused him to cringe. He realized that the shooting was happening in a building close by and pricked up his ears, trying to hone in on the location. He raised an eyebrow when he realized that it was coming from the small house with the word 'Doctor' written on the door.

"Must have found some hideaways," said Brandt, following the linguist's gaze to the doctor's office. He steered Uwe away from the building and towards the gathered Jews. "We evacuated the infirm before you arrived."

Uwe, wanting dearly to believe him but still having his suspicions, was about to beg for the Major's absolute assurance. Before he could, however, Brandt turned him to face the myriad of Jews. The other *Ordnungspolizei* circled the huddled horde, their guns at the ready.

"Now, Herr Litten," said the Major. "If you would kindly instruct the men to separate from the women and children."

He gestured to the Jews, to the fathers that held their wives and children, and although Uwe's instincts begged him not to question any more orders he had to ask, "W-why?"

"We need to have some semblance of organization here, Herr Litten," said Brandt, his bright (if a little stressed) tone not wavering. "It will make sorting go faster."

Sorting? Uwe thought. He was about to question the Major's explanation, but a gleam came to Brandt's bright-green eyes.

It was a threatening gleam, reminiscent of one that might come to a predator's eyes when another creature dared to provoke it. It caused Uwe to shiver and mutter a hasty, "Yes, Major," before turning to the Jews and switching to Yiddish as he begged them to split apart.

Major Brandt gave a small nod of approval, the predatory glimmer evacuating his eyes as his orders were obeyed.

Separating the families was a horrible affair. Some quietly obeyed, taking only a moment to embrace and kiss one another before they tearfully parted. Others, however, clung to one another, weeping loudly and begging to stay with their loved ones. The *Ordnungspolizei* wasted no time marching over to those people, ripping them apart and shoving them to their respective sides, often having to wrestle the husbands and fathers to the ground as they fought to stay with their wives and children.

Uwe wanted to shut his eyes, but they refused to close. It was almost as if they wanted to witness all that was occurring, terrible as it was. He watched unwillingly as the *Ordnungspolizei* slammed the rebellious men onto the cobblestone street, pressing the barrels of their guns to their heads and kicking them with their steel-toed boots until the fathers were finally forced to crawl to their side.

As he watched the policemen act with such cruelty, Uwe couldn't help but remember that most of them were fathers themselves. He recalled how they had talked with such excitement and affection about their own wives and children. Surely, if somebody were to go into *their* neighborhoods and try to separate them from their beloved children, they would fight with all of their might.

Yet now the fathers and husbands were tearing families apart.

Because they're Jews? Uwe thought, watching the injured and sobbing men as they gazed longingly over at their families, empathy grasping his heart as he helplessly observed. *They're still fathers like them. Don't they see that?*

When the Jewish families had finally been separated, Brandt gave a small nod. "Excellent. That usually takes twice as long. Thank you very much, Herr Litten."

Uwe attempted to say, 'You're welcome', but his throat was so thoroughly clogged with a lump of dread that it came out as, "U' 'el 'ca."

"Now," said Brandt, "ask for skilled workers. Artisans, welders, blacksmiths, seamstresses, anybody who could be useful at a work camp."

That made Uwe pause and raise an eyebrow. "But I thought everybody in this area was to be resettled. I thought we weren't sending anybody to a concentration camp."

"*Work* camp, Herr Litten, *work* camp," corrected the Major with a small chortle. "They're not being sent there for correction, after all! They're being sent to *work*. Since there's no railroad here it's not feasible to send every Jew in the area to a work camp when only so many of them would actually be useful for production. We can use the trucks to send the skilled workers to a camp so they can help us. We have a country to defend, after all."

And a country to conquer, thought Uwe, though of course he didn't articulate such an opinion. Instead, he turned to the Jews and asked all the skilled workers to stand while the rest sat down. The Jews slowly obeyed, and over twenty Jewish men and women were left standing.

Brandt waved to one of the nearby trucks. It drove close to the crowd, and a few policemen ran to open the back. Uwe glanced from the standing Jews to the inside of the selected truck and realized that the ride to the work camp would be more than a little crowded.

"Order them to get onto the truck," the Major commanded, and Uwe reiterated the directive to the standing Jews.

The *Ordnungspolizei* started to push them onto the trucks. Several went quietly, with their hands raised and only a whimper of protest. Others struggled and needed to be harshly subdued before they were shoved into the trucks. Uwe winced with every smack and clenched his teeth every time their cries of pain reached his ears.

One woman, with a steely expression that immediately brought the iron-eyed Matthias to Uwe's mind, stood with her head high and her arms wrapped around a little girl. The girl, who Uwe could safely assume was the woman's daughter, gripped her mother's apron, tears leaking from her great brown eyes.

Uwe winced. The girl was even younger than Uriel, and her wide brown eyes reminded him of Trudi, his daughter, when she was only a small child. Trudi had always been daddy's little girl. She would run to hug him when he arrived home, cheerfully greeting him and announcing his presence to the entire house. She would cling to his jacket, giggling and waiting for him to lift her up and kiss her cheek. When she had a nightmare, she would run to him, tears escaping her chocolate-colored eyes as she gripped his shirt and begged for his protection and comfort.

A scream from the brown-eyed Jewish girl snapped him back to his senses. Two *Ordnungspolizei* men were trying to rip the mother and daughter apart. The little girl wailed and buried her face in her mother's chest. The mother looked from German to German, helplessly pleading with them in her native tongue.

Uwe jumped in front of Major Brandt.

"She refuses to leave without her child," he said. "Major, *please…*"

Brandt, apparently deciding that this trouble wasn't worth his time, exhaled in exasperation and waved for the policemen to stop. "Let the child go with her," he instructed. "It doesn't matter."

The policeman released the child, and once Uwe assured the woman that she and her daughter could go together she gave a small nod and gripped the little girl's hand, leading her to the truck and helping her on. Uwe caught a brief glimpse of the child's chestnut eyes resting on him before the doors were shut. The truck sped away with such haste that Uwe had to wonder if the work camp was short on labor.

Once the future laborers had been taken away, the rest of the Jews became the focus. Putting them on the trucks, though, was a slow process even though they had plenty of trucks. Uwe had to wonder why they only seemed to be loading and transporting a dozen or so Jews at a time. They gathered the women and children first, slowly herding them onto the trucks while ordering Uwe to assure them that they would be reunited with their family members soon.

Unable to restrain his curiosity, with the Jews still steadily being pushed onto the trucks and driven away in the backdrop, Uwe turned to Major Brandt.

"What's going to happen to them?" he asked, gesturing to the horribly confused and horribly frightened people. Brandt gave a casual shrug.

"As I've said previously, Herr Litten," he said, once more sounding like an eternally patient teacher. "They'll be resettled. Once they're no longer needed, the ones who were taken to the work camp will be resettled as well. They'll be reunited, Herr Litten, don't you worry."

"Where are they being resettled then?" asked Uwe. "Here? In Poland? I thought this land was supposed to be *Judenfrei*."

"Only until further notice. Until we can figure out a better way." Brandt's green eyes twinkled almost playfully as he said, "I've heard it said that the higher echelons plan on sending the Jews to Madagascar! Now *that* would be an interesting solution to this problem. A beautiful island country all to themselves…a shame *I* wasn't born Jewish in that case!"

The Major laughed at his own joke and Uwe tried to command his vocal cords to at least fake a chuckle, but they stubbornly refused to humor the Major.

Madagascar or no, the Jews had been beaten, abused, robbed, torn from their homes and families. Even if they were reunited later, that wouldn't undo all the trauma they had suffered. They would likely have nightmares about it for the rest of their lives.

And I might too, he thought.

A loud crash nearly made Uwe jump out of his shoes. Major Brandt gave a derisively amused snort. Uwe turned towards the commotion and saw that while half of the policemen were moving the remaining Jews to the trucks, the other half were running in and out of the vacant houses, haphazardly tossing the buildings' contents into the streets, forming a huge pile of miscellaneous goods.

"You boys are getting greedy again!" Major Brandt bellowed to the men as they shoved a few more crates and trunks onto the loot pile. "Already behaving like a bunch of bandits before the job's even complete."

He gestured to the not-yet-evacuated Jews, who dolefully looked from their property to the waiting trucks. The covetous Germans grinned impishly.

"Sorry, Uncle Günter, but if you're going to call us boys, then we're going to act like boys!" said one of the policemen. Brandt rolled his eyes and waved for them to pillage to their heart's content.

"C'mon, let's go!" one driver shouted down to a fellow policeman as soon as his truck was filled with Jews. The young policeman stood still, nervously gripping his green cap, and Uwe recognized him as the youngest of the bunch, the one with a fiancée in Hamburg.

The young man didn't listen to his comrade. Instead, he scurried over to Major Brandt and whispered something into the Major's ear. Brandt nodded and gave the young officer a small pat on the shoulder.

"Very well," he said, his voice curt yet kind. "Go ahead and look in the loot pile instead."

The young man sighed with relief and darted to the mountain of goods while the truck he was supposed to be on drove away, its driver looking rather irritated.

"Looks like I'm getting a bonus for all my hard work!" chuckled one of the Germans, shaking a small jewelry box like a Christmas present before eagerly opening it and beaming at the shimmering necklaces and rings inside.

"Who would have known that Jewesses had such finery!" he laughed.

"They stole it from the *goyim*, obviously," said another policeman, shaking his head condescendingly, as though his comrade was an idiot for not knowing such an apparent fact.

One man opened an ancient trunk and his eyes brightened.

"Hey, guys, look at this!" he said with a good-humored laugh, holding up his find. Uwe had to raise an eyebrow when he saw what it was.

An old cloak. Made of faded threads that might have been red long ago, before age had turned it burgundy. It looked like the sort of thing that an actor in a Christmas Nativity play would wear. Uwe wondered if perhaps it was a costume piece, or maybe part of some Jewish ceremony that he wasn't aware of.

Either way, he could see that it was in fairly good shape for something that was clearly older than he was. There were no holes or patches, no stains, and no moths had nibbled on the threads. Although it wasn't very attractive, it was an interesting piece.

The policeman seemed to share Uwe's opinion. He put it on over his uniform, straining the stitches slightly but not causing any to snap. Some of his fellow officers chuckled at his antics while the others rolled their eyes as he gestured dramatically.

"Stand aside, peasants!" he proclaimed. "I am the great and mighty prophet of the Lord! Bow before my boundless wisdom and divine insight!"

One of his comrades responded by tossing a sock at the false prophet's head. The cloaked German shot him a glare.

"Hey, great and mighty prophet," said the sock-thrower. "Take that thing off. It's probably crawling with lice."

The cloak-clad policeman opened his mouth to respond, but before he could, something bright white came at him. The policeman let out a rather unbecoming scream and fell to the ground as a small bird flew just inches above his ear. Uwe's eyes followed the bird as it fluttered in a circle and then settled on the branches of a tree that stood on the side of the street. It was quickly joined by four more of its kind.

The policeman panted as though he had nearly been shot. One of his comrades, laughing so hard that it was a wonder he didn't collapse, ran to help the cloak-clad German to his feet.

"Oh, what is it with you and birds?" he asked. His ruffled comrade dusted the cloak off and heaved a deep breath to calm himself.

"I have ornithophobia!" he whined, glancing at the five birds as though they were enemy soldiers.

"You're pathetic," said the other policeman, rolling his eyes skyward. "Honestly, do the Poles only require a canary in a cage to gain your surrender?"

"Hey, when I was a kid a whole flock of the things nearly pecked my eyes out! Damn demons with wings!"

"Oh, watch out!" cried the other policeman sarcastically. "They might *sing* at you! How utterly terrifying!"

"If you're so scared of the birds, then maybe you should take that cloak off," another policeman suggested. "It might have belonged to the village birdwatcher or something, or maybe they're just attracted to the bugs that are probably stuck to it!"

The cloaked policeman shuddered at the thought of the birds diving at him again and hastily tossed the garment back onto the pile. Uwe, meanwhile, had hardly been paying attention to the policemen's exchange. He was gazing up at the birds.

Doves. He normally couldn't tell a raven from a hawk, but he could easily recognize those five birds as doves. The birds of peace.

His eyes darted from the doves to the dozen or so Jews that were waiting to be herded onto the trucks and sent to heaven-knows-where. He noted that only the men were left. The women and children had all been taken away.

The remaining Jews looked down at the abused holy books that lay in the street. Uwe saw their fingers twitching. They obviously wanted nothing more than to scoop up the damaged Torahs and hold them close to their hearts.

He almost wanted to pick up the holy books for them, but he resisted the urge. Instead, he forced his eyes back to the doves and pondered their presence.

Along with being the birds of peace, he had heard it said that the dove was the symbol of the Jewish People, God's Chosen People. The Jews were often compared to birds. Hunted, caged, killed. But with God's help, they always escaped the fowler's trap. They always managed to flutter out of danger and live another day.

He narrowed his eyes at the doves. Were they here, perhaps, to give the Jews hope?

Or maybe to mourn for their human counterparts.

Or maybe it was just a coincidence.

Still, he couldn't help but notice that their beady black eyes seemed to linger on him. Their gazes almost seemed accusatory. *You're helping them to do this. You're their linguist. You're responsible.*

He shook his head at such a ridiculous notion. Animals couldn't be critical, and they couldn't be aware of what was going on.

Yet his throat still constricted and became arid as a desert.

"I'm thirsty," he declared so quietly that he was surprised when a soldier heard his comment and gave him a small smile.

"No problem, Herr Litten," said the policeman. He turned to one of the remaining Jews and barked, "You there! Jew! Fetch some water!"

The policeman pointed to the well and the Jew, who had been gazing longingly at the trodden-down Torah scroll, looked up and gave a timid nod. Uwe, however, stopped him before he could step out of line.

"No! No!" he insisted. "I'll get it myself! I'll get it myself!"

"Are you sure about that, Herr Litten?" asked the soldier, glancing at Uwe's skinny arms and probably thinking Uwe wouldn't be able to lift an empty bucket, much less one filled with water.

"Yes, I'm sure," said Uwe, running to the well before the soldier could insist that he let the Jew do it for him.

Uwe grabbed the end of the rope and tried to hold in a frustrated grunt as he struggled to lift the hefty bucket from the bottom of the well. He didn't want to show how hard it really was, so he clenched his teeth together until they nearly cracked and pulled with all his might. After a subdued struggle, he hauled up the bucket.

Sighing with relief, he set the bucket down on the side of the well and took a long, refreshing drink.

Uriel emerged from the thicket and yelped in surprise as he was nearly run over. A truck barreled down the dirt road, and apparently the driver was an evil one since he didn't see the boy.

Uriel jumped back, dodging death by mere inches as the truck flew by. The boy panted and made sure that he still had all his parts before he jumped back into the center of the road and turned to look at the truck's rear. Although it disappeared quickly, Uriel caught a glimpse of an eagle insignia, one that he recognized from other vehicles he had seen in the past. The truck was German.

Since the doves had flown ahead, and since they had said that the village where the Mantle was located wasn't far, he surmised that the truck was leaving that village. He briefly wondered where it was going, but decided that he had more important things to see to than the destination of the truck that had nearly flattened him.

The boy raced in the direction that the truck had come from and soon came to a small village. He heard a chirp and a squeal that rather reminded him of how the little girls in Zingdorf had sounded when scared. He was too far away to see who had screamed and why, but he could recognize the chirp. It was one of the doves.

This is the village, then, he thought, glancing at the German trucks and biting the inside of his cheeks.

Bad luck. Uwe and the Major will be here. I have to be careful or Uwe will spot me. I've already given him enough trouble.

He moved carefully, ducking behind buildings and trucks to avoid being seen. The German soldiers weren't a problem, but he had to keep an eye out for Uwe and any Jews that were still in the village.

At last, he crouched behind a truck and peeked past the hood. He saw Uwe standing by a well, struggling to yank the bucket out. The boy gave a slight smile and a sigh of relief. Uwe was distracted.

The boy's eyes moved to an immense pile of assorted goods, clothes, and boxes. He looked up and saw that the birds were perched on a tree right next to the material mountain. The doves bobbed their heads to indicate the pile.

Uriel nodded and hurried over to the heap, walking right in front of the smirking Major, who watched Uwe's attempts to pull out the water bucket with disdainful amusement. Uriel shot him a glare and briefly considered slapping him in the face, but thought better of it.

He settled for stepping on the Major's toe as he ran by. The boy looked over his shoulder and smirked when he saw the Major nearly jump out of his boots, surprise shooting out of his emerald green eyes as he felt the child's sixty-seven pounds land brutally on his foot. Were the Major's boots not lined with metal Uriel might have given him a broken toe or two. Instead, all he did was give the Major a bit of pain and a mighty scare.

While the Major looked from side to side, rubbing his temples to clear his mind of any more painful hallucinations, Uriel reached the mass of loot. He hid behind it, peeking out to make sure that Uwe and the remaining Jews hadn't spotted him.

When nobody even glanced in his direction, he smiled and let his golden eyes scan the mound, searching for the Mantle. He could safely assume that, like the Book of Blood, there would be something about the Mantle that would set it apart from any other garment. A cloak that had belonged to a man as great as Elijah would surely possess a holy aura of some sort.

Finally, he saw it. A cloak. Royal red, it glittered as though made of rubies. His eyes widened and he grinned. A mantle fit for a prophet. He had to wonder why the greedy Germans hadn't taken it for themselves.

He slowly reached out, stretching his fingers and trying to grab the cloak without standing up. Uwe had finished his drink. Even though the linguist's head was down and he appeared to be staring at the bucket, deep in thought, Uriel still didn't want to risk being spotted.

A hoot of delight nearly caused him to retract his hand, but he scoffed and continued to reach when he realized that it was one of the Germans. He had found the village jeweler's personal stock. Uriel almost wanted to snatch the gold right out of the wicked German's grasp. It would serve the gleeful robber right. The boy resisted the impish urge, however, and grasped the red cloak.

A feeling of pure holiness enveloped the child's hand and traveled through his entire body once he touched Elijah's Mantle. It felt nothing like the Book of Blood. Elijah's Mantle felt warm and seemed to glow with a generous and gentle aura that made Uriel want to bury his face into the holy garment.

He decided that doing so wouldn't be respectful, however, and instead held it to his heart, allowing the sacred energy to seep into his body. He smiled widely and prepared to leave.

A cry made him pause. His smile crumbled as the scream was promptly followed by a bout of depraved laughter.

Uriel peeked above the pile and his grip on the sacrosanct garment tightened when he saw what was happening.

Two cackling Germans shoved an old Jewish man against a wall. At their feet was a scroll. Looking closely, Uriel realized that it was a Torah scroll. His immediate desire was to run out and grab the holy scroll, get it away from the sinners before they could harm it anymore.

But his golden eyes flickered to Uwe, and he realized that he too was observing the scene. Uriel couldn't move.

Grinding his teeth together, he hugged Elijah's Mantle and fought for control of his emotions. The Jewish man had a beard that went down to his belly button and kind, sorrow-seeped eyes. He looked so much like Papa that Uriel wanted to run into his arms.

Instead he stood still, watching as one of the Germans gave the Jew such a harsh slap across the face that it left a lavender mark on the man's cheek.

"Hey, Jew-dog!" the German barked, pointing to the scroll at his feet. "You want this scrap of shit so bad?"

Uriel wanted more than anything to have a sword or a knife in his hand that he could throw at the sacrilegious man. He had never had such murderous thoughts about anybody, but seeing the Holy Torah derided in such a manner by his people's murderers made him wish that he were the Angel of Death for just a moment.

Uriel's anger only increased when the German asked his friend for a matchbox. While the old Jew watched with woe, the German lit a match and threw it upon the Torah. The sacred paper smoldered.

"Stomp on it now, Jew!" ordered the German with a laugh, clapping as the flames spread across the scroll, as if this was some sort of game and he was winning.

The Jew, not wishing to step on the Torah, instead dropped to his knees and patted the flames out with his hands. Uriel saw pain in his eyes, but he wasn't sure if that was because of the fire touching his flesh or the fire touching the Torah.

The Jew killed the fire before it could completely consume the scroll, but the sacrosanct text was horribly singed. Uriel felt tears prick his eyes. The Torah should have been safely stored in the synagogue, protected from all the elements, waiting to be undressed and adored by the entire village come the Sabbath.

Instead, it lay in the street, half destroyed and yet still loved by the few Jews who could see it in its mournful state.

As soon as the fire was gone, the two Germans grabbed the Jewish man and pinned him against a wall. The one with the matchbox pouted like a small child whose fun had been spoiled.

"I said *step on it,* you stupid Jew!" hissed the German. A cruel grin came to his face once more as he lit another match.

"It's all right. I still have plenty of matches."

But instead of tossing it onto the Torah, he touched the match to the old man's beard.

The man screamed and thrashed about, but the Germans, laughing like monsters, held his arms to the wall and didn't let him move. Some of the other policemen joined in laughing, some averted their eyes, and some were too busy stealing or shoving the other Jews onto the last truck to spare a glance at the burning Jew and his tormentors.

The poor man's beard was engulfed in hellish orange as the flames spread across his face. Uriel started to stand, prepared to throw caution to the wind and rescue the man, even despite the chaos and confusion that would surely follow. But try as he might to rise, he found himself unable to move. It was as though an invisible hand had grabbed hold of him and was keeping him down.

Wait, it seemed to say. *Not yet. Watch.*

He waited, he watched.

Then there was a mighty splash. The Jew and the two Germans were drenched, the flames were put out, and Uwe was standing there, holding the now-empty water bucket.

For a moment there was complete silence. The Germans stood, dripping wet, their mouths open. The Jew trembled as he and everybody else stared at Uwe.

Then the Germans broke the silence as they released the Jew, rubbed their eyes, and whined.

"Ugh! *Herr Litten!*"

"I'm *soaked!*"

The Jew touched his singed beard, his eyes meeting Uwe's for a single moment. Uriel saw the man move his lips, but he couldn't tell what he was saying.

While Major Brandt ordered the drenched policemen to stop mocking the Jew and get him on the truck, Uwe dropped the bucket and everybody else went back to their business. Uriel couldn't help but smile as he crouched down and kept his eyes on his German guardian. Of course. He should have expected that much. A man righteous enough to see past the hamsa wouldn't stand by and do nothing.

He held Elijah's Mantle close and slowly slipped away from the Germans and the village. He had a Shamir to catch.

God bless you.

If Uwe hadn't been looking right at the Jew, he wouldn't have seen his mouth move to form those three words.

God bless you. For what? For putting out the fire?

It made little difference when the man was still shoved onto the truck by the sopping, livid Germans and driven away from his home. It made little difference when the village was rendered *Judenfrei*, free of Jews. It made little difference when the Torah was still on the ground, burned and beaten.

One little merciful splash of water fixed nothing. It didn't banish the *Ordnungspolizei*. It didn't bring the murdered man whose body was still concealed behind one of the ransacked buildings back to life. It didn't stop the policemen from resettling the whole village, including the pious man who had blessed the linguist. It didn't keep Uriel safe. It didn't stop Matthias and his people from starving in that little cave.

I don't deserve any blessing, he thought, watching as the last truck disappeared into the distance. *I'm helping the Order Police and sitting on my hands while people are starving.*

It felt good to have helped that man even a little, but at the same time it created a hole in his heart, a hole he knew would not be filled by only focusing on Uriel's welfare.

Uwe's thoughts were interrupted by the sound of somebody clearing his throat. He turned and barely resisted the urge to rudely step away from Major Brandt.

"Your good heart got the better of you again, Herr Litten," the Major casually remarked, not sounding at all annoyed with Uwe's action. He took a quick sip from his flask before adding, "You really need to learn how to control it. It's alright, though. I understand. Personally, I don't like it when the boys do that, but I understand the need for it."

Disgust and anger stirred in Uwe's stomach, but he kept them from invading his voice as he said, "Need for it?"

"Oh, you don't realize why they do things like that?" asked Brandt, a very slight smile playing at the corners of his lips, as if he was talking to a child who didn't yet understand some brand of basic life lesson.

"N-no, sir, why?" asked Uwe, sensing that he wasn't going to like the answer.

"Because they hate that the Jews are humans," said Brandt. Uwe raised an eyebrow.

"I…" he intoned. "I thought they weren't humans, sir."

The Major laughed. "Oh, they're humans all right! That's why we call them *untermenschen*. An inferior race must be human or else it wouldn't be a race at all!"

Brandt's smile became thinner and his pupils rose towards the sky as he pondered how to properly explain this to the linguist.

"It's like…" he said after a moment of pause and contemplation. "Like…a dog."

The Major's smile brightened, as if to compliment his own brilliance. Uwe only stared at him with a creased brow and a steadily growing suspicion that the man he was working for had been hit on the head one too many times.

"A…dog, sir?" he said, struggling to keep every iota of respect from evacuating his voice. The Major nodded.

"Yes," Brandt confirmed. "Dogs are the same species, they just have different breeds, different *races* if you will. But some dogs are stronger and better behaved than other dogs. In nature the better, stronger dog would survive while the weaker, rogue dogs would die off, but in our dog-loving society we don't allow that."

"But imagine for a moment that you have a strong, intelligent, well-behaved German shepherd. You wouldn't let that German shepherd breed with a weak, mottled, ill-tempered mutt, would you? Of course not! You wouldn't want to pollute the good dog's bloodline. In fact, you'd be more likely to put down that ill-tempered mutt, or at the very least sterilize it so it can't make any more of itself! The problem is that for the last hundred years or so we've allowed all the ill-tempered, weak, disease-ridden mutts to run rampant and breed with our best purebreds and have as many pups as they want and spread out everywhere."

"The result," he said, waving his hand to subtly indicate the vacant village, "is that now we have these mutts everywhere, biting people and spreading rabies. Naturally, we have to do something about such a problem or it puts us and all the other good dogs at risk. Jews are humans, but they're not the kind of humans you want living beside you."

His eyes traveled down to the trampled Torah, gazing at it with icy indifference. "That's why the boys do things like that. I don't like it myself. Too childish, and more often than not it causes trouble, causes us to take more time on these operations than we need to. But I understand. They need to mock them, to put them down like that, so that they don't have to look at them too closely and recognize that the Jews might be a different breed, but they're still the same species as us. If they realize that, if they focus on that, their jobs will become impossible. It's a problem I have with the newer recruits, something they have to get over with time and a bit of bullying."

His eyes returned to Uwe and a smile returned to his face. "Which is why I don't wag my finger at them. I just tell them when they're taking it too far. I personally wouldn't have stopped them right then, but I realize that you are unaccustomed to how we conduct our operations here, Herr Litten. You did a marvelous job today, and you kept a level head the whole time. I'm very pleased. You'll do well, Herr Litten."

Uwe hardly heard him. His own ruminations were clogging his ears. The hole in his heart widened as he thought more and more of what he was doing and what he wasn't doing.

He was helping a man who saw humans as dogs to be bred, neutered, and put down at will.

Meanwhile, Matthias and his people were dying, and he was doing nothing.

That, Uwe thought, biting his tongue as Brandt continued to praise him and led him back towards the car, *is going to have to change.*

Before he could make it to the black vehicle, however, his foot collided with a small humanoid figure that had escaped the pilfering pile.

A doll, well-worn and well loved, lay right in the middle of the street, right at Uwe's feet. With unnatural speed, Uwe bent down and scooped the toy up, his fingers circling possessively around her waist, as though he was afraid that one policeman would see it and try to steal it from him.

He bit his bottom lip as he scrutinized her. Her dress was made of faded blue fabric that was covered in dust and stained with dirt. Her eyes were mismatched buttons that were clearly not the ones that had originally adorned the toy, but served as replacements for the eyes that had surely fallen off during the hours of play that the little girl and her doll had enjoyed. The doll's black hair was lovingly combed and tied into two clumsy pigtails. Her threaded mouth smiled almost somberly up at Uwe, as if she was happy to meet him but at the same time sad that her owner was gone.

Brandt looked down at the doll and snorted. "It's probably not something your son will appreciate, but maybe one of your daughters will find it amusing. Even teenage girls might value a present. Keep it if you like, Herr Litten. You deserve something."

Uwe responded with a slight bob of the head that served as an accepting nod. His grip on the doll tightened, and he kept his eyes on her even as he climbed into the backseat of Brandt's car.

She was just too reminiscent of the dolls he had gotten for Marlene when she was little. He had always been sure to have enough money saved so he could run down to the doll shop come Christmas and find one that would surely make her squeal with delight. The look of pure joy that would come to her eyes as she squeezed the toy to her chest and proclaimed that she had never seen such a beautiful doll was always worth every penny. By the time Marlene was old enough to lose interest in dolls, she had an entire shelf lined with them. Even though she didn't play with them anymore, she couldn't bring herself to give even one away. They were all her best friends.

This little doll had been some little girl's favorite (and perhaps only) doll. He wondered if her father had bought it for Hanukkah. He wondered if she had shrieked with jubilation, hugged it like a precious treasure, kissed her father's cheek and thanked him so many times that her grateful proclamations echoed through his head whenever he saw a doll.

But however the little girl had received the doll, she was now without it. There would be no shelf of nostalgic honor on the girl's future wall where she could place her precious toy. Wherever she was being resettled, she would be missing her best friend.

Uriel thanked Hashem for making the Shamir such a heavy sleeper.

He couldn't quite understand why the creature was using its newfound freedom to sleep in a cave. Had *he* been trapped in a teeny cup for a century and only recently freed he would be bounding about, smelling the grass, climbing trees, and stretching his legs as much as possible before somebody could catch him again. The Shamir had plenty of legs to stretch, so Uriel couldn't comprehend why the beast didn't even bother to leave the cave.

He couldn't complain too much about the Shamir's lackadaisical nature, however. He crept back into the cave without alerting the Jews to his presence, found the snoozing Shamir, and threw Elijah's Mantle over it before it could even blink its six eyes. He scooped up the Shamir, using the Mantle as a sack. The Shamir hissed and screeched and chewed as much as it could, but it couldn't make a hole in the holy garment. Eventually, it gave up and went limp. Uriel smiled triumphantly and slung the captured Shamir over his shoulder before hastily escaping the cave and making his way to Samael's clearing just as the light of the stars struck the shadows.

Samael was even surlier than usual when he took the Shamir from Uriel. He refused to touch Elijah's Mantle, instead ordering the boy to release the Shamir. The boy obeyed and the ugly creature crawled over to the Angel of Death like a dog that had been summoned by its master. Judging by its hissing, however, Uriel could tell that the Shamir would have preferred to stay in the cave. He felt a pang of pity for the beast, but Michael was more important than the comfort of the stone-cutting creature.

"You're fortunate," said Samael, gathering the Shamir into his arms. "Hashem Himself decreed that your conversations with the birds don't qualify as cheating."

His eyes narrowed into spiteful slits as he snarled, "Even without Michael in the Host to vouch for you, He still favors your people."

Uriel draped Elijah's Mantle over his shoulder, holding his head high and giving the Angel of Death a curt little nod. *Next challenge.*

With the edge of his mouth twitching maliciously, Samael said, "Very well then, Angel-Finder. Bring me the Golden Tree."

Knowing full well that the Angel of Death would not give him any clues and recognizing that letting his confusion show would only amuse Samael, Uriel stayed stony-faced and gave another small nod. The Angel of Death gave him a glare and a rather annoyed grunt before slipping back into the shadows, taking the Shamir with him.

Uriel allowed his placid facade to fall away once the Angel of Death was gone. A curious crease formed on his brow. He glanced at the trees surrounding him, half hoping that one of them would spontaneously reveal itself to be the golden one that Samael desired. But while his golden eyes scanned them, they all remained dull brown.

He looked at the branches, but didn't see any flecks of white or hear any cheerful twittering. The birds weren't there. He clicked his tongue and sighed.

Oh, well, he thought. He could do nothing more tonight. Hopefully, the doves would arrive tomorrow and tell him what he needed to know about the Golden Tree.

Once he climbed back into Uwe's room, Uriel ran to unlock the door. It was late, and Uriel felt guilt sting his heart as he realized that Uwe had probably been waiting for him. Although he wasn't looking forward to another probably well-deserved scolding, the child opened the door wide.

He was surprised to see that Uwe wasn't standing in the hallway, waiting for the boy to return so he could be properly rebuked. The boy's keen ears picked up the sound of movement downstairs and he curiously stepped out of the room. He stood at the top of the stairs and realized that the sound was coming from the kitchen.

Curiosity overcame his urge to obey Uwe's wandering-the-house prohibition. He darted down the stairs and into the kitchen.

He was only moderately surprised to see that it was Uwe who had been making all the noise. The kitchen was in an odd state of organized disarray. Jars and cans that had been stored neatly in the cupboards now stood on the countertops. The cupboards' contents had been placed into different piles, categorized somehow, but not in a manner that Uriel could identify.

Uwe, who had been putting a can back into a cupboard, looked up when Uriel entered. A slight flinch was the only sign that he gave of being startled by the boy's arrival. His blue eyes flickered about for a moment, making sure that they alone had spotted the boy, before they swiftly shifted back to Uriel's golden irises. The linguist silently commanded the boy to shut the door behind him.

Uriel obeyed and then stepped forward, his mouth caught between a nervous smile and a guilty frown as he approached the German. Uwe looked at the child for a moment, squinting slightly, as though he had the wrong glasses on and couldn't see the boy clearly.

Then he heaved a great sigh. "I'm never going to get you to stop running into the woods, am I?"

Deciding that he had fibbed far too often, Uriel gave an honest nod.

Putting his hands up as if to surrender, Uwe shook his head. "Fine then. You seem to have a knack for slipping past the guards. They're not doing their job well if both you and I can run into the woods unnoticed."

Uriel nodded in agreement, his lips quirking upwards.

"Just be sure to stay safe, and be sure to stay by the house," Uwe ordered. "Make sure you're not followed."

Uriel cocked his head to the side, wondering why Uwe was having such a sudden change of heart. Uwe looked at the boy and a bitter smile came to his stern features.

"Given the fact that I'm about to put us both in danger for something brave and foolhardy, I can hardly fault you for doing the same thing," he said, reading the question in the tiny tilt of the child's head. "I don't know what you keep looking for out there, but I won't try to stop you. I was doing a very poor job at that anyway. You're free to do as you like, Uriel. Just stay safe."

The last three words of Uwe's declaration were spoken in a soft and concerned tone that made Uriel's heart wrench and his eyes twinkle with happiness. He half wanted to rush forward and hug the German, but he decided against that. There were too many cans and jars that could be loudly and destructively knocked to the ground if he did so.

Uwe's eyes left the boy's beaming face and inspected the rest of his body to make sure he wasn't injured. He barely subdued an amused snort when he saw a dull burgundy cloak hanging around the boy's shoulders like a cape.

"What is that you're wearing?" he asked, pointing to the cloak. Uriel's eyes flickered to Elijah's Mantle, and he blushed when he realized that he had forgotten to take it off once he got into Uwe's room. The ruby-red garment sparkled like a galaxy of scarlet stars. The boy was rather surprised that Uwe wasn't stunned to see him wearing something so brilliant.

Uwe examined the old cloak. It looked almost damningly familiar. Although the terrible things he had seen today dominated his memories, he could still faintly recall the cloak that the policeman had put on while prancing about and pretending to be a prophet. It had looked identical to the one that Uriel was wearing.

That had to be a coincidence, however. There was no way that the boy could have gotten close to the village without being spotted by one of the soldiers. Although the boy was good at avoiding detection, he couldn't be *that* good. Perhaps he had found the cloak during his excursion into the woods. Perhaps it was indeed part of some Jewish ceremony or festival. If that were the case, it would only make sense that there would be more than one.

Uwe's eyes glistened as the burgundy garment gave him an idea.

"Uriel, so long as you're down here, come and help me," said Uwe. "Lay that cloak on the counter. We can use it to bring the food up to my room."

Uriel's forehead furrowed with inquisition and hesitation. *He* wasn't so hungry that he needed a cloak to carry his dinner to Uwe's room. True, Uwe's day had been arduous, but was he truly *that* ravenous? Besides, Uriel didn't want to disrespect the Prophet-Angel's cloak by using it as a grocery bag. He had used it to capture the Shamir only out of necessity.

Seeing the child's uncertainty, Uwe begged, "Please, Uriel. This is very important. There are people hiding in the woods, your people. They're stuck hiding in a little cave. Nobody's keeping them safe or bringing them food. They're starving. I'm going to bring them something to eat so they get better, but I need something to carry the food with."

Uriel's eyes brightened. He had no doubt that Uwe was talking about the Jews from the same cave that the Shamir had been hiding in. Uwe had mentioned finding fugitive Jews while he had been scolding Uriel for running off, but he hadn't gone into detail about their situation.

Of course, Uriel was only too willing to help his people. He doubted that Elijah would mind his mantle being used for such a task. After all, giving food to the hungry was a *mitzvah*.

He carefully spread Elijah's Mantle out on the counter and assisted Uwe in piling the food he had selected onto it.

"Good boy, Uriel," said Uwe. "Now listen, I know you want to see your people, but I don't want them to know about you. I'm afraid that if they know I'm hiding you, they'll insist I leave you with them. You won't be as safe with them. I'm very sorry..."

Uriel didn't even give the slightest indication that Uwe's decree upset him. He just smiled happily and gathered a few more cans into his arms. Uwe's smile widened ever so slightly. That was easier than he thought it would be. He had thought the boy would need to be tied down to keep him from scuttling into the forest and visiting his kin. At least Uriel was, for once, being compliant.

"Good boy," said Uwe. "Matthias cares about his people, and I'm sure…"

There was a horrible clanging, one that nearly made Uwe hit the ceiling as his body gave a frightened jolt.

Uriel had dropped all the cans he had been holding. His eyes had become round as the full moon, his body rigid as a statue.

Uwe hissed several German words that he would normally hesitate to use in front of a child, but Uriel didn't seem to hear him. He simply stood, staring at nothing, his arms hanging limply at his sides.

"Uriel!" growled Uwe, "Be careful! Brandt might not be here, but the guards are still at the front door! You have to keep quiet."

It seemed like an odd command to give a mute boy. *Keep quiet.* Especially since Uriel had become totally silent. Even his heartbeat and lungs seemed to have stilled.

"Uriel?" muttered Uwe when the boy's shell-shocked state began to worry him. He grabbed the child's shoulders and gave him a rough shake.

"Uriel!"

The boy seemed to snap out of his trance. He finally blinked and his eyes fell upon Uwe.

"Uriel, what's wrong?" asked the German. The child quivered as if a frosty current had seeped into his bones, but he shook his head and squirmed out of Uwe's grasp. He bent down to pick up a few stray cans that had stopped rolling across the kitchen floor and put them on the cloak. Uwe watched him, his mouth tightening with concern. He almost asked the child what was wrong once more, but before he could the boy gathered up the food-filled cloak and tried to lift it.

"I've got it, I've got it!" Uwe insisted, taking the heavy makeshift sack from the little boy before he could hurt himself. The child allowed the cloak to slip from his slack fingers. Uwe opened his mouth, prepared to question the boy about his sudden melancholy, but the child opened the kitchen door and gestured for them to get going.

Reluctantly, Uwe obeyed and hastily made his way up the stairs. The boy followed, his eyes downcast.

And when Uwe stole a backwards glance, he could swear that he saw tears cascading down the child's cheeks.

BROTHER

He had never wanted one. He didn't think having one would be a curse, but he had never particularly desired one.

So when he was told that he was going to get an older brother, he at first didn't know what to think.

He should have seen it coming. His sister, sweet Adina, was sixteen. Marrying age. His parents had taken her to the matchmaker, who had gushed that she knew the absolutely positively perfect man for their little girl to wed.

Uriel had eavesdropped on the conversation, shaking his head ever so slightly the whole time. Were he a man of marrying age, he would never agree to wed somebody like Adina.

Not because he didn't love her. He loved her. She was his sister, after all. Yet she and he had never been very close. While he adored his mother and father, his relationship with his sister had always been somewhat cold.

That was mostly because Adina frustrated him to no end. She had been blessed with a voice, and yet she almost never used it. Whenever a conversation or a squabble arose her eyes would glisten in a way that Uriel recognized. It was a hint of a hidden urge. An urge to join the conversation, to speak her mind.

But she never did. She only ever said two words at once.

"Yes, sir."

"No, sir."

"Yes, ma'am."

"No, ma'am."

And that was it. Nothing more. She never asked any questions, made any arguments, or even conversed just for the sake of conversing. Even when she prayed, her lips would move, but he never heard her actually speak.

Everybody else saw a sweet, demure girl who would make a wonderful wife. Uriel saw a girl who was wasting her precious vocal cords by staying silent when she didn't have to. In fact, it might have been better if she were a mute and not Uriel. She would probably be happier if she didn't have to speak at all, and everybody would probably think she was even more perfect.

The quieter the woman, the better the bride. That seemed to be the matchmaker's philosophy.

As for Uriel, he could only hope that his bride would be a blabbermouth. He would go insane if his wife was as silent as Adina.

But that time was very far away. His parents already had their hands full with Adina and her groom. The matchmaker informed them that the man she had in mind was actually from another village, one that was far away from Zingdorf. The suitor's father was a poor peddler who often passed through Zingdorf in search of clients. More recently, he had also been searching for a potential daughter-in-law.

Mama and Papa were hesitant. They knew full well that if their daughter married a man from another village, she would have to move away from Zingdorf and live with him in his house. They didn't want their little girl to live so far from them, especially if her husband turned out to be a louse.

The instant they met the potential groom, however, any reservations they might have had vanished.

Matthias was one of the sweetest boys that Uriel had ever met. Nothing at all like the rowdy idiots that many unfortunate girls were matched with. He was the bashful, polite, and terribly awkward sort. The sort that would always run to hold open the door for somebody else and then stuttered an apology in a rather adorably awkward fashion once he ended up nearly hitting them with said door.

He also loved Adina the moment he laid eyes on her. Uriel couldn't deny that his sister, while infuriatingly quiet, was beautiful and kind in her own way. He could tell from the instant that Matthias and Adina's eyes met that they were soulmates whose mortal bodies had at last been united. He saw the same warmth in Matthias' eyes that he saw in Papa's eyes when they fell upon Mama. It was the sort of warmth that let him know that this man would be a loving husband, not an abusive drunkard.

Which was good, because even if Uriel and his sister weren't close, he would never let her marry a man that he knew would be cruel to her. Even if he had to drag her away from the wedding canopy, he wouldn't let that happen.

Dowries were exchanged, contracts were signed, and the wedding was planned.

Normally, after all that was done, Matthias would go back to his home and neither his bride-to-be nor his future in-laws would see him again until the day of the wedding. It was common that a bride and groom met once, maybe twice, before they were wed.

Matthias, however, suggested that he visit Adina's family for a few days. He wanted to get to know them before he joined their fold.

He especially wanted to befriend his future brother-in-law. Matthias had heard that Adina's brother was a mute and wanted to learn more about him. The boy was going to be his little brother soon, after all. He might someday be responsible for the child's welfare. He didn't want Uriel to be shy around him.

So, he stayed at Uriel's house and had many a one-sided conversation with the boy. Uriel didn't find many of Matthias' stories to be very interesting (though he listened and politely nodded, feigning fascination for his future brother's sake). Still, the boy took an instant liking to Matthias. Even if the tales he told weren't as riveting as Papa's, his demeanor was so pleasant that Uriel gravitated to him like a frigid hand to a warm candle. His soft gray eyes and gentle voice were comforting to the child, and Uriel decided that he would be more than happy to have Matthias as a brother.

Matthias seemed to take interest in Uriel's writing obsession. It was fairly unusual for a child to adore writing as much as he did. Uriel snatched any spare sheet of paper he could find and filled it with words.

The result of this was, unfortunately, many lost stories. Uriel didn't have a notebook at the time, and thus his stories were stuffed under his bed, crammed into his drawers, and spread around his room like paper snow. Because of this, he couldn't always find a story if he wanted to read it to himself. Uriel wasn't the most organized boy in the world, and so keeping his stories together was hard for him.

Fortunately, Matthias took note of this.

The day of the wedding came. Uriel was quite relieved that the groom's family agreed to have the ceremony in Zingdorf. Uriel didn't like the idea of being so far away from home for such a long time. He had only left his village once or twice, and each time he did so an ache would come to his heart that wouldn't vanish until his feet touched the familiar cobblestone streets again.

Uriel had heard it said that a bride's wedding was supposed to be the happiest day of her life. While Adina and Matthias were both overjoyed, Uriel was the one who felt that this was the happiest day of his life.

After the ceremony was officially conducted and the festivities began, Uriel found that he couldn't keep still. The excitement and happiness that floated through the air seeped into his bones and caused him to bound about, his eyes glittering with glee as he made a point of tasting every dish and shaking every person's hand. All the adults doted on him, flashing him their biggest smiles and chuckling with amusement when he ran up to greet them.

There was dancing, too. Some men placed bottles on top of their heads and Uriel gawked in amazement as he watched them move about with slow, graceful motions, the bottles balancing on their heads as stably as the Stork on the synagogue roof. Once they were done, Uriel immediately ran over and gestured for one of them to give him a bottle so he could try it too. The bottle dancer laughed affably and acquiesced, handing his bottle to the boy.

The child somehow managed to balance it on his head. As soon as he tried to move, however, it fell down and shattered at his feet. He cringed and went scarlet with embarrassment, but then smiled as everybody laughed. Not cruelly, but happily. Nobody was taunting him today, even when he did something silly. They just seemed to find it adorable.

At one point, Adina and Matthias sat in two chairs in the center of the crowd. Before Uriel could even make a guess as to why, the surrounding guests grabbed the chairs and lifted them into the air. Matthias and Adina laughed as the chairs bobbed up and down. Uriel grinned from ear to ear and once the bride and groom were done, he ran to the chair and sat down, waiting for his turn and eliciting a few laughs from the onlookers.

"No, no, Uriel," Matthias chortled. "That's only for the bride and groom."

Uriel clasped his hands together and batted his eyes, putting on his cutest pleading face. Matthias simply couldn't refuse.

"Oh, all right! Come on, everyone!"

Uriel felt his stomach somersault as he was lifted into the air six times. By the time he was set back down he was both horribly dizzy and delirious with joyous laughter.

"Come here, Uriel," said Matthias, catching the light-headed boy before he could fall on his face and leading him over to a table. Once the child's head stopped spinning, he smiled at his new brother and noticed that Matthias was holding his hands behind his back.

"Even though it's my wedding," said Matthias, a generous glitter in his gray eyes, "I want to give you something. Since we're brothers now."

He held out his gift and Uriel's heart stopped.

It was a notebook, but not just a simple old notebook. Even a simple old notebook would have made Uriel happy, but this was far more than that.

It was the single most beautiful notebook that Uriel had ever seen. Its cover was gold, the same shade as his eyes. The sides of the pages were gold too, glittering as though they were made of pure sunlight. On the cover was his name, written in perfect black ink.

URIEL

It was a notebook for him and him alone, and it was the single greatest gift he had ever received.

"Do you like it?" asked Matthias as the boy took it with trembling fingers. "You can write down all your stories now. You won't lose any of them."

Uriel could only look up at the man—his brother—who had given him such an amazing gift and wrap his arms around his neck, giving him the warmest hug that he could offer.

After the wedding, after Matthias and Adina went back to Matthias' home village together, they still visited often. During holidays and birthdays, they would come, often bearing gifts, but no gift was ever as wonderful as the golden notebook. Though being able to see Matthias again and hug him once more was a gift in its own right.

But then, not long after the Germans marched into Poland, the visits stopped.

Uriel started to hear whispers exchanged between his mother and father, whispers that were so quiet that even his acute ears could not pick up everything. Just fragments. Pieces that he couldn't quite put together to form a complete picture of his brother's fate.

Then, one day, another piece was added to the puzzle of words.

"Pogrom."

A word that caused the heart of every Jew to become cold with dread.

When he heard that word, Uriel rushed to his room and held the golden notebook close to his heart, tears leaking from his matching eyes as he realized that he no longer had a brother.

9.

Uriel was going insane.

It had been days since Samael had given him his latest mission, but the birds had yet to show up. He had been forced to remain in Uwe's room, his mind twisting itself into a thousand frustrated knots.

He tried to write, but even his favorite activity had become unbearable. Every time he picked up a pen and his eyes fell upon the golden notebook, his hand would tremble and he would shove his stories away, burying his head in his hands, unable to look at the gift from his brother.

His brother who was still alive.

His last living family member was so close. Uriel could almost feel his brother's comforting embrace and hear his sobs of happiness as he realized that he wasn't alone anymore.

His soul begged for that embrace, begged him to run back to the Moving Mountain, to find Matthias. He wanted to see his brother. He wanted to have a family again.

But he couldn't.

He couldn't.

He couldn't and it was driving him mad. He couldn't get sidetracked. He couldn't go see his brother. Not when Michael and every Jew in Europe needed him to stay focused and finish Samael's blasted tests as fast as possible. Not when the Major and his minions were still making the Jews suffer.

Not when doing so could put Uwe in even more danger.

The boy buried his face in the soft gray blanket and released a furious moan. If he were searching for the Golden Tree, time wouldn't be ticking by at such a torturously slow pace. If he could go out and *do* something, then being away from his brother would be less painful.

But all he could do was sit, his eyes occasionally wandering to the doll that Uwe had placed on the nightstand right beside the golden notebook. She reminded Uriel of the dolls that the little girls in his village would play with.

And as he inspected her, he couldn't help but think that she looked very much like his sister. Long black hair, a slightly patchy dress, and a mouth that was always shyly smiling, always silent.

Thinking of his sister only succeeded in bringing Matthias back to his mind, and though the boy desperately tried to banish his brother from his brain, he still saw those soft gray eyes shining gently, begging Uriel to find him.

The child ran to the closet and grabbed Elijah's Mantle, which had been serving as both a sack for the food that Uwe brought to Matthias' men and a blanket for Uriel. He buried his face in the crimson fabric, letting the holy aura caress his cheeks as he tried not to think of his brother or look at the golden notebook.

"I must say, little linguist, you surprise me."

They exited the interrogation room, Uwe wiping away the beads of nervous sweat that had accumulated on his forehead and trying to erase the mental images of the abuse he had just witnessed. Brandt spoke in a bright, almost teasing manner. Uwe looked up at him and nearly shrunk back when he saw a devious glow in the Major's emerald eyes that didn't match his light-hearted tone.

"W-why so, sir?" asked the linguist, trying to shove the anxious stutter off of his tongue and failing miserably.

"You're thin as a rail," replied Brandt. "I had thought your appetite must be nonexistent, and yet my kitchen's been growing emptier by the day."

Uwe felt his stomach seize up in fear and struggled to give a casual shrug as he said, "Oh…yes, that. Please forgive me, Herr Brandt, but I get hungry when I'm stressed and I suppose these interrogations are making me restless…"

He observed Brandt's reaction closely, praying that he would buy it. The Major's brow furrowed ever so slightly and the wicked gleam in his irises flashed like a dying star's final flux before vanishing, replaced once more by the typical amiable twinkle. He gave the linguist a pat on the shoulder that was a bit harsher than usual.

"Ah, well, forgive *me* then," he said. "It doesn't bother me if you want to use up my stock. Doesn't bother me at all. My home is your home."

There was a distinctly foreboding edge to his tone that made Uwe's spine shiver. Before the linguist could even think of responding, however, there was a cry from the upper floors. Uwe couldn't make it out clearly, but he could tell from the volume alone that something was wrong.

Brandt could tell as well. Fear, surprise, anger, and determination flashed across his face in quick succession before he turned on his heel and rushed up the stairs. Uwe followed, nearly getting several spider webs caught in his hair as he tried to keep up with the Major.

He was rather disturbed that a cringe was his only reaction to what he saw. He reasoned that he had seen so much blood at this point that he was almost morbidly accustomed to it, but still the fact that his reaction to the grisly sight that greeted him was so minimal bothered him.

Two policemen were lying on the ground, their bodies riddled with what at first appeared to be bullets. Upon closer inspection, however, he could see that they had only been shot once or twice. Most of their wounds had been inflicted by a rushed knife-wielder. Whoever had injured the men either preferred not to use guns or, more likely, simply didn't have much ammo to spare.

While the company doctor and a few soldiers tried their best to help their injured comrades, Brandt knelt beside them. One of the injured policemen, whose wounds were less severe than those of his partner, groaned and looked up at the Major.

"Uncle Günter…" he mumbled, gritting his teeth as though the mere act of talking doubled his pain.

"Lie still and tell me what happened," ordered Brandt in a deadly calm voice. Uwe shuddered. He could tell by the fire in Brandt's eyes that he was livid, but his rage was a quiet brand, one that frightened Uwe much more than a flurry of angry snarls and waving fists would have.

"Poles…" moaned the policeman. "They ambushed our car…tried to take us as prisoners…but we wouldn't let them."

"Good man," muttered Brandt, placing a surprisingly gentle hand on his soldier's shoulder before inhaling deeply through his nose, practically stoking the furious fire that was blazing inside of him.

"They'll pay for this," he said, more to himself than to anybody else. The Major's somewhat sinister vengeful tone caused panic to clutch Uwe's heart. Fear and the groans of the soldiers that were currently writhing on the floor kept Uwe from making any comments, however. He could tell that Brandt was in a venomous state right now. Provoking him would be perilous.

"Hannes," Brandt said to one of his men. "I want a reprisal. Make it twenty… no, fifty! Twenty-five for each policeman injured."

Reprisal. That word made Uwe's blood congeal. There was something ominous about it. It almost felt like a villainous ultimatum, like an irrevocable spell cast by an evil sorcerer in one of Uriel's stories.

The soldier, glancing warily at Uwe, leaned over and whispered something in Brandt's ear.

"Both," the Major responded, his eyes traveling to the linguist. "And while you're at it, take Herr Litten back to the house."

The Major's infuriated eyes locked onto Uwe's as he said, "I'm sorry you had to see this, Herr Litten. But now you know why we need to take out those partisans."

Uwe forced himself to nod, but as the soldiers ushered him away from the wounded men and out of the occupied schoolhouse, he couldn't help but recall that those two men had jeered at the Jews just days ago. They had robbed them, beat them, ripped them away from their families.

Uwe sighed grimly as he thought that, perhaps, this was some form of divine retribution.

Uwe knocked on the door, half expecting that Uriel wouldn't be in the room. He was relieved when he heard shuffling as the child slowly slumped to the door and unlocked it.

A pair of gloomy golden eyes greeted him. The linguist forced a smile onto his face, hoping that the boy would return it, but the child refused to mirror him. Instead he turned around, walked over to the bed, and fell face-first onto the mattress, releasing a muffled moan.

"Well," said Uwe sarcastically, shutting the door behind him, "sounds like somebody's having a wonderful day."

Uriel looked up from his position of misery, his eyes giving an irate glitter, as if to say, 'Don't mock me right now.'

A frown clung to Uwe's face as he examined the boy. The child's bright smile had seemingly been snuffed out. The usually cheerful and friendly boy that Uwe had grown attached to had either suddenly grasped the gravity of his current situation or something else was causing a cloud of misery to hover over his head.

Whatever it was, though, Uwe was getting concerned. Something was wrong with Uriel. He always seemed to be daydreaming, and yet whatever he was thinking about seemed to frustrate and sadden him. Whenever his eyes would become cloudy with contemplation, he would shake his head and bury his face into the old burgundy cloak that now served as a comforting blanket of sorts.

He hadn't asked Uwe to read a story from his golden notebook in days. In fact, he seemed strangely averse to opening the notebook. When Uwe had picked up the book and asked what story they should read before bedtime Uriel had all but shielded his eyes, gesturing for the German to put the book away.

Uriel adored hearing his stories told aloud. Something was wrong. Terribly wrong. He wouldn't refuse a reading otherwise.

Uwe had left the boy alone for the past few days, assuming he would be fine in no time, but this bout of depression wasn't dissipating and he wanted his jovial Uriel to return.

He sat down beside the boy and playfully ruffled his hair.

"Have you even gone outside today?" he asked.

The boy gave a slight shake of the head.

"You haven't gone outside for days, have you?"

Uriel shook his head, peeking up at Uwe with one eye while the rest of his face remained planted on the bed.

"Just as I give you my blessing to frolic about the forest you decide to mope around inside instead!" chuckled Uwe. "Are you just insistent on doing the opposite of what I tell you?"

He was relieved to see a teensy smile tug at the child's lip. *Good,* he thought. *Getting somewhere.*

"Uriel," he sighed. "Come on now, sit up."

He gave the child's collar a yank. The boy gave a surprised squeak and then a sigh before he slowly obeyed and sat up, staring down at his one shoe.

"Now, you've been lying down and moping for days," said Uwe, folding his hands together and speaking in a carefully calm tone, the same tone he used whenever he needed to interrogate Jürgen about potential bullies or problems at school.

"That's not you, Uriel," he continued. "You're normally such a cheerful boy. You almost always smile, and you almost always seem to…have hope. That's it. You always seem to have optimism and hope. And I like that about you. I like to see you happy, and when you're upset, I get upset."

Uriel winced and finally raised his eyes, meeting Uwe's in a rather apologetic manner.

"I'm not mad," Uwe explained. "I'm just concerned because I'm your friend and I'm responsible for you."

The boy's eyes glittered with surprise at that. For a moment Uwe hoped that a wide smile would break out across his face, but the child just gazed at him, stunned.

"So I want to know what's wrong with you," said Uwe. "Did I say something to make you upset?"

Uriel vehemently shook his head.

"Well," said Uwe, "then does it have something to do with your exploring the woods?"

Uriel paused for a moment, biting his bottom lip and looking down at his shoe once more before giving a shrug and a feeble nod.

"I see," sighed Uwe. "Are you…trying to find something out there? Are you having trouble finding it?"

Slowly, Uriel gave another nod.

"Uriel…" muttered Uwe. "Whatever or whoever you're looking for, you might find it and you might not. I don't want you to get hurt trying to find it. Whatever it is, it isn't worth your life."

Uriel shut his eyes and shook his head so hard that Uwe was afraid he might hurt his neck. Uwe grabbed the boy's chin and forced him to look up.

"It's not," he insisted. "You're much more important than any object, that's for sure. And even if it's another person…you might find them, you might not. They may or may not still be alive. I know that sounds terrible, but we're living in a terrible time. But *you* are here, *you* are alive, and I don't want you to give up your life for something or somebody else."

Uriel's head gave a barely visible twitch that Uwe had to assume was a nod.

"That being said," he continued, "I also don't want to see you giving up on whatever you're looking for. It seems to give you hope, and I don't want you to lose that either. I don't want you to go too far and get hurt, but I also don't want to see you just sitting in here all day with your face in that old cloak. You're a rather clever boy, Uriel. And very good at sneaking about and avoiding detection. And very good at staying alive…though much of that can be attributed to me."

He gave a rather teasing smile and dramatically gestured to himself. Uriel, at long last, gave a small giggle and shook his head.

"No? What? I'm sorry, but who's the one keeping you safe?"

Uriel pointed up at the ceiling.

"The roof is keeping you safe?"

Uriel shook his head and pressed his hands together in a prayer position.

"Oh, God? Well, I'll give you that. But still, I do a lot of work."

Uriel, smiling impishly, pressed his thumb and index finger together. *Only a little.*

"Why you little ingrate!" cried Uwe with false fury and an irrepressible grin, grabbing the boy and tickling him, "That's it! I'm handing you over to the Major! Major! I have a delinquent little Jewish boy here! Oh! And he's ticklish too!"

Uriel squeaked and laughed until his face became crimson, wriggling about until he finally escaped from Uwe's tickle-torture and landed on the floor.

"Oops! Are you all right?"

Uriel promptly sat up, his face-splitting smile back where it belonged, causing relief to sweep into Uwe's chest.

"Much better," said the German. He glanced over at the nightstand and grabbed the golden notebook, holding it out to the boy.

"How about instead of roughhousing," suggested Uwe, "we read one of your many amazing stories?"

The child's smile began to dissipate and his eyes moved towards the floor once more.

"Uriel, come now," said Uwe, not wanting the smile he had worked so hard to resurrect to expire so rapidly. "These are your stories. Reading them will probably make you feel better. You love these stories, don't you?"

Uriel looked up and nodded without hesitation, like a parent that had been asked to confirm his affection for his child.

"Well," said Uwe, getting into his reading position and patting the spot beside him, "don't neglect the thing you love."

Uriel looked at the golden notebook for a moment, longing and indecision mixing in his eyes. Slowly, as if worried that the book would turn to dust if he seemed too eager, he took his place next to Uwe.

"There we go," said Uwe. "All right, little writer, any preferences?"

Uriel shook his head.

"Then I'll just pick a random one and we'll read that for tonight. Sound good?"

Uriel smiled and nodded.

"Okay," said Uwe, casually flipping to a page, "Then…how about…this one here! *The Story of The Angel of Repentance.*"

"Very long ago, before God, in His wisdom, restricted the actions of the angels, He created two sister angels, the Angel of Revenge and the Angel of Repentance. Though they were twins and identical in appearance, their respective sacred tasks and their personalities were anything but. The Angel of Revenge, bitter and mistrusting of all but her own sister, looked upon every soul with disdain. The Angel of Repentance, meanwhile, regarded every soul with gentle care and urged them to cease their sinful ways while they still drew breath.

The Angel of Repentance loved every human, from the most innocent of children to the most vile of warlords, as a mother loves her own child. But while the Angel of Repentance loved humanity, she did not have faith in them.

Generations passed and the Angel of Repentance watched as the humans she loved refused to repent and damned themselves over and over again. Her belief in humanity's ability to remain wholesome dwindled until she came to think of mankind as lost children in desperate need of correction. She therefore began to steal the souls of sinners before they even had a chance to repent and wiped their souls clean, turning them into fragile, docile little puppets.

But Hashem saw what she did and was furious with her, for she had meddled with mankind's free will. He demanded that she agree to never forcibly purify a soul again, but she refused, saying, "Humanity would be better off if You, O' Omnipotent Lord, would make them all into righteous men and women from the moment they are born instead of permitting them to choose evil. Better I drag them away from their sin kicking and screaming than let them skip their way into Sheol!"

"Ah, My child," said Hashem with sadness. "Had I desired to make a race of mindless pawns, I would have done so instead of creating Adam and Moses and Pharaoh and Goliath. You have not saved those souls by purifying them in such a manner: you have only rendered them incapable of saving themselves. Since you yourself refuse to acknowledge your sin, I will strip you of your rank and banish you from the Host. You shall be welcome back on the day that you see your own sin instead of dwelling on the sins of others."

And so it was that the Angel of Repentance fell from the Heavens and into the Underworld, where she dwelled among the demons. She made herself a little home and continues to live there to this very day, hoarding the 'purified' human souls and refusing to cease her supposedly noble work.

The Angel of Revenge wept when her sister fell, but Hashem comforted her with the assurance that she could visit her sister at any time, particularly if it meant encouraging her to give up her crusade.

"O, Hashem!" cried the vengeful angel in fury. "Those souls were sinful either way! Even if their purification was cruel and wrong, did they not earn their pain?"

"Not for time eternal," Hashem replied gently. *"For even a soul blackened with sin has a pinprick of light, and I shall never lose faith in the power of that light."*

Uwe couldn't help but smile forlornly. *A pinprick of light, hm? Pretty optimistic.*

Uwe looked down at Uriel, prepared to ask him where he had come up with such a tale, but the child was already leaning against the linguist's arm, his eyes shut, his chest gently rising and falling as a sleepy rhythm set in.

Optimistic…right, Uwe thought as he gazed down at the sleeping child's serene countenance. *Do you think the Major has a pinprick of light in him, Uriel? The people who murdered your family? Do you believe in them, Uriel? I bet you do, you damn little angel.*

The boy seemed content once more, which meant that he would likely go out and try to find whatever it was he was seeking tomorrow. Uwe unconsciously put a protective arm around the overly optimistic boy's shoulders and gave a gentle squeeze, looking down at his lap and praying that he hadn't made a mistake by cheering the child up. He didn't want Uriel to be miserable. He didn't want him to lose hope. At the same time, he didn't want the Major and his men to get their hands on the terribly smart and terribly sweet boy. Pinprick of light or no, Uwe wasn't willing to wager Uriel's life on the strength of that flicker.

I wonder how long I'll have to hide him, he thought. He prayed that something would happen, a miracle of some brand that would let him take Uriel somewhere safe. He couldn't keep the child at the Major's house forever. If he could take the boy back to his house and hide him there he would, but that might be impossible.

Still, Uwe hoped that he wouldn't have to separate from the child. He wanted to watch Uriel grow up. He wished that someday he could introduce Uriel to Jürgen. He was certain that they would get along marvelously. Marlene and Trudi would think he was adorable. ("And the best part," Marlene would almost certainly say, "is that he can't ramble on about stupid things like Jürgen always does!" Then a great argument would erupt between Jürgen and Marlene.) Perhaps they could read and enjoy Uriel's stories.

He glanced down at the sleeping boy and wondered if he would enjoy such a life, if he would like meeting Jürgen, Marlene, and Trudi. He wondered if the boy would even live to adulthood, if he would even live long enough to meet the Litten children.

"Uriel…" whispered Uwe, although he knew that the child couldn't hear him. "You know…someday, perhaps, I won't be the only one reading your stories. Stories are meant to be shared, and it's best to share them with more than one person. Maybe someday millions of people will read your stories. They'll read them and say, 'This boy, Uriel, he has a gift. He's a great storyteller.' Being a storyteller is a wonderful thing, Uriel. Your words will still be here, even after you're gone. It's like living forever."

FRIEND

In Zingdorf, he didn't have one.

He had neither friends nor enemies. There was the occasional bully, but even the other children, cruel as they could be, thought bullying a mute boy for more than a day was pathetic and shameful.

He had playmates. The children had no objection to letting him in on their games as long as he tried hard and wasn't a whiner. So long as his mother wasn't hovering over him with a purse full of bandages, Uriel could take part in all of their crazy and stupid games.

Most of the games, though, were relatively tame. Their favorite activity was during the winter. Zingdorf was right on top of a hill, and when it snowed their town was perfect for sledding. The children would scrounge about for hours, finding the perfect plank of wood and pulling out the splinters so it could serve as a proper sled. Some of the wealthier children even took the time to paint theirs. Only to show off, though. They always threw the sleds away by the end of winter. Keeping a sled would only ruin the fun of finding and making a new one next year.

Uriel could recall many happy hours spent sliding and tumbling down the giant hill. He remembered the year he had actually come in second place during their great annual sled race and how his playmates had all happily tossed snow over his head like confetti as they cheered for him. He remembered falling down one year and needing the help of several playmates to make it back up the hill so he could get home.

But although he had so much fun with them, they were playmates and nothing more.

They never went over to his house. They never comforted him when he was sad. They never stood up for him when he was getting picked on. They never got worried when he was sick.

Many of them didn't even know his name. They just called him 'The Mute Boy.' That was all he was to them.

Playmate. Second-place sledder. Mute Boy.

Not Uriel. Not friend.

He wondered if, when all of this horrible business was done, when Michael was free and the Major was gone, Uwe would be willing to find a decent plank of wood and go sledding with him.

After all, he was his first and only friend.

It was well past midnight when Uriel awoke to a tapping at the window.

His eyelids fluttered open and he was surprised to find that he was not laying on his usual bed of socks in the closet, swathed in Elijah's Mantle. Rather, he was still leaning on Uwe's shoulder, and Uwe's arm was lying limply around his shoulders. The linguist had fallen asleep, ostensibly having been too tired to carry the boy to his usual sleeping place before nodding off. That or maybe that story had just been a dreadfully boring one. Uriel hoped it was the former. "The Angel of Repentance" was one of his favorites.

Regardless, Uriel carefully grabbed Uwe's arm and lifted it off him. He gingerly set the German's arm at his side and got up slowly as possible so as not to wake the slumbering linguist. The boy smiled when he saw the peaceful expression on his friend's face, quite a contrast to his usual fretful visage, and made sure to pull the blanket snugly over Uwe before he ran to the window and welcomed in the crisp night air.

Five birds fluttered about outside. As soon as they saw the Jewish child's wide grin, they landed on the windowsill, twittering happily. Uriel shushed them, gesturing to the sleeping Uwe.

"Forgive us, Angel-Finder," said one dove, bowing. "We were excited. We're sorry to have kept you waiting so long, but gathering information on the Golden Tree's whereabouts was more difficult than we had anticipated."

Uriel offered the birds a bright smile, one that clearly communicated that all was forgiven. He waved for them to tell him everything they had learned.

"The Golden Tree that Samael seeks has no properties of its own," said the dove. "God gave it to Father Adam and Mother Eve as a gift for their wedding, and it was passed down for many generations until it finally went to King Solomon the Wise. King Solomon placed it in the Holy Temple, but when the Romans sacked the Temple, they carried it off. Right now, the Golden Tree is in the Golden Cavern."

Uriel cocked his head to the side, a request for elaboration.

"The Golden Cavern is nearby, but getting into it and even picking up the Tree will be dangerous," said the dove. "The Cavern is guarded by a great beast, a serpent that could swallow a synagogue. It is called the Akha, and if you step close to the Cavern, it will devour you. Then, if you can make it past the Akha, the door to the Cavern can only be unlocked with a Boundless Key."

Boundless Key? Uriel thought, an inquisitive crease forming on his brow.

"A Boundless Key," the dove explained, "is a key that can unlock any door just by tapping it. Fortunately, it is possible to make a Boundless Key out of a regular key. Angel-Finder, do you have a normal key of some sort?"

Uriel nodded, pulling out the silver key that Uwe had given him.

"Wonderful!" chirped another dove. "But making the key will also involve some risk. To make a Boundless Key, you must soak the key in both Darkness and Light, which cannot be impeded by doors. Holding the key you have up to the sun will do for Light, but to soak it in pure Darkness you will have to take it to the Pool of Shadows."

Uriel was getting bemused, but he forced himself to stay focused and nodded for them to explain.

"We can lead you to the Pool of Shadows, but you must be cautious," said one of the doves in a tone of high-pitched severity. "The Pool of Shadows is a direct gate to Sheol. If your flesh touches the waters, you will fall straight into the Underworld."

An icy dread clawed at Uriel's heart. *Sheol.* He had heard enough terrible stories about the Realm of Darkness to know that being sent there was a fate far worse than death. Rather than fire and brimstone, Sheol was a place of loneliness and fear, where the cold fingers of your own sins scratched at your eyes and flesh. The thought of being close to such a horrifying place almost made Uriel want to shake his head and bury his face into Elijah's Mantle once more, but he couldn't just give up. He would have to go through with it.

"And," the dove continued, "there is a way to get past the Akha. Beloved King David put the creature to sleep with his harp. If you play David's Harp, you can put him to sleep as well and enter the Cavern without fear. We figured out where the Harp is hidden, and so tomorrow we can take you to the Pool of Shadows and to David's Harp."

David's Harp to put Akha the giant snake to sleep, Pool of Shadows and Boundless Key to open the door. All right. Uriel nodded.

"One more thing," said the dove, "the Golden Cavern is a cursed place. It is filled to the brim with golden treasures and trinkets, but if you touch anything in the cave you yourself will turn to gold. You must find some way to carry the Golden Tree without touching it. Once you get it out of the Cavern, you will not have to worry, but while you are in there, you mustn't touch a thing or you will be frozen forevermore."

Uriel pursed his lips, his mind already whirring with ideas on how to get past such a curse. An idea struck and a smile curled at the edge of his lips. He gave the birds a nod of assurance. He would manage.

"Fantastic," said one of the birds, "Then we will see you early tomorrow, Angel-Finder. Oh! And one more thing…"

One dove hopped off the windowsill and fluttered down. When he, with some difficulty, flew back up, he was clutching something in his claws. Uriel's smile became as wide as the sea when he saw what the mud-encrusted treasure was.

His missing shoe.

Papa had always been an honest businessman. Plenty of shoemakers in other towns made sure not to put too much effort into their work. Oh, they made the shoes durable and desirable, but they had to make sure their footwear wouldn't last forever. After all, if they lasted too long then business would die down!

Papa, though, made the best shoes in Zingdorf, possibly all of Poland. He had always been proud of his profession and aimed to please everyone. Even Poles from other villages would sometimes stop by the tiny Jewish town, just because they wanted shoes that wouldn't wear down.

Of course, the master shoemaker had made sure that his little boy had only the best. Uriel's muddy left shoe took only ten minutes to clean before it was shining like a gem and could be happily reunited with his foot.

Once his shoe cleaning was finished, Uriel set off before Uwe could wake up. He didn't like leaving without saying goodbye (especially since he might get sucked into the Underworld today, which, to say the least, would distress Uwe), but he had been cooped up for days and was eager to make himself useful once more.

It felt so good to be outside again, to be on the hunt. He felt the twigs crack at his feet and the hamsa swinging back and forth as he chased after the birds and breathed in the forest air. He felt like he had been sick for a week and was only now emerging to view the world in all its splendor once more.

It was a beautiful world, a beautiful forest. He hoped that, after Michael was free, he could have a chance to just explore. Climb the trees, listen to the birds singing (or arguing, as he found they often did), try to catch cute woodland creatures. It would be nice to admire the forest when he didn't have doom looming over him at all times, when he didn't have to worry about Michael or Samael or the Major. Perhaps Uwe could come along if that time came. He might like the woods as well.

But soon, the forest became darker, and not in a natural manner. The light hadn't simply vanished. It almost seemed like it was being *eaten* by the shadows that surrounded him.

The birds led him to a curtain of thin, withered vines. While the doves settled on a gnarled tree branch and whispered warnings about touching the water, Uriel slowly parted the curtain and entered.

He found himself standing at the threshold of some sort of morbid grotto. Before him was a small, circular pool filled with swirling black water. Although it was a pool of pure Darkness, it gave off an eerie glow that bathed the grotto in a strange black light. Above the pool there was a flat stone etched with dreary black letters.

Surely Every Man Walks in His Shadow

He recognized those words from a psalm, but he couldn't recall which one.

The air itself was saturated in a Darkness that was thick as water and threatened to drown Uriel before he could even reach the Pool. He stooped down and coughed, horrible black clouds escaping his lips like dark wisps of winter mist.

Uriel covered his mouth and nose with his hand, hoping to filter out the Darkness with his fingers. It helped, but he could still feel the Darkness sneak into his mouth and rest on his tongue. Its taste was unholy, and his heart began to pound as he felt the Darkness make its way down his throat and into his body.

He heard a sound. Distant, like a whisper from the wind. Looking up, he noticed several silhouettes on the walls of the grotto. Some stood still, others moved about in a gloomy dance, wandering here and there, as if trying to find the bodies they were supposed to be attached to. Only Uriel's own shadow continued to do his bidding. The others swept by, hissing and humming and whispering words in a tongue that no linguist could hope to decipher.

He could hardly stand it all. The Darkness was grabbing his lungs, slithering towards his hammering heart. He wanted to flee, but he knew he couldn't. Breathing as little as possible, he knelt before the Pool of Shadows and took his hand off his mouth long enough to rip a thread off his shirt. He reached into his pocket and pulled out the silver key to Uwe's room. He tied the tightest knot he could around the key before holding it above the waters, careful not to let his fingers graze the liquid Darkness as he slowly lowered the key into the Pool of Shadows.

As the key disappeared beneath the surface, Uriel found himself looking into the dark depths. He could see more figures, more sorrowful silhouettes. They reached up to him, their long fingers beckoning, begging to be pulled from the Darkness.

He gasped with surprise when his own image appeared on the water's surface. At first it was merely a reflection, a black mirror that showcased his shocked expression, but then it morphed rapidly. He could see every little sin he had ever committed in his young life. Sticking his tongue out at his teacher, running off to catch the Stork in the middle of the night, pushing another child out of the way during a race, disobeying and worrying Uwe over and over again.

Uriel started to lean forward, moving closer and closer to the black water, closer to Sheol.

But his short litany of sins ended. He gasped, pulling back before his nose could brush against the dark liquid. He yanked the key from the gloomy depths. The silver metal had become black as the waters it had bathed in.

When he saw that the key had absorbed more than enough Darkness, Uriel leapt to his feet and fled the grotto, ignoring the moans of dissent from the shadows that begged him to stay and join them in the Dark.

He basked in the sun, letting the Light seep into his skin and warm his cold-with-fright heart. While the Light banished the lingering Darkness from his trembling body, Uriel held up the blackened key to the great star.

The sun's brilliant beams of Light wrapped around the little key until it turned from black to gold. When that happened, Uriel tore it from the thread and held it in his palm. It had an odd sort of energy to it. Neither cold and dark nor warm and bright, but a peculiar vibe of neutrality.

The doves twittered happily. "Very good, Angel-Finder! You have a Boundless Key now! There's no room that you cannot enter. You need only tap the lock with the Key."

Uriel exhaled. *Then I guess it was worth it,* he thought, carefully placing the Boundless Key into his pocket. *Now I need to find David's Harp.*

He looked up at the doves and nodded for them to lead him to the instrument. The birds, however, observed that the child was panting. Uriel's throat hadn't recovered from being flooded with Darkness, and he wasn't sure if he would be able to run very fast in his current condition.

Fortunately, the birds noted this and one of them chirped, "Angel-Finder, there is a small stream not far from here. You can have a quick drink before we continue forth. Being near the Pool of Shadows is a horrible experience. Surely you need fresh water."

It certainly would be nice to see water that wouldn't send him to Sheol if he touched it. His throat begged him to consent and so he nodded. The birds fluttered forward, being sure to fly slowly for the boy's sake.

Uriel carefully stepped over some barbed bushes, glancing over his shoulder as he did so, making sure that the Pool of Shadows was far behind him. He looked down at the smooth stream and relief flooded his weary body.

He knelt before the little stream, cupping his hands together and lifting the cool, clear water to his lips. He enjoyed the sensation of the pure liquid moving down his battered throat and removing the last traces of Darkness.

Uriel was about to take a final sip when a scarlet stain on the surface of the stream caught his eye. He slowly stood and took a step away from the water when he realized that it was blood.

Uriel turned and, in the distance, he could see a few figures standing on the other side of the stream, on an old bridge. The child approached slowly.

A gunshot rang out. A body bobbed to the surface of the water. Uriel froze and gawked, his eyes following the still form as it floated down the stream, turning the clear water crimson.

It was a woman, shot in the head by two men in identical green uniforms. Order Police. The Major's men.

Three more murdered maidens joined the girl in the stream as three more gunshots echoed across the woods. Fear grabbed Uriel's lungs in a tight grip and forced him to breathe in short spurts through his mouth. He watched the limp figures as they floated away and then listened to the soldiers.

One of them sighed. "There we go. Reprisal over. Fifty Jews and Poles."

"I can't believe Ackerman made us go all the way out here just to top it off!" huffed his partner. "Just because we 'only' got forty-six yesterday! Damn perfectionist."

"*'The Major specifically ordered exactly fifty!'*" squeaked one of the men in a high-pitched, derisive tone. "Bah! As if forty-six wouldn't get the message across! The Poles are never going to learn their lesson about attacking us!"

"Right," sighed his comrade. Then, in a quiet and reflective manner, he asked, "Do…you think Karl and Dieter will be okay?"

His partner sighed. "I hope so…but…I don't know. Those Poles got them good."

"Damn Poles…" hissed the other German, spitting into the stream, no doubt aiming for the bodies of his poor victims.

"Let's head back. Uncle Günter's going to be waiting for us…"

Uriel shook his head, feeling woozy as he turned on his heel and fled back into the woods. Tears filled his golden eyes, his throat burning as the images of bodies and blood were burned onto his brain and the Germans' words echoed through his mind.

Reprisal over. Fifty Jews and Poles.

Reprisal…Reprisal…

RAT

The first time Uriel saw death, it was a rat.

If rats had been a precious commodity, Zingdorf would have been one of the richest villages in all of Poland. Unfortunately, the rodents had no value, and the townspeople moaned daily about how the troublesome rats had gotten into this or that.

If only God had never made rats, they often said.

Uriel, though, had been told many times that every creature, no matter how obnoxious, had some place in God's grand scheme. So, while he thought badly of the rats when they got to his cookies and cakes before he did, he couldn't find it in himself to hate them.

But then there were the cats.

There were hardly any dogs in Zingdorf (in fact, Uriel barely knew what a hound's bark should sound like), but there were cats galore. To combat the rats, the residents of Zingdorf brought in cats and let them loose.

The first time he saw death, a cat had been the killer and a poor little rat was its victim. Uriel could recall being three years old, sitting on the floor of his father's shoe store and playing while Papa chit-chatted with some customers.

He had been fiddling with the heel of a boot when a rat scurried across the floor in front of him. It had been a little white rat with a dirt-matted coat and black eyes that twinkled with a cautious sort of curiosity as it emerged, driven by hunger to leave the safety of its hole.

He had watched the creature with fascination as it flitted towards the table. But before it could even hope to scrounge about for crumbs, a cat leapt down from the open window and tore it to shreds.

Uriel had been mortified. He had run to his father, wailing and pointing to the mauled corpse of the rat that dangled from the cat's bloodstained mouth.

His father and the other men had chortled with approval and smiled fondly at the murderous feline. Papa had even given the cat a platter of milk to reward it for getting rid of the rat.

The others had tried to calm the traumatized Uriel down. They assured him that it was just a rat.

Vermin. Nothing more.

They said that so casually, but every time Uriel thought back to that day, he couldn't help but think they would have had a much different opinion if God had made them rats instead of men.

He had almost become Saint Nikolas to them. A figure that carried a burgundy sack filled with food and hope. One who always greeted them with a forced smile, his thin glasses failing to restrain the empathy that glistened in his azure eyes as he rationed out the provisions.

Uwe still had trouble picking up names, but he could remember a few of them. The one who had accused him of being a German spy and had argued against letting him live was named Solomon, and since Uwe had become their provider, his tone had noticeably changed. He welcomed Uwe into their hideout with a broad grin and sweeping gestures, assuring him over and over that he was nothing like the rest of the German bastards.

Uwe didn't mind. In fact, he was glad. He couldn't find it in himself to be bitter towards Solomon. Not since the Jewish man had told him about his village's fate.

"Since I'm a hunter, I was in the woods looking for game," he explained. "When I came back home, the village was empty. A few windows had been broken, the houses looted, the synagogue destroyed, and a few people had been shot in the streets, but everyone else had just vanished. I looked everywhere, but they were just *gone*. My wife and daughter as well…"

Uwe tried to offer him hopeful condolences. At the same time, the linguist couldn't help but wonder where the villagers had gone. The Poles, when they attacked the Jews, did so in town with knives and axes and plows. Solomon's village would have looked more like Zingdorf if they had been the ones to attack. It could have been Brandt and his men. In that case Solomon's wife and daughter would have been resettled. Brandt was brutal, but he had said that he and his men didn't behave like the Poles did towards the Jews. Solomon's wife and daughter could be waiting for him wherever they were, though Uwe didn't tell him this. He didn't want to risk Solomon doing something hasty to reunite with his wife and daughter, especially since Uwe wasn't even sure where they could be or if Brandt had even been the one to take them away.

Solomon, though, was the only one who spoke directly to Uwe about what had happened to him. The others would occasionally mutter something about a brother or sister or mother or child that they had lost forever, but none of them were willing to go into detail about what or who had taken them. Matthias, for his part, never even whispered about any lost family members. The only hint that he even still had human emotions was the forlorn spark that sometimes melted his arctic eyes for a few milliseconds when he heard another Jew speak of a wife or brother.

As the linguist handed a small loaf of bread to the youngest of the lot (Uwe was relatively sure that his name was Haim) and asked if he was feeling any better today, Matthias stood in the shadows, his arms folded over his chest. His gray eyes followed Uwe, giving the German an increasing sensation that those icy irises were studying his soul.

"I'm feeling so much better, Uwe," said Haim, his sky-blue eyes glittering up at the German with gratitude. Uwe wasn't sure why, but he was surprised that Haim and a few of the Jews had blue eyes. Perhaps he had been spending too much time with Brandt and the *Ordnungspolizei*. Their racial assumptions were, to a slight degree, starting to rub off on him.

"I'm glad to hear it," said Uwe, handing the rest of the food to Matthias so he could ration it out until the German returned with more. Indeed, the health of the hidden Jews had improved fantastically since he had started to bring them food. Their eyes and cheeks were still sunken in and they were still ghostly pale, but they were no longer barely breathing skeletons waiting for starvation to steal their lives.

He was about to bid the Jews farewell and make his exit when Matthias placed a firm hand on his shoulder, one that made it clear that he wasn't going anywhere until he did what the Jewish leader wanted. Uwe swallowed and nervously turned to face the commander.

"Litten," said Matthias, who was insistent on calling the linguist by his last name, something that made Uwe distinctly uncomfortable owing to how aloof such a designation appeared.

"I want to have a word with you," said Matthias, gesturing to his corner of the cave, where they could speak in relative privacy. Uwe inhaled and reluctantly followed. He didn't like to dally. He preferred to simply enter, give the Jews their food, and exit as fast as he could. He didn't take the time to truly converse with the Jews. The longer he dawdled, the more time Brandt had to return, find him missing, and potentially discover either Uriel or the location of the fugitive Jews.

He had to wonder how Obadiah had managed to feed a hundred Jews for so many years. It seemed hard enough to feed twenty.

Nevertheless, Matthias' metallic voice made it clear that no argument would sway him to release Uwe before they could talk, so he followed without complaint. He sat cross-legged in front of the Jewish leader while Matthias sat on a small wooden stool. Uwe almost felt like a young child, sitting at the foot of a wise schoolmaster and preparing for a lecture.

Far from lecturing, however, it was Matthias who pried for information. He asked the German if anything of great importance had transpired since they had last spoken.

"Two of the Major's men were ambushed by the Polish partisans the other day," said Uwe. "They were badly injured. They might die, and if they do…well… either way, Brandt's already ordered a reprisal of some sort. He and his men are meeting today to discuss what to do about the Poles in the area. They're still looking for the partisans, but I'm not sure what they'll do about the civilians."

"Probably ship them to concentration camps, just like they did to us. It would serve them right," spat Matthias, anger coming to his voice even as his face remained eerily placid.

"But not the women and children," Uwe pointed out. "And not all the Poles. Some of the Poles are fighting hard against the Germans…"

"Some. And some killed our families."

"Some Germans did too, and look at me," said Uwe.

"Fair enough," said Matthias. "But you're one very interesting exception. The Poles have hated us for years."

"But they are a thorn in Brandt's side," said Uwe. "I noticed, though, that the men they attacked were stabbed with knives and only had a few gunshot wounds. Do you think they might be running out of bullets?"

"Likely," said Matthias. "The Polish army tried to beat the Germans back during the Invasion, but they were outmatched, and they're still outmatched now. If they *are* running out of bullets, though, they won't be able to hold out much longer. The Germans certainly don't lack bullets."

"I suppose my country *is* doing well right now," sighed Uwe. A thought struck him as his eyes traveled to Matthias' tattered army outfit.

"Matthias," said Uwe slowly, "I…was wondering. Some of the Poles are fighting the Germans. If you had weapons…would you fight too?"

He almost immediately regretted opening his mouth. He was approaching treasonous territory. Although he had technically already betrayed his nation by hiding Uriel and helping Matthias' men, there was a major difference between hiding Jews and suggesting that they attack German soldiers.

I didn't say he should, Uwe reasoned. *I just asked if he would.*

As much as he had come to hate the Order Police and everything they did and stood for, he wasn't sure that he could support killing them outright. The Order Police were only doing what they were told, after all. Besides, they all had wives and children back in Germany.

"If I could, I would," said Matthias. "I'm sure that the others would, too. But we can't."

"No weapons?" Uwe surmised. The Jewish leader gave a solemn nod.

"None. We only have Solomon's hunting rifle, and *he* only has three bullets left. We don't even have any knives. We have nothing…."

Matthias' own words seemed to strike his heart. His frozen eyes cracked for a mere second and he looked down at his hand, his fingers twitching, doubtless recollecting something and doubtless bothered by his memory.

He came back to his senses and his gray eyes met Uwe's blue once more. "I wish we could fight back," he declared. "We have nothing else to live for. It's either stay trapped in this cave for the rest of our lives or get shot by the Germans…"

"They would probably send you to a camp…" Uwe started to say, but his comment only caused Matthias' eyes to flash.

"Well, *that's* better," said Matthias, the sarcasm in his tone clashing unpleasantly with his steely voice.

"Don't give up hope yet," said Uwe. "We—the Germans, I mean—we might be doing well right now, but we have the Western forces *and* the Russians to fight. It could turn around. Even if it doesn't, something else might happen. You could still end up free by the end of all this."

"Free," hissed Matthias, as though such a word had become a curse rather than a blessing.

"If you got a chance to leave this cave and go anywhere, where would you go?" asked Uwe, desiring to inject some hope or happiness into their conversation.

The Jewish leader's iron-gray eyes softened thoughtfully. He looked up at the dank ceiling of the cave and pondered the question for a moment before quietly responding, "I would look to see if I have any family left…and if not… then I would have no reason to stay. I think…I would like to go to Jerusalem."

"Jerusalem? The Holy Land?"

"Yes," said Matthias. "I want to visit the Western Wall. They say that the Divine Presence always rests there. You can apparently *feel* it if you touch the stones. You can feel God's eyes on you. I want to go there and see if that's true. I want to go there and see if I feel anything at all."

"Then," said Uwe, at last rising to his feet and tucking Uriel's burgundy cloak under his arm, "may you and your men make it out of this unscathed, and I hope you make it to Jerusalem. I really have to go now. Goodbye…"

"Very well," muttered Matthias, meeting Uwe's eyes once more, holding him in place with his gaze. The Jewish leader stared straight into Uwe's pupils and Uwe waited for him to break eye contact before he turned to leave.

"Uwe," Matthias finally said, and Uwe was stunned that the commander uttered his first name. "Make no mistake: we are more than grateful for all you've done. You saved our lives. You've been like a guardian angel."

Uwe blinked and felt a laugh tickle his throat. He could barely suppress it as he shook his head.

"Angel?" he repeated, "No, no. I don't think so. I'm no angel."

With that, he turned and exited the dim cave.

He had spent too much time in the cave. That or the sun was particularly bright today. Either way, when Uwe stepped out into the sunlight he was nearly blinded by its brilliance. He whipped off his glasses and rubbed his eyes, waiting for the bleary dots that danced in his corneas to dissipate as his vision adjusted to the light.

The first thing he saw when he finally opened his eyes all the way was a tiny figure in the distance. He squinted and saw a familiar child flit through the trees.

Uriel, he thought. He opened his mouth to call out to the child, but then closed it, curiosity nagging him as he watched the boy bolt into the thicket. He was running away from the house. Where was he going?

*I wonder…*thought Uwe. If he followed, he could find out where Uriel had gotten the burgundy cloak. He could figure out what the boy was looking for. Perhaps he could even help.

He took off after the boy. Low branches swung at him as he dashed, but he dodged their blows and kept his eyes on the dark blur that was the boy. Whatever Uriel was running towards, he was in quite a hurry. Uwe nearly set his lungs on fire trying to keep up with him. The cloak almost got caught on a bush several times, but he stopped just long enough to safely remove it. For one reason or another, he didn't want to leave the old cloak behind. Perhaps just because it was important to Uriel and he would feel horribly guilty if he upset the boy by losing it in the forest.

Such delays, however, allowed the boy to run further and further ahead until Uwe eventually lost sight of him. The linguist panted and paused, resting his hands on his knees, leaning down and trying to catch his breath.

That was when he heard a gunshot and felt something red-hot fly right above his ear.

By instinct, he fell to his knees and raised his hands. In three languages, he informed the shooters that he surrendered.

Polish voices responded, and within seconds Uwe was shoved to the ground, his hands bound tightly behind his back.

All he could do was sigh and moan, "Not again."

The Polish partisans were about as ragtag as Uwe had expected. It was hard for him to tell how many there were since they kept moving to and fro and he had trouble telling one unshaved, scrappy-uniform clad man from the other. Judging by the number of tents clustered around the large, unlit fire pit in the center of the camp, however, he could tell that there were at least thirty of them.

He wasn't given much of an opportunity to get an exact count, of course. He was led right to the center of the camp and unceremoniously deposited at the feet of five men who had been in the middle of a hushed conversation. Their debate ended swiftly, and they turned their attention to the German as he raised his eyes to meet their surprised gazes.

"Who's this?" asked one man, addressing the partisan who had tied Uwe up and giving the German a glare that could cause flowers to wilt.

Before the partisan could respond, Uwe straightened up and tried his best to give them a hard stare (even though he knew he looked more silly than dignified, what with his glasses lopsided and his hair matted).

"My name is Uwe, Uwe Litten. I'm a linguist, not a soldier or a spy. I'm not here to hurt you, in fact I'd prefer to help you," said Uwe in terse and perfect Polish. He squirmed slightly as he felt the worn ropes dig into his wrists.

"Could you please tell your men to untie me?" Uwe added. "These ropes hurt."

He was surprised by how calm and almost weary he sounded. Although he felt a twinge of fear, he couldn't find it in himself to be terrified of these desperate men, especially since he had already been through this once. In fact, he was much more concerned about Uriel. Given everything Matthias had told him about Polish-Jewish relations in this area, Uwe was afraid that these Poles would be like the ones who had destroyed Zingdorf.

The glaring Pole sniffed resentfully, offended that the German was speaking to them in such a manner without even having the decency to cry and beg for his life. He opened his mouth to threaten the linguist, but another Polish man, one with a bandage on his forehead and a curious spark in his chestnut eyes, stood up and spoke.

"*Pan*…Litten, did you say?"

Uwe nodded.

"*Pan* Litten," said the Polish man, gazing intently into Uwe's eyes. Uwe made sure not to blink, allowing the Polish man to freely examine him. He had nothing to hide.

The Polish man gave the slightest nod, as if to indicate that he approved of what he saw. He waved for the other partisans to untie the German. Instantly, his comrade turned to him with fury.

"Patryk!" he snarled. The calmer of the two, Patryk, didn't even glance at his enraged cohort.

"Oh, be quiet, Felix," said Patryk, speaking in a manner so condescending that Uwe could tell they were brothers. That or Patryk substantially outranked Felix.

"He's a *German*, dammit!" growled Felix, pointing an accusatory finger in Uwe's direction. "The *Germans* are the ones trying to kill us! Did your brain get damaged too?"

He gestured to the bandage on Patryk's forehead. Apparently not offended (or at least not offended enough to show any sign of umbrage), Patryk merely rolled his eyes.

"My brain is perfectly intact, though I sometimes have to worry about yours," replied Patryk crisply. "I realize that he's a German, but you'll notice that he speaks perfect Polish. If he knows Polish, then logically he must know a Pole."

He turned his brown eyes back to Uwe and asked, "Is that correct, Pan Litten?"

"Yes," said Uwe, rubbing his burning wrists once a partisan untied him and threw the rope aside. Uwe sighed sadly and glanced down at the cold embers of the campfire.

"I come from a town at a crossroad," the linguist confessed. "There used to be people from all across Europe that passed through. Many, many Poles as well. That was a long time ago, though. Before all of this Hitler business…"

Another weary sigh escaped his lips before he looked back up at the pair of Poles.

"Major Brandt—he's the one who commands the German forces in this area—he took me away from my home and family. I know Polish and Yiddish and Russian, and he wanted to use me as a translator…"

"See? He admits it himself!" barked Felix, who was starting to remind Uwe of Solomon before he became cordial. "He's one of the Major's men…!"

"He didn't say that, Felix," muttered Patryk, pinching the bridge of his nose as if attempting to restrain an oncoming migraine. "Let the man talk, he might be useful to us."

"I'm willing to help you," said Uwe. "I don't want to bring harm to anybody. I hate Brandt. I hate what he does. I've seen him do terrible things to some of your men while interrogating…"

"Wait, they're alive?" cried Felix, his eyes widening with wonder. "The ones they captured are still alive?"

Uwe nodded. Felix clenched a determined fist.

"We have to rescue them!" he declared. "Litten, where are they? Where are they being held?"

"One moment, Felix…" Patryk began to say, but Felix's eyes flashed.

"Don't tell me to wait, Patryk, you bastard! I've done enough waiting! If the others are still alive, then we *have* to rescue them! Those are *our* people! Besides, they might tell…"

"They haven't given much information yet," Uwe interrupted. "Brandt still doesn't know where you are."

The fire in Felix's eyes died down ever so slightly when he looked towards Uwe. The precious gift of information concerning his captured fellows had soothed his anger, if only a little.

"And," said Felix, "you're not going to tell him where we are, are you?"

Uwe shook his head.

"Swear?"

"To God," replied Uwe with such conviction that none of the gathered Poles had difficulty believing that he wouldn't break his vow.

Felix and Patryk sat across from Uwe, crossing their legs and, in Felix's case, gazing at him with somewhat begrudging acceptance.

Glancing between the two, Uwe narrowed his azure eyes and queried, "Which of you is the leader of the partisans?"

The duo exchanged a grim glance before Patryk replied, "We don't have a leader anymore."

Uwe arched an eyebrow. "What do you mean by that? You two seem like leaders. The other partisans took me right to you when they captured me."

Patryk gave a chuckle so devoid of humor that it made Uwe wince. "That's because we're the actual leader's cousins. Our commander was just killed yesterday."

"Oh, I'm sorry…" Uwe mumbled, but Felix shook his head.

"Don't bother. He died honorably. I'm sure he'd have no regrets," sighed Felix, his eyes flickering up to the cloud-streaked sky, as though he expected to see his cousin's content spirit smiling down upon them.

"How did he die?" asked Uwe.

"You didn't notice?" said Patryk, surprise and slight concern creeping into his voice, "I thought you worked with the Major."

"I do, Major Brandt, though I haven't seen him since yesterday."

"Well, Adrian—our commander—he attacked the Major's car, and he was killed…"

The memory of the stabbed and shot policemen lying on the schoolhouse floor in a puddle of their own blood flashed through Uwe's mind. He gasped and speedily shook his head.

"I know what you're talking about!" cried Uwe. "But that wasn't Major Brandt's car you attacked! It was just two policemen. They're badly injured. They might die, but Major Brandt is still alive!"

Patryk tightened his jaw, biting back a long string of curses. Felix wasn't so poised and let every Polish swearword that Uwe knew (and several he hadn't previously) roll off his tongue.

"Then Adrian died for nothing!" cried Felix, slamming his trembling fist onto the forest floor as though it was to blame for all their misfortune. "Now we're all good as dead! We'll never make it while they have their leader and we don't!"

"There's no reason for you to stay leaderless!" said Uwe. "One of you can take over…"

Felix gave a rather bitter snort, as if the suggestion was so ludicrous that it didn't even merit a politer response. Patryk shook his head.

"I can keep a level head—unlike my brother here." He gestured to Felix, who muttered something under his breath as he shot his brother a poisonous glare.

Patryk ignored his brother's bristling and confessed, "But I'm not a good leader. None of us are. We can't plan or inspire or think on our feet, not the way Adrian could. We thought it wouldn't be so bad as long as the Germans lost their leader too. We figured we might have some time to come up with something before he was replaced. But now…"

"Is there something I can do?" asked Uwe with genuine concern, glancing from brother to brother as hopelessness slowly conquered their eyes. "I'm already helping some other people that are on the run. I bring them food. It might be hard, but I could bring you some food as well."

"That would be nice, *Pan* Litten," said Patryk with a small nod of appreciation. "But we're not *really* on the run. We're trying not to get caught, but we're not going to hide and hope we aren't found. We're fighting back."

"This is our country," declared Felix. "Our home. The Germans are taking it away from us, and we're not giving up until they've turned tail and run back to Berlin."

"That's very brave of you," said Uwe, neglecting to mention that there were no Berliners among Brandt's men.

"Thanks," sighed Felix, a very small and awfully sour smile coming to his face as he muttered, "Though as long as you're offering us help, I don't suppose you've got any weapons we could use…"

Uwe shook his head. "Nothing, sorry. I noticed that the German soldiers your people injured had been stabbed but barely shot. Are you running out of bullets?"

"Yes, unfortunately," said Patryk. "Adrian attacked those policemen out of desperation, but it seems even he didn't have enough bullets to finish them off. The rest of us aren't faring any better."

"We'll be lucky if we don't have to resort to hitting the Germans with sticks by the end of the week," said Felix. A tiny flicker of light appeared in his pupils and he turned to his brother.

"Though," he said, "if we're *really* lucky we might find Crazy Old Julek's…"

"*Enough* about Crazy Old Julek, Felix, that's not going to…" Patryk started to say, rolling his eyes skyward. Uwe interrupted him before he could demean his brother any further.

"Who's Crazy Old Julek?" asked the German.

Patryk gave a rather annoyed sigh and prepared to elaborate, but before he could do so Felix grinned and leaned forward.

"In our hometown," Felix explained, "there was an old man, everyone just called him Crazy Old Julek. He'd seen hell twenty times, lived through war after war after war, and it all made him go nuts. Paranoid. Once Poland became independent after the Great War, he started babbling on about how it wouldn't last and how *he* was going to be prepared when the bad guys arrived."

"He used to buy bullets and weapons by the truckload," said Patryk. "He took them into the forest and hid them somewhere. I think he was planning on starting an insurrection or something. He was expecting this sort of thing to happen."

"Sounds like Crazy Old Julek wasn't so crazy," Uwe observed. The brothers solemnly nodded, a spark of shame coming to their eyes. They no doubt regretted belittling their foresighted neighbor.

"What happened to Julek?" Uwe asked.

"Died of a heart attack just one week before the Invasion," said Felix with a shake of his head. "Missed his right to brag by just a week…"

"But he never told anybody where he hid all his weapons," said Patryk. "His cache could be anywhere. We have no clue."

"No clue at all?" asked Uwe.

"Well," said Felix, "there is the note…"

"Oh, *that*," snorted Patryk. "That hardly qualifies as a clue."

"Note? He left a note? That's the best sort of clue!" said Uwe.

"Not the one he left," said Patryk as an odd smirk tugged at the edge of his lip, one that conveyed a strange sort of sardonic somberness.

"Hey, Nacek!" Felix bellowed to a rather skinny partisan. "Do me a favor and go get Crazy Old Julek's stupid note!"

"Sure thing, Felix," replied the Polish man, chuckling darkly and shaking his head before scurrying into one of the tents and quickly returning with a crumpled piece of paper in his hand.

"Give it to our guest," said Felix, gesturing to Uwe. Nacek's smile faltered for a second as he looked down at Uwe, but he did as he was told.

"Nacek here's from our village," Felix explained while Uwe struggled to smooth out the wrinkled paper so he could read it properly. "He lived right next to Crazy Old Julek. Sometimes helped him clean his windows."

"He used to pay me in coal and hot chocolate," Nacek chuckled nostalgically. "Nice old man. Insane, but nice. Unfortunately, since I lived right next door, I always had to listen to his ravings. This one time he invited me in for hot chocolate and I just saw this gigantic box of bullets sitting on his couch. I thought it was funny, and I asked him where he was gonna take it. He said he'd give me a 'clue.' That note's the clue, though it hasn't done any of us much good."

Uwe could see why. The note was a sloppily scrawled mess of Russian, German, Polish, and even a few Yiddish letters. The partisans, most of whom probably didn't know a word of Yiddish or German, would never be able to unscramble the strange semantic code.

"But…" Uwe mumbled as his mind almost immediately started trying to mold the foreign letters into something comprehendible. He couldn't see an obvious translation, but given time he could piece it together.

"I think I could figure this out," he said, looking up at the partisan brothers. Patryk glanced from the letter to the linguist and a hopeful gleam made its way into his irises. Felix's nose crinkled.

"You? How?" he asked.

"He's a linguist, you moron," sighed Patryk before Uwe could open his mouth to explain his qualifications. Felix's eyes widened and his bitter smirk became moderately optimistic.

"Ah, right," he said. "The note's in Russian."

"And Yiddish and German. All languages I know. Julek must have picked up some languages over the years," Uwe assumed.

"Makes sense," said Patryk. "He picked up a bit of the enemy's language in every war he fought."

"So what's it say?" Felix eagerly asked. Uwe squinted at the paper, trying to spot some hidden message in the bizarre splash of letters, but he couldn't figure it out just by looking at it.

"It seems like a bunch of random letters right now," said Uwe. "But give me a few days and I might be able to solve it."

He looked up at Nacek and politely inquired, "May I keep this?"

Nacek smiled cynically and gave a small shrug of acquiescence. "Go right ahead. It's no good to me."

"Thank you," said Uwe, folding up the letter and tucking it into his coat pocket. "Then I'll try my best to figure this out and I'll tell you if I find anything. Until then, will you let me leave? I need to get back to the Major or else he'll get suspicious, and he might come looking for me."

"I'm willing to trust you," said Patryk. "What about you, Felix?"

Both Uwe and Patryk turned to Felix, but the other Pole wasn't paying attention. He was sitting up slightly, squinting, trying to look over Nacek's shoulder.

Uwe's heart skipped a beat when he thought that the Pole might have spotted Uriel.

"Pardon me!" the German cried a bit too loudly. Felix flinched and looked from Patryk to the German. He took a deep breath to recover from the scare Uwe's outburst had given him and then gave the linguist one last soul-searching stare. After a moment, he heaved a small sigh.

"Fine, sure, sorry…I thought I…never mind. I'll trust you for now, Litten. Don't make me regret it."

"I swear I won't," vowed Uwe, standing up. "Is there anything you need to know before I leave? Anything that might help you?"

"How many men does Brandt have left?" asked Patryk right away.

"And where are they?" added Felix.

"Brandt has a little over forty men," answered Uwe. "They use an old schoolhouse as a base of operations, but the soldiers sleep in an old manor, down the street from the house where the Major and I sleep."

"Forty men?" repeated Patryk, "That's far less than we expected."

"The Order Police aren't as big and powerful as the SS, but they're still very brutal."

"Still, they seemed so much bigger," said Felix. "We thought there were a hundred of them."

"This is good, then," said Patryk, "We're not as outnumbered as we thought."

"We're still outmatched, though," Felix pointed out rather pessimistically. "As long as they have weapons and a leader…"

An idea struck Uwe. A risky one, a plan the Poles were unlikely to accept, but it was a possibility. The word 'leader' summoned a memory of an iron-eyed man that had led his people and kept them hidden for weeks, kept them alive when they should have died or been captured within days.

"I'll keep an eye out for Julek's cache," said Uwe. "But until then, I think I might have a solution to your lack of good leadership."

A mixture of curiosity and suspicion flooded Patryk and Felix's eyes in unison.

"I hope you're not going to suggest that *you* become our leader," said Felix. "No offense, Litten, but you're not exactly a fighter…"

Uwe laughed at the mere notion. "And I know it. No, not me, I had somebody else in mind."

Patryk and Felix glanced at one another before nodding for Uwe to go on.

"There's a group of people hiding in the woods," said Uwe. "I've been bringing them food, and I know their leader. His name is Matthias. He's very strong and very brave. He's kept his men alive for weeks with no food or weapons. He's an outstanding leader, and I'm sure he would make an excellent commander for you and your people."

"This sounds too good to be true," observed Felix, a very slight smile forming at the corner of his mouth. "There has to be a catch."

"Not really," said Uwe, nervously biting the inside of his cheek. "Not unless you make it a catch."

"What's wrong with this Matthias?" asked Patryk.

"Nothing, nothing whatsoever. He's Polish like you, and he hates Brandt and his men…."

"*But…*" Felix started, waving for Uwe to stop beating around the bush.

Inhaling deeply, Uwe confessed, "He's a Jew."

He expected Patryk to give a thoughtful (if slightly hesitant) nod as he pondered the matter while Felix would explode into a flurry of Jew-hatred and refusals.

He was surprised when the opposite occurred. Felix's eyes flashed with slight surprise and discomfort before he brought his thumb up to his mouth and pensively chewed on his nail. Patryk, on the other hand, threw his level-headedness behind his back. His eyes flared like a raging inferno and his face contorted in anger, as though the three-letter-word was the foulest curse one could utter.

"*Jew*," he spat hatefully. "As if we would *ever* let one of those communist Christ-killers lead us…"

Uwe cringed. He could see now what Matthias meant when he emphasized the anti-Semitism of his gentile neighbors. Patryk had gone from a calm and understanding man to a red-faced bellower as he listed off every grievance he had with Matthias' people. Nacek mumbled something that Uwe couldn't hope to hear over Patryk's tirade before backing away and slipping into his tent. Uwe envied him.

Felix let his brother rant until Uwe looked ready to curl up in a fetal position. When that happened, Felix was finally the one to roll his eyes and order his brother to shut up.

"I will not 'shut up'!" snarled Patryk, "It's those filthy bastards' fault our country was taken over in the first place!"

"Oh, just because Father and Pastor What's-His-Name would never shut up about 'the satanic Jews'…" sighed Felix.

"Just because *you* never paid attention in church doesn't mean *I* didn't!" snapped Patryk, "You don't care about the Lord, but I…"

"I didn't say I don't care about the Lord," said Felix, "But Jesus *did* preach forgiveness and all that. It's been a thousand years since Christ was crucified. I say let bygones be bygones, especially if the Jews can help us now."

"The Jews only ever help themselves," hissed Patryk, turning his smoldering irises down to the campfire's dead embers. "They bleed us dry and stab us in the back every chance they get!"

"Now he's just repeating what our father used to blabber on about," said Felix, turning to Uwe and jabbing his thumb in his brother's direction. "Really, he's as stupid as Father…"

"Father was *not* stupid, and neither am I! I'm only being reasonable!"

"This is not reasonable, this is foaming at the mouth," grunted Felix. "I don't care if the Jews are communists who worship the god of the moon. If they can help us against the Germans, it's worth working together just once."

"I'm not asking you to love the Jews—and I'm not even sure that Matthias will agree to be your leader if I ask him…" Uwe started to say.

"Of course he won't," said Patryk, crossing his arms over his chest. "Jews don't help *goyim*."

Uwe felt a blade of anger pierce his chest. He glared at Patryk and said, in the calmest tone he could muster, "The Poles attacked his village, killed his family…"

"He shouldn't have been in Poland in the first place," replied Patryk. "He and his people don't belong here. They don't belong *anywhere*."

"Listen here, you self-centered…!" Uwe snarled, his wrath boiling to the surface as Uriel's cheerful giggle rang in his ears. Fortunately, before any kind of fight (verbal or physical) could break out, Felix hopped to his feet and stood between Uwe and his brother.

"We'll think about it," he said. "I'll try my best to talk some sense into him. For now, just please go. Come back if you have any more information about the Major or the cache."

Uwe bit his tongue and met Patryk's scathing glare once more. He inhaled deeply to quell the fire in his chest and gave a small nod.

"Fine," he muttered. "But think hard. Matthias might very well be your only chance. I'm only a linguist, I can only help you so much."

Felix hurriedly bade him farewell before turning to his brother and beginning a heated debate on Matthias and the Jews in general. Uwe grabbed the burgundy cloak, grasping it tightly. His heart beat furiously as he stomped away from the campfire, barely resisting the urge to go back and give Patryk a good smack in the face. Even if he had been kind to him before, Uwe couldn't stand such prejudice. It was bad enough that he had to hear it every day from Brandt and his men, but to hear it even from the Reich's enemies was maddening.

He got away from the Polish camp and tarried a moment, just in case Uriel ended up needing him. Pity and resentment mixed in Uwe's mind as his thoughts jumped from the boy, to Patryk, to Matthias and his men.

Forcing Brandt out of this area may be the only way to keep Uriel safe, and Matthias' men too, thought Uwe. *I don't like betraying my country, but what we're doing just isn't right. Uriel's my main priority, anyway.*

He could only imagine the scolding his wife would give him if he somehow made it out of this unharmed. If Brandt didn't kill him for all this, then she likely would. He had gone directly against her orders, after all.

Head down. Do as they say. Be safe.

I'm sorry, darling, he thought. *I'm going to have to disappoint you this time. I just can't be Brandt's good little linguist. I just can't.*

He sighed and kicked a small bush, idly wondering if Julek's cache was right under his nose.

Hopefully, I can make sense of the note. Then I can find the cache. Please, God, let me find it. These people need weapons. They need to fight.

But they wouldn't be able to fight well if Matthias and the Poles couldn't come to an agreement. *Damn it. Damn Patryk and everyone like him! They're destroying themselves and the Jews! Poor Matthias. Poor Uriel. I can't imagine my own neighbors wishing me and my children…*

A small shuffling of leaves interrupted his thoughts. He turned and smiled down at Uriel, who offered him a smile that was slightly weaker than usual, but still all around sunny.

"Hello, little writer," Uwe said, patting the boy on the head. "Is this where you've been going every day?"

Uriel shook his head and held up his index finger. *Just this once.*

"Well, nevertheless, don't come back here," Uwe instructed. "I don't know if you heard our little argument, but many of those people don't like Jews. They might hurt you if they catch you snooping around their campsite."

Uriel nodded grimly, his smile vanishing on the spot. No doubt the boy was also thinking of what had happened to Zingdorf.

Uwe noticed that the boy was holding something at his side. Upon closer inspection, he saw that the child was clutching a small, drab wooden harp.

"Uriel!" he chortled. "Did you steal that from the Polish camp?"

The boy glanced down at the instrument before flashing the linguist his widest and most innocent smile. Uwe couldn't help but laugh. Though he would normally be upset and insist that Uriel return the stolen harp, he instead put a hand on the boy's shoulder and started to lead him back to the house.

"Well, I'll let you get away with it this time. Why a harp, though? Of all the things to take…"

Uriel just flashed one of his cryptic smiles, and before Uwe could interrogate him any further, there was a horrible clap of thunder. The child cringed and let out a peep of fear, clinging to Uwe's arm.

"Oh, dear…" sighed the linguist, looking up at the sky and noticing that the formerly friendly clouds had become thick and gray. Uriel, who was evidently afraid of thunder, started trembling something terrible, holding on to Uwe's arm as though the thunder was an old enemy that he did not wish to face alone.

"Let's run back," said Uwe. "It's going to rain soon."

The boy nodded, gripping the wooden harp tightly with one hand and grabbing Uwe's arm with the other. Uwe dragged the child away from the Polish camp and back towards the Major's house just as the sinister clouds swirled overhead and rain began to fall.

By the time they got back to the house, the rain was coming down in buckets. Uwe actually began to entertain the notion that God was once again so disgusted by the evil of the human race that He planned on wiping them all out with another Great Flood, just like in the Noah story.

Uriel was absolutely quaking with fear and cold. The thunder beat above them, forming a frightening rhythm that made the child squeak every time the sky seemed to combust. When they finally arrived at the house and Uwe ordered the boy to climb up to their room, Uriel refused to let go of the linguist's arm. Eventually the boy consented, but only after Uwe gave him the burgundy cloak that he seemed to love so much. He used the cloak as a sack so he could carry the harp he had stolen up the tree and into the room. Uwe watched him climb, twitching with fear every time the boy almost slipped. As the child climbed, though, Uwe noticed that the boy was no longer missing a shoe.

That's odd, he thought. *He must have found it while he was out today. Well, at least it seems to make climbing easier.*

Once the boy was safely inside, Uwe crawled through the first-story window and into the sitting room. He wiped his soaked glasses off so he could see properly and immediately noticed that his shoes were coated in mud. Every step he took formed a grimy shoe print in his wake. He cursed, but decided that there was nothing he could do about it except run upstairs, wash off, and try to run back down and clean up his tracks before Brandt returned.

"Horrible weather, isn't it?"

He froze at the foot of the staircase and tried his best to keep his fear from his face as he turned.

Major Brandt leaned casually against the doorway of his office, smiling in a manner that rather reminded Uwe of a wolf that had just cornered a helpless lamb. There was a terrible moment of complete silence as the Major and the linguist stared each other down, Brandt waiting for Uwe to break.

When the linguist refused to crumble, Brandt exhaled in a rather exasperated fashion, though his smile didn't wane. His eyes traveled to the mud-stained floor.

"Awfully rude of you," said Brandt. "Leaving footprints all across the floor. I thought you were tidier, Herr Litten."

"Forgive me," said Uwe, bowing his head slightly, not daring to take his eyes off the other man as he did so. He kept his voice at an even pitch, struggling not to let any anger or alarm slip into his tone. "I'll be sure to clean it up."

"That you will," said Brandt. "I didn't hear you come in through the front, Herr Litten."

"I thought I heard something in the backyard."

"So you went to investigate? Very brave. Me, if I were in that situation, I would simply call the guards. You know, the ones at the front door."

Swallowing and grinding his teeth together, Uwe looked down at his muddy shoes in pretend shame.

"All right," he sighed. "I wasn't *completely* honest."

"Honesty is always a virtue, Herr Litten," said the Major with a devious glow in his emerald eyes. "Surely you learned that during our interrogation sessions."

Resisting the almost overwhelming desire to ball his hands into furious fists, Uwe forced himself to give a small nod. "Yes. In truth, Herr Brandt, I was getting claustrophobic staying in the house. I wanted to get out for a moment. I didn't stray far, but when it started raining, well, I came back as fast as I could."

Praying that his performance was convincing enough, he looked up and into the Major's eyes. The Major, at first, was deadpan, the soft, sinister glitter in his green eyes being the only indication of his emotional state.

Then, however, his wide, welcoming smile gracefully returned to his face.

"Ah, well, why didn't you say something, little linguist?" he asked. "I could have had my men look after you."

"I didn't want to be escorted," said Uwe. "I just needed some time by myself to get some air. You understand that, don't you? I live in a small town in a rural area, so I've never had difficulty finding a place to walk and think before. But now it's different, and it's a bit overwhelming."

"Of course, of course," said the Major with a genial wave of his hand. "Nonetheless, I would advise against doing such a thing again. After all, it will be hard to gather your thoughts if one of those Polish partisans sneaks up on you and puts a bullet through your brain!"

He chortled at his own morbid joke and Uwe wasn't sure if he should offer a false chuckle or stay silent. He opted for the latter and it seemed he made the right choice. Once Brandt finished his brief bout of laughter, he became severe.

"Especially," he said, "after what they did to my men yesterday."

That was supposed to be you, Uwe thought, but he summoned as much genuine concern as he could and asked, "Are they going to be okay?"

The Major's eyes darted to the front door for a mere second, as though he was tempted to bolt from the house and go see his injured soldiers.

"I'm not sure yet," he muttered. "They are fighters, strong men, and they've gotten even stronger since…."

He seemed to remember himself as he shook his head and offered Uwe a petite smirk. "Well, never mind. I'm sure they would appreciate your concern, Herr Litten. Not to worry, I'll be sure to tell you how they are faring."

He clapped his hands together so suddenly that it made Uwe wince. His eyes sparkled like stars as he exclaimed, "Ah! That *does* remind me! Wait here a moment, little linguist!"

He retreated into his office and Uwe considered running up the stairs to escape before something else went wrong. Before he could even put his foot on the first stair, however, Brandt returned with a large box tucked under his arm.

"Here you are," said Brandt, holding the box out to the linguist, "It's a lot uglier than it was initially. One of the boys found this while they were handling the Reprisal in a Polish town and thought you would appreciate it. Made sure to wrap it up and everything, but naturally I had to tear all the ribbons off since I had to see what he was giving to you. Make sure it wasn't a grenade or bomb, though I doubt one of my boys would give you something lethal."

Uwe took it carefully, as though it really was a bomb or live grenade, and removed the lid.

He gasped in surprise and nearly threw down the box when a snarling creature scowled up at him. He sighed, however, when he realized that the ferocious face was frozen in death.

While Brandt enjoyed a few chuckles at his expense, Uwe took the gift out of the box and held it up. It was a lion pelt, about as big as Uwe when unfolded, complete with a snarling lion's face on the top. It looked like the sort of thing that a proud hunter would hang on his wall, or that a particularly decorative person would lay down as a rug.

It was also the sort of thing that Uwe's lion-loving Jürgen would adore.

"I must have let it slip that lions are your son's favorite animal," said the Major. "Have you sent that doll off to your daughters yet?"

Thinking of the poor, lonely doll that sat next to Uriel's notebook in his room made Uwe want to glare at the Major, but instead he kept his eyes locked on the lion pelt and shook his head.

"I can send the pelt and the doll off tomorrow if you like," said Brandt. "I have a box I can pack them in."

Uwe didn't even look at the Major. He stared at the pelt, wondering if whoever had owned it previously had been the one to bring the noble beast down. Had he traveled to Africa and shot the lion personally? Perhaps it had been a gift from a faraway family member. Perhaps it wasn't even real. Perhaps it was simply an ornamental piece that he or she had seen in a store window and bought on a whim, hoping to make their dreary living room look more exotic.

Either way, it was supposed to be in somebody else's home. Somebody who had been a victim of the *Ordnungspolizei's* 'Reprisal.' He couldn't imagine giving a stolen item to his sweet little son. Jürgen would love it. He would probably carry it around wherever he went. He would probably sneak it into his backpack and try to show it off to all of his friends at school.

And Uwe would never be able to live with himself if that happened, if he gave his son something that the Order Police had tainted with their touch. Something they had taken from its rightful owner because they thought they had a right to whatever they wanted, be it land, labor, or a lion's hide.

Uwe folded up the pelt and put it back into the box. He stepped forward with care, as though he was a zookeeper that was passing a piece of meat to a vicious carnivore, and placed the box at the Major's feet.

"It is very thoughtful," he said, stepping back. "But I can't accept."

The Major's eyes shifted from the box to the linguist. Uwe made sure to keep his expression calm, struggling to hold in the disgust and anger he felt roiling in his stomach.

The Major eyed him carefully, his smile morphing into a thin frown.

"Why so, Herr Litten?" he asked.

"I…I…" Uwe stumbled, trying to think of an acceptable excuse. "My…my wife is very passionate about animal rights. Like the Führer, you know. She can't stand hunters killing animals for sport. She…she wouldn't be too happy if I sent her a pelt."

"That so?" asked Brandt, and though his tone was light, his eyes betrayed his skepticism. Uwe hadn't answered fast enough. He wasn't buying it.

Uwe swallowed nervously and was about to insist that he was telling the truth, but before he could the Major's lips curled into a smile that could have made a live lion squirm.

"I disagree, Herr Litten. I'm sure your family would appreciate the pelt," he said. "Not just your boy, but your girls and your lovely, animal-loving wife as well. It would be an assurance that you're doing well. That you're staying close and following orders. That you're well-liked by me and my men. That you're *keeping your head down*. That's how your wife put it, yes? Very intelligent woman. I would heed her advice, little linguist."

Uwe's nostrils flared. He almost wanted to take back the pelt and throw it in the Major's face.

"You were listening to me and my wife talk!" he growled.

"Well, I realize that *you* thought she was talking quietly, but my hearing has always been…"

The Major prattled on about his near-perfect perception and all Uwe wanted to do was stomp his foot on the grimy ground and cry, "Enough!" He wanted to berate the Major for trying to use his own wife's words against him. He wanted to declare that he would never accept a stolen gift. He wanted to shout at the Major, to call him what he was: an arrogant thief.

But all he could do was listen, his breathing becoming laborious as he felt anger seep into his stomach and fill his lungs. Every little statement that he wanted to make but couldn't struck at his heart and he could feel his organ pound furiously, begging him to lighten its load by saying something, anything, to make the Major understand that he would not be accepting the pelt.

He inhaled, forced his furious thoughts to cool, and managed to say in a firm but respectful tone, "Major, I just can't accept. It isn't right."

The Major stopped bragging and for a moment the pitter-patter of rain on the rooftop was all that could be heard. Brandt stood, stunned into silence, taken aback by the disobedience of the normally docile and easily intimidated linguist.

At last, the Major moved. He bent down, keeping his narrowed eyes locked on the linguist, and scooped up the box at his feet.

"If that's the way you feel, Herr Litten," he said. "I suppose my Hans will appreciate this, even if he prefers tigers."

Uwe's eyes threatened to flicker towards the picture of Brandt's wife and son, but he kept his pupils pinned on the glowering Major.

"Furthermore," said the Major, "we have another operation tomorrow. We need to clear out a small Jewish village—Haldrets, I believe it's called. I expect you to be awake and ready to depart no later than ten in the morning."

Normally Uwe's survival instincts would encourage him to silently agree to Brandt's terms, but the urge to keep his head down was strangely silent. All he could think about was the blood of the murdered man from the last operation, the mountain of loot that the policemen amassed, and the somber-eyed Jewish man whose beard was nearly burned off moving his lips to form three words: *God bless you.*

"No."

Brandt had been ready to return to his office when the single word fell from the linguist's lips like a pound of bricks. He turned. Uwe, knowing better than to stand his ground for too long against the beast that was an angered Brandt, was already walking up the stairs.

"Excuse me?" said the Major, umbrage and pure surprise layering his tone. He might as well have said, 'How dare you defy me?'

Once he was safely at the top of the staircase, Uwe turned and looked down at the Major. Having the high ground gave him a small burst of courage, enough to respond without stuttering like a fool.

"I'm sorry," he said, though he truly wasn't. "But I just can't handle an operation like that again. Resettlement or not, you and your men are stealing those people's homes and possessions. I can't help you with that. Interrogating a captured enemy is one thing, but I can't help you hurt innocent women and children."

"The Jews are hardly angels," retorted Brandt in a manner that was astoundingly composed considering the toxic brew that was boiling in his eyes.

"True. Nobody is an angel. But you said it yourself: the Jews are humans. I don't support treating humans like animals, so I can't help you with any more of those operations. I'm sorry."

"But we need a translator!" said Brandt, startling Uwe by sounding more desperate than incensed.

"You got by without me before, Major Brandt," replied Uwe impassively. "I'm sure you won't have a very hard time getting by without me tomorrow."

Careful not to fully turn his back on the Major, he scurried to his room and slammed the door behind him.

"Herr Litten!" he heard Brandt shout as he looked over at the trembling Uriel and desperately gestured for the boy to give him the key. "Don't you walk away from me! Don't disobey me like this, Herr Litten!"

The child hesitated for only a moment to flinch as another stroke of thunder echoed outside. He then fished through his pocket and pulled out a small golden key. Uwe was idly confused at first since he had been sure that the key was silver and not gold, but he ignored the key's color and swiftly locked the door. Both German and Jew slowly backed away, terrified that the Major might march up the stairs and break through the wooden door.

He didn't. Instead, the Major shouted, "Fine then, Herr Litten! If you wish to be a *coward* and a *weakling,* then that's your decision! I suppose you aren't a *soldier,* after all!"

His voice became slightly softer as he cried, "But I *am* a soldier, and my men are soldiers! We have duties here, Herr Litten! Not *pleasant* duties, but *necessary* duties! If you won't come with us tomorrow, you're making this harder for us and your country! We're all Germans, Herr Litten! Consider that!"

With that, the thoroughly frustrated Major gripped the box that held the lion pelt and marched back into his office. He needed a drink from his flask to muddle his maddened mind a bit before he prepared to mail the lion pelt to Hamburg.

Once his heart stopped racing with worry and he was certain that Brandt wouldn't be bursting into his room tonight, Uwe settled down on the side of his bed and took out the note that Nacek had given him. Uriel had taken his rain-stained cloak and retreated into the closet, no doubt to cower in fear while the storm continued its tirade outside. Uwe had considered going to the closet and trying to coax him out, but the child wasn't being troublesome and wasn't in any danger. It would be best, the linguist decided, to leave him be and let him come to terms with his own phobias. Uwe couldn't always coddle him.

Besides, the child's absence gave the linguist the time and solitude he required to get to work on deciphering the strange note.

He unfolded the crumpled paper and leaned close to the light, examining the faded ink script and trying to uncover a pattern. It seemed like just a random assortment of foreign letters that formed no words, but he was certain that Crazy Old Julek, epithet aside, hadn't just scribbled nonsense onto the page. It had to mean something.

Uwe studied the paper for half an hour, testing different patterns and potential codes in his head before he came to a discovery. He found that when he crossed out every German and Russian letter, the remaining letters formed a sentence. He chuckled.

"Well, makes sense," he said, writing the leftover letters down at the bottom of the page. "Cross out the enemies."

He looked down at the letters and after a bit of racking his brain for correct pronunciations, he translated the clue.

THE CAT RAISES THE ROCK

His triumphant smile became crooked with confusion and he checked his translation over three times to make sure he hadn't made a mistake. After three inspections, however, he could safely confirm that his translation was correct. The clue was right in front of him.

It just made absolutely no sense.

"The cat raises the rock..." he muttered. A riddle of some sort? Perhaps there was a landmark or a nearby town that was named after a cat. Were that the case, he could ask Matthias about it. Being a native, he would likely know.

He glanced at the closet and smiled as he entertained the notion of asking Uriel. The boy wandered about so much. He would undoubtedly be familiar with the area and its various landmarks. Uwe nodded and considered opening the closet door, but then he shook his head. Not now. It was late, and if the poor boy wasn't asleep, then he would probably be too terrified to focus on anything but the frightening blasts of thunder that continued to resound through the region.

Tomorrow, Uwe decided. He folded up the paper and placed it safely under the doll he had picked up in the little Jewish village. Tomorrow he would ask. For now, his eyes were hurting. He needed some sleep.

It sounded like the sky was exploding.

Uriel half expected to open his eyes and see the roof in shambles, but every time he raised an eyelid, he found himself safely curled up on his bed of socks in the closet, Elijah's Mantle wrapped tightly around him. Even as the holy aura gently cradled him, his heart was on edge and his mind refused to submit to slumber so long as the storm was still raging outside.

Another mighty *boom* struck Uriel's ears. His fingernails dug into the sacred fabric of Elijah's Mantle, but it just wasn't enough. He wanted Papa to tell him a story about storms that would make him feel better. He wanted Mama to hold him and sing her song so that he could focus on her voice instead of the destructive claps outside.

His eyes burned with tears and his throat tightened as sobs wracked his small body. Every bang made his heartbeat stop for a second before resuming at a frighteningly rapid pace. He thought his eardrums were about to burst, and the very last thing he wanted was to lose his hearing when he already lacked a voice.

He wondered if Uwe was able to sleep with all this terrible thunder.

That stray inquiry quickly became a torturous curiosity that he knew wouldn't leave him be until he peeked outside of his closet. He slowly set Elijah's Mantle aside and stood, his legs wobbling so much that it was a wonder he didn't collapse.

It was dark, and only the flashes of light that managed to slip through the closed curtains brightened the room to any considerable degree. Uriel opened the door a centimeter wider so that he could see his friend. Uwe was indeed asleep, though he was tossing and turning so much that Uriel had to take a small, cautious step out of the closet so he could see clearly enough to confirm this.

Almost the instant he ventured from the safety of the closet, the loudest thunderclap yet crashed across the countryside. Had he dared to look outside, he knew he would have seen a great ripple of light as pure fury from Heaven struck the earth in the form of a lightning bolt.

His heart did a backflip, but rather than retreat into the closet to curl up with Elijah's Mantle he dashed forward and grabbed Uwe's shoulder, shaking him desperately. Uwe awoke with a flinch and a gasp, looking up with panic flooding his azure eyes, as though he expected to see Major Brandt towering above him with a loaded gun.

Instead, his eyes fell upon the sobbing child's tear-stained face. The thunder snarled outside, and the child sat beside Uwe, burying his face into the linguist's shoulder, weeping wildly.

It took a moment for the groggy German to realize what was going on, but once he did, he placed a hand on the wailing child's head.

"Hush, Uriel!" he hissed, gently stroking the boy's hair, trying to sound firm and calming at the same time. "You can cry, but don't be so loud! Brandt might hear!"

The boy (who found it rather ironic that he of all people was being too loud) nodded and bit down on his lip to muffle his sobs. It was a wonder that he didn't flood the room with his tears. He was so scared and so sad.

He felt much better when Uwe gave him a small and slightly awkward embrace. At first, the linguist seemed moderately uncomfortable, but he quickly relaxed and settled into comforting the crying child.

"It *is* a terrible storm out there, Uriel," muttered Uwe, his eyes wandering to the window. He was silent for a moment before he quietly mused, "Do you think God is angry?"

Uriel stole a quick glance at the window and sniffled, giving a small shrug before hiding his face once more.

"He has a lot to be angry about. Maybe He'll flood the world again, like in the Noah story. Or at least just Germany. We deserve some sort of…"

Uriel shook his head fervently and put his index finger on Uwe's chest, pointing right to his heart and giving a small, scared smile.

Uwe couldn't repress a chuckle. "You think I have a good heart?"

Uriel nodded. Uwe's mind briefly brought up Brandt and his constant sneers about the linguist's good heart. The child, though, was completely genuine, his eyes glistening gently as he looked up at his guardian.

"Thank you, Uriel," sighed Uwe. "From you, that means a lot."

Another burst of thunder, another crack of lightning. The child squeaked in terror and hugged Uwe, a series of sobs causing his body to shake.

"It's all right, Uriel, it's just a storm. Shhh, shhh. You *are* a strange child, you know. Scared of thunder, but not Major Brandt."

But then, all children had odd fears. Jürgen was terrified of beetles (not spiders or flies or any other creepy-crawly creature, just beetles). Whenever his son spotted such an offending insect, he too would burst into tears and run to Uwe, seeking comfort and protection.

"It's all right, Uriel. Just a storm. It'll pass. Don't cry, shhh. It's all right…"

THUNDER

Thunder didn't scare him.

Neither did lightning. When he was very small, before he even knew what death and destruction were, he would peek out his window so he could see the brilliant bolts fall from Heaven. He imagined God wielding the lightning bolts like throwing daggers, tossing them down to warn the humans below of the storm's severity and creating a dazzling display of light.

Thunder and lightning didn't frighten him. It was what the thunder and lightning portended that he came to fear.

Zingdorf was a tiny village, a poor village. A village that couldn't afford buildings and houses and shops made of stone. Everything but the cobblestone street was made of wood.

And lightning was merciless. It couldn't see the struggles of the little village and choose not to strike.

It wasn't the thunder or lightning that scared him. It was the memories. Memories of a crash that would shake the whole town. Memories of the horrible screams that would inevitably follow. Memories of peeking out his window to see whose house was ablaze this time. Memories of praying that he wouldn't be next, praying that the lightning would spare him and his family.

That was the first time he felt smoke and ash mount an attack against his throat and lungs. When he stood near the smoldering house and listened to the wails of the poor woman who had lost everything to the storm. His father hustled him back into his thankfully intact home before he could stare much longer.
"Do not gawk at another's misfortune, Uriel," he muttered as he pulled his son away from the burning house while the volunteer firefighters of the village scurried here and there, trying to find enough water to put out the fire before it

could spread. Mama ran to give them their water barrel (which, fortunately, was then devoid of fish).

Uriel craned his neck, gazing intently at the fire even though seeing it made his chest clench up and his heart twist itself into several knots.

Sooner or later, the lightning would find him too.

But lightning, at least, was easily sated. One house, one building, that's all the flames would take.

Not like the hateful fire that the mob started one cold night, while Papa was out visiting his friends and Uriel was asleep.

Not like the fire that made sure Uriel never saw his father again.

Not like the fire that barely gave Uriel enough time to grab his precious golden notebook before Mama pulled him from their flame-filled home.

Not like the fire that caused a stampede that separated him from his mother and left him standing in the middle of the burning town.

Alone.

It was well past midnight when Uriel finally woke, huddled beside the now-asleep Uwe. The storm was still brewing outside, but its anger had abated. It simmered with the occasional crackle of thunder, but otherwise it stayed silent. Only the pitter-patter of rain against the window served as a constant reminder that the storm was not yet finished.

Although Uriel hesitated to go out in the storm, he had lounged about in Uwe's room too long. He was finishing his third mission tonight.

Before he could do that, though, he needed just one last thing. Now that it was late, much too late for anybody except an Angel-Finder to be awake, he could finally get what he needed.

He slipped out of Uwe's slack embrace and carefully crept back to the closet. Once there, he grabbed Elijah's Mantle and David's Harp, putting the Harp on the Mantle and grabbing the holy garment like a sack. He patted his pocket to make sure he had the Boundless Key and once he was certain nothing was missing, he scuttled to the window and crawled out onto the slippery branch.

Climbing down the tree was rather difficult while it was still drizzling, and the normally rough branch was so slick that it was only by the grace of God that Uriel didn't fall and break his neck. The boy made it down, unscathed and thoroughly soaked. He ignored the water filling up his shoes and scurried not into the woods, but to the front of the house.

The guards were not at the front door. Instead, they were sitting in a car, looking terribly bored. Uriel smirked and tapped on the windshield six times, causing the nearly asleep policemen to flinch and sit upright. Satisfied with the scare he had given the wicked men, Uriel hurried down the road, leaving them to quiver in the car.

It took a bit of scouting, but he found the house that the rest of the Germans occupied. It was even bigger than the Major's, a manor in its own right, and Uriel had to wonder who had lived there previously. He knew that there were several wealthy gentiles in the area, but he couldn't imagine why somebody with as much wealth as the house's former occupant would want to live in such a poor and isolated area.

Either way, sneaking into the house wasn't very difficult. The doors and windows were all locked, but since he had the Boundless Key with him, that was hardly an obstacle. He did as the birds had said and tapped the lock with the Key. A small streak of golden light moved from the Key to the lock and there was a quiet click as the door was unlocked.

He slipped in and shut the door behind him. The house was so dark that the boy had difficulty finding the staircase. Once he located it, though, he scurried up the stairs and listened closely.

Finally, he heard the sound of men snoring. He smiled and followed the obnoxious noise.

He came to a large room that six policemen shared. One of them had taken the bed while the others were curled up on sleeping mats. Two or three snored, but the others had apparently gotten used to that since they didn't even stir.

Moving carefully (even if he *was* invisible, he still didn't want the policemen to wake up and possibly get in his way), Uriel started to rifle through the soldiers' bags, putting the items back when he couldn't find what he wanted but not being particularly precise. The Germans wouldn't think that a little Jewish boy had snuck into their abode and searched their possessions. They would be more likely to blame each other, and if that happened, good. A bickering batch of Germans would be easy for Matthias and the partisans to defeat.

Finally, Uriel peeked under the bed and grinned widely when he saw what he was looking for: a jewelry box.

He pulled it out and his eyes danced with delight as they fell upon the dazzling diamonds and glittering golden adornments.

He paused only to admire his find before reaching in and grabbing every golden chain he could see.

Once he had what he needed, Uriel ran back to the Major's house. He was more than relieved to find that the birds were already perched on the branches of a nearby tree, snoozing with their heads tucked under their wings, no doubt waiting for the morning so they could lead the Angel-Finder to the Golden Cavern.

He surprised them by kicking the tree until they finally felt the branch beneath them shake and awoke. He mimed almost desperately for them to take him to the Golden Cavern. The sun would be up soon. The stars would disappear. If that happened before he could complete his quest, he wouldn't be able to give Samael the Golden Tree until tomorrow. The Jews couldn't wait for their Guardian Angel.

The birds hesitated. "Angel-Finder…are you certain? Are you ready to go now? The room will turn you to gold if you touch anything, do you not…?"

He nodded and waved energetically, his eyes nervously flickering to the sky just to be sure that stars still dotted the darkened heavens.

Though he could sense their apprehension, the birds obeyed and alighted from their branch, fluttering and chirping for the Angel-Finder to follow.

"Remember the Akha!" one of them cried once they started to get close. "Do you have David's Harp?"

The boy nodded, gripping Elijah's Mantle and feeling the weight of the silver instrument that had belonged to the noble king.

The birds stopped at a wall of bushes.

"The Cavern is just past here," whispered the doves. "Be cautious, Angel-Finder. The Akha is awake."

Uriel nodded and pulled the Harp out of the Mantle. He carefully tucked Elijah's Mantle under his arm and slowly stepped through the bushes.

The Cavern itself was small and rather unimpressive. He couldn't imagine that there were mountains of gold in there, enough gold to tempt many an adventurous man to run in without thinking. It hardly looked bigger than Uwe's room.

He only spared the small cavern a glance before his eyes shifted to a giant, green-scaled body that was wound around the cave.

He heard a hiss. The body moved.

It slithered around the cavern and the hissing grew louder and louder until, finally, the great snake's face appeared.

It raised its head, gazing down at the little boy with sickly yellow eyes. Its thin pupils dilated subtly. Its forked tongue popped out of its giant mouth as it let out a curious hiss.

It was even larger than the White Eagle. It could have *swallowed* the White Eagle. Uriel would be nothing more than a crumb to it. Not even an appetizer. He wouldn't satisfy the mighty snake's hunger in the slightest. Its stomach would hardly notice the presence of such a morsel.

Uriel was so fixated on the great snake's face that he hardly perceived its body beginning to circle him. He finally noticed, but when he averted his eyes in order to look at the long body that was surrounding him, the snake let out an unearthly hiss, baring its man-sized fangs. He quickly looked back at the Akha's face, swallowing nervously as he realized that it was trying to trap him, keep him focused on its face so that it could ensnare him and wouldn't have to give chase if he wisely chose to flee.

He quickly raised David's Harp, his fingers trembling as he sensed the Akha's body coming closer and closer, and clumsily played a few notes.

The Akha stopped moving. Its body stopped encircling the child. The mighty snake cocked its head, its yellow eyes focusing on the silver harp.

Inhaling deeply, the boy plucked at the strings a few more times, creating a simple rhythm. His golden eyes widened when he realized what tune he was unconsciously bringing forth from the Harp.

His mother's lullaby. The same one she sang to him every night.

A warm sensation settled in his stomach as he played, hardly feeling the strings touch his fingers. He could hear her sweet, lovely voice and feel her hand affectionately stroking his hair as she lulled him to sleep.

Sleep, my little bird

Shut your little eyes

Eye-lu-lu-lu

Eye-lu-lu

The Akha hissed sleepily, its giant eyelids drooping until they finally fell. It lowered its head and used its own body for a pillow. Its breathing became gentle as it listened to the heavenly sound of David's Harp, the tender lullaby of Uriel's mother.

Sleep soundly, my child

Sleep and be well

Eye-lu-lu-lu

Eye-lu-lu

Uriel finished the song. Her voice faded. He smiled and wiped a tear from his eye.

Thank you, Mama.

He crawled over the Akha's body, careful not to wake the slumbering serpent. The Akha hissed softly in its sleep. A serpent's snore. It somehow didn't sound so bad.

Uriel made it past the sleeping snake and to the Golden Cavern's door. He put David's Harp down on the ground and took out the Boundless Key. The child tapped on the lock of the wrought-iron door (he had imagined that the Golden Cavern would have a more impressive entrance). Once the amber light from the Key caused the lock to click, he turned the handle and threw it open.

His jaw dropped.

The inside of the Golden Cavern was glorious. As big as Major Brandt's house, with mountains of gold piled high to the ceiling. Golden items of every sort. Golden vials and pots and vases. Golden clothes and chairs and desks. Golden seashells and bricks and millions upon millions of golden coins.

How a cavern that had seemed so small on the outside could be so gigantic on the inside he didn't know, but Uriel paused for a moment to take in the marvelous sight before his pupils scoured the Cavern, trying to find the tree.

But as his eyes wandered about the lair of precious metal, he saw several golden forms that made his amazement turn to nausea. Figures that were kneeling on the ground or crouched by the golden heaps, their frozen fingers barely brushing against the treasure, their metallic faces contorted in pain.

People. Men whose greed had overcome them. Men who had been turned into the very thing they craved: gold.

If he so much as touched any of the twinkling, tempting treasures in the Cavern, he too would be trapped there forever.

Even the floor of the Cavern was made of gold. Several humanoid statues stood by the Cavern's entrance, having been transformed before they could even touch the Cavern's loot. Merely stepping on the ground without any sort of shield against the Cavern's terrible power had sealed their fate.

Uriel took in as much air as his lungs could hold and took off his shoes. He knelt down beside the Cavern's threshold and pulled out the golden chains he had taken from the German soldiers. He picked up his left shoe and meticulously wrapped the chains around it, covering it with chain after chain until it was covered in gold. He figured that, though the Cavern turned flesh into gold, it couldn't turn gold into gold. The golden chains around his shoes would, he hoped, let him walk on the Cavern's precious and potentially deadly floor.

Once he covered his other shoe in gold, Uriel tied Elijah's Mantle around his neck like a cape and stood. He looked down at the golden floor and, forcing courage into his heart and legs, gingerly reached his foot out and touched the golden ground with his gold-wrapped toe.

When his skin remained soft and didn't morph into precious metal, he released a sigh and stepped onto the floor.

As soon as he entered the Cavern, he spotted it. All the way across the Cavern, at the end of a long aisle, he could see the Golden Tree glittering gloriously, inviting him to rashly rush right towards his ultimate prize.

But he knew that he needed to be cautious. The path to the Golden Tree was littered with golden trunks and boxes and trinkets. The eternally frozen men served as a grisly warning of what would happen if he tripped or touched anything.

Wrapping Elijah's Mantle around himself, the child slowly moved forward, keeping his head down and being sure to watch where he was going, careful to only touch the golden items with his gold-covered shoes. He stepped over an odd golden statue (a man from the waist up, a horse from the waist down; his mind started whirring with potential stories he could write about such a creature) and cringed as he nearly bumped his forehead on a golden lamppost. He stepped back and gasped, gripping the Mantle and listening to the comforting sound of his heart hammering. It was an assurance that he was still flesh and blood.

Vaguely wondering who on earth would want a golden lamppost, he continued, wincing when he drew close to the men-turned-metal and saw their wide golden eyes, their mouths open in a last cry of agony. He shivered, but forced himself to focus on the floor, praying to God in his mind.

Sh'ma Yisrael Adonai Eloheinu Adonai Echad....Sh'ma Yisrael Adonai Eloheinu Adonai Echad....Sh'ma Yisrael...

By the time he reached the Golden Tree, Uriel decided he hated gold.

Still, the Tree was beautiful, even when compared to the Cavern's other wonders. It looked more like a sapling than a full-grown tree, only reaching Uriel's chest, but it was brilliant. Its leaves shimmered and swayed, seemingly alive despite being made of metal. Buds made of glittering white diamonds dotted the Tree's limbs, causing it to sparkle almost haughtily.

Uriel untied Elijah's Mantle and reached down, being careful not to kneel lest his knee touch the Cavern's cursed ground. Using the Mantle, he picked up the Golden Tree. Relief once more came to his heart when he lifted the Golden Tree off the ground without being turned to gold. Elijah's Mantle, being a holy garment, was also immune to the Cavern's power.

Getting back to the other side while carrying the Golden Tree was even more nerve-racking than getting to the tree had been. He could hardly watch where he was going while carrying the surprisingly hefty tree, and he had to be careful to only touch it with Elijah's Mantle. It wouldn't be safe to let his skin brush against the Golden Tree until it was out of the Cavern.

He panted and felt sweat slide down his cheek. He was so tired. He wanted nothing more than to put down the heavy tree for just one second and sit down, let his aching arms rest.

No, no, no! I have to get out of here! he thought, gritting his teeth and putting all of his focus and energy into getting safely back to the door.

At last, after what seemed like an eternity, he reached the exit.

As he exited the Golden Cavern, he was surprised to find that the Golden Tree went from being a terrible burden to being light as a feather. Nonetheless, he dropped the Golden Tree and collapsed onto the grass, taking deep breaths and waiting for his throbbing arms to regain their strength.

The birds fluttered cautiously over the Akha's still-slumbering form and perched on the Golden Tree's thin branches. They waited a moment for the boy to catch his breath. When the child lifted his head and smiled wearily at them, they gave him several soft, admiring twitters.

"Wonderful work, Angel-Finder," said the birds, their beady eyes nervously darting towards the Akha even as they praised the child. "Very clever, using the golden chains in such a manner."

Uriel smiled and gave a small bow to thank them for their compliment. He took the golden chains off of his shoes, stuffing them back into his pocket where he wouldn't have to look at them. He was sorely tempted to throw them into the Cavern just because the sight of gold sickened him now, but he decided not to. He still had two missions to go, and he might need the golden chains again.

The child collected Elijah's Mantle, David's Harp, and the Golden Tree and put them aside. He looked back at the Golden Cavern and shook his head. If only there were a way to shut the door forever and be sure that no poor fortune-seeker found this wretched trap.

All he could do, however, was close the door and tap the lock with the Boundless Key, sealing it shut for the moment. He gathered his things and prayed that the Akha would frighten future wanderers away before they could enter the cursed Cavern.

Samael was stunned.

He tried to hide it, to make sure that the only emotion on his face was hatred, but Uriel could see in the Angel of Death's amethyst eyes that he was stunned.

Stunned that the boy was still made of soft skin. Stunned that only his eyes were gold. He hadn't expected the boy to make it past the third challenge. He had thought the boy would either give up or foolishly try anyway and end up in the stomach of the Akha or forever frozen in the Golden Cavern.

Instead, the boy arrived just as the black sky began to turn orange and the last stars faded from sight. He arrived tired, with sweat on his brow and dark circles under his eyes, but triumphant as he shoved the Golden Tree into the Angel of Death's arms and impatiently gestured for Samael to give him his next quest.

For a moment, Samael was so stunned that he couldn't speak. He wondered if this was how Uriel felt: desiring to say a million things but being unable to produce even a measly sentence.

Samael, however, found his voice, but even when he did, he could only use it to mutter two words. His fourth request.

"Joseph's Goblet."

And then he was gone, slipping into the shadows just as the last star disappeared in the wake of the sun's majestic appearance. Uriel glowered at the spot where the Angel of Death had been standing, annoyed and surprised. Samael would normally sneer at him, or at the very least get angry. He had expected the Angel of Death to curse him. Instead, the dark angel had been almost alarmingly direct and quiet.

I guess, thought Uriel, turning and striding back towards Brandt's house, *he didn't expect a Jewish boy to get this far. Hashem, please let me get further.*

Uriel looked up at the sky, where the stars had disappeared, replaced with the glorious light of day. He inhaled deeply, and a smile came to his face as he took a moment to admire the sunrise and hope that today would be fruitful.

LIGHT

At night, there were three sources of light. The moon and stars that Hashem provided, and the lamps lit by Shylock.

Nobody knew where Shylock, Zingdorf's beloved lamplighter, had gotten his nickname. Everybody had called him that seemingly since the day he was born. It wasn't his real name, everybody knew that, but how he had acquired the epithet was the subject of many anecdotes.

Some said that he had gotten it while visiting a Polish town, where a little Polish boy had laughed at seeing the religious Jew and called him a 'Shylock.' A few others said that he had been in a bookstore, came across a play with a Jewish character by that name, and liked it so much that he started calling himself that.

Whether or not those rumors were true, however, Shylock wore his name with pride. He liked it much more than his birth name, which was so long and hard to pronounce that even Uriel couldn't recall what it was.

And while his name suggested stinginess and deceit, Shylock was anything but selfish. Although he was a nocturnal soul, and thus was rarely seen except when he was sitting bleary-eyed at synagogue, he always greeted everyone with a smile. What little spare money he had was always given to the poor, and anybody traveling late at night could always depend on Shylock and his old glass lamp to guide them safely to their destination.

The night that Uriel was born was pitch black. The moon had hidden its luminescent face and charcoal clouds obscured the stars. Fortunately, Shylock had heard Mama's screams of pain and ran to their door, offering to light the way to the doctor's office.

Papa and a few friendly neighbors had carried Mama. Led by Shylock's lamp, they made it to the doctor's house. Only an hour later, Uriel was born, healthy and silent.

Mama and Papa had been so grateful that they named their newborn son in the lamplighter's honor. Uriel, Hebrew for 'Light of God.'

Uriel was told many times of how Shylock had saved him and his mother, and of course he was thankful. He always made a card for Shylock on every holiday, and whenever he saw the lamplighter, he made sure to greet him with his brightest smile.

When he started writing, he began to feel a kinship with Shylock. The lamplighter went from lamppost to lamppost, using his own precious lamp to carefully light each and every one until the entire street glowed. He always seemed so happy while he was doing it, as though spreading light gave him the greatest feeling in the world.

Perhaps, Uriel thought, Shylock felt the same way he did when he wrote a story. Bringing light and life to a dark, blank page and continuing on until the spark in his mind died out and the pages glowed with words.

At one point, he even considered going to Shylock and becoming his apprentice. Being a lamplighter wasn't nearly as lucrative as being a shoemaker, but if he could find a profession that felt anything like bringing life to lifeless pages, he would be happy.

Uriel planned on asking Shylock about a potential apprenticeship after his bar mitzvah, when he would officially become a man.

But he never got the chance. One day, he woke up to the sound of great metal machines roaring overhead, causing the roofs to shake and causing the Stork's abandoned nest on top of the synagogue to finally fall.

The Germans were invading.

Zingdorf was such an insignificant town that it hardly got any attention from the German troops. A few passed through demanding supplies, but at first that was all.

"When the Germans invaded during the Great War," he heard Mama whispering to Papa one night, "they were very kind, very civilized. I'm sure all will be well."

Papa, though, responded grimly. "Many things have changed since then."

Only days after he eavesdropped on that conversation, Uriel woke in the middle of the night to the unfamiliar sound of dogs barking and people screaming. When he dared to look out the window, he saw men in dark clothes ramming on doors and pulling people out of houses. He ran to his parents' room and, much to his distress, found Papa missing.

"He's hiding, little bird," Mama had whispered, holding him close and kissing his forehead. "They're arresting men, I think. I don't know why...we've done nothing wrong..."

The night continued on torturously until daylight finally broke and the Germans left the little village, having fulfilled whatever quota of Jewish men they were supposed to arrest.

Papa crawled out from under some loose floorboards once Mama assured him that the soldiers were gone. They insisted that Uriel stay in the house, but the boy's curiosity wouldn't leave him be until he stepped outside for just a moment to see what damage had been done.

The first thing he heard was weeping. The mothers, daughters, and sons of the men who had been taken were wailing to the Heavens, praying to Hashem, begging Him to bring their loved ones back.

The first thing he saw, however, was Shylock, his sparkling eyes dulled by death.

The lamplighter was sitting up against a lamppost, his eyes wide and his mouth agape. Perhaps his last breath had been used to gasp in shock. His precious lamp *lay uselessly at his side, its glass shattered. Several shards were stuck in his hands and chest.*

Why the Germans had killed the kindly lamplighter was a mystery. Perhaps he had stood up for the men being taken away, perhaps he ended up being part of their quota, or perhaps they just decided that any Jew who brought light and hope needed to be dealt with.

But whatever the reason, the lamplighter had been extinguished.

Horrified and heartbroken, Uriel wailed and ran back into the house, right into his parents' arms.

10.

Major Brandt was not having a very good morning.

First, he had the headache of last-minute preparations, being sure that everything was organized and everybody knew what to do (and, more importantly, what *not* to do) during the operation. Then he had to break up an argument between a few of his men. Apparently one of them was missing a mass of golden chains that he had swiped during the last operation, and he was certain that his roommates had committed the theft.

Once Brandt got them to stop shouting at one another (though glares were still exchanged and he could tell that it would take longer than a morning to get them back on speaking terms), there was the matter of the linguist.

He had thought---well, he had *hoped*---the little linguist would come to his senses by the morning and agree to help with the operation. Unfortunately, Herr Litten was more hard-headed than a metallic mule. No matter how much begging, coaxing, and threatening Brandt did, the linguist refused to even open his door.

"I'm warning you, Herr Litten!" cried Brandt, banging on the door three more times. "You're refusing to follow orders!"

The linguist, after a lengthy period of complete silence, finally spoke. "As you said last night, Herr Major, *I* am not a soldier."

"You are a German and you're refusing to aid a soldier during a time of war!" Brandt replied, anger almost making him bark like a furious hound. "That's *treason*, Herr Litten!"

There was a moderate pause and Brandt smirked. Litten knew what a charge of treason could do to a man in the Reich. Perhaps that accusation would make him snap out of this bout of stupidity.

Then, quietly enough that Brandt had to put his ear to the door to hear properly, the linguist countered, "You're the only trai..."

Uwe seemed to realize what he was saying and silenced himself before he could complete his retort. Nonetheless, though it took a moment for the incomplete comeback to register in the Major's mind, he could surmise what the linguist had intended to say. All the Major could do was let out a half furious and half incredulous, "*What?*"

"You can break down the door and drag me to the village, Herr Major," the linguist said, and Brandt could practically hear him obstinately holding his head high. "But you can't control my tongue. You can't force me to translate for you, Herr Major."

For a moment, Brandt was tempted to take Uwe up on his offer and break down the door, but he took a deep breath and thought better of it. He was no brainless barbarian and wouldn't act as such. Besides, the linguist had a point. Short of aiming a gun in Uwe's mouth (which was an option, but not one that Brandt wanted to hastily resort to) there was no proper way to force him to do what they wished. In his current mood Uwe would likely be an unreliable translator anyway, and the last thing Brandt needed was even more disorder.

Turning to his men, he tersely said, "Fine then. Come along, boys."

"But, Uncle Günter..." one of them began to object, his eyes darting to the linguist's door.

"Forget him," said the Major, "We've managed without a translator before, we'll manage today. Come now, we're behind schedule."

With that, Brandt and his men turned and left the linguist to his own devices. As he passed by his office, however, Brandt spotted the package he had sealed last night.

"Ah, right!" he cried, smacking his forehead and chuckling at his own forgetfulness. He wanted to send the lion pelt as soon as possible and so he ran to grab the package. As he exited the house, he handed it to one of his men.

"Make sure this goes in the mail truck today," he said.

"Of course, Uncle Günter," said the guard, taking the box from Brandt. "What's in here?"

"A present for my son," replied the Major. "Not much time to explain. Stay alert today. Check the backyard every once in a while. Make sure our little linguist doesn't go wandering about the forest."

"Yes, sir! Good luck with the operation today."

"Thank you," sighed Brandt, making his way to his car and rubbing the bridge of his nose, already sensing a migraine's approach. "I have a distinct feeling that I'm going to need plenty of luck today."

Soon after the Major and his men left, Uwe told Uriel he had to leave.

"I need to ask Matthias about this damned note," muttered the linguist, tucking the letter into his pocket. He glanced warily out the window and made sure that the curtains were closed once he saw one of the guards walk through the backyard. "But more importantly, I need to convince him to lead the Poles. It won't be easy, but it might be our only chance to get out of this safely. I've really been digging my own grave since I got here."

Uriel glanced down at his shoes, his cheeks reddening with guilt. Uwe noticed this and smiled softly.

"No, no, not you," he said, gently gripping the boy's shoulder. "I'm glad I decided to hide you."

The boy raised his head and smiled, his golden eyes glittering.

"Ah, Uriel," said Uwe. "I don't suppose you know the meaning of the phrase, *'The cat raises the rock'*, do you? Is there a landmark nearby that's named after a cat? Or is that an old riddle or story of some sort?"

The boy, flummoxed, shook his head.

"That's all right. Maybe Matthias will know. I'll figure it out, eventually."

Uriel grinned optimistically and gave Uwe a small pat on the shoulder, as though to communicate that he had faith in him. Uwe chuckled and thanked him for his confidence.

"Listen, though," said Uwe, gesturing to the window. "If you go outside today, you need to be very careful. There's a guard circling the house. I'm going to slip past him, but you'll need to be very, very cautious climbing down the tree, all right? It's a big house, so you'll have some time before he circles back to the backyard, but move quickly and make sure you're not seen."

Uriel nodded obediently.

"Good boy," Uwe said, affectionately tousling the child's hair before running to the door. He looked back at the boy.

"Got the key?" he asked. The child pulled out the Boundless Key and held it up for the linguist to see.

"Good," said Uwe, opening the door and stepping out. "Be sure to lock the door behind me. I promise I'll be back soon. Stay safe!"

With that, he shut the door and Uriel ran to peek out the window, holding his breath and praying that the wicked patrolman wouldn't spot Uwe.

Fortunately, once the guard exited the backyard Uwe skittered out of the house and into the woods, disappearing behind the thicket. As soon as he was gone, Uriel opened the curtains so he would notice when the birds arrived to give him word on Joseph's Goblet.

He didn't want to start on a new story since he had a feeling that the birds would arrive any minute, and he didn't like to stop when he was in the middle of writing. Instead, he perused his old stories and tried to select one for him and Uwe to read once night arrived.

Just as he finished reading through one of his early stories, he heard a quadruplet of chirps. He quickly set the golden notebook down next to the Adina-like doll on the nightstand and scurried to the window, flashing the four doves a welcoming grin.

"Good day, Angel-Finder!" twittered the birds. "We've heard of Samael's latest challenge. It's quite odd, in fact."

Uriel quirked his head to the side. *How so?*

"Joseph's Goblet," explained the birds, "belonged to Joseph, son of Jacob. Joseph used it to see what was going on in places far from where he stood. When the Goblet is filled with water, the holder can look into it and see and hear what's going on in another room, city, or even country!"

Uriel's eyes glittered. *Hm,* he thought, *I might want to use it before giving it to Samael, then. I could use it to help Uwe and Matthias.*

He shook his head. *Well, I could use it once, but the best way to help Uwe and Matthias is to give Samael the Goblet right away and free Michael as fast as I can.*

He nodded for the birds to continue their elaboration.

"The Goblet, however," said one of the plumper doves, "is hidden under the Burden Boulder. The Burden Bolder is made of the same type of stone as the Hailstone Cup. It would take twenty men to lift it off the ground."

Uriel released a frustrated sigh. Recalling how heavy the Hailstone Cup had been, he prayed that the birds had some sort of item in mind that would help.

Fortunately, one of them twittered, "But there is a way to lift it without so many men. If you can acquire Samson's Pelt, then you can easily lift the Burden Boulder."

"Samson the Strong killed a lion with his bare hands," said another dove, its beady eyes sparkling. "After he did so, he skinned the beast and wore its pelt at all times. Even after he died, some of his strength was left behind in the pelt, just as some of the Prophet Elijah's holiness was left on his mantle even after he ascended to Heaven."

Uriel's eyes flickered over to the closet, where Elijah's Mantle was neatly folded up, and then shifted back to the birds. He opened his arms wide and waved towards himself, gesturing for them to tell him where the Pelt was.

"We searched everywhere for the Pelt," said one dove, and Uriel could almost hear a slight squeak in the bird's high-pitched voice that was reminiscent of a chuckle. "But then we discovered that the Pelt was stolen by the commander of the Germans! Samson's Pelt is right downstairs!"

Uriel's eyes shimmered with delight and relief.

"We know where the Pelt is, we know where the Burden Boulder is," said one of the doves. "This quest may be over by nightfall. Compared to getting the Golden Tree, this will be simple."

Uriel breathed in deeply. A simple quest was exactly what he needed. He wondered why Samael would give him an assignment that was so easy to complete. Perhaps he had just been so arrogant that he hadn't even thought the Jewish boy would make it this far. Smirking, Uriel turned and prepared to go downstairs and grab the Pelt.

Then there was a terrible squawk that made Uriel's eardrums ache. A fifth dove, the gangliest of the bunch, flew in, flapping his wings desperately.

"The box! The box with the Pelt!" he squealed, "The Germans are about to take it away in one of their black machines!"

Uriel's heart lurched. He bolted out of the room, down the stairs, and out of the house.

He saw the truck, which was filled with boxes and two sacks of letters, and he saw one of the guards carrying a small package and placing it in the back.

Narrowing his eyes with determination, Uriel ran towards the truck, nearly knocking over the guard that remained by the door. The guard yelped and took out his gun, his eyes flitting to and fro in search of whatever had bumped him. Uriel hardly paid him any mind, however, as the other guard shut the mail compartment door and waved for the driver to go ahead.

The engine started up. The truck began to move, picking up speed while the child desperately tried to catch up. He couldn't lose it. He had to run faster.

Just a *little* faster.

He reached out. He could almost touch the rumbling machine. Smoke from the vehicle blew in his face and nearly blinded him, but he held in the cough that the smoke tried to summon and grabbed the back of the truck.

He pulled himself on and sputtered a bit, spitting in an attempt to get the terrible taste of smoke and gas out of his mouth. Once he could see and breathe again, he gripped the truck with one hand and pulled out the Boundless Key with the other. The truck began to jostle and jolt, nearly knocking the boy off and nearly causing him to drop the Key. He maintained his grip, however, and tapped the lock on the back of the truck.

The door clicked. He shoved the Key into his pocket. He threw the door open and rolled inside so he wouldn't risk being thrown to the road.

Uriel looked up and growled in frustration. He knew the size of the package he was looking for, but there were at least ten packages of the same size.

He looked at the address on each box and finally found the one from Günter Brandt. Tearing it open was a moderate challenge without a blade of any sort, but he managed and pulled out the cold, furry hide.

It was huge, which was to be expected since it had belonged to the strongest man ever to walk the earth. He could feel a great power radiating off it. Otherwise, however, it didn't seem to be anything more than the skin of a defeated beast. It didn't glitter or glow like Elijah's Mantle. Aside from the strength left behind by its conqueror, the lion was lifeless.

The boy looked outside of the truck and cringed when he saw how fast the road was moving beneath him. Jumping would be dangerous, but he had no choice. There was no telling when the truck would come to a complete stop. He couldn't risk being taken right to Germany. Uwe would go mad with worry.

He wrapped Samson's Pelt around his body and summoned every iota of bravery he possessed before leaping off the back of the truck.

He landed painfully on his side and rolled a bit. A few bits of gravel sunk into his cheeks, but otherwise the Pelt protected him.

Slowly recovering from shock, he stood up, trembling. He could feel power pulsing through his body as the Pelt fed his every muscle. He felt like he could rip a tree in half like a twig, like he could conquer the country if he so desired.

He shook his head and turned his eyes to the sky. When he didn't see five white birds fluttering overhead, he looked at the surrounding trees. Unfortunately, the helpful doves were nowhere to be seen.

I must have gotten too far ahead of them, he thought. Uriel looked down both roads, but he had been tossed and rolled about so much when he jumped from the truck that he couldn't even recall which direction led back to Major Brandt's domicile.

The boy bit his lip with worry, but he refused to panic. Instead, he looked at the forest and, making sure that Samson's Pelt was securely wrapped around his small body, he marched into the woods. He figured that he would either come across a landmark that would lead him back to the house, or the birds would find him and lead him to the Burden Boulder so he could claim Joseph's Goblet.

But that didn't happen, and soon Uriel found himself horribly, horribly lost.

Uwe could feel himself being watched.

Perhaps it was just paranoia, but he couldn't leave out the possibility that Brandt had ordered one of the policemen to follow him wherever he went. If that was so, then Uwe could end up leading him right to Matthias and his men.

He couldn't let that happen. So, instead of going right to Matthias' cave, he went the opposite way and wandered about the forest for so long that he lost track of the time. He kept changing course and glancing over his shoulder, listening closely for an extra pair of footsteps.

When he finally verified he wasn't being followed, he sighed in relief and decided to make his way back to Matthias.

But by then he was horribly, horribly lost.

He growled in frustration and cursed himself for taking such a complicated detour without even bothering to make sure he knew where he was. He had been so focused on trying to hear a potential follower that he hadn't even considered setting up a landmark or a trail so that he wouldn't have to wander about in a hopeless attempt to find familiar territory, likely getting even more lost in the process.

He comforted himself with the knowledge that Uriel always managed to make his way back to the house, no matter how far he seemed to stray. If the child could somehow track Uwe from Zingdorf all the way to Brandt's house, then Uwe could find his way through the woods.

Then again, the child was very smart and had a good sense of direction. Although Uwe was certainly smart, he had never needed a great sense of direction since he had previously never needed to leave his little town. The forest was a seemingly endless mess of trees and bushes and stones that all looked the same. He couldn't tell if he was going in circles, getting closer to the house, or fumbling further into the forest.

He hoped to bump into Uriel or the Polish partisans soon. He was getting dizzy, and he needed some company other than the chittering bugs or the squawking birds overhead.

Birds…

He paused for a moment and looked up, squinting at the branches above. The caws from the birds were eerily familiar. They weren't songs. They sounded more like screeches from a sadistic peanut gallery.

Looking closely at the branches, he made out a few black forms sulking above.

Crows.

He swallowed and a few pearls of sweat formed on his brow. He hadn't seen any crows since arriving in Poland. In fact, he rarely *ever* saw crows.

The last time he had seen a crow was when his neighbor's dog died. Or, rather, right *before* his neighbor's dog died. The dog had been on death's doorstep for a week, and the crows had been drawn to his neighbor's house like maggots to a carcass.

It was as if they could sense the approach of the Angel of Death. They could smell it and felt the need to show up like cruel spectators, jeering at the future victim and cheering for the grim reaper as he slowly but surely arrived.

Dread fell upon Uwe's stomach like a pile of bricks.

Someone was going to die.

He followed the crows' cries, morbid curiosity causing his legs to move toward their screeching.

He crept forward, further and further, until the caws faded. He paused.

Perhaps he had imagined it. Perhaps he was being paranoid again.

But before he could even entertain the hopeful notion that the crows had portended nothing this time, he heard a scream.

Gasping and crouching down, he crawled forward.

The screams grew louder, clearer, closer. He could hear women and men sobbing, little children crying that they wanted their mama and papa.

And as the linguist hid behind a bush and began to peek through the foliage, he heard another voice, sharp as a knife and impatient, like a teacher whose students were taking far too long on a test.

He would recognize that voice anywhere.

Major Brandt.

Uriel stumbled over a fallen log and hissed in frustration as Samson's Pelt got caught on yet another bush. The Pelt was so large that, even wrapped around the boy like a royal robe, it dragged on the forest floor, getting snagged every other minute and forcing Uriel to pause his desperate search in order to disentangle it.

Once he had successfully pulled the Pelt from the bush, a sound hit his eardrums. At first his heart rose with hope. Perhaps the doves were searching for him.

As he approached the caws, however, his smile faded, his blood became icy.

Not doves, but rather crows were perched on the branches above. They spoke to one another in a devilishly excited series of squawks, hopping from foot to foot as if to celebrate a merry occasion.

When he heard their cries clearly, the air left his lungs.

"Samael is coming! Samael is coming!"

Samael.

Although he knew that running towards the Angel of Death was dangerous, the hamsa and Samson's Pelt gave him courage. Whatever was causing the dark angel to appear, Uriel knew that he could handle it.

He stumbled over the shrubbery and finally, the crows' cheerful chants vanished.

Replaced by screams and wails.

A familiar voice called out over the din. "Be quiet! Hurry up!"

The Major, thought the child. He hid behind a thin tree and gripped the Pelt tightly as he peeked out.

Every bit of strength that the Pelt gave him evaporated when he saw what was happening.

The Order Police stood over a group of twenty Jews, each soldier aiming his gun at one Jew's head. The soldiers shoved the Jews to the ground, forcing them to lie on their stomachs.

Brandt himself also stood over a Jew, a woman with wavy black locks that immediately reminded Uwe of the picture in the hallway, the picture of the Major's own wife.

Brandt pressed the barrel of his gun to the back of her neck almost without looking. He watched his men as they copied him, moving their guns to aim at the back of their Jew's neck.

Men, women, and little children wept and cried out. Their pleas struck Uwe's heart one by one.

"Please, please just spare my little boy! He's only five!" one mother begged.

"*Sh'ma Yisrael Adonai…*" an old man prayed, pressing his forehead to the ground, sobs causing his body to shake and making his voice crack.

One little girl, who he could tell was ten years old at most, her tearful cries were worst of all. Over and over again she sobbed, "I don't want to die right now! I don't want to die right now!"

Uwe wanted to cover his ears, but he felt paralyzed, as though he had been turned to stone. He wanted to burst out of the bushes. Do something. Anything.

But before he could rise, Brandt gave the order. Twenty guns were fired.

And as the bullets met their victims, a dark figure that only Uriel could see appeared. In a single swift motion, he drew his blade and cut through the heads of every murdered Jew, removing their lives and souls in one fell swoop.

As the Angel of Death sheathed his sword, he seemed to sense somebody watching him and turned towards Uriel.

Mauve eyes met gold, and yet Samael did not open his mouth to mock the horrified Jewish boy. He didn't sneer or even smile.

Instead, he almost seemed surprised.

Surprised and, in a strange way, embarrassed. As though he had hoped that the boy wouldn't have to see what his post entailed.

But the Angel of Death did not tarry. He spared the Jewish boy a glance only for a second before he slipped into the shadows and disappeared.

The guns echoed through the forest, and in the distance, Uwe could hear crows cheering gaily.

A bit of blood had gotten on Brandt's ruffled uniform and those of his fellow soldiers. One of the men had shot sloppily, shooting the head rather than the neck, and his uniform was covered in scarlet stains and bits of shattered skull. The shooter trembled and gawked at his handiwork with wide eyes. He looked like he was about to retch.

It was the man from Hamburg, the one with a fiancée waiting for him back home. He looked down at the woman he had murdered and stumbled back, fidgeting as though he wanted to tear off his bloodstained uniform.

It was obviously his first slaughter.

The other men quickly put away their guns. A few muttered something about their victim being troublesome, but other than that they were casually silent. As though they had just finished filling out a very long and tedious form.

There wasn't a hint of disturbance or disgust at what they had done.

Brandt glanced down at the small crimson stain on his pants with mild annoyance before putting his gun away and announcing that everybody had done a fine job just now.

Clean. Quick. Except for the youngest of the group, who had shot his Jew in the head.

"Wash off when you get back to the house," said Brandt, gesturing to the policeman's gore-covered uniform. "That's why you shoot the neck, not the head."

The man slowly nodded, though he seemed to only barely hear his commanding officer. His eyes were still locked on the woman he had killed.

Uwe gazed at the murdered Jews, hardly listening as Brandt explained the logistics of why a shot to the neck was so much cleaner than a shot to the head.

These were no partisans. These were no threat to Germany.

*Except...*he thought slowly. *All Jews are a threat to Germany.*

Dear God...

Every hint he had failed—or, perhaps, refused—to spot. Every sentence Brandt had spoken concerning the Jews. Every rumor he had heard about what the Nazis planned. Every Hitler speech he had rolled his eyes at and dismissed as a lunatic's ravings.

It all came together, and he almost wanted to rip his own eyes out so he wouldn't have to look at the grisly evidence before him. So he wouldn't have to look in the mirror and think of how *gullible* and *stupid* he was for believing that the Germans were above mass murder.

He wanted to curl up and cry. He had helped them. He had helped them round up the Jews. He had helped them ship them off. He had helped them lead those poor people to their own execution.

He wanted to look away, but before he could another figure right across from him caught his eye. A small figure wrapped in a pale pelt, barely hiding behind a tree that was almost as thin as he.

Uriel.

All it would take was the slightest turn of Brandt's head, the slightest shifting of one of his men's eyes, and the child that Uwe had come to care for would join his fellow Jews as a corpse on the forest floor.

Without a second of thought or hesitation, Uwe jumped to his feet and bellowed, "*Brandt!*"

It worked. All heads snapped towards him. All eyes landed on him.

Go, Uriel

The child paused, his eyes bulging in terrified surprise, but he then seemed to realize what the linguist was trying to do for him.

He ran.

As soon as he saw the boy flee, relief came to Uwe's horrified heart.

At least, he thought, stepping out from behind the bushes, *he'll be safe.*

He took a moment to meet the eyes of every policeman, casting every ounce of anger he had upon them, shaming them with his stare. A few raised their eyebrows, as if they didn't know what they had done that was so damning. One or two squirmed uncomfortably, and the one who had shot his victim in the head looked down at his blood-coated shoes, shutting his eyes so he wouldn't have to face the furious linguist.

Finally, Uwe turned his azure eyes on Brandt. The Major, at first, stared at him like he was a strange spirit that had emerged from the wood, like he didn't quite know what Uwe was. His emerald eyes scrutinized the linguist for a moment before briefly flickering to the corpses that were lined up on the forest floor.

For a moment, nobody spoke. Uwe waited for Brandt to say something. To sputter an excuse, to snarl at Uwe for spying on them, to insist that this was all a wild misunderstanding, to try and justify himself, *anything*.

But the Major said nothing.

Uwe broke the hush. He gestured to the bodies and whispered, "What are you doing here? *What have you done?*"

The Major's eyes followed Uwe's arm and settled on the slaughtered Jews for a moment before he turned back to Uwe and coolly replied, "Resettlement."

Resettlement. It all came back to that. Uwe recalled the last operation, when he had asked Brandt about what the Germans would do to the Jews.

They'll be resettled. Once they're no longer needed, the ones who were taken to the work camp will be resettled as well. They'll be reunited, Herr Litten, don't you worry.

Good God. It all made sense. Terrible, terrible sense. Every rumor he had heard about the concentration camps was right and, at the same time, an awful understatement.

They milk as much work as they can out of the useful ones, thought Uwe, *and then kill them, just like they kill their wives and children. Reunited. Resettlement. Good God, if I hadn't hidden Uriel…*

And if this was how the simple, neighborly *Ordnungspolizei* treated the Jews under their control, he could only imagine what the maniacs in the SS were doing to the Jews in the camps and ghettos.

But he couldn't dwell on that. Not now, at least. Not while Brandt stood before him, impassive, *shameless*.

"You're a monster," Uwe hissed.

A mirthless smile came to the Major's lips. He laughed.

"I'm a soldier, Herr Litten," he replied. "Monsters don't exist."

Uwe was hardly given a second to respond as Brandt suddenly grabbed him by the arm. The linguist writhed and desperately tried to escape, but the Major dragged him to a nearby truck.

"You don't understand yet, Herr Litten," said the Major. "That's fine, most of my men don't at first. You will, though. And when that day comes, you'll thank us for what we've done here."

"Let me go! You're a murderer! Child-murderer! You deserve to go to hell and burn!" spat Uwe, trying to free himself from the Major's grasp. Brandt, however, refused to yield.

"Be silent, Herr Litten," he replied, sounding more irate than offended. "I'm taking you home now. You did a bad thing, running this far. Very, very dangerous."

Uwe at last stopped struggling once he was unceremoniously pulled onto the truck and driven back to Brandt's house. Tears streamed down his face as the screams of the murdered Jews echoed through his mind and the image of Uriel's wide golden eyes caused him to gnaw on his bottom lip.

Please, God. Please, if You're here, bring him home. Please, please bring him home safe.

When they finally arrived at the house, Brandt berated the two guards who were supposed to make sure that Uwe didn't sneak out, but the guards hardly paid attention. One was blubbering about something bumping into him while the other tried to calm his comrade down.

Brandt's frustration with them distracted him enough that Uwe was able to run upstairs and slam the door to his room shut. He pushed the nightstand in front of the door and grabbed the doll and the golden notebook.

He cradled the golden notebook to his heart, hoping that holding it close would somehow bring Uriel back safe, and stared down at the sadly smiling doll.

Her best friend was gone forever. Shot in the neck. Lying somewhere in the woods. The little girl hadn't even been allowed to hold her precious doll while she was murdered.

He started to cry. Every Jew that had been banished from his town. Every Jew that he had helped to send away.

Gone, gone, gone.

Uriel, don't be gone. Uriel, please, please come back.

He cried until he ran out of tears and then, only then, did he hear a branch creak and leaves rustle.

He looked up and saw Uriel. The child closed the window and turned to face Uwe. His eyes had lost their glitter, his smile was gone, and he was no longer wearing the pale pelt.

But he was alive, he was safe, he was unhurt. That was all that mattered.

"Uriel…" Uwe sobbed, alighting from his seat and embracing the boy so tightly that the child gave a small squeak of protest. Once he had held the boy long enough, he knelt before him and brushed back his ebony hair, making sure that he was really there.

"Uriel," he said, his voice almost breaking. "No more going outside, okay? No more going outside."

And although Uriel hated making another promise that he knew he would have to break, he nodded.

DEMONS

He had always believed in angels.

He had always waited eagerly for the Rabbi to get to the Torah portions that mentioned them.

He had always felt especially jealous of his fellow boys when they were able to sing songs about angels and he wasn't.

He had always read the stories of Elijah the Prophet-Angel and daydreamed about becoming a member of the Heavenly Host just like him.

He loved angels.

He knew they were real even before he could see them with his own eyes.

Demons, on the other hand, he had never believed in.

He often heard mothers tell their small children stories of demons that would come and steal them away if they stayed out past sunset or didn't obey their teachers. He had always smiled and shook his head when he heard somebody spin such a cautionary yarn.

Demons, to him, were story creatures and nothing more. They existed only on Papa's lips when he told spooky stories and on the pages of the golden notebook.

But they weren't real.

Not like angels.

He knew now that he had been wrong.

Demons were real.

Before the sun had even fully risen the next day, Uwe snuck out of the house. He needed to leave early, lest Brandt stop him or send somebody to follow him. He needed to tell Matthias and the Poles what he had seen.

He needed to get them to work together. He needed to get them to fight Brandt.

It was the only way to save them and Uriel.

Uriel, meanwhile, didn't dare leave the house. Although he had Samson's Pelt and knew that the birds must have been close by, he didn't want to run out just yet. If Uwe came back and the child was gone, he would be devastated and terrified.

Uriel didn't want to give his dear friend any more pain. He had to wait just a little, just until nighttime when Uwe went to sleep.

Wait.

Wait.

Wait.

For once, his golden notebook wasn't helping. He held it close, but no burst of inspiration came. No stories were born.

He could only think of his people lying on the forest floor, blood pouring from their necks. He could only think of the grim Angel of Death levitating over them, meeting his eyes before he vanished into the darkness.

Wait.

Wait.

Wait.

He wanted to kill the clock. Seconds felt like millennia. His people were dying. They needed Michael. They needed him *now*.

Wait.

Wait.

Bang.

A knock on the door caused the boy to wince and cease his gloomy rumination.

Three more knocks followed. Uriel stared at the door, dread taking over his stomach like a weed in an unkempt garden.

He heard a voice.

"Can you get it open?"

Another answered, "Yes, just a minute."

Uriel's heart jumped into his throat. He was only given enough time to leap off the bed before the door burst open.

The Major and two of his men marched straight into the room. Brandt took a quick sip from his flask and then waved towards the closet, bed, and drawers.

"Search everywhere," he ordered. "Look for anything suspicious."

"Yes, sir!" said one of the soldiers. He and his comrade scuttled over to the drawers and started roughly pulling everything out, tossing Uwe's folded-up shirts to the side.

Uriel stood in the middle of the room, still as a stone and unseen by the wicked men. Brandt brushed right past him, pausing for only a moment as his elbow touched the child's head. He stopped and looked down. The boy didn't move, too frightened to do so as the Major unknowingly met his sun-colored eyes.

The Major tightened his lips and shook his head, his eyes moving away from the invisible child and to the closet door. While the Major opened it up, Uriel slowly began to tip-toe towards the window, holding the golden notebook under his arm and listening closely to the Major as he searched the closet.

Brandt shoved an overcoat to the side and immediately noticed a small pile of socks in the closet's corner. He snorted and critically wondered why a man who claimed to be very tidy would leave his socks lying on the floor.

A frown came to his face. He glanced towards his men, who were ruffling up Uwe's neatly organized shirts. The rest of the room was completely orderly, the clothes properly folded and put away.

Except the socks.

It was atypical, and anything atypical was, in Brandt's eye, suspicious.

He knelt down and noticed a small burgundy garment lying beside the mound of socks. He unfolded it and arched an eyebrow when he saw that it was an ancient-looking cloak. That the linguist would own such a cloak was strange enough, but seeing the garment also gave the Major an odd sense of déjà vu. He was certain that he had seen this cloak (or at least one very similar) somewhere before, but he couldn't remember where or when.

Shaking his head, he tossed it to the side and looked over his shoulder. His men were searching the bed now. He noticed that the little doll Uwe had picked up during his first operation had been knocked to the floor. The Major's lip twitched upward at seeing that, but his smile didn't last, and severity quickly conquered his countenance once more.

"Find anything of note?" he called to his men.

"Not yet, Uncle Günter."

"Be sure to keep your eye out for a black book. It's my copy of *Mein Kampf.*"

"Yes, sir!"

A cool breeze brushed against the Major's face before he could turn back to the sock pile. His eyes wandered to the window and sparkled with surprise when he saw that it was wide open.

"Hey," he said, "did one of you open that window?"

The two policemen paused their raid to glance at the open window. They, however, seemed just as taken aback as Brandt.

"No, we didn't," one of them replied.

"Was it open when we came in?"

"I…don't remember, actually," muttered one policeman, looking closely at the window and almost taking a cautious step back.

"Do you want us to close it, sir?" asked his comrade. Brandt gazed at the open window for a moment, listening closely, but when the whistling of the wind was the only sound that struck his ears he shrugged casually.

"No, leave it open. It's stuffy in here."

Uriel sat on the unsteady branch, peeking into the room, his heart pounding so loudly that it was a wonder the Major didn't hear it.

The Major's looking for the Book of Blood! Oh, no! I'm going to get Uwe in trouble! Uriel thought, wanting to smack himself on the head. He couldn't, however, since a sudden movement could cause him to fall, drop the golden notebook, or shake the branch so much that Brandt would become suspicious.

He instead moved slowly, carefully backing away from the window, clutching the golden notebook close and praying that Brandt would find nothing incriminating in his bed of socks.

Good thing I left Samson's Pelt in the bushes last night, the boy thought, glancing down at the shrub where the lion's skin was hidden. He hadn't carried it up with him because it would have been hard to climb the tree while wearing the large lion's hide. Besides, seeing the Pelt might have distressed Uwe if he thought that the boy had stolen it from the Major (which he technically had, but then again he had stolen it from a murderous thief and the murderous thief was none the wiser).

He held the golden notebook tightly and backed up a bit more, thanking God that he had been holding his stories when Brandt and his men had burst in. If they saw something, anything, with Hebraic script in Uwe's room, they would accuse Uwe of harboring or helping Jews.

As his golden eyes skipped from German to German, however, a small scrap of paper caught his eye and made his heart stop.

Something had fallen out of his golden notebook. He hadn't even noticed until now.

But there it was, lying barely a foot away from Brandt's men. All it would take was a turn of the head, a lowering of eyes, and Uwe would be in more danger than ever before.

As quickly and cautiously as possible, Uriel crawled back to the windowsill. The shaking of the tree branch and the crackling of the leaves was almost painfully loud to him, and once or twice one of the soldiers would look over at the window. Fortunately, they seemed to dismiss it as an action of the wind and went back to their search.

The boy climbed down from the windowsill, his eyes landing on one of Brandt's men. He was taking a step back. Just one more step and he would tread on the paper. Uriel could practically hear the slight crunch that the paper would make under the German's boot and the German's cry of triumphant surprise as he grabbed the paper and presented it to his commander.

As the boy snuck towards the paper, the Major shifted through the socks, keeping an eye out for his precious black book that had been missing for far too long.

He didn't find the book, but he did find a small wooden harp. He held it up, experimentally ran his finger over the strings, and cringed when the noise that came forth sounded more like a screech than the soft melody that harps were known to produce. He tossed the harp to the side, right next to the old cloak, and continued his search.

Uriel's fingers had almost touched the paper when the Major played on David's Harp. The child shuddered as a scream issued from the Harp and memories of yesterday's slaughter bolted through his mind. The Harp had, for a moment, sounded just like the screams from the people Brandt and his men had killed.

Brandt grabbed a sock and was quite astonished when he lifted it up and felt how heavy it was. The Major held it up and saw a huge bulge on the bottom. He turned it upside down and emptied its contents on the floor. His eyes widened when a pile of golden chains fell out. He picked up the tangled mass of gold and narrowed his eyes at the jewelry when he recalled the argument between his men yesterday concerning stolen golden chains.

He stuffed the chains into his pocket.

One of the policemen started to take a step back, his boot looming over the paper. Uriel's heart jolted. With a swiftness that surprised even him, he snatched the paper up and shoved it into the golden notebook before the boot could crush it. Once the paper was safely hidden, he scurried back to the window and climbed onto the branch.

Uriel managed to make it down. As soon as he was safely leaning against the trunk of the tree, he pulled out the precious piece of paper that the German had almost stepped on.

It was yellowed from age, folded once down the middle. Although old, it had been lovingly placed between the pages of Uriel's notebook for a very, very long time and was thus without a wrinkle or tear.

Uriel gently unfolded it and beheld a single, slightly faded Hebrew word. The first word that he had ever written. A word that he wouldn't have spoken even if he had a voice to speak with.

The Ineffable Name of God.

He tenderly stowed the Ineffable Name back where it belonged and put the golden notebook in his pocket. With his stories and the Name of God safely nestled in his coat, the boy ran to the bushes and grabbed Samson's Pelt.

It wasn't long before the birds arrived. "Angel-Finder! There you are! We lost you yesterday! We were worried! We're so sorry!"

Uriel nodded to show he accepted their apologies, gesturing for them to quickly lead him to the Burden Boulder. As long as Brandt and his men were scouring Uwe's room, there was no reason not to finally go out and finish Samael's fourth quest.

INEFFABLE

There was one word that no man, woman, or child in Zingdorf dared to utter.

It was a word that was too holy for sinful human lips to speak. A word that could curse and kill just as easily as it could bless and bring life.

It was to be used only by the highest of prophets and angels. Mere mortals had no right to freely speak the Ineffable Name, the True Name of God.

That was why they called Him 'Hashem', 'The Name.' Because saying the True Name was both disrespectful and dangerous.

The Name of God was power, and it fascinated Uriel from the moment he saw it written in the Torah.

He, for once, had an advantage. The others had to guard their lips and be careful never to speak the Ineffable Name. He did not have to exercise such caution. He couldn't have spoken the Name even if he wanted to.

But while he couldn't speak, he could write.

And it was the Ineffable Name that made him write. Before then, his parents had taught him some letters, but he was still a small child. His hand trembled terribly whenever he wrote, and his letters were never legible.

But one day, an urge gripped him and refused to let go. An urge to write the True Name of God.

He took the Torah, a scrap of paper, and a bottle of ink and, for the first time, he wrote. He wrote by himself. He took his time, moved carefully, and made something beautiful.

Even though it was only one word, it was the most important word in existence. He had written it, he had written it properly and wonderfully, and he had loved writing it down. He loved taking a plain pen and a blank sheet of paper and turning it into something beautiful, holy even.

From that day on, he practiced his writing. He practiced until it was as perfect as he could possibly make it, until he could make even everyday words beautiful.

And the paper with his first word, the Ineffable Name, he placed under his pillow. He hoped that the holiness from the word would seep into his skull as he slept and a miracle would occur. He would wake up with a voice.

Many years passed and no such miracle occurred, but still he kept the Ineffable Name close. Whether it gave him a voice or not, it was a powerful word, a sacred word, and it was his first word.

So when Matthias gave him a beautiful golden notebook, the first thing he did was tuck his beautiful first word between the pages.

The Jews were moderately surprised and awfully scared when Uwe showed up out of breath, alarmed, without a crumb of food to give them, and demanding to speak to Matthias alone.

The Jewish commander immediately granted the German audience, and before long they were back in Matthias' corner of the cave. Matthias offered Uwe a seat on his little wooden stool, but the German refused.

"Not tired," he replied, "I'd prefer to stand."

"You certainly look tired," Matthias observed, his metallic voice giving way to a hint of concern.

"I'm *not tired*," Uwe insisted, his tone becoming somewhat irate.

"How much sleep did you get last night?" asked the Jewish leader, folding his arms over his chest.

"*None*, all right? I didn't get *any* sleep! My sleep schedule *isn't* important!" snapped Uwe. "There's a good reason I didn't get any sleep!"

"Which is?"

Uwe's annoyance evaporated, replaced by eyes wide as a full moon and a shiver that wracked his entire body. He slowly sunk down to the cold floor, staring at Matthias' shadow as though he feared Major Brandt might leapt out of it like a monster from one of Uriel's stories.

"Yesterday," he muttered, "I...found...something out. While I was coming to bring you some news...I..."

He swallowed, the memory of the children's screams causing his stomach to stir and forcing tears to spring to his eyes.

"I saw Brandt and his men...killing Jewish women and children...shooting them in the neck..."

He took in a shuddering breath and looked up at Matthias, trying to blink the bitter water away as he said in his most serious tone, "They've been doing that to every Jewish village. Sometimes they work with the Poles, sometimes they don't. But either way, they take the Jews they want, ship them to labor camps to work until they die, and then kill every Jew that they don't have use for. All the elderly, the sick, the women and children..."

His heart clenched painfully as the faces of all the Jews he had helped to round up came to his mind. Bowing his head in shame, he didn't notice that Matthias' expression hadn't changed. There was no hint of shock or horror or disgust.

Instead, the Jewish man paused for a moment before frigidly inquiring, "What did you expect?"

Uwe ran his rough sleeve over his face to dry his tears and looked back up at the iron-eyed man. It suddenly struck him that Matthias' cold countenance must have been brought about by a slaughter just like the one he had witnessed yesterday, one that had taken the Jewish commander's family and any warmth he might have had before.

Empathy for the Jewish commander flooded Uwe's heart. He almost wanted to apologize, but instead he bit his lip and shook his head.

"I don't know. I was stupid for not even suspecting…but…right now that's not important." His own eyes became steely with resolution. "What matters now is that every Jew in this area is going to be killed, you and your men included, unless we do something. We have to get rid of Brandt and his men. You *have* to fight them, Matthias."

"Believe me, Uwe," said Matthias, a touch of exasperation entering his tone, "I would cherish the opportunity to fight the Germans, and I talked to my men about it too. They want to fight. They feel so much better now thanks to the food you gave us, and they want to avenge their homes and families. But we *can't.*"

"You have no weapons, I know," said Uwe. "Hopefully, I can fix that."

Matthias' head tilted inquisitively to the side.

"The other day," Uwe explained, exhaling and preparing himself for the backlash he was sure to receive. "I met the Polish partisans."

Matthias' eyes heated up like steel in a kiln. "What?"

"I got lost, it's a bit of a long story," sighed Uwe, still not wanting to mention Uriel lest Matthias insist on taking him. "But they told me about a man from their village, Julek. He died before the Invasion, but before then he made a weapon cache somewhere in the woods. Ah! And speaking of which!"

He pulled the cryptic note out of his pocket and handed it to the Jewish leader. Matthias' fury faded, and he looked at the letter with the barest hint of bewilderment.

"What's this?" he asked, glancing down at the strange sentence.

"A 'clue' of some sort. The Pole, Julek, he gave it to his neighbor. I managed to translate it, but I don't know what it means. Do you understand it? Does it mean anything to you? I thought it might be a reference to a landmark or riddle or something."

"'*The Cat Raises The Rock*,'" Matthias mumbled. His rain-cloud-colored eyes scanned the five-word message three times before his lips thinned in defeated frustration and he gave it back to the linguist.

"It means nothing to me," he said. "Ask the others. One of them might know."

Uwe nodded brusquely and turned away from Matthias. He proceeded to hopelessly jump from Jew to Jew, handing them the bizarre hint and asking if they knew its meaning. The Jews each studied the note as carefully as they could before asserting their cluelessness.

Once he had fruitlessly interviewed every Jew under Matthias' watch, Uwe returned to the Jewish commander's corner, his shoulders sagging subtly enough that he hoped Matthias wouldn't notice and lose what little hope he had managed to hold on to.

"Okay," said the linguist, rolling his shoulders in an attempt to brush off his physical demonstration of despondency as a mere case of stiff joints. "They didn't know anything."

"I noticed," said Matthias in a manner so impassive that Uwe might have laughed were the situation less dire.

"Regardless," said Uwe, "it *must* point to something. I'm sure I can figure it out somehow."

"I don't doubt your intelligence, Uwe," said Matthias with a small nod that Uwe couldn't quite define as encouraging. It came off as a sign of both trust and a bit of condescension.

"I'll look as hard as I can," Uwe swore. "I'll read over this damn note until my eyeballs fall out if I have to. If I can find the cache, I can give you the weapons and you can fight back."

"Yes," Matthias said with a thoughtful nod. "That would be helpful. *But* even then, we'll be terribly outnumbered. There are at least fifty Germans and only twenty of us, and we're not trained soldiers. We would need either a miracle or…"

"That's the other thing," Uwe interrupted, his heart starting to beat faster as apprehension pulsed through his veins. "The Poles lost their leader the other day while they were attacking some of Brandt's men. They don't have a suitable replacement available, even though there are plenty of partisans who want to fight Brandt."

He paused, hoping that Matthias would get it. The Jewish commander, however, stayed silent, his sharp breathing being the only hint that he hadn't been completely paralyzed.

"They need a leader," Uwe said. "They need you, Matthias."

Matthias' calm demeanor dissolved.

"*No*," he said, not screaming or snarling or shaking his fists, but speaking in a tone so layered with hate that it made Uwe flinch.

"Please, Matthias!" begged Uwe, clasping his hands together and slowly rising to his feet so that he could be at eye level with the Jewish commander. "The Poles need a leader!"

"I don't care what they need!" snapped Matthias, wrath and agony dancing in his formerly dull gray eyes, his trembling hands curling into fists. "As far as I'm concerned, they deserve…"

"Matthias! I'm not going to pretend that all of the Poles are angels…"

"*Angels?*" He was shouting now. Uwe took a step back. The fire in Matthias' irises could have burned down five forests, could have consumed a country.

"Angels? Angels! You're just as blind now as you were before, Litten! They're not even devils! Devils are born evil! They can't help it! The Poles *chose* to follow the Germans! They *chose* to burn down our houses and slaughter us like rats! They *chose* to do that because they hate us more than they love themselves! They hate us more than they hate the Germans! They've always hated us! They've always wanted to kill us! The Germans just gave them the chance. How could you even *think* of asking me to even *look* at them after everything they've done to me and my people?"

Tears were streaming from his eyes and he seemed to realize this as he turned away from Uwe, pressing his forehead against the stone wall.

"Do you know what they did?" he growled, his voice slightly muffled. "They came to my village, howling like a pack of wolves. They torched our synagogue, killed our Rabbi with an axe, chopped his head off like in the Dark Ages! They took my wife and cut her open. She was *pregnant* and they cut her open with a knife! They *slaughtered* my wife and child! The only reason I survived was because *I ran*! I ran! *I hid,* and they somehow didn't find me! I survived because *I ran* and that's it! But they *would have* killed me, they would have! Just like they killed Adina and the baby and everybody else!"

He wept, and for a few moments the only sound in the whole cave was the sound of his weeping. Even the other Jews, who surely must have heard him, held their breaths and didn't say a word.

Then, slowly, Uwe approached.

"Matthias…" he said, choosing his words with exceptional care. "You're right."

It took a moment for Matthias to catch his breath and hold in his sobs. He wiped his face off and turned to Uwe, surprise spilling from his red-rimmed eyes.

"You're right," Uwe said. "There's no way I can relate to you because—thank God—I've never been through anything like that. You're right that the Poles who did that and the Poles who support that and the Poles who hate Jews are worse than devils. You're right that they don't deserve to even look at you."

He paused for a minute before declaring, "But Brandt is worse than a devil, too. He may not howl like a wolf and wave an axe, he may be *orderly* about murdering Jews, but he's just as bad as the Polish mobs. *He* is *our* enemy. If we don't stop him, he will kill *every* last Jew in this area, including you and your men, including women and children and expecting mothers! I've talked to the Polish partisans. There are pitiful, stupid men among them, but there are some that are willing to obey you if you're willing to lead them against Brandt. This is the only way to stop the Germans, the only way to save all of our lives."

"I can't trust them," whispered Matthias. "Not after everything."

"You don't have to trust them, but do you at least trust me?" asked Uwe. "Matthias, I swear to God…"

"God doesn't exist!" snapped Matthias, his eyes smoldering and shifting swiftly to the ceiling, as though he meant to direct his declaration to the Heavens.

Uwe heard one or two men gasp behind him, probably the more religious ones. A few of them muttered in Hebrew, likely apologizing to God on their leader's behalf. When he stole a glance at the Jews, however, Uwe could see some give grim nods of agreement. A few looked curiously upwards, wondering if there was a Creator above.

Uwe turned back to Matthias, inhaled deeply, and softly said, "Maybe. Maybe not. But you'll have to make it to Jerusalem before you can say that for certain. You have to live, Matthias. You and everybody else."

He waved his hand towards the other Jews in the cave. He had spoken too quietly for them to hear what he said, but when they saw him gesture towards them, they turned their eyes expectantly to their leader.

The flames in Matthias' gray eyes died out like a duo of doused candles. He looked down at his hand, his fingers twitching twice before he curled them into a shaky fist.

"I trust you, Uwe," he muttered, slowly raising his eyes. "But I don't trust them. What's stopping them from turning their guns on us once the battle is over?"

"You," replied Uwe. "Because when I find the cache…"

"*If* you find the cache," Matthias said, his voice returning to its familiar metallic tone.

"*If* I find the cache," Uwe corrected, "I will give it to you and your men. I won't tell the Poles where it is. *You* will lead the Poles, *you* will decide who gets what weapon, *you* will decide how much ammo to give them. The Poles will depend on *you*. And even once you defeat Brandt and his men, the higher-ups will eventually send more soldiers here. The Poles know that. They'll need weapons and ammo then, and if they hurt you or your men, they'll be helpless because you have the weapons and ammo that they need to survive. And I'm going to make *sure* they know that their lives are in your hands."

Matthias' eyes briefly darted to his fists before he released a submissive sigh and crossed his legs.

"Sit," he said, gesturing to the spot in front of him. He finally pulled the maps that sat so dangerously close to a candle away from the flickering flame and laid them out in front of him.

"Sit," he insisted a bit impatiently. "We have to make a plan."

Once he had spoken with Matthias and they came up with a basic plan of attack, Uwe thanked the Jewish commander and promised to return soon with either news from the Poles or news on Julek's cache.

He knew he should go look for the cache, or at least find the Polish partisans and tell them that Matthias was willing to lead if they were willing to follow. But he thought of Uriel and worry invaded his mind, refusing to evacuate until he laid eyes on the boy.

Uwe approached Brandt's house warily and looked up. He saw the window open and anger filled his soul as he immediately (and justifiably) assumed Uriel had once again disobeyed him and run off, purposely putting himself in mortal danger.

Then, however, he heard voices drifting out of the open window. Voices that couldn't belong to the little mute boy that should have been hiding there.

He didn't even feel his legs move or register jumping through the downstairs window and running up to his room. One moment he was outside, gazing up at the open window, terror filling his veins as he realized that Brandt was in his room, and the next second he was standing in his untidy quarters, trying his best to look offended rather than afraid.

His eyes traveled to the open window and then to each of the policemen. His room was in a state of disarray, with clothes tossed here and there and turned inside out, but the Jewish boy was nowhere to be seen.

He disobeyed me. He left the room. He left before Brandt could burst in. Thank God…

As relief rushed through his body, he turned to Brandt with icy eyes.

"This is trespassing, you know," he said in a tone so composed that even he was surprised. Brandt crossed his arms behind his back, holding his head imperiously high.

"You would know something about that, Herr Litten," he replied. "Forgive us for breaking in, but you were out again. You have difficulty listening to me, Herr Litten…"

"I needed to get some air," retorted Uwe, elbowing past the two policemen and going over to the window as casually as possible. He shut it and closed the curtains just in case the boy chose the worst possible time to return before turning back to Brandt.

"It's suffocating in here," he hissed.

"True enough," said Brandt, a tiny, vindictive smile coming to his lips.

"Is there any particular reason," Uwe asked, "that you and your men chose to invade my privacy?"

"*Invade* is a bit of a strong word, Herr Litten," said Brandt with a shrug. "It's my duty as a soldier to make sure that nobody under my watch is harboring anything…detrimental."

"And you suspect me of being 'detrimental'?" Uwe said, glowering at the Major.

"Considering the fact that yesterday you told me that I—oh, how did you put it? 'Deserve to burn in hell', I believe?"

"Considering the *fact*," growled Uwe, taking an aggressive step forward, "that yesterday I saw you and your men *murdering* women and children, I think my *comment* was justified!"

Brandt's men flinched, but the Major only smirked. "*Jews*, Herr Litten," he said. "Pups of ill-tempered mutts will inevitably grow into ill-tempered mutts."

"*Humans*," snapped Uwe. "Like you said before, Herr Major, same species…"

"But different breeds," Brandt interrupted with a galling grin. "Remember that part of our conversation, Herr Litten?"

"Please get out of my room, *Herr Major*," said Uwe, pointing to the door. "I'll clean up *your* mess by myself!"

He gestured to the clutter. Brandt glanced around for a moment before his gaze settled on Uwe.

"Very well, Herr Litten," he said. "I'll give you a day to simmer down before we discuss this properly, but you will not go outside. I am going to stay downstairs to make sure you don't crawl through the windows again. Furthermore, I still have one or two prisoners to interrogate and I expect you to come with me and provide an accurate translation of their confessions. Is that clear?"

Although he dearly wanted to spit on Brandt's boot and tell him to go to hell again, Uwe merely nodded. He needed to be at least somewhat cooperative or else he would only put Matthias and Uriel in more danger.

"Rest assured, Herr Major," said Uwe, "I'll perform my duty as a linguist to the letter."

The warm and welcoming smile that Uwe had previously known Brandt for spread across the Major's face.

"Wonderful," he said. "And not to worry, Herr Litten. You won't have to see anything grisly again. We're almost done in this area, which means soon you'll be able to go home to your lovely wife and children. I envy you, Herr Litten."

"Right," muttered Uwe, not trusting the Major for one moment. "Now please, leave me be."

The Major gave a single nod and waved for his men to follow. Once they were out the door, Uwe slammed it shut and shoved the nightstand in front of it since he lacked a key.

Damn it! Uwe thought. *If he was telling the truth, if we leave soon, what will happen to Uriel? How soon is soon? Ha! And as if he'll send me safely home to my family when I know this much! He'll either ship me to a camp or 'resettle' me. I hope he's lying. I hope I still have enough time to find the cache.*

The cache. His fury and frustration promptly morphed into a sinking sensation of helplessness. He backed away from the door and sat down on the side of his rumpled bed. He drew Julek's enigmatic note from the depths of his pocket and began to desperately scrutinize it, focusing on every minute detail of the sentence and letters until his corneas ached and his temple throbbed in protest.

But try as he might, he couldn't find anything that made him leap to his feet and proclaim eureka. The note was just as nonsensical as before, and the linguist felt his already heavy heart become weightier when he thought that perhaps there was no meaning to be found.

After all, nobody who lived in the area could understand the clue. The only people he hadn't asked were the Poles, and he couldn't ask them. If they knew the meaning of the sentence, then they would be able to figure out where Julek's cache was. They would have the weapons, and he would lose all leverage. Matthias wouldn't be willing to lead the Poles if he didn't have a Sword of Damocles that he could use to keep them in line.

Besides, if Uwe ended up telling the Poles where the cache was then he would run the risk of accidentally arming any anti-Semitic loons that resided in the ranks of the Polish partisans. A Jew-hating fool like Patryk might be eager to take his anger out on any Jews he came across. If such a Jew-hater happened to find a golden-eyed little Jewish boy—worse, a *thieving* little Jewish boy…

Uwe hissed wrathfully and crumpled up the useless clue, tossing it across the room. It landed pitifully on a small pile of socks.

Uwe groaned and grabbed his sore head. He couldn't do it. He couldn't figure out the clue. He couldn't find the cache. He couldn't help the partisans. He couldn't save the Jews. All that was left was Uriel, and he was gone, in the woods, the same woods his people had been butchered in just yesterday.

Uwe looked up at the window and clasped his hands together, bowing his head and praying as hard as he could that Uriel would return soon and safe.

The Burden Boulder wasn't very far from the house. It only took Uriel some time to get to it because Samson's Pelt kept getting caught on every branch and bush he stumbled over as he followed the twittering doves. He had to wonder if Samson himself used to have this much trouble while traveling because of the lion's skin.

Pelt problems aside, though, he made it to the Boulder. The Burden Boulder was large, but rather unimpressive. It was hardly the mountain that Uriel had been expecting given the name, and it didn't look at all spectacular. It just looked like a big rock in the middle of the forest. Certainly not the oddest thing he had seen so far.

While the birds landed close by and confirmed that Joseph's Goblet would be right beneath the rock, Uriel made sure that Samson's Pelt was wound tightly around his body. He felt the Pelt providing him with more strength than any small child could naturally possess. His minute muscles suddenly felt more powerful than a bolt of lightning.

He crouched down and grabbed the bottom of the Burden Boulder. Grinding his teeth together, he slowly stood, lifting the huge rock. He could tell that it was heavy, yet lifting it was no more difficult than lifting a table or chair. A bit of effort was needed, it wasn't like picking up a feather, but it was no insurmountable task as long as he had the Pelt.

He moved the rock to the side and looked down. A gasp of shock leapt from his throat when he saw what the Burden Boulder had been hiding.

Under the Boulder was a deep, deep hole filled to the brim with boxes and guns of every shape and size. The boy set down the Burden Boulder and knelt beside the hole, gawking at the hidden munitions with awe.

He had to wonder who had hidden the weapons, and how they had managed to lift the Burden Boulder in the first place. Either there were at least twenty gun-collectors that liked to hide their wares in the woods, or whoever had owned Samson's Pelt previously had decided to keep an arsenal of his own under the ancient stone.

Wait a minute, thought the child. *These must be the hidden weapons that the Poles told Uwe about!*

A great smile grew on Uriel's face. *Good! I can show these to Uwe, and he can give them to Matthias! That way he can fight back against the Major!*

But before he did that, Uriel needed to find Joseph's Goblet, and doing that would involve digging through a small sea of weapons.

He cringed and hesitated, afraid that if he stepped on one of the guns, it would fire off and either injure him or attract unwanted attention. He didn't have much of a choice, unfortunately. There was no way that he was going to be able to find the Goblet without sifting through the weapons. He took a deep breath and slowly stepped down, balancing on the barrel of a rifle.

Trying to find a metal cup in a mountain of metal firearms was a bit like trying to find a single silver ring in the Golden Cavern. He had to be extraordinarily careful while moving the guns out of the way since he had no clue if they were loaded or not, and the last thing he wanted to do was to lose a hand or foot. Uwe would be more than upset if he returned hobbling or missing a few fingers.

At last, he moved a hefty gun to the side and saw a cup buried under a few boxes of ammo. He yanked it out and meticulously examined it.

It didn't seem particularly powerful. He couldn't feel any energy, benign or otherwise, emitting from the artifact as he held it in his hand. He could tell it was silver, but even then, it was tarnished and dirty. Had he seen it lying on the side of the road, he would have probably passed it by, never suspecting that it was special.

Nevertheless, he climbed out of the cache hole, clutching the ancient cup. After moving the Burden Boulder back over the cache so it would remain hidden, he held the cup up to the birds for confirmation that it was indeed Joseph's Goblet.

"That seems to be it," chirped one of the doves.

"Test it," suggested another. "Fill it with water and then try to see something or someone. You needn't speak to the Goblet, simply think of who or what you wish to see."

Uriel nodded and trudged about a bit, looking for some water. He didn't have to look for long as he quickly came across a large puddle left behind from the rainstorm a few nights ago. He scooped some water into the Goblet and sat down, holding the cup with both hands and gazing at the murky water.

All right, he thought. *Goblet, show me the Archangel Michael.*

Nothing happened. The water remained still and grimy. Uriel sighed in disappointment.

Okay, he thought. *In that case, Goblet, show me my brother Matthias.*

Hardly had he finished his mental command when the water in the cup began to ripple and swirl. Uriel leaned in, his eyes wide and fascinated. The now-clear water seemed to glow. Color came to its surface, whirling until an image formed.

He could see his brother sitting down in a cave by a flickering candle with some papers spread out in front of him. Seeing his brother, alive and unscathed, brought stinging water to Uriel's eyes. His tears dropped into the cup and caused the image to falter before coming back into focus. Another man approached Matthias and opened his mouth. When he spoke, his voice echoed out of the water, wobbly and distant, like a call from far away.

"Matthias, is Uwe going to be back soon?"

"Not until he talks to the Poles and finds the cache."

"When's the attack?" Uriel couldn't tell if the man was nervous or eager. His voice sounded so strange coming from the Goblet's water.

"Whenever he finds the weapons. *If* he finds the weapons."

Uriel's heart ached. Even with Matthias' voice altered by the Goblet, the boy could tell that his brother was speaking sternly. It hurt him to see his warm and shy brother so solemn. He could only hope that the joy Matthias would surely feel upon seeing his little brother-in-law again would make him smile and laugh once more.

The child wiped the tears from his eyes and looked down at the waters again.

Goblet, he thought, *show me Uwe Litten.*

The water rippled and Matthias' image dissolved, soon replaced by another. Uwe sat in his room, which was in a chaotic state, with clothes and papers scattered to and fro. He had his hands clasped together and his head bowed, praying, only interrupting his supplication to glance at the window. Guilt grasped Uriel's heart when he realized that the linguist was praying for his safe return.

He stood up and was about to throw the water out of the Goblet and run back to Uwe when another thought occurred to him. He clenched his lips together and scowled at the cup.

Goblet, he thought, *show me the Major, Major Brandt.*

The water swirled and Uwe's room disappeared, replaced by the Major's tidy office. The Major stood behind his oaken desk while two of his men stood in front of him.

"…so we're really going to be leaving soon, Uncle Günter?"

The Major gave the policeman a small smile and a curt nod. "Yes indeed. We've almost completely cleaned out this area. Once the Sweep is over, we'll only have one or two more villages to handle before we can safely declare this area free of threats."

"And when that happens…when we move on, I mean…we're not going to keep Herr Litten as…"

"I'll decide what happens to our little linguist," the Major declared, and Uriel's blood boiled at the thought of the evil man hurting Uwe.

"Don't concern yourselves with him," the Major continued. "You should focus on the Sweep and be ready."

The Sweep? thought Uriel, his brow knitting curiously. He wasn't the only clueless one, it seemed. One of the Major's men bit his lip and bashfully spoke up.

"Uhm…Uncle Günter," he muttered. "Forgive me, but I was out topping off the Reprisal for Karl and Dieter when the Sweep was discussed. I don't know the specifics."

"Moron," his companion hissed so quietly that Uriel was sure the only reason he heard was because of the Goblet's powers. "Why didn't you ask earlier? It's in two days!"

The Major, however, only chuckled a bit and smiled warmly at his soldier. "That's all right, Josef. My fault, actually. I should have made sure that somebody got you up to speed. Well, it's not very complicated. Essentially, those Polish partisans have been attacking us for far too long. They're making us waste time and energy, and we're getting behind schedule as a result. Not to mention the irreparable damage they've caused by injuring and killing our comrades."

"Fortunately," he said, and his smile curled in a manner that made Uriel quiver, "our little linguist upstairs helped us more than he knows. The Poles we interrogated together gave us just enough information to narrow down where the partisans are. We don't have an exact location, but we have a general area. And in two days we're going to sweep through that area and take out any resistance we find, Jews and Poles alike."

Uriel's stomach tied itself into nineteen nervous knots. Two days. Was that enough time for the partisans to mount an attack? Would the Germans find Matthias during the Sweep?

He listened for more information, but the conversation had quickly turned away from the Sweep and back to Uwe.

"But sir, if we're already doing the Sweep then why are you going to take Herr Litten to interrogate the prisoners some more after tomorrow?"

"To make sure there's no crucial information that we didn't pick up during past interrogations," replied the Major. "But more than that, to make sure our little linguist hasn't completely abandoned all loyalty to the Reich and his people. I will confess that what he saw yesterday was shocking, and that's why I'm giving him a day to cool off. I'll be sure to have a long talk with him after tomorrow, and if he goes back to being a good translator then fine and good. I've never believed in dispensing corporal punishment right away. When my little son acts out of line, I always give him some time to come and tell me that he did wrong or overreacted. It's only if he persists in his stubbornness and insubordination that I give him a smack or two. I'd prefer it if we spoke cordially, he came to his senses, and confessed to his wrongdoings."

He put his hand into his pocket as he said all this and Uriel could hear a teeny clinking noise, like many bits of metal hitting one another. The boy's heart began to pound as he realized that the Major must have found the golden chains he had taken from the Germans. He cursed himself for not throwing them into the Golden Cavern like he should have.

"You're very kind, Uncle Günter."

"Thank you. Though I hope he comes to his senses fast. My patience is wearing thin, especially with his little romps in the woods. I don't know what he's doing, but I don't like it. In fact, Johann, I want you to stay here tomorrow and guard the living room. He keeps slipping out through the window there, so just be sure he doesn't and keep your eyes open."

"Yes, sir!" laughed the soldier, visibly pleased about being assigned a post that would let him sit on a comfortable sofa while on duty.

"That being said, good night, boys…"

Having heard enough, Uriel turned the Goblet upside down. The water fell to the ground and turned the dirt at his feet into mud. He watched it for a moment, thinking that perhaps, if he looked closely, he would see the Major's face in the muck.

He didn't, and when he was certain that the Major's visage was gone for good, he shoved Joseph's Goblet into his pocket. He pulled out his golden notebook and gazed at it for a moment before clasping it to his chest and taking off towards the Major's house.

As soon as Uriel climbed back into the room, he was engulfed in a hug so tight that he almost thought he heard one of his bones crack. The embrace wasn't entirely unexpected, however, and he returned it as much as he could with his arms pinned to his sides and his lungs slowly being crushed.

When Uwe finally released him, he gave the boy a small kiss on his brow. The child smiled widely. That was the kind of affectionate gesture his mother and father would provide when they were worried about him. Or when they were happy to see him. Or when they had to say goodbye.

"Uriel," Uwe laughed, crouching down before the boy and smiling in a manner that seemed more conflicted than joyful. "I'm not sure if I should be angry or glad! While you were out Brandt came in to search my room…he almost found you…"

His smile slowly melted into a guilty frown. "Damn. Maybe I should bring you to Matthias…"

Uriel grabbed Uwe's arm and shook his head as vigorously as he could. Much as he wanted to see his brother, he still had one quest left, and besides he didn't want to leave Uwe yet.

Uwe smiled, touched, but before he could say anything Uriel remembered Brandt's objective and pulled rather roughly on the linguist's arm, his eyes round and frantic.

"What's wrong?" asked Uwe, concern coming to his voice. The boy gestured for a pen.

It took a bit of digging since Brandt and his men had left the room in such a hectic condition, but Uwe unearthed a pen and handed it to the boy.

The child turned to the back of his golden notebook and, looking exceedingly pained, ripped out a blank page. Uwe flinched and panic promptly pinched his heart. Uriel would never tear a page from his beloved notebook, not unless the situation was truly dire.

The child closed the notebook and used the sheet of paper he had ripped out to write a quick, neat note. He handed it to the linguist. Uwe read it over.

Heard the Major talking. He has an idea of where the Poles are. Going to do a sweep of the forest area. Will kill anything he comes across. May find Matthias and the Jews too.

Sweep will be in two days. He's testing you with interrogation. Wants to see if you 'behave.' He also put a soldier down in the living room to make sure you don't get out.

I found the hidden weapons.

Uwe, overwhelmed, felt his head spin. How had the boy gotten all of this information? How had he eavesdropped so thoroughly without the Major taking notice? The child was good at sneaking past the Germans, but he hadn't thought the boy could possibly be *that* good.

The linguist had to read the last line three times to be sure he hadn't gotten the translation wrong, but once he got through the third read, he was certain. The hidden weapons. Uriel must have meant Julek's cache. How on earth had he found the weapons? Was that why he had gone out? Perhaps the note hadn't been complete gibberish to the child after all. Had he thought about it while Uwe was out and, after realizing what the letter meant, disobeyed Uwe in order to see if his hunch was correct?

Uwe looked up and prepared to ask Uriel one of the thousand questions that the child's written proclamation had raised, but when he lifted his eyes, the boy was already sitting on the windowsill, climbing onto the branch. The boy looked back at the German and urgently gestured for him to follow.

Uwe hesitated, his mouth open, trying to ask a question that refused to exit his lips. He closed his mouth and inhaled deeply, deciding that the boy was right. This wasn't the time for questions. He trusted the child, and so he had to hurry. He only had two days to get everything together.

"Right," he muttered, folding up Uriel's note and shoving it into his pocket. "Then let's go. Show me where the cache is."

Uriel nodded and skittered down the tree like a squirrel. The boy hopped down and looked up at the German. Uwe could see him nervously chewing on his bottom lip. The linguist looked at the branch with apprehension. The branch, he could tell, was just barely strong enough to support the boy's weight. Although Uwe was a small man, his weight coupled with his poor tree climbing skills could amount to a nasty fall, and he certainly couldn't afford to break a leg or, worse, his neck.

But he didn't have much of a choice, and so he emptied out his lungs and cautiously crawled onto the branch. It wobbled awfully and he could hear it moan and crack, but by some miracle it didn't snap. He was able to crawl to the trunk and slowly climb down.

He inhaled appreciatively once his feet touched the earth. Climbing down wasn't as hard as climbing up, but either way he knew that getting in and out of his room via the tree wasn't going to be very pleasant.

More pleasant than having to explain myself to Brandt if he catches me sneaking out the living room window, he thought, trailing Uriel as the boy scurried into the undergrowth. He made sure to follow the child's every step, knowing that he had to stay out of sight and knowing that Uriel was an expert in that area.

Before they continued through the forest, the boy paused to fish something out of the bushes. Uwe was quite surprised and confused when the child threw a lion's pelt over his shoulders. The same pelt, he was sure, that Brandt had offered him earlier.

"Uriel, how did...?" he started to ask, but the child was already running ahead, huffing in exasperation when the pelt got caught on a bush or branch. Uwe helped free the pelt when that happened, but he still had to wonder how and why the boy had acquired the pelt. Hadn't Brandt shipped it off to Hamburg? How on earth had the child managed to steal it without the Major noticing? And why on earth was he so determined to take it with him while he showed Uwe the cache?

Since Uwe knew that the child both couldn't and probably wouldn't answer any of those questions, he decided not to bother with asking. Besides, Brandt had stolen the pelt in the first place. If Uriel stole it from the thief, Uwe could sympathize.

Yet he couldn't help but think of the note that was currently resting on a pile of socks in his room. *The Cat Raises The Rock.* He wondered if there was some sort of connection, but quickly decided that even if there was, he didn't care. As long as the cache was found and secure, the old man's letter was meaningless. More meaningless than it had been before, anyway.

It wasn't long before the German and Jew were standing in front of a large rock.

"Is this it?" asked Uwe. The child nodded, darted to the boulder, and crouched down beside it, making a lifting motion.

"Oh, it's under the rock?" Uwe asked, moving next to Uriel and squatting down beside him. The child smiled and nodded.

"How in God's name did you lift a rock this big before, Uriel?" queried Uwe. The child's smile widened and his golden eyes glittered mysteriously. *Sorry, it's a secret.*

Uwe rolled his eyes and shook his head. "Of course. Well, at any rate, let me help you this time. Don't want you to break your back."

Uriel gave a small nod of agreement and grabbed the bottom of the boulder. Uwe did the same.

"All right," he said. "On three. One, two, *three!*"

Both lifted in unison and Uwe was surprised. The boulder must have been some kind of hollow rock because picking it up was so easy that it was almost startling. It felt more like a small wooden chair than a boulder six times his size. Uriel seemed to be having even less trouble than he was.

I suppose that explains how Uriel was able to lift it all by himself, Uwe thought as he and the child set the light stone to the side.

Dusting his hands off, the linguist looked down into the hole that the boulder had been hiding and his eyes bulged when he saw the bounty of firearms. Crates of ammo and heaps of guns. Crazy Old Julek had certainly been prepared for the absolute worst. One could conceivably take on a large troop with all of these weapons.

Uwe laughed and clapped his hands together. He looked down at the boy, who was beaming merrily, and yanked him into another tight embrace.

"Uriel, you blessed boy!" he exclaimed, kissing the child's forehead once more. "You've saved all of us!"

Uriel blushed and looked down at the ground, kicking a small puddle of water and giving a bashful shrug.

"Oh, don't be so timid!" chuckled Uwe. "You really have! We can fight back now, but we have to put the plan into action fast! Come, help me put the boulder back over the cache. I want to make sure that you, me, and Matthias are the only ones who know where it is."

Uriel nodded in wholehearted agreement and happily helped Uwe put the Boulder back over the cache. Though he was concerned about how Uwe would lift it without Samson's Pelt, Uriel knew that the linguist would manage.

Matthias had about twenty men with him, and according to the doves that was enough to lift the Burden Boulder even without a garment from the strongest man who ever lived.

Still, just in case, the boy took off the Pelt and put it down next to the Boulder. If Uwe needed it, he could use it.

Uwe hardly noticed the boy place the lion's hide on the muddy ground. He was too focused on estimating where the cache was in relation to Matthias' cave.

"Right," he muttered once he made a mental map. He turned to Uriel.

"Uriel," he said, kneeling down in front of the boy and grabbing his shoulders, "Run back home, okay? Wait for me at the house. I'll be back soon, I promise, but first I have to get Matthias. I have to show him where the cache is. We all have to hurry."

Uriel nodded and spun around, running back towards the house. Once Uwe was out of sight, however, the boy stopped and changed his route. He glanced up at the sky just as the first stars emerged from the blackening heavens.

Uwe was indeed right. They *all* had to hurry. Uriel pulled out Joseph's Goblet. It was time for him to get his final quest.

Samael was not overtly shocked when Uriel arrived. He merely stretched out his arm and opened his hand, waiting for the child to give him the Goblet.

The boy placed the Goblet on the Angel of Death's palm and Samael's spider-leg thin fingers curled around the cup. He examined the ancient dinnerware for a moment, his purple eyes wandering across its tarnished surface before he sighed and gave a small nod, accepting that it was indeed what he had asked for.

His eyes returned to the boy, and the child braced himself for a sneer or an insult. He was surprised when the Angel of Death muttered a rather reluctant, "You've done well so far."

Uriel's brow furrowed. He shook his head, sure that he had heard that wrong. The Angel of Death would never give anything akin to a compliment to anybody, much less a Jew.

"Better," the Angel of Death confessed, "than I thought a little mute Jew would…"

His voice trailed off. He glanced up, meeting Uriel's golden eyes. The boy recalled meeting Samael's violet eyes during the massacre. Just yesterday those eyes had shimmered with something resembling shame as he stood over the bodies of the murdered Jews and performed his grim duty, unaware that his little opponent had been observing the whole time.

He wasn't sure how, but Uriel could tell that Samael was remembering the same incident as he stared at the boy. After a lengthy pause, Samael opened his mouth and Uriel could tell that he was seconds away from letting a comment about the slaughter fly from his lips.

The Angel of Death, however, seemed to remember himself. He shut his mouth and his eyes became hard and cold as ice.

"It's time we finish this," he hissed. "Don't you agree, Jew-boy?"

Uriel gave a stiff nod.

"Then one more task," said Samael, "and we'll see if you live up to the title that the rest of the Heavenly Host has bestowed upon you."

His lip curled and the sneer that Uriel knew Samael for returned to his face.

"*Angel-Finder*," he scoffed. "Your last task is this: bring me a jug of water from the Eternal Fountain."

The ice in his amethyst irises melted and a cruel fire burned in its place. Uriel felt a shiver snake its way up his spine, but he refused to show the fear that the fire in the Angel of Death's eyes was giving him. He gave a small, curt nod and turned to leave before the Angel of Death could even disappear.

Samael stared at the child's receding form, unwillingly admiring his courage.

Or maybe it's stupidity, he thought as he watched the boy march through the thicket. *Angel-Finder, you should know better. Never turn your back on the Angel of Death.*

PRAYER

To many people, prayer meant one of two things: praise or request.

They prayed to thank Hashem for His many miracles, for His mercy, for His eternal love and kindness.

They also prayed when they wanted something. Uriel couldn't count the number of times he had seen the naughtiest boys in his class, the ones who wasted their precious vocal cords on constant cursing and vile jokes, bow their heads like pious little angels when they were presented with a test they hadn't studied for. Papa often said that tribulation turned robbers into rabbis.

But Papa taught him that prayer could also be used to ask questions. Hashem, he said, did not consider honest and respectful questioning to be a sin. He had let Moses and Abraham question Him because they had done so in a loving and reverential way. Papa always encouraged Uriel to ask God any questions he had on his mind while praying. Perhaps one day he would receive a divine answer.

Uriel, therefore, always made sure to ask God a question during his prayers. After he finished thanking Hashem for all of His mercies and kindnesses, he always posed a query.

And more often than not, he would ask why God had made him a mute.

The bullies that taunted him would often say that God didn't love him and that was why He had made him a mute. Although Uriel didn't believe those bullies, he had to wonder why, if God didn't hate him, He hadn't given him a voice.

It couldn't be a case of oversight. The omniscient Lord of all life wouldn't be so forgetful.

Perhaps it was a blessing in disguise. Without a voice, after all, Uriel could never curse or say anything cruel. Hurtful words, once said, could never be taken back and they could often fester like an open wound. Without a voice, he couldn't cause such pain.

Perhaps it was something for him to overcome. Papa had once told him that Moses himself, the greatest prophet of them all, had a terrible stutter. He had freed the Jewish People and become a prophet even with such a disadvantage. Surely Uriel, even without a voice, could manage to do well.

Whatever the reason (and Uriel refused to believe that there was no reason), he never heard a justification for his muteness whispered in his ear. No gentle voice ever muttered an explanation in response to his query, and the dreams he had following his nighttime prayers never answered his burning question.

Nevertheless, he prayed and he asked, hoping that one day he would either be answered with a reason or a miracle. Perhaps it had been a heavenly error. Perhaps, if he asked about it enough, Hashem would take note and Uriel would wake up one day with a voice to sing and pray with.

It was doubtful, but Uriel was an optimist.

Uriel normally only prayed in his mind. He didn't like to mouth anything. Mouthing always felt like cheating to him, and a rather cruel form of cheating besides. All it did was remind him that even if his lips could form the words, he would never be able to speak them.

But there was one prayer that he did mouth. Although when he did so his heart would sink and he would feel like a hypocrite for hating cheating so much when he, in his own way, cheated every night. Nevertheless, he would always mouth the prayer once before he went to sleep.

'God of the First and God of the Last

God of all creatures

Master of All Generations.

Hashem neither slumbers nor sleeps

He makes the mute speak.'

He only mouthed it after Mama had tucked him in, once she thought he had completed his prayers and asked Hashem all of his questions.

One night, though, she was so tired and stressed that she neglected to give him a kiss goodnight. Although he felt bad and waited awhile for her to come and peck his brow like she normally did, he eventually grew tired of waiting and knelt down before the window, mouthing his nightly prayer.

He was so focused on his prayer that he didn't notice his mother walk in until he had finished. Once he did so, he turned red as a beet in embarrassment. She had seen him mouthing his prayer. He didn't like to reveal how much he wanted a voice, knowing full well that his muteness worried his mother and father enough. He didn't want to appear unhappy. He was happy. He would just be much happier if he could talk and sing like the rest of the children in Zingdorf. He would even be content if he could just know why he was made a mute in the first place.

She smiled, and it was one of the strangest smiles he had ever seen in his life. It wasn't a forced, sad smile that was barely hiding the fear she felt on behalf of her little son. It wasn't a smile of pure joy or amusement. It was an odd smile, one that conveyed love and confusion and certainty all at once.

She walked over to him, knelt in front of him, gave him the kiss that his forehead had been craving, and looked him right in the eye.

"Little bird," she said. He expected a speech or a story or at the very least a witty proverb like Papa would provide.

Instead, she spoke only a single sentence, one that filled him with more hope than any long-winded sermon would have.

"What you do not have in this world, Hashem, blessed be He, will give you in the next."

"What you do not have in this world, Hashem, blessed be He, will give you in the next."

It was hard for Uwe to brush off 'his' finding of Julek's cache when Matthias asked him how he had discovered it so fast. The linguist claimed he had simply been lucky enough to find a lion's pelt that just-so-happened to have the location of the boulder written on the inside. When Matthias saw the lion's skin lying on the forest floor, he snuck a peek and quickly discovered that the hide had no such map. When confronted about his apparent fib, Uwe simply asserted that the pelt had been left in a muddy puddle and the writing that had been there before must have washed off.

The Jewish commander was noticeably suspicious, and had Uwe not evolved into a decent liar he might have been forced to bring up Uriel. Since the boy was so determined to stay with him for now (and since Uwe wanted to put off moving the child into the dank, dirty cave for as long as possible), he took credit. He could always give the credit back to the boy once he and Matthias met, but until then it would be best to avoid any further complications.

Getting the weapons became a bit of a problem, one that involved two trips. Initially, thinking the boulder was unusually light, he only took Matthias and Solomon. However, much to Uwe's astonishment, it appeared the stone had become ten times as heavy during his absence. What had been light as a piece of wood while Uriel was with him was now impossible to lift even with two fairly strong grown men assisting him. He almost thought he had led them to the wrong rock at first, but Matthias found the lion pelt that Uriel had stolen lying in the mud right beside the boulder, confirming that it was indeed the same stone.

Although he insisted that he had been able to lift it by himself before, they were eventually forced to go back and get reinforcements. It was dangerous, marching through the woods with twenty Jews, and Matthias' men were noticeably jumpy, cringing at the mere hoot of an owl or whisper of the wind. Uwe had to keep reminding himself that most of them hadn't stepped out of the cave in weeks, maybe months.

Even with twenty men, lifting the boulder was a struggle. They managed, though, and once they laid eyes on the weapons, it was all the Jews could do to stop themselves from cheering. They grabbed as much as they could carry and pushed the rock back over the cache.

Once they were back at the cave, they laid out what they had on the floor. Uwe confirmed that what they had gathered would be more than enough for both the Poles and Jews to use against the *Ordnungspolizei*. However, he warned them that they had to move quickly, informing them that the Sweep was in two days.

"I'll tell the Poles about you and the cache first thing tomorrow," Uwe vowed. "For now, we have a plan…when do we put it into effect?"

"We have two days, and we'll need at least a day to set up the rendezvous point and get everything ready," said Matthias. "The day after tomorrow, at midnight. That's when they'll be off guard, and since we know where they're sleeping, we can surprise them."

"That's cutting it close," Uwe sighed.

"We have to cut it close! We don't have a choice!" said Matthias. "Just make sure the Poles are ready. Make sure they know we have the cache."

Uwe vowed that he would and then promptly left the cave, returning to the house to get some much-needed sleep and make sure Uriel was safe. Climbing up the tree was indeed much harder than climbing down, but by imitating Uriel he was able to hoist himself up and climb back through the window without being injured or seen.

The next day involved more climbing, and Uwe wasn't sure if he loved or hated that tree. On one hand, it was saving his life and had saved Uriel's several times in the past. On the other hand, it was a pain to climb. If the war concluded and he was alive by the end, he wasn't sure if he would honor the tree or turn it into firewood.

But for now, the tree was Uwe's salvation. He slipped out of his room early in the morning and scurried into the woods, praying that the Major would do as he promised and leave him alone for a day.

After a bit of searching and retracing his steps, he found the Polish camp. Following a brief interrogation, he was brought to Felix and Patryk.

Wasting no time on pleasantries, he ignored Patryk and faced Felix.

"I found it," he announced. Felix's eyes widened with hope.

"Crazy Old Julek's…?"

Uwe nodded and Felix let out a joyful laugh.

"See now, Patryk?" he snapped at his brother. "I told you we would find it!"

"*We* did not find it," Patryk said with a slight roll of the eyes. "Pan Litten did. We're very grateful, Pan Litten."

Since he wasn't beholden to Patryk, Uwe decided not to dignify the Jew-hater with a proper response. Instead, he intentionally said something that he knew would infuriate him.

"I gave the weapons to Matthias and his men. The Jews have them now."

Patryk, struggling to suppress a furious shout, gritted his teeth and glowered at the German. Felix was visibly shocked.

"*What?*" he cried. "How could you do that?"

"Not to worry," Uwe said. "I talked to Matthias. He's willing to lead you if you're willing to follow, and if you're willing to follow then he's willing to arm you."

"But…"

"Because," said Uwe, keeping his voice even and unyielding, "you can trust Matthias, but he can't trust you."

"Trust a Jew…" he heard Patryk mutter. The linguist turned to him with a glare so potent that the Polish man actually took a cautious step back.

"I don't want to hear it from you!" he snarled. "Listen here: the Major and his men are going to do a sweep of this whole area in two days! We have *two days* to mount an attack, and you have no choice but to join with the Jews. Unless you hate the Jews so much that you would rather get shot in the head than work with them, you had better keep your bigotry to yourself!"

"Wait, two days…?" muttered Patryk, fear coming to his eyes though his tone was calm once more.

"Two days," Uwe confirmed.

"How do you know…?" Felix started to ask, suspicion creeping into his voice. It was Uwe's turn to roll his eyes.

"I'm the Major's linguist. I hear things," he answered. Felix glanced at his brother and gave a slight shrug, as if to communicate that he believed the linguist but wanted Patryk's opinion as well.

Patryk nodded dourly. "I see…two days…"

"We have a plan," Uwe said. "Matthias and I. We know where the Germans are resting, we know when and how to attack, and we have the weapons to attack. But we need more men."

"I talked to the rest of them," Felix said, gesturing to the camp. "We're… split. Some of the men are willing to follow Matthias if he's got a good plan, but the others don't want to work with Jews. They might go along with it if Patryk does, but he's hardheaded."

"Fine then," said Uwe, raising his shoulders nonchalantly. "Gather the men who are willing to work with the Jews. We don't need Patryk."

"Hold on a moment!" cried Patryk, finally allowing umbrage to slip into his level tone. "I'm a good Pole and a good soldier. I want to fight the Germans, but I don't want to work with the same people who are destroying my country…!"

"The Germans are the ones destroying this country," said Uwe. "The Germans and people like you! Listen here, Patryk: the other day I saw Brandt's men murdering women and children. They shot them in the neck because they were Jews, and if you think they won't do that to your women and children once they finish off the Jews, then you're as blind as I was."

"I realize that, but that doesn't mean…"

"*Yes. It. Does.* The Germans got this far because of people like you. If all of you had helped the Jews instead of killing them or looking the other way, you would have made the Germans' jobs all the harder. Instead, people like you helped them destroy villages, and now their work is almost done. They only have a few villages left, and then there's you. The Poles."

He paused, waiting for Patryk to cut in, but when the partisan remained stoic and silent, he heaved a great sigh and spoke in a quieter tone.

"Now look…you're brave. You are. You're facing the Order Police and fighting for your country. You're right to fight for your country, that's admirable. But if you want to stay alive and if you want Poland to stay alive, then you can't afford to pout in the corner like a small child when an opportunity is presented. Matthias and his men are not deicidal bloodsuckers or evil communists waiting to stab you in the back. They want to live and be free as much as you do, and right now they're *your* only chance. If you want to fight, fine. You'll just have to accept a Jew as your commander."

A pregnant pause followed as Patryk stared at the German, gradually taking in everything Uwe had said. Slowly, he looked down at his mud-covered boots and took a deep, acquiescent breath.

"Very well," he muttered. "If it means surviving and finally getting rid of the Germans, I'll go with Felix and the Jew."

"Matthias," Uwe corrected sternly, crossing his arms over his chest.

"Matthias," huffed Patryk. He looked up at the German, his eyes brimming with humiliation and ire as he hissed. "But if I even *suspect* that this Matthias is a traitor or a communist, I'm going to put a bullet in his…"

"No, you won't," Uwe interrupted, "Because even if you take out Brandt and his men, the higher-ups will eventually send replacements. And when that happens, you'll need Matthias, and you'll need more weapons and ammo.

Matthias is the only one who can give you the weapons you need. If you shoot him, you might as well shoot yourself."

He waited for a comeback from Patryk, but the partisan had been rendered retortless.

After the silence had gone on far too long, Felix mercifully cried, "Good then! We're both onboard! Then let's hear a bit about this great plan that you and the J---er, Matthias—came up with, Litten."

"Right," said Uwe. "I need a map."

The two partisans quickly provided him with one and gathered around as he marked off where the two target houses were.

"First, though," he said. "We need a rendezvous point where you can meet up with the Jews, somewhere close to these houses. Have anything in mind?"

He pointed to the two houses that the rendezvous point needed to be close to. The brothers stroked their chins and glanced at one another before Patryk suggested, "There's that old tree. Big, gnarled black thing. Been dead for years, but it's still standing. Impossible to miss it."

"Can you mark it off?" Uwe asked. Patryk nodded and did so. Uwe looked at the mark and a smile crept onto his face.

Perfect, he thought. It was close to the houses, and also relatively close to the cave where Matthias and his men were hiding. They could easily carry the weapons to the tree.

"That's good," he said. "You'll meet Matthias there at midnight, and he'll give you everything you need before the attack."

"All right," said Felix with a nod. "Then let's hear all about this attack plan."

After everything was sorted out with the Polish partisans, Uwe met with Matthias to tell him that the Poles were ready to follow him and to give him the rendezvous point.

Once Matthias had all the information he needed, Uwe hurried back to the house. There was still one last thing he needed to do.

Uriel was still in the room when he returned, sitting on the bed and scrawling in his precious golden notebook. The child took a moment to finish a paragraph before he jumped up and ran over to greet the linguist.

"Hello, little writer," chuckled Uwe, allowing the boy to wrap his arms around his waist and give him a small hug. The boy stepped back, his smile bright and his eyes inquiring. *Well,* he seemed to ask, *how did it go?*

"Everything's almost done," said Uwe, crossing the room and sitting down on the bed. He picked up the golden notebook and looked down at it, running his thumb along the spine.

"Tomorrow night," he muttered. "That's when the attack takes place. Midnight exactly. By midnight tomorrow you and I will have to leave. I'll introduce you to Matthias. I'm not sure what's going to happen after the attack, but we'll stay with Matthias for some time. I'm sure you'll like him."

Uriel's heart sashayed with joy. Midnight. By midnight tomorrow, the Major would be gone. He could finally embrace his brother. He hoped that he could find and free Michael before then or else complications could arise. He had been waiting all day for the birds to lead him to the Eternal Fountain, but the doves hadn't come. He assumed they needed a day to gather information and figure out what completing the final quest would require. He would just have to wait until tomorrow.

He sat down next to Uwe and pointed to the golden notebook and the linguist's mouth. Uwe smiled.

"Of course," he said. "This is the last night we're going to be able to read like this, you know. At least for a long time."

Uriel gave a small nod and gingerly took the book from Uwe.

"Pick a good one," said Uwe. "Well, they're *all* good ones of course…"

Uriel's golden irises sparkled and he nodded obediently, his eyes roaming across the titles as he searched for a suitable story.

"You know…" sighed Uwe, "It feels like we've been doing this forever…"

The child paused his hunt for a moment and looked up at the German, a teensy twinkle in his amber eyes, one that communicated a bittersweet agreement. He would miss this nightly ritual as much as Uwe.

"Well," muttered Uwe, "hopefully we can still read together after the attack."

Uriel nodded. *Hopefully.*

The boy handed Uwe the golden notebook. Uwe thanked the child and exhaled nostalgically as he recalled the first time he had flipped through the little book. He glanced at the boy as the child got into a comfortable position and leaned on the linguist's shoulder. Uwe smiled fondly as he remembered the first time he had read a story aloud to the boy. It seemed like it had been so long ago.

He shook his head. Now wasn't the time for reminiscing. Now was the time for reading.

"Long ago, in the land of Israel, the Greeks had conquered the Holy Land. The wicked King Antiochus, ruler of all the Greeks, despised Hashem and all who followed him.

'My gods should be worshiped by all,' he decided. 'Therefore, place a statue of Zeus in every synagogue and even in the Great Temple in Jerusalem. Force every Jew to abandon Hashem and worship Zeus and Hades and Poseidon instead. If they will not, throw them into a kiln of fire and let them burn as a warning to every other Jew who might refuse to worship my gods.'

So the Greeks went to every Jewish town and placed a statue of their false gods in each synagogue. They took all of the residents of the town and said, 'Worship our gods, or you will die in the fire.'

Many Jews, such as Judah the Maccabee, fled from the Greeks and returned as fighters. Some others fell and worshiped the Greek gods in order to save their lives.

But in one little village there was a mother. She had seven sons, all of them handsome and smart. She loved them all and raised them as good Jewish boys. She taught them the Torah every day, and even though they were all young, they were well-versed and eager to become rabbis someday.

But the Greeks soon came to their little village, and before any of them could hope to flee and join Judah the Maccabee and his fighters they were dragged to a great statue of Zeus.

As the Greek governor looked over the Jews, the seven handsome brothers caught his eye. He spoke to them a bit and realized how intelligent they were.

'They,' the governor decided, 'will make wonderful Greeks, and once they become Greeks and worship our gods it will encourage the rest of the village to do so as well.'

So he called up the oldest of the brothers.

'Young man,' he said, 'if you bow down before Zeus and worship him as your god, I will make you a great official and give you many pounds of gold. You will have more power than you can dream of.'

But the eldest said, 'Your god is made of marble. I only worship Hashem, and I will never betray Him by bowing to you or your gods! Do what you like to me!'

The governor became furious and ordered his men to kill the eldest. The youth was tortured and thrown into the fiery kiln.

The governor summoned the next son. 'Young man," he said, 'see what happened to your brother when he refused? Your God did not save him, and He will not save you either! But if you worship my god, I will let you live and make you rich.'

'Be silent, monster,' replied the second son. 'You murder my brother and now you think I will betray him and Hashem at the same time? Throw me into the kiln if you like, but I will not bow!'

The governor became even more furious and had the second son tortured and burned like his brother before him.

He called up the third son, but he too refused and was murdered. The fourth, fifth and sixth sons refused and cursed the governor even as they were thrown into the kiln.

Finally, the seventh son and his mother were the only ones left. The seventh son was merely a child, only eleven years old. The governor thought, 'This one is only a child. He'll see what happened to his brothers and gladly worship Zeus, and then all the other townsfolk will worship our gods as well! But in case he refuses, I'll threaten his mother.'

So he ordered his guards to hold the boy's mother by the fire while he spoke to the seventh son. 'Now, my son,' he said, 'you can worship Zeus and live a long life, or you can refuse and both you and your mother will suffer as your brothers did.'

His mother cried out, 'My little son! I raised you from birth to love God as much as you love me!'

'Yes,' said the boy, then he turned to the governor and said, 'I will not betray my mother, I will not betray my brothers, I will not betray my people, and I will not betray my God. You have lost, governor.'

Furious, the governor himself shoved both mother and son into the kiln, but as he did so he himself fell in and burned to death.

When the villagers saw the sacrifice of the seven sons, instead of being filled with fear, they were filled with bravery and fought back against the Greeks, joining Judah and his fighters. The mother and her seven sons were rewarded greatly once they reached the Throne of God, but the Greek governor was tossed into Sheol and sentenced to stay in the Darkness of the Underworld for eight thousand years, a thousand years for each child he threw into the kiln.

Hashem was so touched by the sacrifice of the mother and her seven sons that, in their merit, once Judah the Maccabee and his forces reclaimed the Temple and lit the menorah, He kept the flame burning for eight days. One day for the mother and each of her seven sons.

So every night of Hanukkah is a day of remembrance for the miracle that Hashem performed, for the freedom that Judah the Maccabee won, and for the sacrifice of the mother and her seven sons."

The interrogation was torture.

Not for the Pole who was being questioned, in fact Brandt was unnaturally composed during the entire session, never even giving the prisoner a smack.

For Uwe, though, once morning came and he left with the Major, the clock seemed to turn into a tortoise, going far too slow for the linguist's comfort.

He so wanted the day to be done. He so wanted to go back to the house and get ready to leave. Today was the last day before the Sweep, and if the attack at midnight didn't go as planned tragedy would surely follow.

He knew this, and therefore he had to be very careful not to arouse any suspicion. If he did something to anger or upset the Major, it could cause a chaotic complication to arise. Because of this, he was forced to smile and nod, to agree with everything the Major said, and to be on his absolute best and most obedient behavior.

Head down. Do as they say.

At least until his job was over for the day and the Major dropped him off at the house. Until then, Uwe had to stomach Brandt's 'explanations' for why killing the Jews was necessary.

"We don't enjoy it," said Major Brandt with a small shake of the head. "But we have our orders and we have to follow through. Leaving the children and women alive at this point will only cause problems down the road. Revenge killings, more partisans, more inbreeding and hurting the bloodlines. If a dog is sick and spreads sickness, you don't hesitate to put it down because it's young or a female. And we're dealing with the survival of the German people—we have much more at stake than just poor dog breeding!"

"Yes," said Uwe, his soul screaming in protest as he forced his face to give the Major a smile. "You must forgive me for my outburst the other day, Major. It's just that I grew up with Jews in my neighborhood and worked with them. You can understand that it's hard for me to grasp all this straight away. I needed some time to think."

The Major took a quick swig from his flask and gave Uwe his widest and friendliest grin yet.

"I'm glad you came to your senses in that regard, Herr Litten," he said. "I completely understand. It was hard enough for me and my boys to adjust. Poor Ludwig is still having nightmares about it. We try to do it fast, keep it clean and orderly. Still, I wish the higher echelons would hurry and come up with a long-term solution, one that's less…personal. That Madagascar plan has some promise, I think, but I've also heard that they're working on something at the camps. Making some adjustments to make it even faster and even more systematic."

Uwe was far too disgusted to ask what sort of new system the leaders were thinking of. All he could do was glance at his watch and mentally curse it for continuing to insist that he still had hours left with the Major.

It was fortunate that Brandt wasn't brutal to the Polish prisoner or else Uwe wasn't sure he would have been able to stand being near the Major for another minute. The interrogation itself seemed rather pointless (particularly given the fact that the Sweep was tomorrow) and went on far too long, but he didn't dare complain and made sure to say whatever Brandt told him to.

Finally, finally, *finally*, Brandt announced that they were done for the day. He took Uwe back to the house and Uwe's gut coiled unpleasantly when the Major didn't immediately leave. Instead, Brandt went into the kitchen.

"Just filling up my flask," he chuckled. "Hope the boys left me enough to get by for the rest of the day. I have to go talk with them for a bit, we have some important matters to discuss. I'll be gone most of the night, but Johann will be right in the living room if you need anything."

Uwe nodded. No doubt the Major's meeting would involve the Sweep. His eyes warily traveled towards the living room. He hoped that Johann was incompetent or would leave to join the rest of his comrades at the meeting soon.

Well, thought the linguist, *he'll have to sleep eventually. By then, Uriel and I will be gone.*

The Major glanced idly at the clock and hissed a few curses.

"I'm late, late, late!" he cried, dashing to the door. "Didn't even realize! I have to run! The boys will be waiting for me! Goodbye, Herr Litten!"

"Goodbye!" cried Uwe. He glanced at the counter and noted that Brandt had forgotten his flask. He almost grabbed it and ran to the Major, but instead he wrinkled his nose and shook his head. The Major didn't deserve such consideration.

Leaving the flask on the countertop, Uwe grabbed as much food and water as he could and scurried upstairs. He delicately kicked the door seven times and Uriel opened it.

"Okay, okay, okay," he muttered, entering. Uriel shut the door behind him and promptly spread out his burgundy cloak. Uwe put all the food down and gestured to the provisions.

"Take something, Uriel," he said. "You need to be careful. There's a guard down in the living room."

The boy nodded, grabbing an apple and taking a big bite. Uriel glanced at the window and Uwe noticed that the child was anxiously tapping his foot.

"Now, Uriel," said Uwe, "are you sure that you want to stay here? I'm going to Matthias and the Polish partisans to make sure everything is ready. I could take you to Matthias right now…"

Uriel shook his head and pointed to the floor. He wanted to stay.

"All right," said Uwe. "I'll come back to get you before the attack starts. Be ready to go. Grab everything you need, have it all packed, be sure to take a nap and eat something. I'm not sure what exactly will happen to us after the attack, but I don't want you to be tired and hungry when we have to move, okay?"

Uriel nodded. He put his apple down and ran forward, giving Uwe one last hug before he left to get everything in order. Uwe gagged as the boy squeezed the air out of his lungs, but then gave the child a fond smile and patted him on the head.

"I'll be back soon," he promised as he grabbed the burgundy cloak like a sack and made his way to the window. Climbing down was even harder while carrying a sack full of food, and Uriel winced every time it seemed that the linguist was about to fall, but Uwe made it and rushed into the woods.

Once Uwe was gone, Uriel shut the window. He stared out of the clear glass for a moment before pressing his face against it and exhaling. He had been waiting patiently for hours, but the birds hadn't arrived yet. He so wanted to finish this mission before the attack brought about uncertainty and change. What if something happened before he could finish the quest?

He sighed again and noticed that doing so caused the window to mist up. Smiling, he occupied himself by drawing faces and shapes in the mist, giggling as he completed a goofy-looking dog.

Once mist art became tiresome, Uriel finished up his apple and decided to help Uwe pack his things. He found Uwe's suitcases and started to (rather sloppily) stuff everything the linguist owned inside. Since he didn't fold everything properly, the suitcases were very hard to shut, but he sat down on top of them and closed them both. He set the two bags by the nightstand and smacked himself on the forehead when he realized that he had forgotten about the Adina-like doll. He had to assume that Uwe would want that as well.

He somehow managed to open one of the bags, shove the doll in, and shut it again with a minimal mess being made. Once all of Uwe's possessions were packed and ready to go, Uriel got his things together. Uwe had Elijah's Mantle for now, but Uriel made sure that he had David's Harp and the Boundless Key. Those were certain to come in handy later. He kept the Boundless Key in his pocket and put the Harp on top of Uwe's bag. He would carry the Harp and the Mantle together once Uwe returned.

Last, but certainly not least, he grabbed his precious golden notebook and put it right on top of the bed. It stuck out like a star against the dull gray bedspread. He wouldn't forget it, but he wanted to carry it himself once they left. He didn't want to shove it into a sack or bag where it could get lost or damaged.

Almost the second he put the golden notebook down, he heard a tapping at the window and his heart fluttered. He bolted to the window and threw it open, smiling widely at the doves that had finally arrived.

"Angel-Finder," they twittered, and although they sounded happy there was an edge of uncertainty to their high-pitched tones, one that dampened Uriel's bright smile.

"Forgive us," they said. "There was not much information to be gathered on the Eternal Fountain. We know where it is, but we're not sure of the obstacles that are there."

Uriel gave a satisfied nod. The location would be enough for now. He waved for them to tell him what they had figured out.

"The Eternal Fountain," said the doves, "is hidden inside of a tree, the Hai Tree. We weren't able to find out anything about the Hai Tree except where it is. It is close, and we can take you there now, if you so desire."

"But you must be cautious!" one of the skinny doves chirped urgently. "The Eternal Fountain is filled with water that can heal even the severest of wounds. If you pour the water on a wound or rub it on your flesh, you will be healed. But the waters can also be deadly. If you swallow even a drop, it will burn you from the inside out and you'll die in agony."

Uriel gave a nonchalant shrug. *Don't drink the water. All right, not too difficult.*

"We're not sure what the Hai Tree will do if you try to enter," said the doves. "We're not even sure *how* to enter, but we will lead you to the Tree if you believe that you are ready."

Uriel nodded and eagerly gestured for them to show him the way. They looked at one another apprehensively, not wanting to lead the Angel-Finder to his untimely doom, but nonetheless they obeyed and alighted from the windowsill. Uriel scampered down the tree and raced after them.

The sun had already started its late-evening descent by the time the birds and Uriel arrived.

It was a little clearing, not unlike the place where he normally met Samael, except instead of grass there was a sea of little stones littering the ground. In the center of the clearing was a tree, with bark black as the night and gnarled limbs that twisted themselves into the most unnatural knobs and knots.

As he stumbled over the stones and approached the Hai Tree, a shiver scurried up Uriel's spine. The Tree gave off one of the oddest auras he had ever experienced. There were gentle, comforting wisps of holiness that seeped from the ancient tree's ebony body, but at the same time he felt an ominous energy emerging from the Tree's twisted limbs. As if the Tree wished for him to come closer, but then remembered itself and used its contorted fingers to warn him. *Stay back. Don't come any closer.*

He ignored its baleful counsel and pressed his hand against the Hai Tree. It felt cold, lifeless, but there was a lingering warmth that, when he focused carefully, he could still sense.

The birds settled on the Hai Tree's warped branches, gazing helplessly down at the boy as he tried to figure out how to open the gate. He put both hands on the Tree's trunk, bowing his head and praying fervently. When that didn't work, he took out the Boundless Key and tapped several places on the trunk, but the golden light that gave him access to every door didn't leap from the Key and find the Tree's hidden entrance.

He pushed the Key back into his pocket and stepped back, staring up at the Tree, his brow furrowing in frustration as he tried to figure out how he could enter.

After what felt like a century of pondering and testing his theories, failing again and again, the boy's anger bubbled to the surface and he stooped down, grabbed a stone, and threw it at the Hai Tree. He thought it would be cruelly comedic if *that* ended up working, but not surprisingly the door did not appear.

"Losing your temper, Mute Boy?"

That voice. Uriel could practically hear the sneer that came with it. Without even turning around he knew what he would see. A black-clad angel with purple eyes that glittered with malevolent mirth.

Surely enough, when he turned to face the Angel of Death that's exactly what he saw. Samael stood in the shade, as if the sun's lingering rays were loathsome to the dark angel.

Samael folded his arms and spoke in a tone so arrogant that Uriel had half a mind to throw a stone at *him*.

"Well," said the Angel of Death, gesturing carelessly to the birds perched nearby, "I suppose your flying vermin friends couldn't help you much this time. To be expected. The secret of the Hai Tree is only known to the angels of the Heavenly Host. Angels such as myself."

He put a hand over his breast, his galling smirk clawing at Uriel's pride and nearly forcing the child's wrath to the surface once more. The boy could barely keep his fury contained as he glowered at the Angel of Death.

"But," said Samael, "since you've been doing so well, I think I'll tell you the secret."

Uriel's anger became astonishment. He gawked at Samael. No. The Angel of Death would never really tell him such a thing. Not unless there was some catch.

The Angel of Death leaned forward a bit and in a sickly-sweet tone whispered, "To open the Hai Tree, a human or an angel must *speak* the Ineffable Name of God."

Uriel felt as though he had been smacked by a ton of bricks. The air abandoned his lungs and his eternally silent lips parted in horror.

Samael's smile stretched viciously. "Oh," he cooed, "but you *can't* speak, can you Mute Boy? And it will only work for a human or an angel, so your little bird friends can't help. What a shame. If *only* God had given you a voice. If *only* He had picked somebody with a voice to be His Angel-Finder. Ah, you were so close too! Frustrating, isn't it?"

He laughed and Uriel couldn't stand it. With tears in his eyes, the child grabbed three rocks and threw them at the dark angel. Samael, surprised, barely dodged the projectiles. He gave the boy one last gloating smile before stepping into the shadows and vanishing.

One of the birds leaned forward and chirped the Name, but nothing happened. Samael had been right. The mouth of a human or the mouth of an angel needed to be the one to utter the Ineffable Name.

Suddenly, Uriel no longer felt like an Angel-Finder. He no longer felt like a brave agent of God sent on a divine mission.

He felt like a ten-year-old boy. A mute, helpless ten-year-old boy with no mother or father to race in and make everything better. He felt the same way he had when he woke up after the pogrom, after Zingdorf was destroyed. He felt hopeless. Lonely. Mute.

He sunk down to the ground and pulled his knees to his chest, burying his face in his hands and weeping like the child he felt like. The salty tears stung the small cuts and bruises that his hands had accumulated since he had begun his quest, but he hardly noticed the twinges of pain. All he could focus on was his own silence. Every insult that every bully had ever tossed his way echoed in his ears and he cupped his hands over them, trying desperately to block out his own memories.

Mute. The word pounded at his mind like a hammer would a nail.

Mute. Mute. Mute.

But then, as his throat began to hurt from sobbing, another voice, familiar and fond, came to his mind and whispered two welcoming words.

Little writer.

His eyes widened. The tears stopped. Slowly, he looked up at the Hai Tree.

A tree. The predecessor to paper.

He shifted his weight and felt the rocks he sat upon. Some were ragged. Some quite sharp.

A memory hit him like a lightning bolt. Being a small child, finding a small scrap of paper, carefully scrawling the Ineffable Name, holding up his finished work and glowing with pride as he looked at the beautiful, holy letters.

He couldn't speak, but he could write.

He grabbed the sharpest stone he could find and leapt to his feet. Wiping the tears from his face and eyes so he could see properly, he took the stone and stabbed at the trunk of the Hai Tree.

The birds twittered in surprise. "Angel-Finder! What are you doing? Don't desecrate the Hai Tree!"

But they realized what the boy was doing and fell silent, leaning forward and watching with fascination as the child expertly carved four Hebrew letters onto the trunk of the Tree.

Once he had finished, he dropped the stone and pressed his hand against the trunk. The Ineffable Name gleamed like a diamond, and he felt the formerly bitter bark become warm as a human hand.

He looked over his shoulder. The sun had disappeared, and the stars were just beginning to shine in the darkening sky. The celestial lights struck the carefully carved Name, and the letters began to glow like stars themselves.

Uriel stepped back as they grew brighter and brighter, forming a small archway of light. The birds twittered with joy.

"Angel-Finder! You've done it! Now enter, hurry! And remember: do not drink the water!"

Uriel didn't even waste time nodding. He ran through the arch of light and for a moment his vision was overtaken by the clear glow.

He rubbed his eyes and found himself standing at the top of a staircase in a room as large as the entrance hall in the Major's house. The walls, stairs, and floors of the room were made of wood, but unlike the outside of the Tree, the inside was a pleasant shade of chocolate brown.

The boy didn't even bother with wondering how such a sizable area could be contained in a small tree. The Golden Cavern had taught him that outside appearances could be deceiving. He glanced around.

Right at the bottom of the staircase, in the middle of the wooden room, was the Fountain. He could hear the water bubbling cheerfully as the Eternal Fountain allowed it to elegantly leap and twirl.

He slowly descended the staircase, keeping his eyes open and staying on guard in case something unexpected happened.

Nothing did happen, however, and he sat at the side of the Fountain, observing the clear waters with fascination and awe. The contents of the Eternal Fountain were obviously not simple water. Without even touching it, he could sense its benign and sinister qualities flowing together. He clamped his lips tighter, not wanting to get so much as a drop on his tongue, and glanced about for something to hold the water with.

He was delighted when he looked down at the Fountain's side and saw three different vessels. One was a giant vase, far too big for the child to carry by himself. The other was a jug that was perfect for his purpose. Right beside the jug was a miniscule vial, barely big enough to hold one sip of water.

He picked up the jug and set it beside him, but then looked down at the little vial and squinted thoughtfully. Samael had commanded the boy to bring him a jug of the water, but Uriel himself might need the water at some point. Water that could heal any wound would certainly be useful when he and Uwe were with Matthias, hiding from the Germans.

Of course, that would only be the case if the water could truly heal wounds. He decided to test it. He looked down at his rough hands, noting the cuts and bruises. The rash he had gotten by touching the weeds had stopped itching long ago, but its ghost still lingered in the form of scarlet skin.

Uriel dipped his hands into the Fountain and watched, not daring to blink lest he miss the miracle.

He gasped in wonder as his wounds healed before his eyes. His calluses vanished and his crimson skin became white once more. He lifted his hands out of the water and wrung them. They had become as soft as a newborn's flesh.

The child made sure to dry his hands off on his pant leg before he grabbed the jug. He dunked it into the Fountain and pulled it out once it was filled to the brim. The jug seemed no heavier than it had been without the water. He set the jug down at his side and snatched up the little vial. He would have to use the miraculous water wisely since the vial would barely hold any.

He filled the tiny container with as much as he could and put a cork on it. He tucked the little vial into his pocket and grabbed the jug.

Uriel took a second to admire the Eternal Fountain, but soon a series of desperate twitters struck his ears.

"Angel-Finder! Angel-Finder! Hurry! The gate!"

He looked over and gasped when he saw the arch of light getting smaller and smaller. Holding the jug tightly and being careful not to spill, he scurried up the stairs and crawled out of the Hai Tree.

Uriel knelt down on the gravelly ground, holding the jug of wondrous water to his chest, a smile blooming on his face as he inhaled and exhaled. He had done it. The final quest.

He lifted up the jug, laughing. He might have danced with glee, but he didn't want to risk spilling the water.

Michael would be free within the hour. His people were saved.

He looked back at the Hai Tree and giggled merrily when he saw that the Ineffable Name was still shimmering on the ebony trunk. He leaned forward and kissed the rough bark of the Hai Tree.

Thank you, Hashem. Baruch Hashem! he thought. While the birds sang a merry song, he held the jug of water close and marched off to Samael's meeting spot. It was time to end this contest.

"Everything's ready."

"Everything?" Uwe asked, inclining his head towards the Jewish commander and peering dourly through his glasses.

"Everything," Matthias confirmed. Uwe breathed out and rubbed his weary eyes.

"Thank goodness," he said. "In that case, you'd better go to the rendezvous point and meet the Poles."

Matthias gave a small nod. Uwe could practically feel the hesitation radiating off the Jewish commander.

"You'll all be fine," Uwe assured him. "The Poles are excellent fighters."

"I'm a little concerned about that."

"They know better than to attack you."

"Even so," Matthias sighed, his gray eyes moving towards his men as they gathered up the weapons, "we're not soldiers. Even with surprise on our side…"

"If you keep thinking about everything that could go wrong, something *will* go wrong," said Uwe. "Stay strong, stay confident. You'll win this. I know it."

"I appreciate your guarantee," said Matthias, and a subtle smile yanked at Uwe's lip when he heard a hint of amusement in the Jewish commander's normally dispassionate tone.

"I'm going to run back to the house," said Uwe. Matthias' brow creased with concern.

"Are you certain that's a good idea?"

"Yes, I have to. Don't worry, I'll be back soon."

"Hold on a moment," said Matthias, grabbing Uwe's arm and pulling him back into the corner before the German could bolt to the exit. He pulled Uwe confidentially close and reached into his pocket.

"Listen," muttered Matthias. "I thought about this for some time…and…as long as you're going back to Brandt's house…"

He pulled a little bottle out of his pocket, a vial filled with dark liquid and marked with a skull and crossbones.

"Poison?" whispered Uwe as the Jewish commander pressed the bottle into his palm. Matthias nodded.

"In my village," Matthias explained, "we would use it to kill rats. Put a few drops on some crumbs and they would fall over dead once they nibbled a bit. This dose here, though, is enough to kill a man."

"Why do you have this?" Uwe asked, rolling the bottle in his hand and trembling when he felt how cold it was.

"For myself," Matthias explained crisply. "In case I ever got captured."

Uwe didn't know what to say. He had been helping with an interrogation mere hours ago.

He wondered if those prisoners he had helped interrogate had tried to commit suicide. He wondered if any of their comrades had bitten a poison pill or swallowed a dose of deadly liquid.

He shook his head, not wanting to dwell on such a dreadful topic at a time like this, and curled his fingers around the bottle.

"What…do you want me to do with this?" he asked. Matthias raised an eyebrow, looking at the linguist as if it were obvious.

"It will be easier to defeat the Germans if they don't have their leader," explained the Jewish commander. "Is there any way you can poison him before the attack?"

Uwe's blood became as cold as the bottle he was grasping. Matthias wanted him to kill Major Brandt.

There was no doubt in Uwe's mind that the Major deserved to die. He deserved to die, go to hell, and burn for eight thousand years. But Uwe was no killer. He wasn't a soldier, he could hardly stand the sight of blood (much less a corpse), and he hated the idea of ending life. He had always been the sort that wouldn't squish a spider if he could help it. Even if the stupid bug crawled into his bed or scared his daughters, he always preferred to toss it outside and let nature be its eventual executioner.

Now Matthias wanted him to kill the spider. His hands quivered at the mere thought of killing a man, even a man as evil as Major Brandt. If one of the Jews or Poles shot Brandt, that would be justice, but the thought of slipping the policeman poison made Uwe's skin crawl. As much as he hated Major Brandt, he didn't want to be the one to end him.

But he couldn't find it in himself to say that to Matthias, and he couldn't find it in himself to lie to the Jewish man either. After all, Brandt *had* left his flask on the kitchen counter. If it was still there, it would be all too easy to poison the Major. He would almost certainly be back by midnight, and he would likely take a sip once he got home.

Uwe swallowed, shrugged, and slipped the poison into his pocket.

"I'll try," he softly mumbled.

"Thank you," Matthias said. "Stay safe, Uwe. I hope we both live through the night. I want to figure out a way to thank you for all you've done."

Uwe smiled. He wanted to say something strong, something inspiring that the Jewish commander could think to himself before and during the battle, when fear and uncertainty clouded his mind.

But all he could say was, "God watch over you, Matthias."

Matthias flinched when he heard the divine epithet. As the linguist turned to leave, however, he heard the Jewish commander mutter something in such a quiet tone that he barely caught the two whispered words.

"And you."

Faintly, Samael was surprised that he had a heart.

It had become so cold after Esau and his children were wiped out that he almost forgot he had one. The only time it came to life was when anger pulsed through his veins and he felt it beat like a war drum. Otherwise it was so quiet that he often forgot it was nestled in his chest at all.

But when he saw Uriel, his heart gave him a brutal reminder of its presence. Not by pounding, but by *stopping*. Even though its beat was always subdued, the sensation of it stopping, becoming utterly silent, was so startling for the Angel of Death that his hand flew to his breast and he softly gasped. It was impossible for the Angel of Death to die, but he didn't like the feeling of a still heart.

He had been waiting in the clearing, expecting the mute boy to arrive with his head bowed in submission, tears dribbling down his pale cheeks as he slowly unfastened the hamsa and gave it to the Angel of Death.

Instead, the child marched up to him, a bright and boastful smile lighting up his youthful features as he cradled a jug of Eternal Fountain water.

For a few seconds, Samael was as paralyzed as his heart. He stood there, his mauve eyes wide with denial and disbelief as he gawked at the golden-eyed boy who was his undoing.

He shouldn't have done it. He shouldn't have underestimated him. He shouldn't have made this foolish bet in the first place.

But it had been too tempting and amusing to resist, and if there was one thing that Samael lacked it was self-control, especially when it came to tormenting Jews.

Gradually, his heart came back to life and its slow, steady and nearly silent pace resumed. He looked down at the boy, whose eyes were sparkling with impatience as he held the jug out to the Angel of Death.

A smile forced its way onto the dark angel's face and a laugh escaped his throat before he could even hope to stifle it.

"Well, well!" he cried. Somehow, he couldn't find it in himself to be furious or even very upset. A thousand years of waiting and trying over and over again to get his revenge on Michael and his people. A thousand years and this mute little boy had ruined it all.

Yet he laughed, and after his initial shock wore off, he found that he wasn't surprised.

"You actually did it," he said, taking the jug from Uriel. He looked down at the boy, who crossed his arms and held up his chin.

Well, I wasn't going to lose to the likes of you!

The unsaid words only added to Samael's strange sense of amusement. He studied the boy's features for a moment. The child looked very much like an Israelite, in fact almost infuriatingly so, but Samael could sense a bit of Jacob's brother within the child.

"You know," he said, "you might be a Jew, but you remind me of Esau."

The child's nose crinkled. He made a small sound of disgust.

"Esau's morals might have been lacking in your view, Angel-Finder," said Samael. "But he was a fighter, always determined. Never the sort to sit down and give up. He never gave up…"

He realized that his voice was softening and the child was giving him a funny look. Uriel gazed at the Angel of Death in confused surprise. It sounded as though Samael was giving him a compliment, but Uriel couldn't believe that the Angel of Death would ever do something so genuine.

Samael shook his head and set the jug down on the ground.

"Well," he sighed, "an angel never breaks a vow that he makes to God. I suppose I should reveal Michael's hiding place now."

Uriel nodded tersely.

"Very well," said the Angel of Death. He lifted his hands and clapped twice.

Uriel waited for a few seconds, but when nothing seemed to happen, he turned to Samael with an accusatory flare in his golden irises.

"Be calm," said Samael. "I simply made my hiding place visible. Return to the German leader's house, where you and your German friend have been staying. Go down into the basement and now you will see a small cupboard. Michael is locked in there."

Uriel's jaw became slack. Michael had been in the basement the whole time! He recalled the ominous aura he had sensed when exploring the basement before.

That must have been Samael! He made the cupboard invisible! I was right from the beginning! Michael was being kept in the Major's house! Right under my nose the whole time!

A strange mixture of anger and pure joy erupted in Uriel's chest and he turned, ready to run back to the house and finally free the Archangel.

"Wait, Uriel!"

The unexpected call made Uriel stop mid-step. Had the Angel of Death referred to him as 'Angel-Finder' or 'Jew-boy' he wouldn't have paused, but the strangeness of hearing his first name fall from the dark angel's lips caused the boy to halt and look back at Samael.

Samael seemed to recognize his slip of the tongue, and Uriel could swear he saw the Angel of Death's cheeks flush for a fraction of a second before promptly returning to their normal shade.

Straightening his back and looking at the boy with deathly severity, Samael said, "Be warned: if you free Michael, you will pay dearly."

It wasn't a threat—Uriel could tell that much just from the angel's urgent tone. It was a true warning. The Angel of Death actually wanted the boy to exercise caution. For a second the child stared at Samael, not sure what to make of him or his comment. *Pay dearly?*

Uriel's heart jolted with fear. Would freeing Michael cause his death?

He inhaled deeply. He didn't want to die. He didn't want to surrender to Samael yet.

But Michael needed to be freed. Now. No matter the cost.

His hands curled into fists as he forced himself to come to grips with the grim notion. If freeing Michael cost him his life, so be it.

He gave a nod of acceptance and turned towards the house.

"One moment!"

Sighing in exasperation, the boy turned to face the Angel of Death once more. Samael gave the child a searching gaze, as if he hoped that his amethyst eyes could peer right into Uriel's soul and see what made him so strange.

"You realize," he whispered, "that I'm going to win. You are a human, Uriel. Mortal. Someday I will have you. That hamsa can't hide you from me. When your time comes, I won't delay, and I will win."

Samael thought that the child's shoulders would sag as he realized that he could never truly defeat the Angel of Death.

Instead, the child flashed Samael a knowing smile, his eyes twinkling like the stars above before he turned and disappeared into the forest.

As soon as Uwe arrived back at Brandt's house, he peeked through the sitting room window and was rather relieved to see that Johann the guard was gone. He assumed that the policeman had either gone to the last-minute meeting with the Major or had gone back to the policemen's house to get some rest before the Sweep.

Uwe tried to open the window, but unfortunately it was stuck. Sighing, he glanced at the tree. *Well,* he thought, slowly and clumsily beginning to climb up, *hopefully this will be the last time I have to climb this damn thing.*

He made it to the windowsill and crawled into his room. Once he tossed the burgundy cloak to the side and dusted himself off, he let his eyes roam the room. He saw two poorly packed suitcases and a tiny smile tugged at his lip. Uriel must have packed them for him. *Good boy.*

But then he noticed something missing. He saw the boy's golden notebook on the bed, but there was no sign of the child.

His stomach coiled as he grabbed the golden notebook and looked on the last blank page. There was no note or message from the boy. He just wasn't in the room.

Blast it! Uwe thought, glancing at the window. Had the child run into the woods? No, he wouldn't have. He knew that the attack was at midnight. Even Uriel, for all the times he had disobeyed Uwe, wouldn't have done so at a time like this, at least not without an extremely good reason.

Perhaps he had run downstairs to get something before they left. Maybe he was in the kitchen.

The kitchen. Uwe's blood froze over. *Yes, the kitchen. Brandt's flask might still be there.*

He stuffed the golden notebook into his pocket, knowing that Uriel wouldn't want to leave his stories behind if they had to flee, and pulled out the cold, dark bottle that Matthias had given him.

He exited his room, trudging down the stairs, keeping his eyes on the bottle as if he expected it to shatter at any moment, covering his hand with the deadly liquid.

He reached the bottom of the staircase. Even from his position he could look into the kitchen and see the little flask still sitting on the countertop. The Major hadn't returned to claim it yet. He was still meeting with his men.

The teensy bottle suddenly felt like it weighed a thousand pounds. Uwe was holding death in his hands and he hated it. He could hardly stomach it, even as he thought of the malevolent Major Brandt and hatred brawled with hesitation.

Uwe wavered in front of the kitchen, his eyes darting from the flask to the bottle in his hand.

He half hoped that Uriel would burst in and interrupt. Then he would at least have an excuse. Perhaps the boy was in the kitchen. Maybe the living room. Maybe the Major's office. Maybe he was right upstairs.

Uwe glanced towards the sitting room and his eyes landed on the picture that hung on the wall, the picture of Major Brandt's little son and his now-expecting wife.

He gripped the bottle, cursed himself, and ran into the kitchen.

Uriel wasn't in the kitchen, the living room, or the Major's office.

Heaving a worried sigh, Uwe ran upstairs. He had to find Uriel.

Matthias could see his men quivering.

At first, he thought (and hoped) that they were simply fatigued from carrying the ammo and weapons, but as he looked into their eyes, he could see flashes of fear. He could see apprehensive creases forming on their faces, and seeing his men so worried made him worried. He tried to think positive thoughts, recalling Uwe's admonition that thinking of everything that could go wrong would only make everything go wrong, but he couldn't stop the pessimistic scenarios that taunted him.

After all, his men were not soldiers. They were carpenters and shoemakers. Solomon was the only killer of the bunch, and even he had only shot at creatures that couldn't shoot back. Most of the men had only learned to shoot yesterday. It would be a miracle if they made it out of this alive. They were brave and wanted to fight, he could sense that much, but it seemed as though the closer they got to the rendezvous point, the more hopeless their situation became.

Hopeless. The word, once summoned by his mind, kept repeating over and over. He tried to suppress it, but the more he fought against it the louder it became. Yes, they had the advantage of surprise, and once the Poles arrived, they would have enough manpower, but still they were not soldiers, and even surprised soldiers could fight more effectively than prepared partisans who didn't have proper training.

The gravel crunched beneath their feet as they finally arrived at the black tree and set down their boxes and guns. Matthias hissed and took a seat on a small crate. The rough wooden crate had felt like sandpaper on his exposed hands. He looked down at his reddened palms to make sure he didn't have any splinters.

As he looked down at his calloused palms, the images that haunted his nightmares sulked through his mind. His hands were scarlet, coated from fingertip to wrist in blood. Adina's blood. He could practically feel her warm body going cold as her tepid blood poured from her fatal wound. He could practically feel the hot tears stream down his face as he tried to do something. Comfort her, save her. He didn't remember what he had been trying to do at the time, but either way he had failed.

He felt fresh tears prick his eyes, but he refused to let them escape lest he demoralize his men.

His sweet, beautiful Adina. So quiet and gentle and kind. Always worried about him, always knowing when he needed comfort or encouragement, always able to lift his spirits with only a few softly spoken words. He had failed her. Failed to protect her and their baby.

He refused to fail her again. He hadn't saved her, but he would avenge her. He would avenge his wife and child.

His stomach twisted as his thoughts wandered to his other family, Adina's family. He hadn't dared to go to Zingdorf after his village was attacked. For so long, he didn't know what had happened to Adina's parents and his little brother-in-law.

That is until Haim joined the group only days before Uwe arrived in their cave. The teenager had been scrappy and starving, but also knowledgeable. He had passed by Zingdorf. He had seen the plumes of smoke rising from the decimated village, obscuring the heavens. Haim had lingered there for some time, but no survivors limped out of the smoldering *shtetl*. Adina's family had joined her in the afterlife.

Her little brother. *His* little brother. Matthias felt tears pound against his corneas once more. Poor, sweet little Uriel! His innocent little brother, his creative and cheerful little brother. He didn't want to imagine what horrors the boy had been forced to witness before his life was viciously ended.

Matthias would avenge him too. Even if he had to fight to the death, even if there was no God to give him strength, he would fight for Uriel and Adina and everyone else.

He was so engrossed in his thoughts of revenge that he barely noticed Solomon nudging him on the shoulder.

"What is it?" he asked. Solomon didn't speak, but instead he silently pointed to the dead tree.

Matthias turned and slowly stood. All the men were staring at the trunk, their eyes pinned to four freshly carved letters. Hebrew letters.

The Jewish commander stepped up to the tree and carefully touched the word, or, rather, the name. It was a name that any Jew with a working knowledge of Hebrew and the Torah could recognize right away, a name too holy to utter.

"The Ineffable Name," he muttered, "The Name of God."

Whispers were exchanged between the Jewish men, worry turning to wonder as they debated the significance of the Name's presence.

"God must be with us," someone said at last, and as soon as the suggestion was spoken even the least religious of the men glanced piously up at the star-speckled sky.

Matthias couldn't bring himself to even suggest that the word had not been written by a divine hand. All he could do was marvel at how quickly one little word could bring hope back into hopeless eyes.

The Poles arrived just before midnight, and to say that the initial meeting between the two groups was cold and uncomfortable would be a great understatement. At first, no pleasantries or greetings were exchanged, just icy glances and suspicious stares.

Then, once the tension became nearly unbearable, one of the Poles stepped forward, grabbing a clearly unwilling comrade by the arm and dragging him along.

"Uhm…" he muttered in Polish, glancing uneasily at the Jews. "Which of you is Matthias?"

A few of the Jews who couldn't speak Polish stared blankly at the partisan. Fortunately, Matthias had learned the language of his neighbors.

"I'm Matthias," he said, aware that his Polish was far from perfect but refusing to pause or stumble as he spoke.

One look into the Jewish commander's steely eyes sent a shiver down the Polish man's back, but nonetheless he held in his fear and shoved his hand forward, offering the Jew a handshake.

This small gesture caused quite a few of the Poles to mutter disparagingly, but Felix merely gave them an annoyed scowl and looked back at Matthias. He tried to force a smile onto his face, but failed miserably under Matthias' wintry gaze.

Matthias made sure to look at the Pole's hand before shaking it, and even then, only gave him a single, swift handshake before pulling his hand away. Felix seemed satisfied (in fact, he seemed happy to have gotten that out of the way). He introduced himself and his brother, Patryk. His brother took a step away when Felix gestured to him, shoving his hand into his pocket, a not-too-subtle indication that he would not be shaking Matthias' hand anytime soon.

Nonetheless, Patryk stared at Matthias, focusing on his face. Matthias had to wonder if the Pole was surprised. Matthias had lived next to Poles, but he knew that superstition and stereotypes were still rampant among them, especially where the Jews were concerned. Perhaps Patryk had been expecting an ugly, hook-nosed, beady-eyed criminal rather than the handsome young man that Matthias was.

Matthias made sure that every Pole had a decent weapon and enough ammo. Once all of his men (he supposed the Poles were technically 'his men' as of now) were properly armed he reiterated the plan of attack.

"We'll go for the house first. Most of the Germans are there," said Matthias. "Once we take them out, we go to the Major's house. Uwe Litten said he would try to kill the Major before the attack, but we can't be sure if he succeeded."

He sighed. "Either way, let's all hope that he's all right."

"Amen," muttered Felix, and Patryk gave a small nod of agreement.

"Everybody is here, right?" asked Matthias, standing on top of a crate so he could see all of the men who had gathered around the ancient tree.

"Almost all," Felix admitted, looking down at the forest floor with embarrassment. "Patryk and I tried to convince everyone to come, but some just refused."

Matthias didn't need to ask why.

There was a terrible moment of silence. All eyes were locked on Matthias as he stood above them on the crate.

"Well…" Patryk said after the silence had become as oppressive as the Order Police. "What now?"

Then he added, almost as an afterthought, *"Commander?"*

Matthias felt a twinge of surprised stage fright as he realized that they wanted him to speak. Were they expecting him to give some sort of grand speech, or were they just waiting for him to give the order to attack?

He had no speech planned, and so he took a deep breath and gestured towards their target.

"Come on!" he cried. "We're going to avenge our wives and children! We're going to kill the German murderers! We're going to fight for our families, for our lives, for our country, for our people, and for God!

None of them cheered, none of them dared, but the determined fire that flared in their eyes as he spoke was enough for him to know that his words resonated.

He jumped down from the crate and gave the order. The attack was on.

Uriel didn't bother climbing the tree back into Uwe's room. He used the Boundless Key to unlock the front door and ran in. It had been some time since he had been in the entrance hall, and he took a second to look around.

It seemed much more ominous than the last time he had stood in the hall. There was no sunlight seeping through the clear windows and casting light on the cobalt carpet, the electric lights had all been snuffed out, and the diamonds that still dangled dangerously from the ceiling were no longer sparkling. The whole house seemed lifeless.

His body wanted to shiver, but he stifled the urge and ran forward, trying to remember where the basement was.

But as he darted down the hall, he passed the kitchen and something caught his eye.

A flask. A familiar flask.

Uriel recalled seeing it during his second quest, when he had been sneaking through the small village, looking for Elijah's Mantle. The Major had taken a sip from it while smirking at Uwe's distress, while forcing the Jews from their homes, while his men trampled the Torah and burned the beard of an innocent man.

He remembered seeing it at the Major's side while spying on him with Joseph's Goblet, while the Major casually explained the Sweep as though it was some sort of sanitary act rather than slaughter.

He recalled seeing it while the Major searched Uwe's room, when his men had almost stepped on the Ineffable Name.

He remembered seeing it dangling from the Major's belt as he held a gun to a sobbing young woman's head and shot her without a hint of hesitation.

And the more he thought about the Major, the more he felt hatred flare in his heart. Uriel recalled every time the Major had taunted and threatened Uwe, every time he had treated the Jews like rabid dogs instead of people, and his hatred grew until it was almost all-consuming.

The Major was a monster. Worse than Samael. He deserved to die. He deserved to burn from the inside out.

The little dose of Eternal Fountain water that he had in his pocket suddenly felt heavy, whereas before it had been weightless. He slowly pulled it out and noticed that the clear water was swirling.

Uriel looked up at the flask. He hadn't been able to punish the Major before, but now he held justice in his hand.

He marched right up to the flask, unscrewed it, and poured in the Eternal Fountain water.

Once that deed was done, he tossed the vial into a nearby wastebasket and continued his search.

He finally found the basement and ran down the stairs so fast that he almost fell.

He saw it right away. Standing against the wall that had previously been blank was a tall, smooth cupboard made of chocolate-brown wood and wrapped in black chains. The basement itself emitted a menacing aura, as if the Angel of Death was still in the vicinity but simply couldn't be seen. The child ignored the threatening sensation and scurried to the cupboard.

The boy tapped the black chain with the Boundless Key and then shoved the Key back into his pocket. He reached out, prepared to rip the chains off of the door and at last free Michael.

But he paused when he saw the dreadful Darkness that coated the chains. It all but dripped from the links like liquid, and he strongly suspected that the chains had been dipped in the Pool of Shadows.

He shivered as the memory of that horrible place came to his mind, reminding him of how he had been mere inches from being sucked into Sheol. His fingers lingered dangerously close to the chains as Samael's dire warning echoed in his ears. Was this what he meant? If he touched the black chains, would he die?

Or worse, would he go to Sheol? He shuddered at the thought of being trapped in such a cold, dreary place for any amount of time.

Uriel shook his head and glowered at the chains. He wasn't going to let fear of the Underworld keep him at bay. Forcing away his fright, he grabbed the chains.

In an instant, the black chains turned gold and the sinister aura dissipated. He gave the chains a tug and they shattered, the links turning to amber dust as they struck the floor.

The cupboard flew open and a wind so powerful that it threw Uriel to the floor swirled around the basement. A light, so pure and bright that it nearly blinded the boy, filled the room.

The light and wind vanished, and the newly freed Michael was gone before Uriel could even see him.

"Uriel!"

Relief caused Uwe's pounding heart to finally settle down as he ran into the basement and saw the child on the ground. He dashed to the boy's side and picked him up.

Uriel seemed dazed. He stared at an open cupboard with eyes as wide and bright as the sun, as if the empty cupboard held something so incredible that looking away even for a second would be sinful.

"Uriel!" cried Uwe with worry, giving the boy a firm shake. The child snapped out of his trance and released a sigh so full of relief that it seemed as though a trillion pounds had been taken off of his small shoulders.

He looked up at Uwe and gave him a smile more brilliant than a universe of suns. A few tears of joy escaped from his dancing eyes as he wrapped his arms around Uwe's neck and squeezed affectionately.

"It's okay, Uriel," said Uwe, returning the hug. "I'm all right."

He grabbed the child's shoulders and pushed him back. "But we have to leave! The attack is happening right now!"

Uriel's smile vanished and he gave a serious nod. The linguist stood up and offered the boy his hand.

But before Uriel could grasp Uwe's hand, both of them heard a rhythmic and terrifying sound.

Footsteps.

Uwe reacted instantly. He grabbed the boy, shoved him into the cupboard, and slammed it shut. Uriel was so surprised that he could only sit in the dark cupboard for a moment. A small sliver of light caught his attention. He peeked through a petite crack in the cupboard.

As soon as Uwe turned, he found himself facing the barrel of a gun.

Major Brandt stood at the bottom of the staircase. Every bit of friendliness that his face had once possessed was gone, replaced by a cold, calm expression that was more frightening than any angry contortion.

Cocooned. That was how Uwe felt right then. Wrapped tightly in the spider's silky web, unable to even wriggle any longer.

All he could do was take deep breaths, treasuring every intake, knowing that it could very well be his last. He met the Major's eyes, allowing every ounce of anger and hatred that he had been holding in to pour from his blue irises.

The Major hardly seemed to notice the linguist's poisonous glare. He held his gun with one hand and kept the firearm trained on Uwe. With his free hand, he pointed upwards.

"There are gunshots," he said, his voice devoid of any emotion except frigid disappointment. "The partisans are attacking, but I suspect you already knew that. I suppose I no longer have to ask where you were going during your woodland walks, little linguist."

"No," replied Uwe in an amazingly tranquil tone. "You don't."

The Major shook his head and stepped forward. Uwe noted that the man's flask was at his side once more. He had made sure to retrieve it before going to confront the linguist.

"It appears," said the Major, "that I underestimated your bravery and overestimated your intelligence. I didn't think you would be *stupid* enough to betray us, Herr Litten."

"Then it appears you were wrong, Herr Major," said Uwe, holding his head high. "As usual."

"I truly didn't want it to end like this, Herr Litten," said Brandt, sounding genuinely upset. "I should have shot you earlier. I should have shot you or sent you to a concentration camp the second you stole from me, but I didn't. You know why?"

Uwe stayed silent.

"Because," said the Major, "you reminded me so much of myself."

His emerald eyes glinted furiously as he hissed, "You don't remind me of myself anymore, Herr Litten."

"Good," said Uwe.

The Major gritted his teeth wrathfully and his green eyes flickered from the linguist to the cupboard.

"Is that where you're hiding your stolen goods?" asked the Major. "Or were you just stealing from me again?"

Uwe felt his heart beating brutally against his chest. His eyes darted to the cupboard behind him for a brief moment before he looked back at the Major.

"I have no clue what you're talking about," he said, taking a step to the side, shielding the cupboard.

"Open it," Major Brandt commanded.

"What?"

"Open the cupboard."

"I don't…"

"Open it," snarled the Major, "or I shoot you."

There was a mere second of hesitation before Uwe replied with a steadfast, "No."

An explosion caused Uriel's eardrums to ache and the thick smell of gunpowder filled the basement.

Uwe felt the air leave his lungs. His pounding heart seized up, and unbearable pain struck his body and spread from his chest to his limbs. His legs wobbled and he stumbled back, falling to the floor and leaning against the wall. He grabbed his chest and felt a warm liquid pouring from the wound. He didn't even need to look at it to know that it was fatal. He could feel his life leaving his body.

Uriel whimpered, but found himself paralyzed, only able to move his eyes to the Major. Brandt lowered his gun and marched right up to the cupboard.

Uwe saw, and the blood that had not yet escaped his body became cold.

"N-no, wait…" he choked, but the Major paid the dying man no mind as he threw open the door.

Complete silence fell over the basement. The Major was staring right at Uriel, green eyes meeting gold. Uriel gazed at the man, his eyes wide with fear, his breath ragged, his hand clutching the hamsa that hung around his neck.

Uwe watched, waiting for another gunshot to end the precious child's life.

The Major turned to look at Uwe and sneered.

"Well, Herr Litten," he said, shutting the cupboard, "it appears you died for nothing."

Uwe's terror turned to complete confusion as the Major moved away from the cupboard where the child was huddled.

He hadn't seen him.

How?

The Major stood over the dazed linguist with his arms crossed behind his back, contemptuously shaking his head.

"I was aiming for the heart, you know," he said. "Your precious good heart. It's given us both nothing but trouble. Goodbye, Herr Litten."

And with that, Major Brandt left Uwe to die alone.

As soon as he exited the basement, Major Brandt felt his parched throat plead for a drink, his aching head begging for the bit of bliss that just a sip of alcohol could provide.

He obeyed his body's wishes and brought his flask to his lips. He took a long sip and felt the cold liquid move down his throat.

As soon as it filled his stomach, it began to burn.

He felt like he had swallowed a hot ember, like his chest was ablaze. Choking, he dropped the flask and the tainted liquor spilled across the floor.

The Major fell to his hands and knees, gasping and gagging so much that he couldn't even cry out in pain as the fire spread from his stomach to his organs, to his lungs. The blaze consumed his heart. He grabbed his chest, screaming in agony as he begged God or whatever deity might be observing his plight to make it stop.

But God ignored the Major's plea, and the pain continued, the fire inside of him spreading as though his insides were made of coal. His heart, his head, his hands, his eyes. By the time the fire spread through his whole body he was howling, begging for a quick death, anything to stop this slow, smoldering torment.

But the torment went on for what felt like an eternity, until Hell itself would have been preferable.

And by the time Samael arrived to savagely rip out the Major's life and soul, Brandt could only thank the Angel of Death for finally quenching the inferno.

Once the Major was gone, Uriel felt his limbs come to life again. He leapt out of the cupboard and knelt beside Uwe.

There was blood. Scarlet liquid covering Uwe's coat and dripping to the floor, forming a puddle of crimson. Uriel sobbed wildly and put his hands over Uwe's wound, as if hoping that he could stop the blood from leaving Uwe's body.

The Eternal Fountain water, he thought as tears scorched his eyes. *I could have saved him if I hadn't given it to Brandt! I could have saved him!*

For the first time in his life, the child cursed. He cursed Major Brandt and himself. He cursed the Major for shooting Uwe and himself for being so brash and angry that he had used up the miracle water without a second thought.

"Uriel…"

Uwe's weak voice forced him to look up and wipe away his tears. He felt Uwe grasp his hand.

"My boy, don't be sad…" Uwe choked, "I don't know…why Brandt didn't see you and I don't care…"

With a trembling hand, Uwe reached into his pocket and pulled out Uriel's most precious possession. The golden notebook.

"Take this," he said, struggling to keep himself from sobbing, "Go, run, find Matthias. You need to stay safe, Uriel. Stay safe for me…"

No, no. He couldn't just leave, not when this was all his fault. The child became blind as tears forced his eyes shut. He held the golden notebook close and threw himself at Uwe, hugging him, sobbing into his shoulder.

"Uriel," muttered Uwe, too weak to return the embrace, "Don't feel so sad… I'm sure we'll see each other again, I'm sure. Go, Uriel. You need to go now…"

Uriel shook his head, pushing the golden notebook back into Uwe's arms and weeping until his lungs and eyes ached.

But then he felt something. He felt an aura so pure and holy that it could only come from one source.

His stinging, tear-filled eyes became wide as he slowly looked up.

A light, brighter and more breathtaking than anything he had ever seen, filled the whole room. Uwe could feel it too, a benevolent sensation that swept over him even as he drew closer and closer to his end.

Uriel gazed in wonder as a humanoid figure appeared along with the light. The light slowly dissipated. The angel's visage became visible.

The Archangel smiled kindly down at the child. He was even more perfect than Gabriel and Raphael. His mere presence caused Uriel's tears to dry. When he spoke, his voice wrapped around Uriel like a warm blanket on a chilly night, soft and comforting.

"Uriel," said Michael. Uriel gave a tiny nod.

Michael's amber eyes glittered like twin suns. He bowed to the boy. Michael, the Archangel, the Guardian of the Jewish People. Michael was bowing to him, Uriel, the village mute, a mortal of no consequence.

Michael straightened up and spoke once more.

"You've done well," he declared. He extended his hand, his palm open.

"Come," he said. "Come with me to the Heavenly Host."

Uriel's heart pulled him towards the Archangel. He slowly stood and walked towards him.

"Uriel…?" Uwe mumbled, concern somehow still finding its way into his raspy voice as he watched the boy walk towards nothing.

Uriel paused just as his fingers were centimeters from Michael's hand. He looked back at Uwe and his gladdened heart sunk once more.

Michael saw this and said in a gentle and reassuring manner, "Do not worry, Uriel. You will see him again very, very soon."

One last tear escaped the boy's golden eyes before he looked back up at Michael.

"Come, Uriel," said the Archangel. "Come Home."

Uriel took Michael's hand and light once more filled the room. The child looked over at Uwe.

And just as the wind swept around Michael and Uriel and the light began to take them away, Michael revealed himself, allowing Uwe to see the Archangel holding the child's hand before they disappeared together.

Uwe stared, his dimming eyes going wide with amazement as he watched the little boy vanish in a torrent of sacred light.

Then he slowly smiled.

Uwe Litten felt completely content when Samael finally came to collect. As the Angel of Death carefully took the linguist's life and soul, Uwe could only look at where the child had once stood and smile, knowing that the cherubic little boy was an angel.

EPILOGUE

Day had barely broken when Matthias and his men managed to make it to the Major's house. They found Brandt sprawled on the ground in front of the basement, his face contorted in agony and his flask lying a few feet away, its deadly contents spilled across the floor.

When they went downstairs to investigate, they found Uwe, still and seemingly comfortable, his eyes calmly closed, as though he was merely resting.

Matthias saw him cradling something. Something gold and familiar. He took it from Uwe's arms and fell to his knees, crying and clutching the notebook to his chest. His notebook. The notebook he had given to his little brother, little Uriel. The notebook that his brother had left behind before vanishing without a trace.

Matthias was so distraught over Uwe's death and Uriel's disappearance that he hardly recognized what an astounding victory he and the partisans had won. The Order Police were taken out. There wasn't so much as a scraped knee among the Jews. They had fought like true warriors. Perhaps seeing the Name of God had given them the strength they needed to fight and survive, or maybe holy hand had guided them during the battle.

The Poles had it worse than the Jews, the most prominent casualty among them being the death of Patryk. Felix couldn't even bring himself to be saddened by his brother's death. His brother had died in battle. Even if it had been a battle led by a Jew, he knew that Patryk would have been happy to die for his country, to die with honor, just like their cousin.

Even after the battle was over, many of the Poles, Felix included, remained with Matthias and his men. They stayed together throughout the war, and by the time Germany surrendered and peace was declared Felix and Matthias had become close friends. So close, in fact, that Felix saved up every spare penny he had to send Matthias to Jerusalem.

Matthias looked long and hard for his brother, even after he moved to Jerusalem. He kept the golden notebook with him at all times and kept his eyes open, waiting for the day that they would finally fall upon a familiar mute child with golden eyes and a bright smile.

But eventually, Matthias' eyes and body became weary with age and he consented that he would not see Uriel until he joined him and Adina in the afterlife.

When he realized that, he finally let go of the golden notebook. He sent it to a publisher and told them all about his little brother, the little writer.

Uriel's stories were published and translated into more languages than even Uwe Litten had been able to speak. The silent child's words were read by thousands of people, often aloud.

Even Samael knew when to accept that he was beaten.

Jürgen Litten and his sisters read little Uriel's stories frequently, often wondering if their father had read them all. There was so much about their father they didn't know. They remembered how loving he was, and they remembered shedding a lake of tears when they were told that he was never coming home, but there was so much that they didn't know, especially concerning his time in western Poland.

What little they knew, however, made them more than proud. While many of their fellows would turn red with shame when their parents were brought up, they could hold their heads high and say that their father had been a righteous man.

Many years later, when Jürgen was an old man, a father and a grandfather, a little museum was opened in the house that Uwe, Uriel, and Brandt had lived in. The museum was so small and out-of-the-way, though, that the only people who ever bothered to visit were the families of those affected by the events that had transpired there.

Jürgen and his sisters made a point of taking their family on an annual trip to the museum so they could tell their children and grandchildren about Uwe. Normally they were the only ones there, but one year Jürgen met a kind old woman only a bit younger than him.

He was more than surprised when the sweet, gentle, quiet woman introduced herself as Sophie Brandt.

Sophie had never met her father, but she knew enough about what he had done to be ashamed of him. She refused to even call him 'my father.' When she referred to him, she simply called him 'the Major.'

"Don't you have a brother?" Jürgen asked her as they neared the museum's biggest exhibit.

She did. Hans. They never spoke.

"He only has good memories of the Major," Sophie explained. Hans refused to believe that his beloved father had ever done anything wrong, and he had become quite the hermit as a result. He rarely left his little house, and he didn't have a single friend. He never spoke to anybody. He just sat by his window all day, scowling through the curtains, glaring at the world that thought his father was evil.

Sophie, though much more sociable than her recluse of a brother, also allowed her father's ghost to haunt her.

"Are you married?" Jürgen asked. "Do you have any children?"

"I wouldn't dare," she whispered. "I don't want to bring another monster into the world."

He wanted to say, 'Monsters don't exist, Sophie. People exist, but not monsters.' However, before he could utter a syllable, one of his grandchildren grabbed his hand and yanked him over to the most prominent display.

"Grandpa, look!" she chirped. "That's *The Book of Uriel*, isn't it? Mama read some of it to me."

"Yes, darling," Jürgen said with a nod, looking through the glass that shielded the golden notebook from the elements. Matthias had donated the original golden notebook to the museum. It was the museum's most cherished artifact.

After Jürgen's family had gazed at it for long enough, they turned and prepared to leave the museum and head back to the hotel. Jürgen, however, wanted to look at it for a little longer.

"I'll meet you back at the hotel," he promised, and his family agreed, taking Sophie with them as they left him alone with Uriel's notebook.

For a long time, Jürgen stared at the golden notebook, thinking of his father and the little mute boy, sensing the connection that they had forged in this very house and sensing that, somehow, it all came back to this little golden book.

A small shuffling of feet startled his old heart. He turned and took a deep breath when he saw that it was merely a small child.

"Sorry," he sighed. "You gave me a bit of a scare there, son."

The child smiled bashfully, his golden eyes glittering as if to apologize.

"Are you okay?" asked Jürgen, kneeling down before the boy and smiling kindly. The child nodded.

"Are you here to see the book?" Jürgen asked, gesturing to the display case behind him. The child's bright smile faltered as he glanced at the golden notebook. His twinkling eyes were filled with longing as he looked at it. He placed his hand on the glass display case that separated him from the precious book.

Pursing his lips and wondering if there was something wrong with the boy, Jürgen asked, "Are you lost, son?"

The child looked back at him, a cryptic smile spreading across his face as he shook his head.

"Are you sure? You know where your family is?"

Sun-colored eyes sparkled softly. The child nodded once more.

"You really shouldn't go wandering off all by yourself," said Jürgen. "You should get back to your family."

The child nodded in agreement.

Jürgen was prepared to offer the child his hand, prepared to help him find his family.

But once he blinked, the boy was gone.

Later, after he had recovered from his shock, he reunited with his family in the hotel lobby. Sophie and his sisters were getting along splendidly, and she was very good with his grandchildren. It was truly a shame that she had never had children of her own. He could tell that she would have been a wonderful mother and an even greater grandmother.

While Sophie and his grandchildren laughed and scurried to and fro, Jürgen approached the innkeeper and asked if he had anything to drink. While the innkeeper filled up a glass for the old man, Jürgen told him about the strange little boy he had seen.

He was rather surprised when the innkeeper informed him that such sightings were often reported by museum visitors. It was always when they stood by the golden notebook. The child would appear for a few seconds before vanishing. Always smiling, always bright-eyed, and always silent.

THE END

Thank you for reading *The Book of Uriel!*
If you would like to read more stories like this one, follow Project 613
on Twitter @Project613Books, on Facebook, and sign up for updates at
Project613Publishing.com!